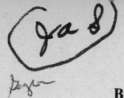

BALEFIRE

It means a signal fire; a funeral pyre.

BALEFIRE

"COMPULSIVE READING! Mr. Goddard's forte seems to be riveting depictions of terrifying violence and his creation of excellent male characters. His prose has sheer explosive energy."

—ERIC VAN LUSTBADER,
author of *THE NINJA*

"A THRILLER THAT GRABS THE READER in the opening pages and keeps him turning them eagerly until the very end."

—*Associated Press*

"HAS THE SUSPENSE OF *THE DAY OF THE JACKAL* AND THE EXPERTISE ABOUT COPS AND POLICE WORK OF *THE BLUE KNIGHT*."

—*San Diego Union*

"I WAS HOOKED. . . . AN INTRIGUING AND GRIPPING READ. AND WHAT A TERRIFIC ENDING!"

—CLIVE CUSSLER,
author of *RAISE THE TITANIC!*

MORE . . .

BALEFIRE

"HARD-HITTING, BELIEVABLE AND VERY DIFFICULT TO PUT DOWN—EVEN FOR SO ESSENTIAL A NEED AS SLEEP . . . Mr. Goddard knows whereof he writes and he writes circles around many others in his field. A beautiful piece of work."

—DOROTHY UHNAK,
author of *LAW AND ORDER*

"*BALEFIRE* COMES AT YOU LIKE A FIRESTORM. It's all there: international intrigue, terrorism, and fear set in a California that none of us has ever seen before, the dark side of Orange County. The action starts fast and then accelerates straight through to the last page."

—JOHN SAUL,
author of *THE GOD PROJECT*

"TAUT, WELL-WRITTEN, A PAGE-TURNER THAT SHOCKS THE READER. . . . From page one, *BALEFIRE* pulls the reader to the explosive climax."

—MARY HIGGINS CLARK,
author of *A CRY IN THE NIGHT*

MORE . . .

BALEFIRE

"Contains elements that are reminiscent of . . . Eric Ambler's love of intrigue, Joseph Wambaugh's feeling for cops and Ian Fleming's passion for technically sophisticated gadgets."

—*Newsday*

"FASCINATING. . . . A FINE ACHIEVEMENT!"

—*Booklist*

"Written by a working cop, *BALEFIRE* offers continuously rising excitement and suspense."

—*Publishers Weekly*

"A TOP-NOTCH THRILLER WITH THE IMPACT OF WAMBAUGH AT HIS BEST. . . . The suspense will keep you riveted to the pages as this fast-paced drama unfolds. Like Forsyth, Goddard creates a truly masterful story of international terror."

—CHARLES ROBERTSON,
author of *THE OMEGA DECEPTION*

AND NOW, EXPERIENCE
BALEFIRE

BALEFIRE

Kenneth Goddard

BANTAM BOOKS
TORONTO · NEW YORK · LONDON · SYDNEY

This low-priced Bantam Book
has been completely reset in a type face
designed for easy reading, and was printed
from new plates. It contains the complete
text of the original hard-cover edition.
NOT ONE WORD HAS BEEN OMITTED.

BALEFIRE

A Bantam Book

Bantam Hardcover edition / June 1983
Second printing June 1983
Bantam rack-size edition / May 1984

Library of Congress Cataloging in Publication Data
Goddard, Kenneth W. (Kenneth William)
Balefire.
I. Title.
PS3557.0285B3 1982 813'.54 82-24483
ISBN 0-553-24029-3

Published simultaneously in the United States and Canada

PRINTED IN THE UNITED STATES OF AMERICA

O   0 9 8 7 6 5 4 3 2 1

To Liebchen and the Squirrel,
who remained confident and supporting.

It does not really matter if the thing
that you fear above all else is really out there—
as long as you believe in your soul that it is.

bale•fire *n*: a large outdoor fire:
a: a funeral pyre **b:** a signal fire

BALEFIRE

Minus 37 Days

Thursday Evening

1825 hours

Ben Maddox, a Huntington Beach patrol officer assigned to the swing shift front desk, had just finished saying good-night to the last of the stragglers going off duty, and was trying to adjust his plaster-bound leg into a more comfortable position when the elderly, timid-looking man entered the reception area of the southern California police station.

"Help you?" Maddox asked, looking up, still trying to position his tender right leg on the stool he had borrowed from one of the Records clerks. Five more weeks, he thought moodily, as he prepared himself to listen, distracted by the knowledge that the lieutenant was going to transfer him out of Motors for carelessly totaling one of the brand-new Kawasakis.

"I am Martin Botts," the man said hesitantly in a broken and heavily accented voice. "I was told to report for work at the . . . first desk?" He smiled hopefully, the wrinkles crinkling on his tired-looking face as he fumbled in his jacket pocket and brought out a small packet of identification cards, one of which indicated he was employed by the maintenance company that held the contract for cleaning the new police building.

"Front desk," Maddox corrected, comparing the ID photos on the cards with the wrinkled, still-smiling face. "Your first day on the job, Mr. Botts?"

"Yes, I am much too young to retire in spite of what my children think." Botts was visibly pleased by the officer's polite use of his surname.

"I know exactly what you're talking about." Maddox

1

nodded, remembering the comments of the orthopedic surgeon who had pinned his leg together. He flipped through the thick stack of well-worn pages on the front desk clipboard, and found the list of Leland Maintenance Services employees authorized to work unescorted inside the security doors of the police building. He immediately noted it had been a while since anyone had taken the time to type up an updated list. Almost every one of the original names had been crossed out and replaced in pen or pencil. As Maddox expected, no one had gotten around to adding the name of Martin Botts to the list. He said as much to the old man.

"Is there anything that I do, officer?" Hiram Gehling—who would be using the name of Martin Botts for the next eight hours—asked hesitantly. "I don't want to cause trouble my first day on the job."

The problem of a security list was unexpected, and it had caught Gehling off guard. The Committee had gone to considerable lengths to arrange for his employment with Leland Maintenance Services and to brief him on the standard police security procedures as well as the floor plan of the building. But a security list had not been mentioned.

"Typical government efficiency, Mr. Botts. It's not your fault," Maddox said, shaking his head. He hesitated, knowing that he was supposed to run a complete security check on the new maintenance man. That, however, would mean at least twenty minutes of painful limping through Warrants and the Records Bureau. Then there was the additional time he would have to spend on the phone trying to reach all of the people necessary to verify that a sixty-year-old retiree was authorized to push a mop and to empty trash cans in the building. And it was six-thirty on a Friday evening.

"Listen," Maddox said, making his decision. "They issue you a room key?"

Gehling fumbled through his pockets again and came up with the key that would open the maintenance storage room in the basement. He held it up to the officer.

"Good enough. Tell you what, you can go to work tonight. But you tell your boss to make sure that he gets your name on the security list before you come in tomorrow. Okay?"

"Thank you very much, officer." Gehling nodded his head

quickly in agreement. "I hope that I'm not going to get you into any trouble over this."

"Don't worry about it, buddy," Maddox chuckled, motioning with his hand for the male cadet assigned to the front desk to come over. "As much trouble as I'm in now, there's not a whole lot you could do to make it worse." He turned to the cadet. "Mike, why don't you take Mr. Botts here through security and show him how to find the maintenance room. Take him on a tour of the building to get him oriented and then come on back."

Fifteen minutes later, having assured the eager-to-assist cadet that he could find his way around now, Gehling pushed his cart into the crime laboratory and pulled the door shut. He paused for two more minutes to correlate his memory of the floor-plan diagram with the actual layout and to make certain that no one had noticed—and was coming to check on—the unfamiliar individual who had just walked into a restricted area. As Gehling waited, he took note of the extensive alarm systems that protected the exterior door and windows of the laboratory. As expected, the actual examination rooms were locked separately.

Finally confident that he would be left alone for at least a few minutes, Gehling removed an elaborate set of lock picks from a packet strapped to his lower leg. The tumblers were difficult; the lock mechanisms had been specially purchased to provide additional security of the evidence in the rooms. Almost eight minutes elapsed before Gehling was able to align the last tumbler. Then he slowly turned the entire internal mechanism until it clicked.

Intently aware of the time-risk factor, Gehling quickly replaced the lock picks into his leg pouch and then entered the examination room. Moving immediately to the single desk phone in the room, he removed the phone cover and went to work. Using a small pocket screwdriver, he worked with careful haste to attach a miniaturized logic chip to a specific pair of thin, red-and-white striped wires. Then he quickly replaced the cover and dialed a memorized number to confirm that the phone still functioned properly. A voice answered. Gehling recited the number on the phone dial, hung up, and rapidly left the examination room.

Eight hours later, having installed twelve of the special

logic chips in predetermined phones throughout the police building, Gehling waved good-night to the cooperative desk officer and walked to his car. Everything was in order. Tomorrow morning, his "wife" would call Leland Maintenance Services advising them that her husband had found the work to be too demanding on his heart, and he would regrettably have to find other employment. By that time, Mr. Hiram Gehling, alias Martin Botts, would be far, far away.

Smiling contentedly at the completion of another job well done, Gehling patted the inner pocket of his jacket, which contained his passport and a stack of soon-to-be-used first-class airline tickets, and began the one-hour drive to the Los Angeles International Airport.

Arlan Marakai, a meticulously dressed man with dark Mediterranean features, strode purposefully through the large glass door of the southern California Pontiac dealership and advanced toward the potbellied salesman who was drinking a cup of coffee with a fellow con man. Eighteen years of competition-hardened instincts spotted a probable sale, and the salesman moved with deceptive speed to block out his competition and intercept the customer in the middle of the showroom.

"Can I help—" he began.

"I would like to purchase an automobile." Marakai spoke in precise Oxfordian English.

"Certainly." The salesman nodded happily, sensing the glare that his associate was focusing on the back of his head. "We have—"

"A Firebird," Marakai stated. "Black. Fully optioned. Five-speed package. Sun roof, of course."

"Of course," the salesman managed to say without actually grinning. "We don't have one in stock at the moment, but—"

"Delivery in five days." Marakai continued as though the salesman hadn't spoken. "Ownership to be registered as indicated on this document." Marakai reached into his immaculate sports jacket and pulled out a folded piece of heavy manila bond which he handed to the stunned salesman. "A simple gift,'' he explained in a tone which dismissed the need for any explanations.

"I'm not sure—'' the salesman tried again.

"I'm sure that you are perfectly capable of dealing with any difficulties that may be encountered,'' Marakai continued firmly. "A one-thousand-dollar premium should cover any additional expenses that you may incur. Payment, of course, will be in cash at the time of delivery.''

"Cash?'' the salesman repeated weakly, not quite able to absorb the direction or the speed of the transaction all at once.

"Certainly. Now then, are we agreed as to terms?''

"Ah, yeah, sure,'' the salesman stammered, abandoning any attempt to gain some semblance of control over the situation. He had no idea how or where he was going to get a black Firebird in five days.

"Excellent.'' Marakai nodded as though he expected nothing less than total cooperation in such matters. "I should also like one in azure blue and another in royal maroon.'' He reached into the jacket for two more pieces of the heavy manila bond.

Forty-five minutes later, Mr. Arlan Marakai entered the Datsun showroom on Beach Boulevard and approached the politely attentive salesman.

"May I help you, sir?'' the salesman inquired.

"Yes, I would like to purchase an automobile,'' Marakai said, reaching into his hand-tailored jacket, taking care not to pull out the packet which contained the airline tickets and his passport.

Bobby Joe Edwards, foreman of the fifteen-man crew from the Los Angeles Department of Water and Power, stepped across the nailed two-by-six forms that would contain the massive cement support slab, jammed his gloved fists against his tool belt, and wrinkled his sunburned forehead in professional satisfaction.

In spite of the latest armload of changes from the City Architect's office, Bobby Joe was satisfied that his crew would meet their deadline with days to spare. The emergency fuel tank was already pressure-tested and buried. The specs for the huge burner had been fed into the grid program and cleared. No one in the valley would run short on gas to heat their hot tubs or grill their hamburgers. As soon as the bare-chested master plumber finished soldering the latest pipe changes, they would be ready to call in the cement crew. No problem.

Bobby Joe sucked in a deep breath through his cigar-stained teeth and grinned happily as he stared into the future.

In exactly thirty-seven days, the 1984 Summer Olympic Games would open in Los Angeles Olympic Stadium. At ten o'clock that evening, a young athlete carrying the symbolic torch would sprint up the thirty-eight tile steps which were now only lines on a sheet of blueprint. At the precise moment that the runner reached the top of the platform, Bobby Joe would open a large brass valve with a firm twist of his heavily callused right hand, keeping his eyes locked on the flow gauge and his left hand on the backup valve. The runner would pause, salute the stadium, and then extend his arm, placing the burning torch against the lip of the massive brass bowl that would be filled with heavy gas fumes. The flame would ignite, and the Games would begin once again, this time with the help of Bobby Joe and his work crew.

Like most of the Los Angeles County residents, Bobby Joe Edwards was loudly and emotionally supportive of the mayor's declaration that the 1984 Olympic Games would be held in Los Angeles, regardless of any threat of boycott, demonstration, or violence by any government or special interest group. "Or any other dissident assholes!" Bobby Joe had shouted one night while watching tv in a local bar with his drinking buddies. He had pounded his thick fist on the bar with glee as the chief of the Los Angeles police department declared his intention to use hundreds of volunteer police officers from neighboring cities in addition to his own officers to make certain that the Games would be held without incident.

"Goddamned right!" Bobby Joe declared as he continued to watch his men sweat and work in the hot sun. As far as Bobby Joe was concerned, the Olympic Flame was a symbol of everything that was right about the Games, and the United States of America for that matter. When it came time for an American athlete to run up those steps, the Olympic torch held high and proud in his hand, Bobby Joe would see to it that the flame continued to burn.

*   *   *

Seventy miles south of Los Angeles, a young man named Baakar Sera-te stepped out of the elevator at the top floor—number fourteen—and stared with undiminished awe at the entryway to his temporary penthouse residence. Still unaccustomed to the richness that enveloped him, the young Arab communications expert allowed himself a few moments of blissful contentment before he carried his armload of last-minute shopping items through the front door of his lavish three-bedroom apartment.

As Baakar Sera-te stepped inside the Santa Ana penthouse, he mentally shifted from the assumed personality of a nervous and shy foreign exchange student to that of a trained, determined, dedicated individual with a mission. Unlike Hiram Gehling and Arlan Marakai—both of whom had been well paid to complete assignments of short duration—Baakar Sera-te had no intention of using his forged passport or his escape route in the near future.

Placing his shopping bags on the wooden kitchen table, Baakar began the series of tasks for which he had trained with single-minded intensity during the last nine months of his relatively short life.

First he set the locks—three separate dead bolts at the top, middle, and bottom of the reinforced door. Forced entry would still be possible, but such an entry would take time, too much time. Baakar smiled with fierce pride.

The electrical circuits were next.

The first series magnetically alarmed the door and the panoramic windows. A green light over the door blinked reassuringly. The alarms were loud and wired in duplicate. Baakar would be awakened within milliseconds of an attempted entry from any direction. He nodded his head in satisfaction.

The second series of circuits were wired directly into the instruments that would comprise the total reason for his existence in the weeks to follow. The instruments represented the latest in computerized communications technology—instruments specifically designed and built for covert communications. Baakar threw the switch, and twelve large, yellow buttons glowed brightly at their selected locations throughout the apartment—there were two in the bathroom and one right next to his bed. All that Baakar would have to do would be to reach one of the buttons, press firmly, and every bit of incriminating data in the memory banks would be wiped irretrievably clean.

The third series of circuits were the most critical. Baakar held his breath as he closed the final switch, and then exhaled with a relaxed smile as the room remained intact. He had wired the circuits himself, and had made the appropriate triple-checks, but one could never be absolutely certain until the loop was actually closed. Next to each of the twelve yellow buttons, twelve red buttons glowed their brilliant affirmation that the explosive devices were armed and ready to obliterate the entire fourteenth floor of the building the moment that such an action became necessary. The stage was now set.

The red buttons might very well be necessary, Baakar knew. The man that the Committee had hired was known to be ruthless and persistent in carrying out his assignments, driven to succeed at whatever the cost. He would be expected to push the opposition with fierce, insidious determination, ultimately forcing them to strike back wildly out of desperation and fear. He also had a reputation for pushing his resources to their limits and expending them whenever there was a tactical advantage to be gained.

The reality of Baakar's mission was that he was a resource—essential to the success of the Project, but at the same time, totally expendable. His task was to maintain a communications link between the man and the Committee, a link which would remain open twenty-four hours a day, a link which would be severed the moment that pursuit of the man placed the Committee—and more importantly, the Project—in danger.

In simple terms, Baakar Sera-te was a cutout. If something went wrong, he would have to die.

BALEFIRE

Minus 37 Days

Thursday Evening

2030 hours

The passenger, whose name was prudently unknown to the ignorant, superstitious, and untrustworthy ship's crew, remained belowdecks in the humid darkness. Lying naked, sweating, and alone on his spartan bunk, he was unwilling and unable to sleep. He listened to the loud, penetrating noises of the ship as she changed course again. He sensed the flow of the cold saltwater against the thin, riveted steel plate that still separated him from . . .

Thanatos shook his head violently, refusing to allow the images to form again. Reaching out, he wrapped his muscular hands around two of the steel pipes that supported his bunk, baring his teeth in savage fury as he strained his arm and chest muscles against the immovable posts, releasing only when his muscles began to cramp with fatigue.

He allowed his head to fall back onto the mattress, his bare skin glistening with sweat as his eyes glared up into the blackness. Daring the images to reappear, he waited, knowing that it was out there, following and waiting . . .

He cursed the ship's cook again, but he knew that he himself was equally to blame for the monster's presence.

The cook had simply been following the morning routine of tossing the weighted garbage bag over the side as the *Hadar Jee* churned northward along the South American coastline. The cook had performed this mundane ritual every day for as long as he could remember. As he watched the burlap sack drop the twenty-odd feet to the water, he inadver-

tently focused on the scarred, greyish-white snout that was
waiting patiently below.

The cook's eyes had reflexively widened as the nightmar-
ish creature rose up out of the water, snatched the tied sack
into its wide cavernous mouth, and then glided smoothly
beneath the surface. The entire deck crew had gathered at the
cook's excited shouting, and had watched awestruck as the
great white shark resumed its patient movements, thrusting
powerfully with its vertical tail fins, slicing its thick dorsal fin
through the water in a path that paralleled the course of the
Hadar Jee.

In the days that had followed, the shark had maintained its
rearguard position, content to follow in the oil tanker's frothy
wake, feasting on the daily garbage sacks and other miscellaneous debris tossed overboard by the crew.

At first, Thanatos had watched from a high perch on the
stern, appreciative of the immense strength that the shark
displayed when it broke out of its gliding pattern to lunge
without hesitation at another offering from the ship. Later, he
had taken to feeding the great white himself, laughing with
the others when a well-directed galley scrap forced the giant
shark into a sharp, twisting, 180-degree turn.

It was much later, as the *Hadar Jee* drew even with the
Baja peninsula, that Thanatos had thought of his mission and
realized that the shark had no intention of abandoning its
newly discovered food source. A hurried and insistent conversation with the captain had resulted in an immediate ban
being placed on the crew; henceforth and until further notice,
all garbage would be sacked and stored in the meat freezer.
Furthermore, no one was to drop anything overboard for any
reason, especially anything that might be interpreted by the
great white shark as being food. In view of the research
conducted by the crew on a great white's feeding habits, that
meant virtually everything.

There had been considerable grumbling among the crew.
Only the Greek captain knew about the mission that his
passenger was to undertake. Thus, only two men had realized
the danger that the trailing beast represented to Thanatos and
the mission. The crew had cursed the captain and the fearsome,
uncommunicative passenger who had spoiled their fun, but
only among themselves and only when they were certain that

both were out of earshot. The feedings had ceased immediately, and the passenger had watched for two days with a tightening chest as the dorsal fin continued to patrol the white foamy wake.

The triangular fin had also become a persistent companion in his dreams. Thanatos had faced the thick mattress in the cold bunk room with reluctance, knowing that he would waken several times in the night, drenched in sweat, and shaking. The dream was always the same. He would be swimming in the darkness, watching, waiting for the conical head and the lifeless eyes to appear, knowing that no matter which way he faced, the horror would always come from behind, knowing that the shark would become visible only when its great jaws opened in anticipation.

On the third day, Thanatos had screamed at the crew, accusing them all of slipping out onto the deck at night to feed the shark. He had ignored their pleas of innocence, informing them that if he saw anything being thrown into the water, the thrower would follow immediately thereafter.

The next day, the deck was empty. The crew, having been informed that the man had the full support of the captain, had found that there was a considerable amount of work to be done belowdecks. The consensus of opinion had been that the obviously insane passenger would fly into a blind rage if one were so much as to spit over the side.

Alone, shaken and exhausted from insufficient sleep, Thanatos had spent the morning and early afternoon on the stern, watching the wake and praying silently when the dorsal fin disappeared, and cursing loudly and feverently when the greyish-white triangle resurfaced.

Late that afternoon, less than twelve hours away from the rendezvous point, he had made his decision. Forcing himself to appear composed, Thanatos had climbed the exterior steel ladder to the bridge and entered the captain's cabin, wordlessly extending his hand to the veteran mariner who nodded his head, sucked on his pipe and reached for a key ring.

The wooden cabinet held two weapons, a .303 British Lee Enfield bolt action rifle, a sturdy relic that had served in two World Wars, and a modern 12-gauge double-barreled shotgun. Thanatos had selected the rifle and a cardboard box of ammunition, then had carefully locked the cabinet before walking silently out of the cabin and back to the stern. There, he had checked over the familiar weapon, a staple training tool in the early desert training camps before the Russian Kalishnikov assault rifles became readily available, noting that the adjustable rear sight was bent slightly and the ten-round box magazine was empty.

The shark was becoming more aggressive, Thanatos had noted as he fed the long, round-nosed bullets into the receiver with practiced hand movements. The dorsal fin was rising higher out of the water as the great white shark whipped back and forth across the wake, searching for the tasty morsels that its primitive brain had come to expect from large objects that produced throbbing engine sounds.

Thanatos had set the rifle across the steel guardrail, feeling the forestock wiggle slightly in his callused hand as he worked the bolt, locking one of the high-velocity rounds into the chamber. He had released the safety and had tightened the buttstock against his unshaven cheek, sighting just below and forward of the moving dorsal fin. Judging the distance to be approximately fifty yards, he had readjusted the rear sight and then had squeezed the trigger smoothly as the fin rose up high again in the water.

He had winced at the sharp ear-splitting crack, having forgotten to stuff his ears with the cotton in his pocket, but his eyes never left the fin. Ejecting the expended casing and feeding a new round, he had watched the spray of water rise up approximately three feet behind and slightly to the left of the greyish-white triangle. Sensing the entry of the bullet into the water, the shark had whipped around, tearing at the surface of the water, expecting food and shaking its head in frustration before turning back into the wake.

Thanatos had watched the shark renew its crisscrossing search of the bubbling white water. It would be days before the shark left the *Hadar Jee* to search hungrily for a new food source. The danger was that the water would dissipate the velocity of the bullets, thereby only wounding and enraging the beast, or worse, the blood would draw more sharks.

Thanatos had taken comfort in the solid familiarity of the firearm as he sighted and fired in a single quick motion. This time water and blood spurted; the dorsal fin suddenly stopped short and then the thrashing torso disappeared in a convulsive spray of pinkish-red foam. For long seconds, the shark had fought on the surface, slashing with frenzied movements at the enemy that could not be seen, giving Thanatos enough time to send another jacketed bullet tearing into the armored flesh. Then, before he could work the bolt action again, the shark had disappeared, leaving only patches of bloodied water that quickly dissipated in the swirling propeller eddies.

Thanatos had remained on the stern of the ship, rifle fully loaded and ready, his breathing rate returning to normal as he continued to watch the darkening water for any sign of the terrifying dorsal fin. Searching intently, he had waited until the sun dropped over the horizon and the reddish-orange reflections on the water diffused into blackness before he left the stern for food and warm clothing. He had returned almost immediately, having left orders for the cook to bring up hot coffee every half hour, continuing to watch the swirling water long after darkness made any sighting possible, unwilling to try to sleep during the few hours that remained before he would have to enter the water.

The *Hadar Jee* wallowed in the swells less than a mile offshore, gently nudged by the giant pair of brass propellers that strained the fully loaded oil tanker against her anchor chains, causing the thick welded links to screech against the ship's rusted metal plates. In the darkness, it was difficult to see the anchor buoy from the bridge, so the captain had to depend upon relayed signals from the seaman at the bow to guide his ship into position for the scheduled transfer.

The captain was a patient man—a trait that was the inevitable result of having spent a lifetime working aboard deepwater vessels—and it did not bother him to spend a few extra minutes positioning his ship so that the pumping of number two fuel oil into the system of underwater pipes leading to the coastline power plant would be carried out efficiently, and most importantly, without a spill.

The captain spoke softly and the engines surged again, dragging the weighted flukes of the anchors deeper into the rocky continental shelf that lay less than fifteen fathoms below the waterline of the ship. The fueling platform was quickly lowered over the side, and the crew scrambled down the rope ladders, working with practiced efficiency to link the pipelines to the intake valves mounted on the anchor buoy. In the darkness that was barely pierced by the distant shore lights, wrenches clanged against non-sparking brass fittings, completely masking the sounds made by the darkened figure as he slowly climbed down the rope ladder that was hung over the side of the ship that was hidden from shore.

Thanatos used his elbows to brace himself against the surging movements of the ship and prevent his air tank from smashing against the riveted side plates while he made his precarious descent. He could feel the intense cold transfer through the insulation of his rubber wet suit as he fought the twisting rope.

He wasn't worried about making noise. The one thing that his entire awareness was concentrated upon was the possibility that the fragile regulator mounted on top of his air tank would be damaged. Without the regulator, he would be unable to descend the ninety-or-so feet to the buoy anchor and follow the underwater pipeline to shore. Instead, he would be forced to make the fifteen-hundred-yard swim on the surface, horribly exposed and vulnerable.

The descent was going to be bad enough, Thanatos thought, pausing on the ladder to make another futile search of the liquid surface that rose and fell less than ten feet from his dangling fins. There was nothing to be seen, and he knew that further delay would only sap what little remained of his resolve to go forward.

He had been trained from childhood to fight, to die willingly without fear, and he had proven himself innumerable times in the north African desert. On land, the enemy was a known and visible entity that could be confronted and fought until one or the other died. But on water . . . He looked down again and shuddered, fighting to control the panic that threatened to turn his thick, muscled arms numb and useless.

In that moment of panic, his tightly controlled imagination disobeyed and formed a mental image of the environment that waited below. He envisioned the huge barnacle-encrusted hull that would be dimly visible in the murky saltwater, looming down from the surface like a preying monster. He would have to swim under this monster to reach the buoy anchor lines and pipes that would be illuminated by the ship's platform lights before they disappeared into the darkness ninety feet below.

It was the swim underneath the corroded and slimy hull and the exposed descent down the buoy cable that Thanatos feared more than he had ever feared anything in his lifetime.

Closing his eyes and uttering a quick prayer, he willed his hands to release the rope ladder, committing himself irrevocably to the water and the nightmare. He fell backward, arms and legs immediately tucking in to cover the package that was strapped to his stomach and to offer some measure of psychological protection, his mind screaming silently until it was stunned into numbness as he hit the water.

As he dropped silently through the liquid darkness, Thanatos remained in a tucked position, fighting to control the panic that threatened to turn his legs and arms into useless appendages as he tensed against the expected rushing attack of the grey form with the rows of serrated triangular teeth. Then survival instincts overrode the paralyzing fear. He sucked on his mouthpiece and began thrusting madly with arms and legs for the underside of the hull, blocking out the part of the nightmare that had the shark drifting lazily beneath the oil tanker.

Eighteen inches away, the barnacles and seaweed strands were clearly visible in his faceplate as he swam with single-minded desperation. He could see the buoy anchor now, a dark line hanging vertically out in the open water, far away from the relative security of the ship's hull. Hesitating only momentarily, he jammed his rubber-protected feet against the encrusted metal and pushed himself away, pulling frantically at the chilling water as he put everything he had into the twenty-yard swim that he knew might take a lifetime to finish.

In the final moments before releasing his grip on the ladder, Thanatos had resolved not to look back. His only accessible weapon was a sheath knife strapped to his leg, virtually useless if the shark was determined to attack. Besides, in the darkness the great white would be invisible until it was almost upon him, leaving him with a few horrible seconds to experience all the terror that he could ever imagine. He had long ago decided that he preferred a death that would be quick and unexpected. He didn't fear the pain. It was the

totality of the fear itself that he knew he could not withstand
much longer.

As he swam into the volume of water faintly illuminated by
the overhead platform lights, Thanatos felt himself trying to
draw inward as though he could find safety by abandoning
the exterior body. Grunting and gasping with exertion into the
mouthpiece, he willed his arms and legs to keep stroking as
he fought to contain the terror that was building in his chest.

Contact!

He screamed into his mouthpiece, almost biting through
the hard rubber as his forward hand struck a massive object
that moved slightly. His eyes bulged and adrenaline surged as
his survival instincts took over, demanding that the body
make a fight for it. But an analytical segment of his brain
recorded the fact that the object had been hard and metallic
beneath the slime.

Pipeline.

He realized that he had swum blindly into the bunched
column of uprising pipes and cables, and that he had instinctively wrapped himself around the nearest slick metal tube.
Shaking uncontrollably, Thanatos clung tightly to the pipe,
sensing the warm oil being pumped downward through the
thin aluminum as he tried to choke back the sobbing deep in
his throat. He wanted to swim upward, to break the surface
that was so close, to keep climbing until he was back on the
deck of the *Hadar Jee*. Instead, he looked around for the first
time, staring desperately into the murky green depths for the
greyish-white streamlined death form.

He saw nothing, but he suddenly realized that he was
exposed, not secure, on the warm throbbing pipeline. Momentarily under control, Thanatos began to descend the pipe
rapidly, hand over hand, welcoming the warm sense of security,
even though he knew it was false.

BALEFIRE

Minus 9 Days

Thursday Evening

1955 hours

Twenty-eight days after the *Hadar Jee* had uncoupled her fuel lines and weighed anchor, another oil tanker maneuvered into position to pump her load of fuel oil into the massive storage tanks of the Edison power plant located at the southwest edge of Huntington Beach.

As the crew worked to link up the thick rubberized hoses, they occasionally stared at the distant shoreline where they could see the street lights that illuminated the crackled paint surfaces of the old buildings that made up the downtown portion of the coastal city.

On shore, the lights cast sharply defined and immobile shadows in the temporary stillness that was a prelude to another torrent of summer rain. It came quickly. First, a few tentative drops, readily distinguishable as they struck pavement and asphalt. Then a sudden, rushing downpour that covered the old downtown area in a blur of wind-driven rain and chilling mist.

Deep in the shadows of an open stairwell that led up to a cluster of run-down rooms, a young, lightly dressed male crouched down in a futile attempt to find shelter from the cold wind and rain. Unwilling to venture into the storm, the youth stared sullenly at the running lights of the offshore tanker.

Shivering in his damp clothing, Toby Williker snorted at the irony of Huntington Beach having to import oil for its power plant. In the forties, the downtown area had been a source of food and shelter for the rough-and-tumble men who

17

built oil derricks as fast as farsighted investors could come up
with the cash or credit to sink a well. Forty years later, the
landscape was still dotted with slowly rocking pumpers, but
the remaining pockets of thick black crude were deep and far
apart. Wells that once pumped barrel after barrel on a daily
basis were reduced to a relative trickle, barely paying the
taxes on land now more valuable to a developer than a driller.

Ultimately abandoned by the wildcatters, Huntington Beach
remained a mecca for surfers, drifters, runaways, transient
criminals, and dopers who migrated to the run-down shops,
two-story flophouses, and the day-and-night pier life. There
they found a warm sun, a cold, murky-green ocean, salt-
laden offshore winds, ever-present sand, a continuous state of
mild hunger, and a persistent sense of loneliness. All these
elements were basic to the southern California illusion that
felt so good as long as the weather was warm. Undaunted by
the surrounding growth of suburbia, the transients continued
to arrive by bus, auto, plane, and thumb, doggedly pursuing
the dreams and myths that nourished the soul even as they
ravaged the body.

At the onset of cold weather—scorned by those who had
fled the below-zero climates of the Midwest and Northeast—
the hunger and the loneliness became more intense to those
who possessed neither the money to remain in comfort nor
the resolve to leave the fabled southern California beach
community. Thus they stayed, sleeping in communal crash
pads that were little more than empty rooms with thin lice-
infested mattresses, selling themselves or a wide assortment
of controlled substances of questionable origin and quality,
while they waited for the warm weather to return.

All in all, the downtown area offered a nearly perfect
environment for those free-living souls who were tied to their
dreams, slightly larcenous of heart, and used to periodic
discomfort. Consequently, the area also provided a perfectly
suitable location for a terrorist to initiate the mission that was
intended to stun an American city and to ignite an international warning that could not be ignored.

Huddled in the damp doorway, Toby Williker knew nothing about the concepts, tactics, or practical applications of

terrorism. He had never read nor had any reason to care about the widely studied doctrines of Mao, Guevara, and Marighella, all of whom emphasized the importance of using the residents within a target area as a source of operational support and sanctuary. All that Toby knew for sure was that he was soaking wet, shivering from the cold, exhausted, and at least twenty-five minutes behind schedule.

He was also more than a little scared, he admitted to himself, as he adjusted the paper shopping bag closer to his body for protection from the rain.

The contents of the paper bag did not really justify the concern that the twenty-one-year-old dope dealer showed for the water-soaked package. The box of plastic 12-gauge Federal rifled-slug shotgun shells, the roll of silvered duct tape, the cans of red spray paint and the other miscellaneous items on his shopping list were far more immune to the elements than his own drug-emaciated body. It was simply the fact that he had been due back at his lice-infested second-story hotel room with his purchases twenty-five minutes ago that caused the nervous youth to act overly protective.

Toby Williker was frightened because the man who had given him the shopping list, the man who had shown up at his front door six days ago with a foil packet of righteous hash and an irresistible job offer, had been very insistent about keeping to the schedule. So insistent, in fact, that Toby had just about convinced himself that the man was capable of carrying out his casually issued threat.

"You screw this job up, my young friend," the man had said the previous evening, as he exhaled a lungful of the rich hashish smoke past his cold, half-closed eyes, "and I will have to kill you."

"Crazy bastard!" Toby muttered to himself for the eighth time that evening, no longer certain whether he meant the man with the disconcerting eyes and the money for good dope or himself.

Toby remembered how the eyes of the heavily muscled man had seemed to stare right through him, especially when he had ordered Toby to repeat the time schedule until he had finally gotten it letter perfect twice in a row. The man was soft-spoken, seemingly indifferent to his surroundings, Toby remembered. A real gentle guy, if it hadn't been for those damned eyes.

The spooky part was that the guy's expression never seemed to mellow out, Toby told himself, trying again to rationalize the nervousness he felt over screwing up the time schedule. Even during the few times they had toked up together on the hash, the glaring intensity in the man's eyes had never dimmed. If anything, the hash only served to make the man's gaze more sharp and penetrating as he drew slowly on the small, polished, stone pipe. Not a normal reaction at all, if Toby's subsequent condition after smoking the same hash was any basis for judgment.

It was one thing to go out and do a job. Everybody he knew, including Lori, had done a burglary or two. Twist a doorknob or pry a sliding glass door, go for the jewelry and cash in the main bedroom, the color tv or stereo in the living room, and then split out the back door and load up the car while the driver kept an eye out for the black-and-whites. No big deal. But it was something else entirely to deliberately fuck with the cops like this guy intended to do. It wasn't like he was being totally paranoid, Toby assured himself. It was just common sense. Everybody on the street, even the barely functional dust freaks, knew better than to mess with the nighttime patrol cops in Huntington Beach.

Daytime, sure. You could get away with all kinds of shit with the daytime cops. Hell, a lot of them would even strike up a friendly conversation with a bunch of dudes when they were making their bar checks. No real hassle at all. Just some friendly grab-ass while they made sure that nobody in the bar was belligerently drunk or bleeding seriously.

Nighttime, however, was a different game with very different rules. At night, after the straights locked themselves into their hundred-thousand-dollar homes, it was just you and the heavy pigs out there. And there wasn't one of them who would hesitate to rattle your skull if they thought you were fucking with them, especially if they found you capering in the tracts or selling dope to the local high school kids.

Toby shook his head in confusion, going over the plan in his drug-numbed mind, trying to reason out what was wrong with the job that had sounded so good a few days earlier.

The distraction was the important part, the man had

emphasized. Had to pull the patrol cops out of the area to make sure that there would be plenty of time to do the house. Distraction was his job, Toby thought with an uncomfortable mixture of pride and apprehension. As instructed, he had made arrangements with three of the local greasers to bust into a downtown liquor store at a specified time tomorrow evening, assuring them the alarm would be cut and they'd have all night to drink and steal to their heart's content. The deal that Toby laid out was that he'd handle the alarm in exchange for the bread in the cash register, money Toby Williker had no intention of ever trying to collect.

First of all, Toby was not about to go anywhere near that liquor store, even if he actually knew how to take out an alarm system without being detected. Which he didn't. Secondly, there wasn't going to be any money stolen anyway. The stupid bastards would be lucky to make off with a couple of bottles when the alarm went off and the area cops started to show up. By that time, Toby and his newfound partner would be busy about two miles away, tying up a retired Laundromat owner who was supposed to have been stashing at least half of his daily receipts somewhere in his house for the past ten years.

If the snitch was correct—and Toby couldn't imagine anyone having the balls to feed his new partner false information—there was at least a hundred and twenty grand in the house, most of it in used tens and twenties. Toby's twenty-percent cut would buy a hell of a lot of first-class dope.

The trouble was, Toby thought, shaking his long, wet hair in frustration, his demented partner really didn't seem to give a shit about the money. The whole idea of the caper was apparently to show the rich bastards that they couldn't get any protection from their high-priced police department. Before they split with the money, the man had explained, he and Toby would paint "Fuck The Pigs" and other appropriate slogans all over the inside of the guy's house with the cans of spray paint.

That was the part of the deal that really scared him, Toby knew. They were going to deliberately give the cops the finger. In spite of the promise of more money than he had ever seen in one place in his entire life, Toby had spent too many years on the streets to believe there was anything good to be gained by pulling a dumb-shit stunt like that.

Still crouched down in the doorway—wet, shivering and scared—Toby Williker continued to watch the tanker lights and the still-falling rain, unable to make a decision. He couldn't decide whether he was more afraid of the uniformed animals who patrolled the quiet Huntington Beach streets in marked black-and-whites from dusk to dawn or the frightening, dope-smoking stranger with the intense, penetrating eyes who called himself Thanatos.

BALEFIRE

Minus 8 Days

Early Friday Morning

0015 hours

Senior Patrol Officer Daniel Branchowski watched the rain drops bead up on the waxed surface of the patrol unit windshield with unfeigned disgust. Branchowski and his younger partner Jacob Farber still faced another two hours of patrol before they could turn their unit back toward the station.

Two hours meant at least four calls, Branchowski thought. At least four opportunities to be confronted by some asshole who was pissed off, drunk, or wired and who was willing to absorb a beating for the chance to whip on a cop. Hell of a thing for a grown man to look forward to, he thought. The irritated police officer shook his head.

This was not to say that the prospect of a confrontation seriously concerned Branchowski. If the truth were known, he actually looked forward to the possibility of a little action, anything to break up the monotony of early-morning swing-shift patrol and the seemingly endless downpouring rain that had been falling for three days and nights without any sign of a letup. He and Farber were now waiting patiently for the bars to close so that they could make a quick deuce arrest and head back to the station for a warm cup of coffee while they booked the drunk.

Eight more days, Branchowski told himself, wrapping and unwrapping his massive hands around the steering wheel. Eight more days, then he and Farber could start their coveted tour of duty as plainclothes security for the Summer Olympics in Los Angeles. An eighteen-day vacation from traffic stops, puking drunks, the uniform, and the goddamned rain.

The rain was the real aggravation. It wasn't the expected confrontation or the fifty-fifty chance of a fight with a drunk that Branchowski objected to. It was the virtual certainty of getting his uniform soaking wet that infuriated the forty-two-year-old patrol officer.

An eighteen-year veteran in the department, Branchowski had long since accepted the ever-present discomfort of the body armor, the heavy gunbelt and the holstered .357 revolver that invariably dug its checkered wooden grip into his rib cage whenever he sat down. He even grudgingly accepted the persistent infiltration of electronic gadgetry into his on-duty home—a black and white, two-man, patrol car. What he could not endure, much less accept, was the repulsive smell and uncontrollable itching that began when the rain flowed down his neck underneath the department-issued yellow raincoat and soaked his heavy wool uniform shirt.

"Jesus Christ Almighty!" Branchowski exploded, striking the palms of his heavy, callused hands against the steering wheel in helpless frustration. "Look at that shit. You'd think we're in the middle of the goddamned winter. Who the hell ever heard of rain like this in July?"

"Careful," Jake Farber cautioned, looking up from his report form with a mischievous grin. "You piss off the man upstairs"—he gestured with his head—"and we're liable to have snow."

Branchowski rolled his eyes, and then looked over at his partner, noting for perhaps the hundredth time that Farber seemed to be impervious to discomfort. Jake Farber would smile if it were hailing horseshit in June, Branchowski decided, watching with undiminished awe as his partner cheerfully updated their patrol log under the small swan-necked dash light. Farber was humming to himself as he double-checked the neatly printed paragraphs.

Branchowski hated to write reports; he hated to write anything for that matter. The mandated departmental paperwork—a seemingly endless stream of constantly revised report forms, log sheets, and supplemental pages—was widely recognized as the number one enemy of the field officer, and it had very nearly cost Branchowski his job on more than one occasion.

Up until the day that Jake Farber had been assigned as his partner, Branchowski would regularly spend one to two hours of unpaid overtime meticulously writing and correcting his crime reports and patrol log. It was only the fear of being put on a desk job in the detective bureau, shuffling reams of paper, that kept Branchowski working feverishly on his own time to complete the hated paperwork.

Jake Farber happened to be one of those rare men who really didn't mind the paperwork. After spending the better part of an evening watching his new partner's agonized efforts to write a simple breaking-and-entering report, Jake had quietly volunteered to write the reports and maintain the patrol log for their unit. In doing so, he made a devoted friend for life.

"Think we're going to get inside duty at the Olympics?" Branchowski asked hopefully, as he continued to guide the black-and-white through the dark, wet streets of the downtown area, watching his side of the street, hoping fervently that they wouldn't come across anything that would involve getting out of the protective patrol car.

"Lieutenant says we're going to be assigned by squads," Farber replied, putting his metal briefcase away and watching his side of the street through the half-opened side window. "We're detailed with Lagucii, so I figure the worst we can get is front-row security for some dignitary. Might even get guard duty at the women's dorms if the white-haired wonder really applies himself."

"Never thought I'd appreciate that SOB's talent for kissing ass," Branchowski nodded, momentarily distracted from his complaining. "You going to take Kathy and the kids to some of the events?"

"Kat's got tickets for gymnastics and women's volleyball. Said she'd share them with us if we put the kids on our laps. You get Janie."

"Hot damn!" Branchowski laughed enthusiastically. "Hey, wait a minute," he asked, suddenly suspicious. "You manage to get her housebroken yet?" Two-year-old Janie Farber loved to tuck herself in her Uncle Branch's lap and fall asleep while her parents talked. Branchowski, a determined bachelor after his first childless marriage, always suffered the inevitable accidents with uncharacteristic good humor.

"Nope," Farber grinned. "But Kat promised to double-wrap her and fix you up with a bunch of spares."

"Fair deal," Branchowski nodded, looking pleased in spite of his irritated mood.

The prospect of spending a couple of days off at the Olympic Games with Jake Farber and his family would have been thoroughly comforting to Branchowski if it hadn't been raining, and if his partner hadn't been cheerfully humming, oblivious to the unseasonal summer cold and rain and the likelihood that both of them would be wet and shivering before their shift was over. Branchowski was about to vent his feelings on these matters at length when the radio interrupted.

"Six Adam, a four-five-nine silent, RD two-six-three, on your teleprinter."

Jake reached for the microphone as Branchowski accelerated the black-and-white down an alley toward Pacific Coast Highway which ran parallel to the ocean, intersecting Main Street at the pier.

Reporting District 263 was right in the middle of downtown Huntington Beach. A generally active area during the day when the streets were filled with the regulars and summer tourists, 263 was abandoned and isolated at night, except for the occasional security guards, drunks, dope dealers, and burglars who crossed paths in their individual attempts to stay warm, earn money, or steal.

"Six Adam, copy," Jake spoke calmly, and then replaced the microphone as they waited for the lighted electronic box mounted below their radio to print out the call.

The teleprinter began whirring. Farber reached over and turned on the TP light so that he could reach the dispatch message as it was contact-printed across the roll of paper.

```
SIX ADAM      459 S     RD:263    0017 HRS CN:139
INF: N/A                 LOC: ALBERT'S LIQUOR
                              275 MAIN STREET
SILENT ALARM ACTIVATED AT 0016 HRS. NOTIFICATION
BY SENTINEL ALARMS. ALARM HAS NOT RESET.
```

Farber waited for the teleprinter to stop, and then reached for the mike. "Six Adam confirming the TP. Our ETA is approximately five. ETA on the backup?"

"Good luck, partner," Branchowski commented sarcastically as he decided against the coast highway route and calmly directed the black-and-white through the poorly illuminated back streets at a rate of speed that just barely kept the tire treads attached to the rain-slickened asphalt. "Charley and Rick pulled out of the area to handle that firebomb about twenty minutes ago." Branchowski quickly checked his watch to confirm his time estimate. "The other two south units just took a family fight call, remember?"

"Maybe they'll send Lagucii out," Farber suggested innocently, and then laughed at the thought. The idea of Patrol Sergeant Patrick Lagucii abandoning his warm office to get his thin, blow-dried hair and crisply ironed uniform wet in order to back up his officers was an old departmental joke that never failed to get a chuckle. Branchowski and Farber were still smiling when dispatch confirmed Branchowski's suspicions.

"Six Adam, be advised no backup units available in the south. Handle with caution and advise when code four."

"No shit, honey." Branchowski grinned as he turned a corner at just above safe speed, allowing the unit to go into a controlled slide while the spinning tires temporarily lost and then regained contact with the slick street as he made minor adjustments with the accelerator. Farber continued to watch the alleys and side streets reflexively, totally unconcerned about his partner's driving habits. He knew from extensive and occasionally bone-rattling experience that Branchowski was a highly accomplished pursuit driver, perfectly capable of pulling out of a skid at much higher speeds.

Every Huntington Beach black-and-white contained certain supplemental items of equipment. One of these items was a Remington pump 12-gauge shotgun with an extended five-round magazine, solidly mounted and locked vertically against the dash on the right side of the radio. Farber unlocked the mount and removed the heavy weapon, keeping his finger well away from the trigger. Humming quietly, his only external display of tension, he quickly confirmed that there was a round of .00 buck in the chamber, that the magazine was full, and that the safety was in the ON position. Then he waited.

Branchowski drove the last five hundred yards with the radio turned down and all of the unit's lights out, depending upon the occasional street light for enough illumination to stay on the road. They turned slowly onto Main Street at Fifth, two and a half blocks north of Albert's Liquor Store, both men tensed and alert for movement. Farber waited until Branchowski brought the black-and-white into position across the street and approximately a hundred yards north of the liquor store, and then he snapped the shotgun safety to the OFF position.

Both officers silently watched the liquor store's front door. Two figures came out, slipped, and then rolled across the wet sidewalk. From their position, Branchowski and Farber could see the broken front window and the slightly open front door. A single light bulb burned faintly in the back of the store, and a flickering street light threw indistinct patterns of light and shadow across the two prone figures lying in the darkened street. One of the figures made an unsuccessful attempt to pass a bottle to his struggling companion who reached out, slipped, and fell flat on the cement.

"What do you figure?" Branchowski whispered.

"Third guy in the store," Farber answered, his index finger tapping lightly against the trigger guard of the shotgun.

"You see him?"

"No. Shadow moved inside, north of the door. Might be a cat."

"No, here he comes."

They watched silently as the third suspect staggered out of the front door of the liquor store, his arms full of bottles. Like the first two, the third suspect appeared to be a typical downtown inhabitant—male, possibly white, long unkempt hair, ragged and loosely fitting clothes, large bulky jacket that appeared to be military. None of the three seemed to notice the black-and-white which had to be clearly visible in the light rain in spite of the fact that all of the interior and exterior lights of the unit were still turned off.

The third suspect started yelling something unintelligible as he tried to pull his two cohorts to their feet. He succeeded only in dropping several of his bottles. Finally giving up in disgust, he threw the rest of his bottles down at the two prone figures and staggered back into the store.

"Jesus, a bunch of stinking biker pukes," Branchowski muttered, adjusting his raincoat so that the scratched and weather-stained grip of his revolver and the top of his holster stuck out through the large slit in the thick yellow raincoat. "Too goddamned drunk to make a getaway."

"Let's just hope that they don't puke in the back seat," Jake suggested, grinning, watching the horrified expression develop on his partner's face as Branchowski considered the olfactory possibilities of wet wool and vomit.

"Six Adam. We are ten-ninety-seven at Albert's," Farber whispered into the mike. "Three suspects observed. All appear to be intoxicated. Three males, possibly Mexican or Latin, unknown age, possibly late twenties or thirties. Four-five-nine confirmed. Will advise."

"Shall we do it?" Branchowski looked over at his partner, and received a nod. The heavy-duty engine of the black-and-white roared as Branchowski accelerated the unit down and across the street from their parked position, sliding to a water-splashing stop in front of the store.

The two drunks on the sidewalk looked up in startled amazement as Farber lunged out the side door before the unit came to a full stop, stomped through the scattered bottles and broken glass, and kicked in the front door of the store with his heavy boot.

Branchowski was out of the unit seconds later, the .357 Smith & Wesson in his thick right hand as he grabbed the wet, stringy-haired suspect nearest to the front of the unit, throwing him sprawling against the brick storefront. The second drunk received the same treatment just as Farber pushed the third suspect out through the front door. Moments later, the three unsuccessful burglars were mumbling incoherently at each other as they stared at the two officers with bleary reddened eyes.

"Watch them. I'll take the store," Branchowski said. Farber nodded, holding the shotgun in a casual ready position, aimed just in front of the sprawled feet of the middle suspect. Until they had been subjected to a cursory search for weapons, the youths would be treated as potentially armed and dangerous, in spite of their outwardly drunken conditions.

Welcoming the opportunity to get out of the irritating rain, Branchowski made a thorough and careful search of the store, confirming that the back door was locked, the cash register was intact, and there were no other suspects in the immediate area. He located the liquor store's emergency number and notified the owner on the counter phone. Then, reluctantly concluding that there was no further reason to stay in the relatively warm and comfortable environment, he walked back outside.

"Store's clear," he said. "I'll call in the code four. Maybe we can get a transportation unit out while we wait for the manager."

"Dream on, partner," Farber said with a laugh, keeping an alert eye on their three meal tickets back to the station. Farber had been a cop too long to let his guard down. As soon as the three were searched, handcuffed, and strapped into a unit, he would allow himself to relax. It meant a little extra effort, but Farber didn't consider that unusual or unreasonable. It paid to be meticulous and careful on the streets.

Branchowski reached in through the open window on the driver's side of the unit and grabbed the mike. "Six Adam."

"Six Adam, go."

"Six Adam. Be advised it is code four at Albert's Liquor. Repeat, code four. We have three in custody for four-five-nine. Requesting a transportation unit. Owner is notified and en route."

Branchowski turned his back to the store, watching the darkened buildings and the alleys for any onlookers who might be involved with the trio, while he waited for a reply from dispatch.

"Six Adam, confirming code four at Albert's. Be advised that all transportation units are unavailable at this time."

Branchowski nodded to himself and was bending over to replace the mike when the concussive roar of a shotgun blast hammered at his street-conditioned reflexes.

"Jake, what the hell!" he yelled, striking the back of his helmeted head against the upper window frame of the unit as he jerked erect, ready to yell at his goddamned partner who knew better than to shoot at a drunk, no matter what the son of a bitch did. As Branchowski got his head clear of the window frame and stood up, the first thing he saw was the Remington shotgun flying crazily up and out of Jake Farber's hands as Farber spun away, his arms outstretched and loose.

As his mind screamed no! no!, years of repetitious training took over. Branchowski unthinkingly dove against the side of the black-and-white, sliding against wet and cold enameled metal as he reflexively jerked his revolver out of its holster and brought it up and across the hood with his arms fully extended.

The suspect that Farber had thrown out of the store was now standing in a half-crouched position, his right hand pointing down at the ground where Farber had fallen. Wide-eyed and snarling behind tightly clenched teeth, Branchowski fired twice from a point-shoulder position, and was immediately blinded and deafened by the flash and the sharp, ear-piercing explosions of the high-velocity rounds.

The semijacketed hollow-point bullets struck chest high, expanding upon contact and slamming the suspect against the dirty white-washed brick wall. His heart muscles shattered and instantly stilled, the suspect bounced off the wall like a limp rag doll. Then he seemed to take what might have been a staggering step forward, had his legs been capable of directed movement, only to fold and immediately drop as Branchowski mistakenly interpreted the forward motion and triggered two more rounds that struck just above the marijuana-leaf belt buckle.

As the first suspect dropped, Branchowski ignored the high-pitched buzzing in his ears and tried to follow the second suspect with the front sight of the Smith & Wesson. The suspect was now on his feet and running frantically toward the opened front door of the liquor store.

The running figure looked hazily dark against a darkened wall; Branchowski's night vision had been temporarily destroyed by the successive yellow-white fireballs that had erupted from the recoiling gun barrel immediately in front of his intently focused eyes. He waited until the twisting shadow silhouetted itself against the dimly lit store window before he squeezed the trigger. Having temporarily blocked out the mental images of Jake Farber, Branchowski's mind was functioning smoothly now, and it immediately recorded the miss as the store window shattered into thousands of jagged flying fragments just behind the suspect's jerking and then accelerating body.

Branchowski blinked and shifted his hands slightly. He squeezed the trigger again just as the figure reached the door and hesitated for a fraction of a second before leaping into the security of the liquor store. Branchowski was aware for the

first time of the revolver recoiling solidly against his tightly
gripped hands as the copper-lead slug streaked across the
relatively short distance, ripping through the old, worn, military jacket just below and between the suspect's shoulder
blades.

As the second suspect was flung headfirst into a display of
cheap jug wine, Branchowski spun back and around to the
rear of the unit, crouching down with his back to the cold
metal. He watched for the third suspect with adrenaline-
widened eyes as his hands went through the well-practiced
routine of unlocking and opening the cylinder of the now
inverted revolver, holding the weapon with extended fingers,
and thumbing the ejector with the same hand to dump the
expended and smoking brass casings. His eyes still searching
for the third suspect's location, he held the emptied weapon
open with his left hand as his right dug a speedloader out of
its leather pouch. He broke off his intense search of the street
and buildings long enough to confirm that the cylindrical
loader had fed the six live rounds correctly, then brought his
eyes back up.

Time was the factor. It had taken Branchowski almost four
seconds to dump empties and reload. Too long, if the third
suspect with the gun was counting shots. It had to be the third
suspect because Branchowski couldn't see any kind of firearm near the first two sprawled bodies. If the suspect was
counting, he would wait for the sixth shot and then make his
move. There was no movement on the street. Branchowski
tried to control his breathing as he snapped the cylinder shut,
feeling a strong sense of relief as the empty speedloader
bounced noisily onto the pavement.

Crouched low and tight against the rear bumper of the
black-and-white, Branchowski searched the darkness once
again, momentarily uncertain, and then moved forward along
the far side of the unit as quickly as he could force his
numbed legs to respond. Reaching the driver's door, he
inched himself upward, revolver held out in his left hand as
he stared out into the street. Seeing nothing, he moved quickly.
Reaching in the window, he jabbed at the small red button
just barely within reach on the radio console, then immediately pulled his arm out and dropped down low against the
side of the unit.

Branchowski was vaguely conscious of the dispatcher's voice, calling to confirm that Six Adam's emergency button had been punched. Accidental emergency alerts were a relatively common occurrence with the two-man units where knee room was at a premium. She repeated the call twice, and then immediately put out a code three alert for backup units when she failed to get a response.

Branchowski started to move forward to the edge of the front bumper, and then hesitated. He knew he was violating basic patrol procedure by failing to notify dispatch that a shooting had occurred, that his partner and two suspects were down, and that a third one was out there somewhere. But to do so, he would have to open the door, reach in for the mike, and let the asshole out there know exactly where he was when the goddamned door hinges on the new unit squeaked. The alternative was to go up again and reach through the window, exposing himself for a head shot.

Poor goddamned Jake, Branchowski thought, as he went down on his stomach and pulled himself underneath the unit, catching and tearing his raincoat on the transmission housing as he tried not to look at his partner's shattered face. Farber was lying on his back, thin streams of blood still flowing from an indeterminate number of wounds in his head and neck, his eyes and mouth silently open. For a moment, Branchowski couldn't take his eyes off of the blood-spattered badge that his partner polished with a silicone cloth every afternoon before going on duty.

The paramedics weren't going to be able to do anything for Jake, Branchowski knew, clenching his teeth and fighting the sudden urge to vomit when his hand brushed across ragged pieces of skull on the pavement as he reached for the Remington.

Calling in didn't matter, Branchowski told himself, knowing he was wrong, feeling the chilling surge of adrenaline as his mind responded aggressively to the cold security of the heavy pump shotgun. Trembling fingers, chilled and barely sensitive, checked chamber, magazine, and safety. His hand brushing against a still forearm that had already begun to lose body temperature, he found five extra rounds in Jake's jacket and transferred the shotgun rounds awkwardly into his own pocket.

Jake didn't need help any more, so the only one left was the asshole out there in the darkness who had probably stashed a sawed-off under his coat. That meant he would have to be close. Branchowski grinned knowingly as he twisted under the automobile frame, smearing his clothing in the accumulated grease and oil as he reholstered and secured his revolver. Then he held the shotgun out in front of his head, one large blood-and-grease-stained hand wrapped around the trigger grip, and began to move forward in an instinctive military crawl.

Branchowski emerged from under the unit behind the left front wheel, crouching behind the front headlight frame as he made a quick survey. Nothing moved on the street or sidewalk except the plummeting rain and the grounded, blood-streaked water. It would be at least ten minutes before the first backup arrived, he estimated. Plenty of time. He could feel his heart pound madly against the tight, padded vest. He paused to brush the rain and the sweat out of his eyes with his free hand. Then he ran.

Five, six long strides, and he threw himself across the sidewalk, grunting from the impact as he slid against the unyielding cement, rolling and flattening out into the classic prone position: heels flat, legs spread, head tucked down, and shotgun sighted, searching for the muzzle blast.

No shots. Bastard! Branchowski thought savagely.

He rolled again, this time coming up to a standing ready position, back against the solid brick wall of the liquor store, boots crunching on broken glass.

He's going to wait, Branchowski nodded to himself. He's going to wait until I'm close. Except that he's going to eat buckshot, Branchowski vowed, inching forward along the wall, keeping an eye on the series of alley openings that separated stores along the street up ahead, watching for any shadow that moved in the drizzling rain.

Miserable little pricks, he thought. Busting into a store, drinking themselves senseless, and killing his partner who wrote his reports.

The third suspect broke from the darkness of an alley, running for the street. Branchowski fired instinctively from the hip, absorbing the jarring recoil with his toughened wrists, pumping and triggering a second roaring explosion as the

figure screamed and tumbled. Branchowski yelled out a mocking cry of victory, and then gasped sharply in shock as his
vest suddenly seemed to cave into his solar plexus.

Can't be. Branchowski's mind rejected the data even as he
was slammed backwards into the wall. Dazed and unable to
comprehend why or how, he tried to raise the Remington to
aim at the still figure that lay face down in the street. But he
couldn't, because the shotgun was too heavy and his chest
hurt too much to breathe. He tried to suck in air, but immediately twisted in pain from a spasmodic cough. He was unaware of the second shot that blissfully terminated the pain
when the heavy slug shattered the side of his helmet.

Thanatos reached out with a gloved hand to take a long
drink from the opened soda bottle that he had placed within
easy reach on the cluttered kitchen table. Then, having satisfied his thirst, he quickly moved back to the partially opened
window, squatting down in the totally darkened room to
avoid being spotted from the street. He raised the small
night-vision scope—capable of magnifying any available light
several thousand times—up to his right eye and quickly confirmed a continuing lack of animated movement in the darkened street below.

He scanned the entire area once more, this time allowing
himself a few moments to enjoy the visual effect of the
magnified, green-tinged raindrops as they struck the wet
pavement with increasing frequency. As he expected, the
street remained dark and deserted. If anyone in this isolated
area of the city had heard the sounds of gunfire, he wasn't
about to make his presence known by walking out into the
street.

Thanatos nodded his head in satisfaction, then quickly
returned the scope to its precut space in the foam interior of
the open suitcase. By the time that Thanatos heard the first
siren in the distance, the suitcase had been snapped shut and
placed next to the door. He paused calmly to take one final
look around the room, checking for the third time to make
certain that everything was in order.

Fifteen seconds later, as the second and third sirens began

to add their shrieks to the late-evening din, Thanatos had shut
the door of the hotel room, traversed the hallway and the
back set of sagging wood stairs, and was within a few feet of
his waiting vehicle.

BALEFIRE

Minus 8 Days

Early Friday Morning

0133 hours

Patrol Officer Keith Baughmann, who drove a one-man unit designated Nine Charles, was the first officer to arrive at the shooting scene.

Baughmann had power-turned onto Main Street three blocks north of Albert's Liquor, and he was approximately one hundred and fifty yards from the store when his headlights picked up the empty black-and-white that was parked at an angle in front of the store and the crumpled dark figures on the sidewalk. He immediately jammed on the brakes, sliding the unit to a stop sideways in the middle of the street, and grabbed for his mike.

"Nine Charles, nine-nine-seven! Repeat, code nine-nine-seven! Officers are down at Albert's Liquor! Backup and paramedics, now!"

"Nine Charles, confirming officers are down at Main and Second. Eight Adam, Four Charles and Twenty-Six Sam, start rolling, code three."

Baughmann was out of his unit and running toward the sprawled uniformed figures on the sidewalk, his revolver in one hand and the portable pack-set radio in the other, before the broadcast stopped. He could hear the other units in the south confirm that they were converging on the downtown area, the radio transmissions distracting as he tried to take in everything at once. One body in the street, civilian, probably dead. Three bodies on the sidewalk, one civilian, definitely dead. Farber, dead. Baughmann turned his head away, numbed by the sight of Farber's shattered face, but instantly stone-

37

walled his emotions as he made a quick survival check of the
area.

Nothing moved on the street in either direction. Baughmann
made a mental note of the alley locations. No movement.
Then, remembering an old academy admonition that cops
usually forget to look up, he scanned the tops of the buildings
on both sides of the street, searching for windows or a
silhouetted figure, anything, while he moved quickly to the
second uniform. Branchowski. Still breathing?

Baughmann looked around quickly once more, and then
dropped to his knees, carefully setting his revolver within
easy reach. He gently touched the bleeding head and neck,
feeling for a carotid pulse; he felt nothing. He then tried his
flashlight, holding the illuminated glass up against Branchowski's mouth. Faintly visible condensation formed on the
glass disc.

"Nine Charles!" Baughmann yelled into the radio, grabbing up his revolver and immediately making another visual
search of the quiet street. "Code three the paramedics! Farber's
DOA. Branchowski's got a head wound. Two suspects down."

He looked up at the open doorway of the liquor store and
saw the twisted, unmoving legs for the first time.

"Correction, three suspects down. Hurry those backups!"
he added unnecessarily, feeling the familiar panic and numbness starting to build. Goddamned Southeast Asia. He kept
staring back into the darkness, instinctively wanting to fight
and hide behind something.

"Easy, buddy," he murmured, setting the radio aside and
running his hand across Branchowski's forehead, pushing the
blood-matted hair away from his eyes. Baughmann had no
intention of abandoning the fallen officer, in spite of his
growing fear of the surrounding darkness.

He tried to stop the flow of blood from Branchowski's
head, using his handkerchief as a compression pad. He tucked
the folded piece of cloth as tightly as he could against the torn
scalp that was exposed, but he was afraid to remove the
shattered remains of the heavy plastic helmet which concealed the major source of the bleeding.

He continued to monitor Branchowski's faint and irregular
breathing. "You're gonna make it, buddy," he whispered,

anger and helplessness pushing aside his fear that the veteran officer was very near death.

"Nine Charles be advised paramedics en route from the north, code three, ETA ten."

"Nine Charles. Is there anything closer?" Baughmann demanded. He was venting his frustration at the dispatcher, even though he knew that the closest paramedic unit would be automatically dispatched on an "Officer Down" call, regardless of any jurisdictional boundary lines.

"Negative. We have two additionals rolling on a mutual aid. All units are code three."

"Eight Adam, Nine Charles. Seventeenth and Pecan. ETA one. Hold on, babe."

"Four Charles. Adam and Mag. ETA three."

Baughmann maintained pressure on the exposed portion of the head wound while he tied a large compress bandage from the first-aid kit around the loosely attached sections of broken helmet and torn skin. He had reluctantly left the mortally wounded officer for a few moments to retrieve the first-aid kit from Farber and Branchowski's unit when he realized that his handkerchief was soaked through with blood. Now that he had the visible bleeding under control, he continued his visual search of the area from his kneeling position, tense and expectant.

Black and grey shadows mixed with the rain and the reflections from the still-rotating red and blue lights on his unit. Nothing else was moving that he could see. He checked the rooftops again, feeling the shakes starting as he tightened his grip on his revolver, wishing now that he had the shotgun that was still in his unit, but it was too far away.

Shotgun?

He swiveled around and stared into Branchowski's unit through the opened passenger-side door. The shotgun rack hung open. Baughmann forced himself to think about the missing shotgun. Farber had been hit by a shotgun blast. Farber and Branchowski both had their side arms holstered and strapped in. Baughmann shook his head. Didn't figure.

By the time that Eight Adam came flashing and shrieking around the corner, Keith Baughmann had made two important discoveries. He had located Farber's and Branchowski's shotgun lying under the front of their black-and-white, almost hidden by the right front tire. He had left it there, unwilling to expose his back in order to reach underneath the unit for the more protective weapon, realizing that its location might mean something to the detectives. He had also discovered that all three of the suspects were DOA and none of them appeared to have a weapon on or about their persons.

Patrol Sergeant Patrick Lagucii was not by nature a decisive individual. Specifically, the potbellied, egotistical supervisor did not like to make decisions in field situations, much preferring to allow his patrol officers to handle the problems on their own whenever possible. According to Lagucii's insistent rationalization, which did have some merit, his hands-off policy would eventually make his patrolmen better police officers. Also, everyone realized, it would ensure that the patrolmen would face the Review Board instead of Lagucii when the inevitable screw-ups occurred.

Lagucii would have preferred to place the entire shooting scene in Keith Baughmann's hands. After all, Baughmann had been the first officer on the scene, and the book specifically stated that the first officer on the scene was responsible for the investigation until properly relieved by his supervisor. Patrick Lagucii had no intention of properly relieving anyone except himself. In fact, he would have been on his way back to the station already to initiate the paperwork and get things organized if he hadn't been the only available sergeant in the field—and if Baughmann hadn't run off to help search the immediate area, after stuffing his field jacket under Branchowski's head and placing his raincoat over the unconscious officer.

It wasn't that Lagucii didn't care about his men. He did care, but only to the extent that their welfare and safety reflected upon his rating as a supervisor. Emotionally, Lagucii maintained a careful distance, never allowing himself to get involved in the prayer meetings and other officer-attended functions that had a tendency to result in disciplinary action. In effect, Lagucii simply looked upon his squad of six officers as city employees who were expected to perform their duties without getting hurt.

The paramedics arrived and immediately formed a tight

ring around Branchowski, working fast with practiced team-work to try and save the officer's life. One paramedic started cutting off the uniform with a pair of heavy-duty surgical scissors, while a second wrapped a pressure cuff around one of Branchowski's arms and a third began working cautiously at the splintered helmet. Lagucii watched from the shelter of the liquor store doorway, lighting his third cigarette from the butt of the second while he waited impatiently for a detective supervisor to arrive. He wanted out of this scene as soon as he could possibly get clear.

Baughmann had advised him that all the weapons located in the area so far belonged to Farber and Branchowski. So now they had three unarmed kids shot and killed during a routine four-five-nine call. A simple goddamned burglary. Much worse, all three of the young victims—suspects, Lagucii corrected himself, well aware that he was likely to be inter-viewed and that an unfortunate choice of words could prove to be very embarrassing—were definitely members of the very vocal and politically influential Mexican-American community.

Lagucii's instinctive sense of self-preservation told him that there would be a charge of unjustified shooting filed on this case. And based upon the growing crowd of spectators standing around the outside of the barrier ropes, it was very likely that newspaper and television reporters would arrive within the hour.

Under less volatile conditions, the photogenic patrol ser-geant would have willingly remained on the scene, making himself available to be interviewed as the supervising uni-formed officer. Using the full effect of the sharply creased field uniform and gleaming badge to present a correctly pro-fessional image, Lagucii had never been one to overlook the effect of positive media coverage on his law enforcement career.

Tonight, however, the officer who faced the reporters and camera crews would be required to answer or avoid some very touchy questions. Sergeant Patrick Lagucii had no inten-tion of being that officer.

BALEFIRE

Minus 8 Days

Early Friday Morning

0206 hours

Detective Sergeant Walter Andersen hated telephones. Had he remained a bachelor into his middle years instead of becoming a husband and a father of two extremely attractive daughters, the Andersen household would have been one of a very few middle-income residences in California to have its telephone cable terminate six inches from the house.

Andersen was one of the new generation of officers in a police department that had grown rapidly from a handful of deputies who casually patrolled a beach town to a modern two-hundred-and-fifty-man police force that used modern law enforcement methods and equipment to maintain order in a city bulging with new coastal developments and people. Relatively young for his investigator's stripes, aggressive, cool-headed, well-educated, protective of his men, Andersen had only one hang-up. He hated to work overtime.

Unlike the numerous officers in the department who were working on their second or third divorce, Sergeant Walt Andersen was totally dedicated to his blond Scandinavian wife and his two daughters. Because he believed strongly that a man was obligated to care for the needs of his family first, he cheerfully accepted the demands that such an attitude placed upon his own free time and saw to it that his off-duty hours were spent on family outings and home projects. Given the opportunity, he would have left the station at precisely 1800 hours every evening, Monday through Friday. Unfortunately for his treasured family life, along with the detective's stripes and prestigious homicide detail came overtime, a constant and unavoidable part of the job, just as the telephone was unavoidable, too.

There were three of the intrusive instruments in Andersen's home. One was mandated. Departmental regulations specified that every member of the homicide division had to be available by phone for a call-out at any time of the day or night. In the event that Andersen left the city on a nonscheduled vacation or was gone overnight, he was expected to leave an emergency phone number with the front desk. The alternative was to wear a beeper, but Andersen detested beepers even more than telephones.

Conforming with the regulations also required that Andersen acknowledge the blossoming maturity of his teenaged daughters—both of whom Andersen thought attracted more than their fair share of male attention—and have a second phone line installed. This resulted in at least one phone number that could be reached in the evening with occasional, though by no means guaranteed, success.

Unfortunately, phone calls at two o'clock in the morning were never for his daughters or for his soundly sleeping wife.

"Andersen," he answered sleepily, trying to separate the confusion of an interrupted dream from the seemingly disjointed statements coming out of the telephone. The first five to ten seconds of a call-out were always difficult. He shook his head, trying to concentrate on the phone. Then the words began to make sense, and he was suddenly very alert and listening carefully.

"All right, I've got it," he finally said, his voice no longer sleepy. His wife had responded subconsciously, and was immediately awake. She reached for him, confused, and recoiled slightly at the feel of his tightened back and shoulder muscles as he listened intently at the phone.

"I want Hernandez, Kretcher, and O'Rorke. Have them meet me at the scene. What about the lab?"

The Watch Commander assured Andersen that the crime lab was being notified.

"Good. See if you can get Sheffield. Tell him I want a full team out there in thirty minutes."

Andersen hung up, noting the time of the call on the clock radio. He scribbled 0215 hours on the small notebook next to the phone. It was the first of several hundred notes that he would make regarding the case before the night was over. He took a deep breath and shook his head, trying to release some of the tightness. He suddenly realized that his wife was awake, her head propped up on her arm, watching him intently.

"What's the matter?" Her voice was gentle.

He released the breath through clenched teeth. "Branchowski and Farber have been shot," he rasped. "Jake's dead."

"Oh, my God," she whispered.

Michelle Andersen played bridge on Thursday nights with Katherine Farber and several of the other officers' wives, her one attempt to maintain some contact with the police environment within which her husband worked. She visualized Kathy— very young, a little uncertain about her husband's career, but very trusting and vocally certain that Jake was too careful to get hurt. Michelle Andersen realized that her hands were clenched and her fingernails had begun to dig painfully into her palms.

She also realized, not for the first time, that she, too, was very trusting and equally certain that her gentle, easy-going husband was very good at his job. She watched him dress, pulling heavy jeans and wool shirt over his solid frame—just barely starting to thicken at the hips and waist—and quickly lacing the waterproofed hiking boots. He quickly combed his short blond hair, only recently beginning to turn white at the temples. Then he reached up on the top shelf of their closet for the belt that held a pair of handcuffs, a folding buck knife, a holstered .45 automatic and two extra clips of ammunition.

Andersen strapped the leather belt and its hardware around his hips, reflexively checking the safety with his fingers, and slipped on the heavy jacket that effectively concealed the tools of his profession.

"See you for breakfast?" his wife asked, forcing herself to talk in a neutral voice and to block out Kathy Farber's laughing face. She understood when he shook his head absentmindedly, kissing her lightly on the cheek before heading for the bedroom door. She waited until she heard the garage door close, gathering her resolve. Then she reached for the phone to notify the Watch Commander that she would be available to assist in notifying Kathy Farber if needed.

*   *   *

Brian Sheffield instinctively reached out to slam the alarm clock into silence and was immediately jerked into a semiawake state of confusion when the jarring noise sounded again. He remained in a sitting position for a few moments, unable to comprehend what or where. Then his mental gears reluctantly meshed, and he identified the sound.

"Meiko, phone," he mumbled sleepily, dropping his head back down on the pillow and groaning as the phone on the opposite side of the bed rang a third time. The warm, soft, and naked body lying beside him refused to stir, and he forced himself to stretch across the unresponding girl to reach the receiver.

"Hello," Sheffield slurred. He tried to speak clearly, but the wine and the late evening love-making had sapped his normal reserves, which hadn't been replenished by the two hours of sleep indicated by the glowing clock face. Sheffield was exhausted, but he had already concluded that there wasn't a chance in the world that it was going to be a wrong number.

"Brian? This is Gilcrist. You awake?"

"No." The answer was spontaneous, his mind reacting independently in a futile attempt to delay the inevitable for a few more precious minutes of sleep. Lieutenant Herbert Gilcrist was the Watch Commander on the graveyard shift, and his voice meant a call-out.

"We need you down here, son. Right away. Full team as soon as possible."

"What have you got?" Ever a scientist, Sheffield's curiosity overcame his fatigue.

"Officer's been killed," Gilcrist said, the words catching in his throat. He had been making similar calls for the past five minutes, and it hadn't gotten any easier. "Jake Farber. Dan Branchowski's critical. Three suspects dead on the scene and maybe others running."

"Shit," Sheffield whispered softly, feeling a chill run through his body that had very little to do with the cool night air coming in from the opened bedroom window. "Where's it at?"

"Downtown, Main and Pacific Coast Highway," the fifty-year-old Watch Commander answered in a strained, but controlled voice. "We need you down here fast. Who else do you want?"

Sheffield forced himself back into his scientist's role. Define the scope of the problem, then evaluate and select the appropriate resources. Trouble was, he wouldn't know how much work would be involved until he got to the scene. But from Gilcrist's brief description, it was going to be a bad one.

"Ed Malinger, Bob Dorsey, Lee Spencer," Sheffield decided, selecting his senior photographer and the crime lab's most experienced identification technicians.

"You got 'em," Gilcrist replied, rapidly scrawling the names on a note pad and reaching for the personnel roster. "Anyone else?"

"I'll bring Meiko," Sheffield answered, vaguely aware but unconcerned that his statement amounted to a confession. Gilcrist had too many things on his mind to worry about a case of boss-worker cohabitation, thought Sheffield as he hung up the phone.

Meiko was going to be difficult to wake up, Sheffield realized. She was lying face down on the bed, her long shiny black hair spread fanlike over the smooth milky skin of her bare shoulders and back, reflecting the painfully bright light from the small bed lamp.

"Come on, bright eyes," Sheffield urged, resisting the temptation to move his hands down the girl's passively seductive body. "Wake up. We've got to go to work."

Meiko mumbled something that was muffled and lost beneath her crossed forearms. Beyond the uncertain vocal response, there was no indication at all that she was going to awaken from a deep sleep.

"It's a call-out, lover," Sheffield whispered next to an exposed ear, and then gently swatted her bottom when he failed to get any further response.

"You go," she mumbled a little more distinctly, trying to maintain her grip on the twilight zone as her normally chivalrous lover continued to try to shake her out of a perfectly satisfying dream.

"We've got a four-body homicide. One of our guys is dead."

He felt her stiffen under his hands. Meiko sat up and

turned to face him, her eyes blinking open in shock, but Sheffield's mind was already two and a half miles away, reviewing in his mind the scene search equipment in the laboratory.

BALEFIRE

Minus 8 Days

Early Friday Morning

0230 hours

It was immediately obvious to the lab team that the scene was still hot. There were four officers from the SWAT unit stationed on the scene, each armed with an M-16 automatic assault rifle. They had positioned themselves at the four corners of the scene's perimeter with their backs to the interior of the scene and their rifles pointed at second-story windows and rooftops. Additional officers were taking names and directing the growing number of blurry-eyed and half-dressed spectators to stay behind rope barriers. In the darkness, wildly illuminated by headlamps, street lights and still rotating red-and-blues, the scene looked like a combination of carnival and war zone.

Detective Rudy Hernandez spotted the arriving lab van and walked quickly over to the curb as Sheffield, Malinger and Meiko Harikawa began to open their equipment boxes. Hernandez had been the first detective to arrive at the scene. As such, he would be responsible for the entire investigation until Andersen arrived and took over.

"Ready to go to work, Doctor?" Hernandez's normally spirited bantering was markedly subdued, but he still made an attempt at their running joke that anyone who ran around in a white coat had to be a doctor. Rudy Hernandez was a good cop who believed strongly in teamwork. Moreover, he was more intrigued than he would admit by the scientific technology used by the forensic team.

Sheffield had worked with Hernandez on several investigations, but this was the first one in which a cop had been

48

injured or killed. Hernandez was frustrated, an easy observation for Sheffield who knew the Mexican-American officer took any assault on a police officer as a personal attack. The fact that Hernandez was the senior investigator on the scene, and therefore not allowed to take part in the door-to-door search for any more suspects, had to be tearing at his sense of professionalism—not to mention his sincere belief in summary revenge.

"Walk-thru?" Sheffield asked.

Hernandez nodded, his eyes momentarily flickering up at a rooftop, hoping. His .357 was within easy reach in his shoulder holster.

"Just a second." Sheffield motioned to Malinger, who was busy strapping on a strobe pack and a camera bag. "Ed, hop up on the van and get some overall shots before we do the walk-thru. Concentrate on the center."

"Gotcha." Malinger nodded and started up the metal ladder welded to the back of the lab van, climbing toward the heavy metal platform that would give him a clear view of the entire street. The photographs would later show the exact locations of the bodies and the black-and-white that sat abandoned in the center of the roped-off perimeter. The strobe light flashed several times, adding to the eeriness as the blanketed bodies were momentarily illuminated before fading back among the street shadows.

The four investigators began the walk-thru at the body that was lying face down in the middle of the street. Hernandez, Sheffield and Meiko walked together; Malinger was behind them taking medium-range and close-up photos.

"This one caught at least one round of buckshot in the back," Hernandez said, lifting up the blanket and using his flashlight to point out the pellet-sized holes in the back of the blood-darkened jacket.

"Branchowski?" Sheffield asked.

"Could be. Their shotgun's under the unit."

Sheffield nodded and made a note on his clipboard.

"The one face down in the store got one in the back, probably a thirty-eight or three-five-seven," Hernandez continued. "Six empty casings and an empty speedloader behind the unit. Farber has both of his loaders in his belt, duty weapon holstered and snapped." Hernandez used his flashlight to illuminate the empty metal speedloader and the casings.

Meiko Harikawa immediately knelt down to place two sequentially numbered location tags next to the speedloader and casings, and then stepped back to allow Malinger to take his photos, a procedure that would be repeated several dozen times during the next few hours.

The part that Sheffield had been dreading was next. He didn't know Farber all that well, but he had seen the veteran officer at several scenes. He knew that the body lying underneath the blue woolen PD blanket would barely resemble the man that he had once observed directing traffic and laughing with some small children. Sheffield sent Meiko back to bag the hands of the first two suspects—to protect the hands from the rain until they had the time to go back and swab for gunpowder residues. He wanted to give Meiko a chance to stay back if she wanted, even though he knew that she wouldn't.

Hernandez knelt down and gently pulled the blanket back from Farber's face. The lifeless eyes stared upward, reflecting the last moments of pain and disbelief. Sheffield used his flashlight to try to count the wounds. At least six in the left side of the face and neck. Two possible ricochets against the helmet. The holes were big, consistent with wounds typically caused by the .00 buck officers carried in their shotguns. At close range, the effects of a .00 magnum load were devastating and usually fatal.

"What do you think, Doctor?" Hernandez asked, using the fake title by reflex. There was no trace of the casual banter left in his voice, which now came from somewhere else, someplace deep and cold.

"Short distance," Sheffield shrugged, his throat feeling tight. "Maybe fifteen, twenty yards. Hard to say." He looked around at the three bodies, making rough estimates. "Could have been any of them. Anybody find the gun they used?"

Hernandez shook his head. "PD weapons only, so far. Found two double-aught casings in the gutter." He used the flashlight again to point out the location of the two expended shotgun rounds, just in front of the blood-spattered sidewalk area where Branchowski had fallen. "Figure the paramedics probably kicked them around while they were working on Branch.''

Sheffield nodded and began talking into his tape recorder. Later, back in the lab, he would use the roughly dictated tapes to prepare a polished and detailed record of the scene, trying to transfer the complexity of a three-dimensional homicide scene onto two-dimensional pieces of white paper.

"What about the windows?" Hernandez asked when Sheffield had finished. He pointed up at the windows of a two-story building across the street. It was one of the old downtown hotels; more accurately, it was a cluster of worn, dirty, and foul-smelling rooms with one shared, filthy bathroom. It had been built in the forties, and now catered to beach bums, dopers and runaways.

Sheffield looked up, quickly gauging distance, and shook his head. "Too far away. From that distance, the pellet pattern would have to spread at least three feet. No way he'd be hit in the head with eight out of twelve."

"Makes sense," Hernandez nodded. He was convinced by the logic, but he still looked back up at the windows across the street with suspicion that was pure cop instinct.

Before Hernandez and Sheffield could get into a discussion about pellet patterns, Meiko came up beside them and knelt down to examine Farber's wounds. Then she gently replaced the blanket.

"Should I bag his hands, too?" she asked hesitantly.

It took Sheffield a couple of seconds. The gunpowder residue test was usually a suspect-oriented procedure. Meiko was assuming that Farber would be treated like any other victim in a shooting, that is, like a potential suspect.

Sheffield looked up at Hernandez. The detective shrugged and looked straight back into his eyes, momentarily revealing a coldness that Sheffield had never seen in the thick-shouldered officer. "Do your job."

"Yeah, bag everyone," Sheffield said. "Including Branchowski," he added, looking at Hernandez again. The detective removed the pack-set radio from his belt and issued the order to the officers who would be standing by at the hospital. If possible, and only if it would not interfere with the operation, the doctors were to be requested to tape small paper bags around Branchowski's hands.

"They've probably washed him already," Hernandez said.
"Yeah, I know," Sheffield nodded, "but we'll try anyway.
I don't want to screw up anything on this one."

When Detective Sergeant Walt Andersen stepped out of his
car down the street from Albert's Liquor Store, the scene
investigation, and the controlled disorder that inevitably accompanied such an undertaking, was well under way. At least
it stopped raining, Andersen thought as he watched Homicide
Detective Hernandez and Patrol Sergeant Lagucii step carefully through the barricades. Andersen steeled himself for the
worst, knowing from past experience that Lagucii was perfectly capable of derailing an investigation at its onset.
"Glad to see you here, Walt," Lagucii said, his nervous
smile a bright contrast to the somber expression of Hernandez.
"This is going to be a bad one. Real bad," he emphasized
with a jerky movement of his hand. "KUTV's got a mobile
team with a mini-cam on their way here now. They're making noise about this being an unjustified shooting with racial
overtones."
Lagucii's nerves were already starting to act up, Andersen
noted. Twitch under the left eye. Probably meant that the
egotistical son of a bitch had things thoroughly screwed up.
"What do we have, Pat?" Andersen asked conversationally.
The homicide sergeant had no real intention of listening to
Lagucii. Any information that he needed he would get from
Hernandez after Lagucii found an excuse to head back to the
station. And that shouldn't take long at all, Andersen estimated,
observing that the twitch was pulsing at an increasing rate.
"Well, the information's a little sketchy," the patrol sergeant began lamely. "Basically, Farber and Branchowski
walked into it. Three, maybe four suspects in the liquor store.
Probably came out shooting. Best I can tell, Branchowski got
two of them before he got hit. Clean shooting, as far as I can
see, but the media boys aren't going for it."
"Who called them in?"
Lagucii shrugged. "You know how it is when these people
get into trouble. First thing they want is a lawyer and a tv
crew." The patrol sergeant smiled knowingly, oblivious to
the malevolent glare from Hernandez less than six feet away.

"Anyway, I talked with them on the phone and said that you'd give them a statement when you had things under control."

"Thanks a lot," Andersen said drily. "You have a county team rolling?"

"You mean the coroner? He'll be here as soon as he rounds up another wagon. Four stiffs . . ." Lagucii's voice trailed off as the enormity of his words registered. Hernandez choked back a strangled sound deep in his throat, turned, and walked quickly away in disgust before his wire-tight control snapped.

"Investigators, Lagucii," Andersen said softly, jaw muscles tightening as he resisted a sudden impulse to drive a clenched fist into the capped and polished teeth that were outlined by the neatly trimmed mustache. "DA's investigators. We've got a dead cop and a critically wounded cop in a shooting incident with three dead suspects. That means that we automatically run a joint investigation. Remember?"

"Oh, yeah, sure." Lagucii tried to act as though the importance of an independent parallel investigation on a cop killing—a situation in which the victim's fellow officers were likely to be biased in their search for additional evidence and suspects—was something that anyone could forget.

"Hey, listen," Lagucii said, placing his gloved hands on his hips, resting his right wrist across the grip of the lightly oiled chrome-plated revolver he religiously cleaned and polished weekly, "I'll get on that as soon as I report back in to the Watch Commander. I figure that Gilcrist'll want a first-hand report as soon as possible. I'll make the call to the county from the station."

Lagucii held his mirror-practiced supervisory pose out of habit for a few moments, until his specialized survival instincts, those dealing with the care and maintenance of his departmental image, alerted him to the fact that Andersen wasn't impressed.

Shrugging self-consciously, Lagucii waved his hand in the general direction of the crime scene activity. "She's all yours, Walt," he said. Then he hurriedly walked over toward his patrol unit without waiting to see if Andersen would respond.

Andersen watched quietly as Lagucii paused momentarily in his flight to say something to the well-known television newscaster who had arrived and was busy outside of the scene perimeter working with his field recording crew, setting up for a background scene shot to highlight his six-o'clock news report. Lagucii spoke briefly in his typically animated fashion, patting the newscaster on the shoulder as he made some final comment before reaching for the door of his black-and-white. The cameraman picked up on Lagucii's pose and quickly recorded a short segment.

"Asshole," Andersen muttered out loud to no one in particular as he watched Lagucii drive rapidly away. He ignored the departing sergeant's waving hand.

"Not enough brains for an asshole," Hernandez commented, having moved up quietly next to Andersen. "An asshole knows when to shut up and not spread crap all over the place."

Andersen grinned briefly at his stocky, mustachioed detective, and then immediately sobered. "What do we have, Rudy?"

"A fuckin' mess, boss," Hernandez spat as they both started walking carefully toward the store, taking care not to step on location tags and the related evidence. "By the way, sorry about the county notification. I shoulda asked."

"Not your job." Andersen shook his head.

Hernandez shrugged.

"I've got O'Rorke, Dukata, and Baughmann checking those rooms," Hernandez continued, pointing up at the second-story windows across the street.

"Baughmann? I thought he was the reporting officer?" Andersen closed his eyes in momentary frustration. Lagucii again. One officer at every major crime scene was supposed to be designated the reporting officer. His job was to assemble, organize and cross-check all the information necessary to write the initial crime report. The job was demanding, and it required the officer's constant attention. He was not supposed to be running around kicking in doors.

Hernandez explained the background on Baughmann's initial actions at the scene, noting that the patrol officer's raincoat and jacket were still laying on the sidewalk next to the spot where the paramedics had gone to work on Branchowski.

"He did a good first-aid job on Branch, Walt," Hernandez added. "I figured I'd let him run a little while longer, seeing as how our good buddy let him loose in the first place. He deserves a chance if there's anyone else out there.''

''What about the crime report?''

''I took a few notes.'' Hernandez motioned with his notebook. At least fifteen pages were flipped back, filled with Hernandez's distinctive block printing. ''They should be finished up there in another ten. I'll sit down with Baughmann and work up the report.'' Hernandez produced a slightly pained smile at the thought of doing the additional paperwork, something that was usually assigned to one of the junior officers at the scene.

''Fair enough. What else have we got?''

''In the meantime,'' Hernandez continued, ''Kretcher and I have done a little preliminary work and come up with a big fat zero. No witnesses, no guns.''

''What?'' Andersen's head came up quickly from his clipboard. ''What do you mean, no guns?''

''Didn't Lagucii tell you?''

''Fuck, no!''

Hernandez muttered something in vulgarized Spanish. ''All we know so far is that we've got three young and very dead suspects. None of them were armed. At least, we haven't found any weapons yet.'' Hernandez looked up at Andersen and shrugged as if to say he didn't believe it either.

''Branchowski and Farber shot three unarmed men?'' Andersen's expression matched the incredulous tone of his voice.

Hernandez silently opened his palms skyward. ''Three unarmed kids,'' he corrected.

''You check the alleys and trash cans?''

''Sure.''

''What about under the bodies?''

''Not supposed to move anything until the coroner's investigator arrives,'' Hernandez reminded reproachfully.

''Is he going to find anything?''

''No, I don't think so. At least, he isn't going to find any rifles, pistols or sawed-off shotguns. Might find a couple of pocket knives.'' Hernandez decided not to mention that he had made a complete pat-down search of the bodies. Better to keep things in their proper perspective. Figuring that Lagucii had probably ignored anything relevant to the case when he

talked with Andersen, Hernandez briefed him on Sheffield's
opinion that Farber's wounds were caused by buckshot at less
than twenty feet.

"Fourth suspect could have collected the guns before haul-
ing ass," Andersen suggested, standing in the middle of the
unevenly illuminated street with his hands in his pockets,
staring at one of the blanket-covered bodies.

"Possible," Hernandez agreed, not believing it either. "But
if he did, he left Farber's and Branchowski's revolvers and
their shotgun. Kinda dark around here to be looking around
for a gun with units moving in. Bastard'd have to be awfully
cool."

"Who do you figure did the shooting?"

Hernandez shrugged as if he were used to being asked
impossible questions. "Farber's revolver is fully loaded—
Sheffield checked. His belt loaders are full. He usually rode
shotgun, so you have to figure he came out of the unit with
the twelve-gauge. Guy in the middle of the street's got a load
of buck in his ass and backbone. Trouble is, Farber looks like
he got hit with buck."

"Might have lost the weapon."

"Yeah, sure," Hernandez nodded. Neither of them could
visualize the veteran Farber losing a loaded shotgun to a
couple of punk kids. "Thing is, they found Branchowski over
there by the wall with a holstered revolver."

Andersen was digesting that bit of perplexing information
when he noticed that the television crew, at the direction of
the newscaster, was dragging their equipment past the wood
and rope barriers that defined the scene's perimeter.

"Hey, where the hell do you think you're going?" Andersen yelled, moving forward and standing in front of the
newsmen who were struggling to lift their minicamera system
over the ropes. The newscaster looked up, startled, and then
extended an opened hand and an engaging smile.

"Jack Paradee, Six-O'Clock News," he said confidently,
but then hesitated as he realized that the angry cop had made
no effort to move aside or take the offered hand. "Ah, your
Sergeant . . . Lagucii, I believe . . . he said it would be all
right to go inside and take some background shots as long as
we watched where we stepped. We won't get in the way."

"You sure as hell won't," Andersen agreed. "This area is

restricted. You and your people will be required to remain behind the barriers at all times, in spite of whatever Sergeant Lagucii may have told you.''

Andersen turned and glared at the cameraman who was working frantically to disengage himself from the rope while trying to get Andersen and Paradee in focus. The glaring floodlights caused Andersen to wince. He quickly turned away to protect his eyes.

"Officer, do you intend—'' Paradee began.

"I am Detective Sergeant Andersen. I am in charge of this investigation, and yes, I do intend to keep you and your crew out of the way of my men.'' Anderson hesitated for a moment, looked around, and then continued. "I might also add that we are not in a position to guarantee the safety of you and your crew.''

The cameraman and the soundman appeared to notice for the first time the SWAT officer standing guard at one corner of the perimeter. They looked at each other and then at the darkened and shadowy surroundings. If Paradee noticed, he didn't give any outward indication.

"Are you aware then, Sergeant Andersen, of the rumors that your department may be trying to cover up an unjustified shooting?'' Paradee's smile had shifted perceptively. The camera lights showed the newscaster's expression to be polite, inquisitive, and persistent. This was precisely the image that was expected of a professional reporter whose primary goal in life was to keep the public well informed and whose career image was about to be enhanced by his choice assignment covering the upcoming Olympic Games.

It was a nicely performed act, but Andersen knew Paradee to be a ruthless digger who was very good at his job, and thoroughly dedicated to the premise that all cops were either barbarians, racists, or liars. Andersen was also very much aware of the theory—confirmed in private by a number of other newsmen in the community—that Paradee was equally dedicated to the prospect of advancing his career into a choice anchor spot on the evening news, preferably over the figurative bodies of several unwary cops.

Resisting his impulse to tell the newscaster what he thought of rumor-mongering hacks, Andersen mentally cursed Lagucii

for the fifth time that evening. Resigning himself to losing a
few more minutes of valuable investigative time, he began
talking to Paradee in a slow, firm voice.

Sheffield walked over to the open door of the ill-fated
black-and-white, and bent down to examine Bob Dorsey's
efforts.

"Get anything off of that shotgun mount?" Sheffield asked
the ID technician. Dorsey's hands and face were streaked and
smeared with black fingerprint powder, as was a major portion of the vehicle's interior.

"A few partials—mostly glove smears. You really think
one of those kids got at their shotgun?" Dorsey asked. He
quickly folded and tore off a four-inch strip of lift tape from
the roll on the seat, then carefully rubbed the sticky transpar-
ent tape over a dusted area on the rearview mirror with his
thumb.

"It would explain a few things." Sheffield shrugged.

"Maybe," Dorsey said, reaching for his blackened Fiberglas brush and redusting the rearview mirror, holding a small
flashlight beam on the smudged area in question with his
other hand. "But it sure doesn't make a hell of a lot of sense.
Farber's shotgun key is still on his belt."

Sheffield's eyes followed the flashlight beam as it played
across the empty lock mechanism of the brass shotgun mount.
He muttered something unintelligible and made another notation on his clipboard. Dorsey nodded his head sympathetically and went back to work as Sheffield stood up and looked
around the scene.

The whole idea was to find a pattern. He had a number of
established points—the store, the black-and-white, the locations of Farber and Branchowski and the three suspects, the
shotgun. The trick now was to backtrack, to find logical
sequences that would explain positions and facts that appeared to be contradictory. The expended shotgun and revolver casings, the empty speedloader, the miscellaneous
debris inside the store and out on the sidewalk, all had to fit
into the pattern.

Sheffield reminded himself that there had to be a logical
pattern as he allowed his flashlight beam to shine on a filmy

piece of torn plastic that he had noticed lying in the gutter in front of the liquor store. He was in the process of trying to decide whether or not the seemingly irrelevant bit of debris was worth another line on his evidence list when Hernandez came up beside him.

"Doing any good, Doctor?"

Sheffield started to answer when a broadcast came over the pack-set in the detective's hand. The voice on the other end was broken—the transmission was partially blocked by the high buildings in the area—but they both heard Hernandez's call sign.

Hernandez brought the pack-set up to his ear and requested a repeat. He listened for a few moments and then looked up at Sheffield with a confused expression on his face.

"That was Gilcrist. He's at the hospital. The doctor just advised him that they found a deer slug in Branchowski's clothing."

Sheffield and Hernandez stared at each other for a moment in shared confusion. The realization hit them at the same time. They both turned and looked out across the street at the row of second-story windows. Sheffield was still staring up at the darkened windows when Hernandez began talking fast into the keyed mike of his radio.

BALEFIRE

Minus 8 Days

Early Friday Morning

0445 hours

The number of people who knew why Jacob Farber had died violently in the middle of Main Street could be counted on the fingers of two hands. At 4:45 that morning, five of those individuals were gathered at an expensively decorated house less than thirty miles south of the killing site.

The home was owned by a Dr. Jacquem Kaem, a skillful and financially successful oral surgeon whose medical career had been utilized to purchase the six-bedroom estate that overlooked the Pacific Ocean from one of Dana Point's more impressive bluffs. The house was accessible only by a narrow road which led up to the exclusive dwelling from a guardhouse that was manned twenty-four hours a day. As a place to get away from it all, the thick-beamed deck house offered more in terms of beauty, peacefulness, and security than any man could reasonably ask.

More important to the five men who had taken extensive precautions to arrive at the coastal retreat without being observed, the expensive home also offered a virtually impregnable degree of security and privacy for their conversations. Above all else, their identities and the very existence of the Committee had to remain a tightly guarded secret if the Balefire Warning was to succeed.

Four of the well-dressed men sat in deeply padded living room chairs arranged in a semicircle looking out over a rock-and-moss garden that suddenly dropped away at the top of a sheer cliff. Fifty feet below the alarmed boundary of the garden, the waves crashed rhythmically against huge broken chunks of rock from the cliff which was now reinforced against further erosion. Sitting in their chairs, the men could hear the pulsing sounds of the ocean and smell the distinctive odors that rose up from the frothy salt water.

The men talked quietly among themselves, sipping carefully at mugs of steaming coffee as they individually fought against fatigue and the lulling sounds of the ocean. They had been up all night arguing and discussing, waiting patiently for the sequence of events they had initiated to unfold properly.

The men waited now with considerably less patience as their host stood silently in the adjoining dining room and held a telephone to his ear. They watched even as they talked, noting the fact that Kaem nodded his head several times before he placed the phone receiver in the recessed cradle of a typewriter-sized computer and pressed a series of raised buttons on the keyboard. After a delay of approximately fifteen seconds, a high-speed printer attached to the computer began to chatter and disgorge paper.

The electronic device finally fell silent, and Kaem quickly tore the extended length of paper out of the printer. As his eyes scanned across the printout, his face remained expressionless.

"It goes well?"

The question had been asked silently by every one of the four professional men as they remained sitting in their comfortable chairs, staring at Kaem. The most imposing member of the select group had vocalized their mutual concern. Zakar Taskanian, a middle-aged lawyer with a barrellike body and a fierce looking black mustache, had a well-deserved reputation for bluntly speaking his razor-sharp mind whenever he pleased.

Taskanian held his ceramic mug poised, his elbow resting on the soft arm of the chair. Only his reddened eyes betrayed the lateness of the hour and the unaccustomed strain upon his courtroom-hardened nerves. Like the others, he too now waited.

Kaem nodded his head, closing his eyes momentarily as if embarrassed by the sudden focusing of eight intelligent eyes upon his face.

"It goes very well," Kaem announced suddenly, raising his eyes to meet the four waiting faces. His face broadened into a wide smile as he stepped forward into the living room and dropped the anxiously awaited message on the low ornate coffee table. "Thanatos has successfully completed the first stage of Balefire. He has returned safely to his house. He now awaits the Committee's evaluation and direction."

Kaem settled himself in the unoccupied sofa with a sigh of satisfied relief as the thin piece of printout paper was rapidly passed from hand to hand as each of the Committee members savored the good news with their own eyes.

Finally, Taskanian held up the now crumpled message in one beefy hand and laughed with heartiness, his eyes glistening with enthusiasm. "You see, it is just as I predicted. The American policemen are trained only to deal with incompetent criminals, dope addicts, drunks, and emotional cripples. They are completely incapable of dealing with a professional like Thanatos. I say again, this business of taunting a small city police department is child's play. We are unnecessarily diverting ourselves from our primary task—the Warning! We should be focusing our assault on the Olympic site itself with equal success!" He slammed his heavy fist down on the solid table in emphasis.

"Ah, my friend Taskanian," Kaem shook his head slowly in mock sadness, his own relief and enthusiasm far too great to mind rekindling an old argument, "you keep forgetting that we have already agreed on this matter several times.

"First of all," Kaem began, placing his forefinger against the thumb of his outstretched hand, "even our Thanatos could not be expected to deal with the legions of federal, state, county and city police officers who will be drawn into Los Angeles to protect the Games. Secondly"—the forefinger moved over to touch its left-handed mate—"how are we to focus our attack when the entire county of Los Angeles has been made into an Olympic village? Instead of generating fear and confusion, a diffused assault would only create anger and a thirst for vengeance among these Americans—a highly dangerous situation. It is better that we select a smaller, more vulnerable target that is some distance away, but still close enough to be seen by every Olympic athlete when we ignite Balefire!"

The other Committee members in the group silently nodded their agreement.

"Finally," Kaem continued, "it is essential that Balefire remain a two-pronged attack. The Warning is critically important to our cause, but also these Americans must be made to realize that they are no longer safe behind their 'thin blue line.' Once we have displayed the inherent weaknesses of the American policeman, the Warning will be all that much more effective.''

"But Los Angeles—'' Taskanian began before Kaem raised his hand.

"No, my friend," Kaem shook his head again, "the city that we have chosen is perfect for our needs. Thanatos will amply demonstrate that the expensive American police forces are helpless to protect even themselves from a single determined terrorist. Once we have demoralized the Huntington Beach police officers and turned their own citizens against them, we will ignite Balefire and chill the very hearts of the people of this country.''

The sounds of laughter, murmured agreement, and clinking of glasses surrounded the table. Then the eldest member of the Committee, Dr. Jain Saekia, a widely published and respected human behaviorist, raised his hand. The celebrative laughter was immediately silenced.

"There is no question that the Americans begin at a disadvantage. The preliminary success that we have won tonight more than adequately confirms our expectations,'' the old man began quietly. "But we must never forget how dangerous the Americans can be, if they are given a chance to unify and direct their anger at an adversary. Also, there may be reason for us to question the capabilities of our terrorist.''

He looked around, one by one, at the now sober and attentive group. "I am very much disturbed by the report from the captain of the *Hadar Jee*,'' Saekia continued. "The possibility exists that our man, fearsome as he has shown himself to be in combat, may lose his nerve under certain circumstances—a weakness not mentioned in his file.''

"But the circumstances were extraordinary,'' Taskanian protested. "Who among us would react differently in the face of such a creature?''

There were general murmurs of agreement around the table.

"But that is not the point, my friend Zakar,'' Saekia spoke gently. "We are bureaucrats, planners, administrators. Not terrorists. Like the American policemen, we too are vulnerable to the fears of the unknown and the unexpected. Look at how we have acted this evening while we waited for the first news of Balefire. Speaking for myself,'' he said, shaking his head sadly, ''very much like a nervous old woman.''

The old man looked around at the sheepish nods of his fellow conspirators before going on. ''The critical thing is that the man we selected for Balefire must be capable of instilling doubt and fear, and not succumbing to that fear himself.''

''If I may say something . . .''

Four heads turned in unison to face the youngest member of the Committee, who waited respectfully for permission to speak. In spite of the fact that the thirty-six-year-old restaurant owner held full membership in the Committee, he did not look upon himself as a bureaucrat, planner, or administrator. Prior to his illicit immigration six years ago, he had fought in the desert until Israeli warplanes had dropped out of the blinding sun to obliterate his camp and most of his assault group. He now walked with a distinctive limp and no longer smoked because of the loss of one lung. But his skills as a leader of fighting men were still valued by the men who had conceived Balefire. They were perfectly willing to listen to his opinions. The old man nodded his permission.

''I understand your concerns,'' the ex-soldier began. ''But I know this man Thanatos well. I worked with him. He is a loner, a man who does not work well with others. True, he has nightmares—about what, I am not certain. But one thing that I am certain of is that he is one of the most fearless and terrifying men I know. If I were his target, I would not relish waiting in the darkness for the inevitable.''

Having finished his quick speech, the young businessman picked up his coffee mug and raised it to the others.

''To Balefire,'' he said quietly. ''It will succeed.'' Each sipped, alone for a moment in his own thoughts, before they joined together in animated conversation.

In a small middle-class, single family home in the suburbs of Los Angeles, an eighteen-year-old American athlete slept and dreamed. In the dream that had repeated itself many times during the past months, Johnny Baumgaertel heard the thunderous roar in the stadium as his muscular legs pistoned up the thirty-eight tile steps once again. His face was tight and sweating as he willed his right hand to remain upraised.

At the top of the steps, he stopped and turned to face the stadium below, holding out the burning torch in salute as he sucked air into his heaving lungs. Then, in the moment that sent adrenaline coursing through his sleeping muscular body once more, he turned and touched the raised torch to the lip of the massive brass bowl overhead and was instantly awash in the heat of the huge flame and the intensified roar of the stadium crowd.

BALEFIRE

Minus 8 Days

Early Friday Morning

0445 hours

The warning broadcast by Hernandez over the pack-set radio had an electrifying effect upon the quiet, methodical activities of the investigators in and around the scene perimeter—and an even greater effect on the search teams who were combing the back alleys on either side of Main Street.

The scene investigators and the SWAT officers detailed to scene security continued to work at their assigned tasks, but the added factor of the deer slug put everyone on edge. Unconsciously, the officers in the street managed to readjust their working positions so that their backs were toward the liquor store rather than the distant row of darkened second-story windows. No one in the department carried deer slugs in their shotguns. Branchowski and Farber certainly hadn't. Which meant that an armed fourth suspect, running loose with a shotgun and rifled-slug rounds, was now a very likely possibility. The security officers fingered the safeties on their rifles as they began to move the spectators further away from the perimeter ropes.

Patrol Officer Keith Baughmann, SWAT Officer Ed Dukata, and Detective Michael O'Rorke were the search team closest to the buildings that overlooked Main Street when Hernandez's warning broadcast came out. They responded by quickly moving to the bottom of the alley stairway that led up to a series of second-story hotel rooms which overlooked the shooting scene. While Dukata and O'Rorke provided cover, Baughmann moved cautiously up the old wooden stairs. He pushed the half-opened door aside with his shotgun barrel, and then lunged forward into the hallway with the shotgun at waist level. Nothing.

Of the nine cracked and irregularly painted wooden doors that were visible in the dimly illuminated entryway, only the two at the end of the hall led into rooms with windows overlooking Main Street. The old hotel was one of several rooming houses in the downtown area that accepted as a tenant anyone who was willing to pay his rent in advance with cash. There was no need to obtain the floor plans for this building. Baughmann had been in this particular hotel numerous times during his law enforcement career, as had almost every other officer who worked the downtown beat, and he had the layout memorized.

Baughmann waited at the top of the stairs, ignoring the indecent smell emanating from the bathroom doorway. From his position, he could see both of the doors that were of primary interest to the search team. He held the pump shotgun in both hands, pointing straight between the two distant doorknobs, as he waited for O'Rorke and Dukata to come up the stairway. O'Rorke carried a short-barreled folding-stock shotgun. Dukata was armed with his SWAT weapon: an M-16.

"Windows were open in both rooms," Baughmann whispered, keeping his eyes fixed on the end of the hallway, waiting for either door to open suddenly. "Which one do we take first?"

They would only be able to take one of the doors using the standard procedure—one kicking the door and staying high, the second going in low, and the third covering the other door—before they lost whatever was left of the element of surprise. It was unlikely that a gunman would remain in the room after shooting at a cop, unless he was suicidal. This was always possible, and it meant that they had to assume that there was someone with a gun behind at least one of the doors.

"We take both of them," O'Rorke answered without hesitation. An experienced cop with twenty-two years behind a badge, Detective Michael O'Rorke had worn out several shoes on run-down hotel room doors. Given the advantage of surprise, he was perfectly willing to take a room himself. But he was not about to kick a door after the inhabitants had been

alerted, no matter how many officers were standing behind
him.

The yelled warnings of "Police! Open up!" were muffled
by the sounds of two doors being ripped loose from their
barely functional, rusted hinges. Baughmann dove to the
floor, rolled, and started to come up when he found himself
staring wide-eyed at a darkened figure in a chair with a
shotgun.

"Gun!"

Baughmann's mind recoiled at the horrible sight of the
shotgun, barely visible in the unlit room, and then registered
the fact that the cavernous barrel was pointed in the general
direction of his forehead. As he screamed the warning, his
military training took over. He threw himself sideways off his
elbows, pulling the trigger of his own shotgun one-handed as
he twisted frantically away from the mouth of the murderous
weapon.

Baughmann's eyes, already blurred from shock, were blinded
by the muzzle blast of the 12-gauge that was almost torn
loose from his grasp by the recoil. Rapidly expanding shock
waves slammed sharply against his eardrums as twelve .00
spheres of lead spewed out at the darkened figure in the chair.
Unable to see the effect of his first shot, Baughmann pulled at
the slide of his shotgun as he rolled on his back, trying to
pump a second round into the chamber. He started to come
up again, then winced and dropped flat as Dukata let loose a
concussive half-clip of .223 rounds at the figure from the
doorway just above Baughmann's head.

Hot, empty .223 casings were still clattering off Baughmann's
helmet when the shotgun in the figure's hands came up and
around in the direction of the two officers. Dukata, momentarily stunned and disbelieving, recovered first and threw himself backward against the wall. Then he fired a second
eardrum-shattering spray of high-powered rifle bullets, disinte-
grating the upper torso of the figure. Blood, bone, tissue,
chair stuffing, and window glass flew in all directions.

In the silence that followed, the figure tumbled forward
and hung suspended in the chair, the shotgun still grasped—
unreasonably—in the dead, limp hands.

When O'Rorke came crashing into the room moments
later, Dukata and Baughmann were still trembling from shock.

O'Rorke's eyes swept the room as he thumbed the light switch on, taking in the sight of the uniformed patrol officer on the floor and the SWAT officer leaning against the wall, both staring open-mouthed at the bloody, shredded figure hanging face down out of the ruptured chair.

"Either of you hit?" O'Rorke demanded, the barrel of his weapon sweeping in unison with his eyes as he checked quickly for a second suspect.

Neither officer responded right away. Dukata was the first to turn and stare at the veteran detective, shaking his head, trying to clear his ringing ears. To Dukata, O'Rorke's voice seemed to be uncharacteristically soft and distant. Baughmann finally looked up, blinking, and then returned his uncomprehending eyes to the figure that remained chained to the overstuffed chair next to the now shattered window, the long-barreled shotgun taped to the lifeless hands.

O'Rorke moved past the two stunned officers and made a quick unnecessary check. Confirming the obvious, he shifted his stubby weapon to one hand and reached for the radio that hung on his belt, being careful to stay away from the window.

The unexpected roar of gunfire and shattering glass that echoed through the downtown street a second time that night immediately set off a number of widely diversified reactions among the people below.

Sheffield had been staring up at the partially opened windows of the old hotel across the street, trying to force his tired analytical mind to recalculate distances and angles of fire—taking into account the new problem of the deer slugs—when the sound of Baughmann's shotgun thundered across the quiet darkness. As the sounds of the two subsequent rapid bursts of gunfire and the breaking glass reached his ears, he turned and dove toward Meiko, sending them both rolling on the wet asphalt behind the abandoned black-and-white.

Spectators screamed and ran as the other investigators on the scene reacted instinctively, diving under and behind vehicles, and into doorways as they searched for the source of the gunfire with quickly drawn weapons.

Paradee was no less hesitant in his bid for self-preservation. However, he was less fortunate because his camera crew

happened to be rooted in a spot directly in line with the
nearest open doorway. Three terrified men and a fragile
camera ended up in a tangled pile of thrashing legs, arms,
and video cable on top of an overturned wooden barrier.

Caught in the open, the SWAT team members assigned to
guard the investigators dropped to their knees and aimed their
weapons at the shattered window, sighting anxiously up into
the darkness, searching for a target with tensed trigger fingers.
As they waited expectantly, the detectives at the scene sprinted
into action.

Andersen and Hernandez were halfway up the back stairs
leading to the hotel, weapons drawn and ready, before they
heard O'Rorke's voice on the radio calling the code four.
They went up the rest of the stairs and down the hallway with
less caution, joining the three officers in the now brightly lit
apartment.

"What the hell happened up here?" Andersen demanded
as he entered the room, and then stopped short as he took in
the entire scene. O'Rorke turned to look at his boss, but
didn't speak.

"Mother Mary," Hernandez whispered at Andersen's
shoulder, as the sergeant walked carefully forward around
Baughmann, who had just started to get up off the floor, and
squatted down to look directly into the shattered face of the
young male who hung vacant-eyed, dripping blood from
numerous severely torn wounds.

"I had to shoot, Sarge," Baughmann said quietly, looking
down at his weapon and then carefully clicking the red safety
button to the ON position. "He had me dead on when we
came through the door."

"Where were you?" Andersen asked, looking up at O'Rorke.

"In the other room," the heavy-set detective said matter-of-
factly. "Wouldn't have made any difference. I'd have done
the same thing."

Andersen nodded, turning his attention back to the taped
hands. "Rudy, get Sheffield up here right now," he said,
standing up. "I want every inch of this room photographed,
dusted, and searched. And I want every room on this floor
checked right now!"

Hernandez disappeared through the doorway, and Andersen turned to O'Rorke. His eyes glared with barely restrained frustration.

"Mike, I want the owner of this building contacted now. Get a blanket permission search for every room that he says is unoccupied. And then tell him to get his ass up here on the double. I also want you and Rudy to start pounding on doors. If anyone is still in any of these rooms, I want them out. And take these two down to Kretcher." He motioned his head toward Baughmann and Dukata, who were standing over in the far corner of the room, shifting their eyes back and forth between the blood-splattered form in the chair and Andersen. "I want complete statements from both of them while everything's still fresh in their minds. Got it?"

O'Rorke nodded and motioned with his hands for Dukata and Baughmann to follow him down the hallway. The pair of shaken officers were almost out of the door, each carrying his weapon gingerly, when Andersen spoke again.

"Hey, you two." He waited until they had both stopped and turned their heads. Their expressions were almost identical. Eyes dulled, jaw muscles loosened, cheeks paled. Baughmann had two years of combat in Vietnam under his belt. Dukata had been an honor graduate from the Los Angeles Police Academy and was an avid hunter. Yet it was obvious that neither of the officers was hardened to the idea of killing a kid who was chained to a chair, whatever the justification.

"You both did exactly what you were supposed to do." Andersen spoke softly. "You did a good job up here, and I appreciate it. So does Branch . . . and so would Jake."

Their eyes flickered at the reminder of the dead officer, each making a halfhearted attempt at a nodding smile. Dukata started to say something and then gave up, nodding his head as he walked out the door. "Yeah, thanks, Sarge," Baughmann managed and then followed Dukata as O'Rorke's burly arm guided them out of the room.

Alone in the room, Andersen stood with his hands in his pockets for a few moments, glaring first at the unresponding youth, then at the locked chain that looped around his waist and back behind the chair. He also took in the heavy silver-grey insulating tape that secured the pale, blood-streaked hands to the auto-loading shotgun, the discarded roll of matching tape on the floor behind the chair, and the two expended 12-gauge shotgun casings scattered across the floor.

He let his eyes roam upward, noting the narcotics-oriented posters on the walls, the plastic water pipes and roach clips on the shelves, the stereo equipment which was too expensive for the rest of the room and probably had its serial numbers gouged out. The bed was unmade; the sheets looked as though they hadn't been washed for several weeks. One corner of the room had been converted into an unsightly kitchen. There was an old refrigerator, a stained linoleum counter, a small steel sink partially filled with dirty dishes and pans, and an old two-burner hot plate. Dirty clothing was piled up against the wall next to the bed.

Aside from the body and the shotgun, and ignoring the extensive damage to the walls and the window caused by Baughmann and Dukata, the room looked exactly like a hundred other crash pads that Andersen had searched during his law enforcement career.

Stepping carefully to avoid disturbing anything on the floor, he walked slowly over to the broken window. Standing next to the chair, directing his gaze in an approximate 45-degree angle toward the street below, he observed the shadowy form of Hernandez walk quickly across the street.

He saw Hernandez shrug off the beckoning arm of Paradee, who was shouting from his position behind the perimeter rope, and walk directly over to the black-and-white where Sheffield and Malinger were kneeling next to Meiko, sitting on the wet pavement holding the side of her head. Hernandez knelt down next to Sheffield and spoke to him. Andersen could see Sheffield turn his head and look up in his direction.

About thirty yards, Andersen estimated, guessing at the distance between the window where he was standing and the blanket-covered body of Farber. Andersen knew a little bit about shotguns, enough to know that Sheffield had been right about the pattern spread of a buckshot round. Too damned far away to have grouped that many pellets into the side of Farber's face.

A deer slug, however, was another matter entirely. A magnum deer slug round was designed to cover a lot of ground and still retain enough momentum to drop a heavily muscled buck in its tracks. Trouble was, a deer slug was

nothing more than a round-nosed hunk of lead th▓▓
shoved out of an unrifled shotgun barrel with little stabilizing
spin. At a relatively close range, the heavy slugs were
devastating. At any distance, they were inaccurate as hell. To
drop Branchowski, the kid had to have hit a target that was
probably moving, twice, in almost total darkness. Hell of a
job for a kid who usually needed at least three tries to shoot a
needle into his scarred veins.

Andersen shook his head slowly, turning back to the room
to look for something, anything, that would offer some proof
that this young man had been a cop killer or at least something more than a typical burned-out doper who had inhabited
the downtown area for most of his adult life. But Toby
Williker was well known by all of the HBPD detectives, and
a burned-out doper was all that he had ever been.

Sheffield stared at Hernandez, the flesh below his eyes
crinkled from fatigue and disbelief. He was physically
exhausted. The adrenaline-launched effort to drag Meiko behind the protective bulk of the black-and-white had finished
off his already minimal reserves of energy. He was cold and
dirty. His clothing was thoroughly soaked with the rain and
the blood that he had rolled into trying to shield Meiko and
himself from the sudden eruption of gunfire. Meiko was hurt;
her head had struck the edge of the unit's bumper when they
had tumbled trying to get behind the heavy black rubber tire.

Sheffield didn't believe his ears.

"You're trying to tell me that Toby Williker shot Farber?
And that little bastard was up there in that room all this time
and you guys didn't know it?"

"Looks that way." Hernandez nodded grimly, his eyes
revealing a mixture of controlled anger and embarrassment,
as he helped Sheffield apply a compress bandage to Meiko's
head. The gash was about two inches long and just in front
and above her right ear. A minor cut, but like a typical scalp
wound, it had bled like crazy for the first few seconds,
momentarily convincing Sheffield that she had been struck by
one of the bullets.

"Walt wants you up there right now," Hernandez said to
Sheffield, motioning with his head at the hotel room, as he

..y tightened the bandage around Meiko's glistening forehead with fingers that were more suited to slamming handcuffs on the wrists of combative suspects than to the application of first aid. The beautiful girl winced at the pressure, inhaling sharply as Hernandez tied the gauze ends together snugly. "Sorry, hon," the detective said softly, using his flashlight to check her eyes again.

"What's he got up there?" Sheffield asked, distracted. He observed for the second time, as did Hernandez, that Meiko's pupils had responded differently—one constricted more slowly than the other—to the sudden beam of light. Probable concussion.

Hernandez described the situation in the hotel room and the position of Williker in the chair as they both carried the dazed girl over to the nearest black-and-white parked outside the perimeter. It never occurred to either of the men to postpone their gruesome discussion until they were out of earshot of their injured associate. In a field situation, Meiko had long been considered one of the boys by the detectives of the homicide detail. They started to lay her down in the back seat, but she balked, trying to sit up.

"I'm all right," she insisted weakly, straining against the supporting hands until a sudden wave of stomach-twisting dizziness forced her to lay back. "I've got work to do." She tried to sit up one more time, but Hernandez ignored her protests, folding a thick blanket behind her head for support.

"Sure you do," Hernandez agreed, pulling a second blanket up over the wet arms and shoulders that had started to tremble slightly under the soaked clothing. "And just as soon as the doctors tell me that they've put that gourd of yours back together, I'll come right over to get you." He spoke with paternal firmness, as though he were talking to one of his own daughters. Then he stood back up, shut the door, and motioned for the uniformed officer to take Meiko directly to Pacifica Hospital, with an admonition to drive carefully and watch out for bumps.

Sheffield and Hernandez walked together across the street, talking in barely lowered voices. They completely ignored the outraged Paradee. As he yelled questions at them, Steve Tarrin, an imposing green-and-black uniformed SWAT officer, stood in front of him, waiting patiently for the obnoxious newscaster to make another attempt to climb over the perimeter barriers. The combination of Tarrin's cheerfully anticipating expression and the fact that the news team's video camera was no longer capable of recording any action on the part of the officer apparently intimidated Paradee. Or perhaps it was the fact that Sergeant Andersen had loudly and clearly issued blanket authority for the officer to arrest Paradee if he made one more attempt to damage the crime scene. In any case, the frustrated newsman was effectively reduced to yelling himself hoarse at a continuing succession of unmindful investigators who went about their business as though Paradee did not exist. From all outward indications, the newsman was more outraged from being ignored than from the physical restraint.

Sheffield and Hernandez were nearly at the alley entrance to the steps when a shouted voice caught their attention. Both men stopped and turned at the sound of the familiar voice, and observed the short, distinctively overweight figure of Coroner's Investigator Lamar Franklin staggering in their direction. The two thick black suitcases that he carried in his deceptively strong black arms almost dragged on the ground as he struggled forward.

"I hear tell you've got some difficult ones for me tonight, Brian," Franklin said, dropping his suitcases at the feet of the two men with an unabashed sigh of relief. "Dispatch said that one of them's supposed to be a police officer?" The fleshy dark eyes that were rarely solemn, in spite of his profession, looked up soberly for confirmation.

Sheffield nodded.

"Too damned bad." The obese face turned and looked out across the street, the perspiration readily visible despite the cool air temperature. "Goddamned folks won't never learn, will they?" The eyes immediately took in the four blanket-covered bodies in the street and on the sidewalk. "They never stop to think that somebody like me's gonna come get them some day. No sense in hurrying that day along." He reached into his jacket pocket for a pen and a card. "Call number's one-three-seven-eight. Want me to put all four on one report?"

"You mean all five," Hernandez corrected in a slightly reluctant voice. Unlike Sheffield, who genuinely enjoyed talking with Franklin under most circumstances, Hernandez had never managed to develop a warm relationship with the fat county investigator who spent virtually every working day of his life dealing with dead bodies and grieving relatives. Hernandez realized in a vague way that his discomfort had something to do with his religious convictions, but he had never cared to dwell on the topic very long.

"Five?" Franklin's voice clearly implied that he had done nothing to deserve this kind of treatment from Huntington Beach.

"We can even give you an exact time of death on this one," Sheffield said as they went through the alley and started up the back stairs. Hernandez carried one of the suitcases, in spite of his personal misgivings about handling anything that involved Franklin's unthinkable career. Oddly enough, Hernandez would have argued violently with anyone who suggested that he and Franklin had very similar occupations. Violence and death in the streets was something that the detective viewed as a natural part of life. A body in a cold morgue was something else entirely. Besides, Hernandez told himself, with all of the fat that Franklin was lugging around, they were liable to have a sixth body clogging the stairs if the perspiring and wheezing investigator tried to carry up both of his suitcases.

"You going to start doing my job for me so I can get my union on your ass?" The lungs puffed but the voice was strong.

Sheffield smiled in spite of himself as he climbed next to Franklin. It was difficult to be serious for any length of time around this man, regardless of the situation. In a way, it helped.

"You'll have trouble guessing wrong on this one," Sheffield tried to banter, feeling himself loosen up a little. "SWAT blew him away while we were working in the street a few minutes ago."

Franklin mumbled something to the effect that he was suitably impressed, saving his breath for the rest of the climb.

When the three men entered the room at the end of the hall, they found Andersen poking at a pair of brilliant yellow nylon panties with the tip of his ballpoint, apparently trying to read the label without having to touch the visibly unhygienic underwear.

"Excellent choice," Franklin commented as he set his suitcase down and took in a deep labored breath. "They'll go very nicely with your shirt." Ignoring Andersen's thoughtful glare, Franklin immediately walked over to take a professional look at the chained body that was still seeping blood from the majority of the wounds, especially the massive ones that exited the back. "Don't really match your eyes, though," he added offhandedly as he squatted down and stared directly into the glazed blue eyes of Williker. Gently, he touched the fingers of one hand to the unmarked pale cheek and then probed tentatively into the shoulder, buttock, and leg muscles.

"Well?" Andersen finally asked.

"He's dead."

Franklin gingerly removed a pair of thin white plastic gloves from one of the huge bulging pockets of his heavy overcoat, and slipped them on over his puffy, dark brown hands. Then he continued to probe at the wounds and softer tissues, being careful not to disturb the position of any of the articles of clothing.

"No shit, Sherlock," Andersen said drily, glaring at the fat investigator. "We figured that out ourselves."

Franklin smiled cheerfully and continued on with his silent examination of the body. "Just in case you have any intention of being useful around here," Andersen added, "you might try coming up with an expert-witness opinion on this one."

"Such as?" Franklin queried, not looking up as he began to write quick notes on his official field report form. Sheffield had joined Franklin next to the body and was in the process of conducting his own examination of the items of evidence that he and the other forensic examiners would be working with back at the crime lab.

"Could he have wrapped that tape around his hands, for a start?"

"I don't know," Franklin answered, suddenly turning serious. He joined Sheffield in visually examining the wrapped hands, both of them manipulating the roll of tape in their minds as if they were holding the shotgun.

"I would say . . . yes, he could have," Franklin finally answered, his voice uncharacteristically hesitant. "But it would have been a bit awkward."

Sheffield was nodding his head in agreement.

"Why so?" Andersen asked.

"The first hand, by the grip," Franklin said. "The right hand. The tape's wrapped around tight and smoothed out. He wouldn't have had any problem doing that with his left hand."

"Okay, so what about the left?" Andersen had evidently observed the same thing that was puzzling Sheffield and Franklin.

"If he was going to try to tape both of his hands to the shotgun," Sheffield interrupted, "it would probably have been easier to have stuck one end of the tape to the stock with his left hand, then grip the stock and flip the tape over." Sheffield made a circling motion with both of his hands as though he were holding a shotgun. "Then all he would have had to do was to press his hand against his leg or the chair to mat the tape down."

"Unfortunately," Franklin finished, "the tape was obviously stuck across the fingers first, and then wrapped loosely around the stock twice."

"Which he could have done by himself?"

Franklin nodded agreeably, chewing on his inner cheek in silent contemplation. Andersen shifted his eyes back to Sheffield.

"Sure, I think so, too, but that brings up the next question. Why?" Sheffield looked at both men. Neither seemed ready to offer an answer.

"Okay," Sheffield continued, welcoming the opportunity to blank out his fatigue and Meiko's bleeding head by forcing himself to work out a logical pattern, "it's probably reasonable to assume that he chained himself to the chair after he finished shooting at Branch and Farber. Agreed? I mean, it would be difficult enough to hit somebody with deer slugs at this distance without the handicap of being chained to a chair. Right?"

"Deer slug?" Franklin's eyebrows raised in surprise. He received a confirming nod from Sheffield and made another notation on his report form.

Andersen regarded Sheffield thoughtfully.

"So he shoots at least twice, because there are two empty

casings on the floor, and then he reloads." Sheffield looked around.

"Behind the chair," Andersen said. "An opened box of twelve-gauge magnums loaded with deer slugs. Six rounds missing."

"Which means that there should be three in the magazine and one in the chamber. So now he's got a fully loaded shotgun and he doesn't run. Instead, he chains himself to a chair and tapes the shotgun to his hands so he won't lose it when the cops come through the door and start shooting. That's suicide." Sheffield waited in vain for an argument.

"What's your problem with this one, Walt?" Franklin had abandoned his accustomed role completely now. He had worked with Walt Andersen for several years. He knew that the sergeant rarely asked investigative questions casually.

"A lot of missing pieces," Andersen said wearily. "First of all, I knew this kid. Name's Toby Williker. Local puke. I arrested him the first time for dope when he was thirteen. By now, his rap sheet's probably three pages—possession, sales, burglary, shoplifting, you name it."

"I don't follow," Franklin said.

"Thing is," Andersen continued, "Williker never did anything, as far as I know, that involved violence. That was his standard spiel whenever he got popped. Always bragged about the fact that he had never hurt anyone when he capered and that he had never carried a gun. I think he had himself pegged as some kind of dope-smoking Robin Hood."

"Yet," Andersen hesitated, looking around the room once more, "as far as we can tell right now, Williker just involved himself in a shooting that killed one officer and three civilians down there in the street and put another officer in surgery. None of the dead suspects on the ground had weapons anywhere around them when the patrol units arrived. The three in the street were apparently shot by one—or possibly by both—of the officers. The officer who was wounded took one deer slug in his chest armor and a second slug across the helmet."

"Match up with all of this?" Franklin waved a thick hand to encompass the entire blood-spattered room.

"Not entirely. Farber caught at least eight buckshot pellets in the side of his face, which our resident criminalist here tells us is inconsistent with the distance involved from this window.''

"Not to mention the fact that there doesn't appear to be any buckshot casings or live rounds in this room,'' Sheffield said, looking at Andersen for confirmation.

"None that I can find. So we assume that either Farber got hit by his own shotgun or we still have a cop killer running around loose. This makes it a little difficult to explain to assholes like Jack Paradee out there what's going on because I don't know either.''

"This kid could have had a death wish,'' Franklin suggested. "Not all that unusual if he's heavily involved with dope. He flips out, does a little shooting, and then puts himself in a box where you people are forced to dump him when you try to pull him out.''

"Fine. So he wants us to do the job for him. Why and how does he manage to get three liquor store burglars involved in the whole mess? Or I should say, three Mexican kids who may have been unarmed and who were probably too drunk to piss in the street accurately. And if they were armed, where the hell are the guns? And if they weren't, why the hell did Branch and Farber start shooting at them?''

"Got me,'' Franklin shook his head sympathetically. "You ready to have this one brought down?''

"No, hold off a while. We still need pictures and a search.''

"Okay, I'll be downstairs with the other four,'' Franklin said. "Give me a call when you're ready.''

"Yeah, we'll do that,'' Andersen replied glumly. He stood up and walked over to the window again to stare down at the darkened street that had already asked a lot of questions but had provided damn few answers.

BALEFIRE

Minus 8 Days

Friday Morning

0612 hours

The long northward leg of the *Hadar Jee*'s journey and the subsequent twenty-eight days that Thanatos devoted to orientation, systems checks, and rehearsal, had provided plenty of time for the terrorist's internal time clock to recalibrate accurately to sunrise. He awoke as the whispery streaks of cloud in the dark grey sky began to reflect a faint reddish-orange light, and then forced himself to remain face down and absolutely motionless on the mattress as the sounds of creaking wood brushed across acutely sensitive nerve endings.

The survival instincts had been hard at work during those last few moments before Thanatos awoke in tightly controlled confusion. Subconsciously, data gathered by his senses—including the smells and background noises of the ocean—had been accumulating for routine evaluation by the forebrain. The creaking noises were noted immediately by his subconscious and quickly compared to the array of background noises recorded during the night. No match. Something new to the environment was putting stress upon wood.

He tensed, listening for a pattern to develop that would tell him what and where. Programmed portions of his mind had already evaluated his position on the yielding mattress, noting the restrictions on quick movement that would be imposed by the single thin sheet which covered the lower half of his naked body. Unlike most men, Thanatos did not possess the psychological need to cover his genitals when facing danger. He had fought for the first time as a naked child in the dirty village streets of his homeland. As he matured, he had contin-

ued to fight bare-handed, with a knife, garrote wire, or
machine gun. The weapon didn't matter. His clothing or lack
thereof didn't matter either. He was trained to stalk, to attack,
and to survive.

The confusion of wakening in a still unfamiliar environment was distracting as he tried to sort out dream data from
surrounding reality. Accustomed to such situations by a lifetime of moving from one strange bed to another, Thanatos
waited patiently for a trackable pattern to develop, ignoring
the self-preserving instincts that demanded immediate action.
The Browning—beneath the pillow and his unmoving head—
was inches away from his still right hand. Too far. Ignore.

The creaking noises seemed to be occurring at random so
far. This was primarily a subconscious evaluation because he
was still slightly disoriented; his memory was a confused and
murky swirl of uncertain images. Heavy steel doors with
rounded corners . . . deep, greenish-black water . . . a menacing grey-white form that waited in anticipation far below
. . . the long gun . . . scarlet dot . . . fire . . . Balefire . . .
Balefire.

The mother liquid in his mind suddenly crystallized and he
sat upright on the bed, confirming with open eyes that he was
alone in the room. He was inwardly annoyed because he
realized that he had not escaped the fear-induced sweat of the
dreams, but outwardly he smiled because the walls of the
expensive Huntington Harbour home continued to creak as
they expanded slightly in response to the late-arriving summer weather. Allowing himself to relax, the terrorist quickly
reviewed in his mind the sequence of events that he had
initiated and then abruptly terminated the previous evening.

To the extent that he had been able to remain in the area
and evaluate, it appeared as though the first objective of
Balefire had been successfully accomplished. He had left two
Huntington Beach police officers and three relatively innocent
civilian victims lying—presumably dead—in the middle of
one of the city's major streets. A questionable suspect and an
assortment of contradictory evidence had been provided to
keep the homicide investigators busy trying to explain the
actions of their two dead officers. Assuming that the Committee had made all the other proper arrangements—and there
was no reason to believe otherwise, considering the well-

planned efficiency of the operation so far—the news media would make certain that the citizens of Huntington Beach were fully informed of the situation.

Nodding to himself in satisfaction, he reached under the pillow and brought out his ever-present companion, a 9mm Browning High Power automatic pistol with the worn and sweat-stained wooden grip. The pistol had been part of the packet that he had carried strapped to his stomach during the terrifying underwater swim to shore. As expected, the waterproof bag had leaked slightly. He went through the familiar motions of field-stripping the heavy black weapon—which he valued as much for sentimental reasons as for the weapon's deadly accuracy and invaluable fourteen-round clip capacity—still thinking about his role in Balefire.

He realized, of course, that he would not know how well the initial phase of Balefire had succeeded until the reactions of the news media and the subsequent response of the local citizens were known. He would have to assume that the parties involved would react as planned, something that the Committee would evaluate carefully before authorizing the next phases of their meticulously planned operation.

He allowed himself the pleasure of visualizing the flashback pictures vividly etched in his memory, confirming in his own mind that the Committee had been brilliant in its projections. He had been particularly pleased with the puppetlike responses of the second officer, responses which had been anticipated and which were essential if the goals of Balefire were to be realized.

Thanatos stretched his arms, flexing the hard muscles, and grinned widely, displaying two even rows of carefully maintained white teeth. He brushed his hands through his ragged hair, remembering that the services of the ship's cook—a reasonably proficient barber in spite of his extremely dull scissors—were no longer available. He would have to make other arrangements.

He remembered now the astonished expression on the second police officer's face as the heavy lead missile caught him full in the chest. The Committee had been absolutely correct in their preliminary evaluations, he thought contentedly. The American policemen were totally unprepared to deal with an unexpected attack by a professional. And if all continued to go as planned, it would be some time before the demoralized officers even realized that they had a terrorist operating within their city. Their failure in basic intelligence gathering would cost them dearly.

Carefully wiping the internal action of the pistol with a lightly oiled rag, Thanatos thought again about his good fortune to have been chosen for a mission of such magnitude.

The Committee had bypassed the readily available Palestinian organizations in favor of a European who could easily conceal himself among the predominantly white, upper-middle-class citizens of the target city. The Committee paid well—very well, in fact—but their substantial cash payment was contingent upon total success. Anything less would not have the desired political effect; therefore, anything less would be compensated only by the down payment: the deed to the prestigious Huntington Harbour home that Thanatos would use as his base of operations.

The statement which remained unspoken—for it was perfectly obvious to everyone involved—was that in the event of failure, Thanatos would most likely be dead, or at best, in no position to enjoy the benefits of a southern California residence. In effect, the home was an added incentive for the terrorist to remain elusive and unseen. As if life itself were not a sufficient reason to be extremely careful, Thanatos thought to himself.

If the pay was high, the demands of the Committee provided more than sufficient justification. The operational plans of Balefire were complex—each phase had a number of options to which Thanatos could resort. The options, in turn, were keyed to the range of anticipated responses from the police, the news media, and the public at large. Undeniably, Balefire would be difficult to accomplish. However, the difficulties were counterbalanced by the recently demonstrated fact that the Americans were complacently unprepared. The idea was to conduct the operations at such a diffused, low-profile level that more dangerous federal law enforcement agencies, such as the FBI and the Secret Service, not to mention the more feared CIA, were unaware until the very last moment that a professional terrorist was in place and operating on the outskirts of the Olympic Village.

Thanatos did not dismiss these difficulties lightly; he sim-

ply placed them into his own perspective. However difficult
the project might become, he knew that the dangers would be
magnified tenfold if he were to attempt the same maneuvers
against a less complacent foe.

He thought momentarily of his colleagues, who had to
contend with the eye-for-an-eye-plus-the-head philosophy of
the Mossad, Israel's highly effective counter-terrorist organization. In comparison, the opposition which he faced was run
by rank amateurs.

He was particularly pleased by the ease with which he had
evaded the vastly overrated police dragnet. His escape—if the
low-keyed action could be dignified as such—was accomplished simply by driving away from the area at a reasonable
speed while carefully monitoring the progress of the police on
the police-frequency receiver concealed behind the standard
AM/FM radio of his vehicle, a dark green Pontiac sedan.

Once he had determined the location and direction of the
responding units, Thanatos had driven the inconspicuous car
to a nearby rented garage space, one of the numerous individual storage units in the city area leased by the Committee.

Having been used once, the Pontiac had been permanently
abandoned in the garage space. It was a minor loss because
half of the leased garage spaces contained an assortment of
brand-new Pontiacs, Porsches, Datsuns, and Toyotas. The
fact that all of the leases were paid in cash, for a period of six
months, ensured that the vehicles would remain undiscovered
long after the successful conclusion of Balefire. Alan Marakai,
the man who had negotiated the leases utilizing a variety of
falsified documents and ID cards, had long since departed the
country on a well-deserved vacation.

After shutting and locking the back door of the rented
garage, being careful to keep his driving gloves on both
hands, Thanatos had simply discarded the key and gloves in
separate nearby trash bins. The specialized equipment that he
had used remained in the trunk of the abandoned vehicle. He
had then calmly walked the few blocks to the location where
his primary vehicle, a very ordinary, tan Volkswagen Bug,
was parked and waiting.

Had he been stopped during the drive home—a possible,
but unlikely event, as very few police officers would expect a
fleeing homicide suspect to use an underpowered VW as an

escape vehicle—the wallet that he immediately removed from the glove compartment of the VW and slid into his rear pants pocket properly identified him as the legal owner of the car. There was absolutely nothing in the Volkswagen to suggest that the owner was anything other than a businessman who preferred to spend his money on something other than expensive automobiles. In the event he was stopped, the name on the driver's license would come back on the FBI's NCIC computer as having no criminal record, and no wants or warrants.

Avoiding the spasmodically assembled blockade of the exit routes out of Huntington Beach had been the easiest part of the operation. The blocking points had been established to keep a fleeing suspect within the boundary limits of the city. Thanatos would never have to try to bypass the blocking units, even if they did manage to respond in time, because he did not intend to try to leave the city. The Huntington Harbour home was well within the boundary limit of the nearest blockade point, and was one of the last places that the police would search for a fleeing killer.

The only part of the operation that was slightly inconvenient was the reporting procedure using the cutout in Santa Ana. The fact that the origins of all long-distance phone calls in the United States were recorded into a computer memory bank for billing purposes necessitated the use of pay phones to call in routine progress reports and to receive instructions.

In order to call in his report, it had been necessary to take a pleasant ten-minute walk along the boat docks to an isolated phone booth near the fueling ramp that served the local boat owners. Leaving the door open to avoid turning on the interior light, Thanatos had dialed one of the four memorized phone numbers, and waited.

Three of the phone numbers accessed the cutout who was the terrorist's primary communication link with the Committee. Once the cutout verified the identity and status codes, he would connect the terrorist to the Committee through a multiloop scrambler that was capable of defeating all but the most sophisticated phone-trace computers and was programmed to signal whenever such a trace was attempted. Even if the CIA's reputed Backtrack computer program was brought into play, the Committee was guaranteed at least two hours in which to go to ground. The cutout, of course, would have no warning whatsoever.

The fourth telephone number represented the panic button. A call to this number would activate an automatic recording device that would record on direct dial, and then transmit ten minutes after the caller dialed an additional four-digit number. This was a one-way emergency system that was to be used only in the event that Thanatos was in serious trouble and was unable to make contact through the cutout. It was only to be used in an absolute emergency, because—unlike the primary system that utilized the sacrificial cutout—this communication link, theoretically, could be traced back to Kaem's Dana Point home.

Thanatos had spoken briefly into the telephone receiver, hearing the whispering background sound of the recorder's take-up reel as it turned slowly in a rented apartment. He had rehearsed his report several times before dialing the number to be certain that he was transmitting only the essential information. Then he had rewarded himself with a slow enjoyable stroll back across the creaking wood docks before returning through his back gate to the house, and welcome sleep.

Now that he was awake, the terrorist finished cleaning and reassembling his trusted weapon, placing it in its accustomed location under his pillow in a loaded and cocked condition. Then he religiously forced himself through a half hour of conditioning exercises.

Required by his career choice to spend much of his life without female company, the exercises provided an acceptable form of almost sexual release. Thanatos actually looked forward to putting his hardened body through the punishing exercises, relishing each explosive effort that he made to push his straining muscles past previously established endurance points. Finally exhausted, he staggered painfully to the shower, sated by the knowledge that only eight days remained, and he had every reason in the world to believe he would succeed.

The breakfast that the suspiciously young and mildly flirta- tious waitress set in front of Andersen, Hernandez, O'Rorke, Kretcher, Sheffield, and Malinger would never be mistaken for the work of a budding gourmet cook. In fact, it was more likely that the cook had only recently graduated from the preparation of refried beans and corn tortillas.

The reason that the homicide investigators continued to patronize this particular eatery had nothing whatsoever to do with the quality of the food, or the enthusiastic attitudes of the poorly paid Mexican aliens and under-age runaways who hired on as cooks and waitresses. The fact was it happened to be the restaurant closest to the police department open twenty-four hours every day of the week. Six-thirty on a Friday morning was no time to be choosy about one's food.

The men sat wearily in the largest of the rear booths as the girl refilled the chipped cups with hot, bitter-tasting coffee. They were tired, unshaven, and dirty. Their stomachs were still queasy from the many cups of lukewarm coffee that had been delivered and left to cool on the hoods of the units. With the exception of O'Rorke, who muttered something impolite through a mouthful of soggy waffle, no one responded to the quality of the offered breakfast.

It wouldn't have mattered if the food had been good. For a number of individual reasons, none of the men had an appetite this morning. They ate simply to fill their stomachs because they knew that they would need the fuel to keep going for the remainder of the day and possibly well into the next evening.

The investigators had stopped by the hospital to check on Meiko and Branchowski before going to breakfast. They were informed that the gravely wounded officer had been returned to surgery when it was discovered that cranial pressure had developed. There was no available prognosis. Meiko had been given a mild sedative and was sleeping soundly. There was nothing the officers could accomplish by waiting, so they left.

Sheffield continued to pick at his food, distracted, while the others directed their attention and comments at the morning paper that was spread out across the aisle edge of the table.

The headlines took up two lines of heavy black type: ONE HB COP AND FOUR SUSPECTS DIE IN QUESTIONED SHOOTING.

"It says here," Andersen read aloud, "that 'two officers

of the Huntington Beach Police Department's Patrol Division shot and killed three young and apparently unarmed downtown residents in an unexplained shooting incident that left a fourth youth dead in an upstairs hotel room. One of the officers was dead at the scene and the other was taken to Pacifica Hospital in critical condition. Police spokesmen refused to provide any explanation for what one source has suggested may be an unjustified use of lethal force.' Shit!'' Andersen slammed the offending paper down on the table, startling the cook and the two waitresses who wisely chose to remain busy at the other end of the dining area.

"Read this part," Hernandez said, pointing to a paragraph located near the end of the inflammatory article. " 'Independent eyewitness accounts suggest that the fourth suspect may have been executed by police officers in retaliation for the death of their comrade-in-arms!' What the hell does he think we are, a fucking military operation?'' Hernandez's eyes glowered with barely contained fury.

"Good old Paradee slipped it to us again," O'Rorke commented, wiping up a remaining egg yoke with the last piece of the waffle.

"Did anyone let him up in that room?" Andersen asked, looking around at the group. They all shook their heads. As far as anyone knew, Paradee had been bird-dogged by Tarrin until the frustrated newsman finally gave up trying to get around the unshakable SWAT officer and departed with his crew.

"Then he's either guessing, or he's got inside information. He knows that Williker had a shotgun, but there's no way he could tell from his position on the street whether Baughmann or the kid fired off a shotgun round before Dukata opened up with that goddamned M-16.''

"You figure Paradee has to be the independent eyewitness?" Malinger asked. The newspaper story had the by-line of one of the paper's less conservative editors, who—as far as anyone at the table knew—had not been anywhere near the scene.

"Who else?" Andersen looked up, questioning.

"I don't know," Malinger admitted. "I just don't see Paradee's motive in giving away all of his good stuff to a morning newspaper instead of saving it for his tv broadcast. He's not exactly the shy retiring type."

"Yeah, you've got a point," Andersen nodded.

"What about a libel suit?" Hernandez asked.

"Against whom?" Andersen shook his head. "All the paper's done, as far as our candy-assed Supreme Court is concerned, is print a few statements made by witnesses that the reporter supposedly contacted at the scene. The fact that these witnesses happen to be unavailable and the fact that this article is a piece of inflammatory shit would get us exactly nowhere. Besides, we're supposed to be investigating a homicide, not tracking down asshole reporters."

"So we just let Paradee and his friends make us look like a bunch of trigger-happy freaks?"

Everyone at the table knew that Hernandez was just letting off steam. They also knew that they had nothing to gain, either as a department or as individuals, by reacting with off-the-wall statements and accusations. Their primary salvation lay in the fact that the entire shooting incident was also being investigated by a joint team of investigators from the district attorney's office and the county sheriff's.

"What we do," Andersen finally responded, "is to figure out what the hell happened out there with Branch and Farber. Which means" —he looked pointedly over at Sheffield and Malinger—"that our lab had better come up with a lot of scientific answers pretty damn quick."

"Our best bet is still in the autopsies," Sheffield said. "Franklin's got them scheduled early. First one will be at nine o'clock." He looked at his wristwatch again to confirm that he still had plenty of time. "Anyone else coming?"

"Not me," replied O'Rorke, stabbing at a half-raw piece of sausage that Sheffield had wisely decided to leave untouched on his plate. "I don't like those things." He popped the piece of indeterminate flesh into his mouth. "Upsets my stomach."

BALEFIRE

Minus 7 Days

Saturday Morning

0858 hours

Sheffield sat forward on the padded square seat of his laboratory office chair, elbows braced against the desk top. His hands supported a quietly humming telephone receiver and a head that had not grown appreciably lighter after Andersen's gift of ten hours of uninterrupted sleep. Settled comfortably, he waited patiently for the County Crime Laboratory's secretary to locate her wandering criminalist and transfer his call.

Andersen's offer of sleep hadn't exactly been a gift. After working on the investigation without rest for slightly more than twenty hours—which included a grueling nine-hour autopsy session—the detectives and lab team were out on their feet. They weren't stumbling or dozing or exhibiting any of the other external body signals most often associated with fatigue. Those symptoms wouldn't begin to show up among the investigators for another four to six hours. Andersen had simply realized that his detectives were no longer alert to the subtle but critical bits of investigative information being continuously gathered for evaluation.

The deterioration was mental rather than physical, and the warning signals were not all that apparent. One of the first involved a seemingly casual response made by a witness, which Andersen discovered when he made a routine playback of an interrogation tape. The comment wasn't significant by itself, but the detective asking the questions should have followed up immediately with a couple of sweep questions to see if there was anything else in the background worth discussing. He hadn't, so Andersen sent him back into the field to recontact the witness in the faint hope that the individual would still be cooperative. He wasn't.

There were other similar incidents, each by itself was relatively insignificant, but they formed a growing pattern of sloppiness that would eventually result in the loss of significant information. The unspoken worry on Andersen's part was that the diminished awareness of his investigators would result in another officer's death if they ran across another suspect involved in the shooting.

So everyone, Andersen included, received a mandatory ten hours off, while a fresh team of detectives ran down developed leads. Eleven hours later at eight o'clock Saturday morning, everyone on the original call-out team—with the exception of Meiko, who was still under the protective custody of a concerned resident neurologist—was back at his desk, shuffling, reading, and organizing loose stacks of reports in an effort to get caught up with the progress of the relief team.

The line clicked and one of the on-duty criminalists answered sleepily.

"Hello, Brian," the voice yawned. "What's up?"

"I thought that one of you guys might have screwed up and worked some of my hand swabs this morning by mistake—the ones we picked up at the autopsies last night."

"Not by mistake," the criminalist laughed. "Cash money. Good old Franklin must have lit a fire under the boss. Joe and I got authorized overtime to run your swabs. Finished them a couple of hours ago, at a considerable sacrifice to my sex life, I might add."

"I sympathize. You got the readings handy?"

"Right on my desk. Ready?"

Sheffield picked up a pen and then began to write quickly as the Orange County criminalist read off his report. Sheffield filled half a page with notes, then blurted out, "What?" at one unexpected set of figures. He asked for a repeat.

"I double-checked," his friend said. "Franklin's already been in and asked for a duplicate run."

"Any chance of an accidental switch?"

"Much as I hate to brag, not a prayer. We ran your batch completely separate. All the blanks and standards check out beautifully. I even double-checked the swab tube markings. Everything matches line for line.''

"You only ran one of the swabs?'' There were two gunshot residue swabs in each of the small collection tubes. They were normally held together as a pair when rubbed across the subject's hands, thus automatically producing a duplicate set of swabs for cross-checking by prosecution or defense.

"Sure. You want the duplicate run?''

"No,'' Sheffield decided, thinking quickly. "You'd better hold on to them. Things are about to get confusing.''

"Yeah, that's roughly what Franklin said.''

Sheffield started to ask another question when Hernandez burst into his office.

"Get your ass in gear, compadre,'' Hernandez said, motioning with his thumb. "Chief wants us at the council chambers as soon as possible. Bring all of your notes, and tell Malinger to get hot on those photographs.''

"I've got a set of contacts,'' Sheffield started to say, "but—''

"Bring 'em,'' Hernandez nodded. "Got to go. I'll meet you there in five.'' He disappeared around the door before Sheffield was able to say anything else.

"Oh, mother,'' Sheffield muttered to himself. "Hey, listen, I've got to go to a meeting. I'll call you back as soon as I get out. I want to double-check the swabs with the clothing. You might be able to get something off of the sleeves.''

"Your case is still good for more overtime, according to Franklin. Bring the stuff by any time. We'll probably be here.''

"Later, friend,'' Sheffield said, and hung up the phone. He stared at the scribbled notes for a few moments, then tore off the top page of the pad and added it to the bulging manila folder. Deciding to make an attempt at reasonable formality, he rummaged through the coat closet for his jacket and a tie before walking across the plaza steps to the city council chambers.

The meeting was already in progress when Sheffield arrived. Technically in executive session, the council members had decided to move the meeting from the public chambers into an adjoining room with a single conference-sized table. Trying to be inconspicuous, Sheffield entered the room through a side door and took a seat in the second row of chairs against the walls that surrounded the long rectangular table. He sat directly behind Andersen, and waited until the mayor stopped speaking for a moment to grab at Andersen's arm.

"I've got to talk with you," Sheffield whispered.

"Not now," Andersen shook his head, and turned his attention back to the mayor who had started to speak again.

"I think that Mr. Hammon has summed up our public relations problem very accurately," the mayor said, looking around at the twenty-odd people who sat in the two rows of chairs around the table. Aside from the mayor and two of the councilpersons—one being a woman who was big on lib terminology—most of the individuals present were from the city administration, including the administrator, the public relations officer, the personnel director, and their immediate staffs. There were four representatives from the police department: Police Chief Lars Sager, a gruff, white-haired, streetwise veteran in his fifties; Sergeant Andersen; Detective Hernandez; and Sheffield.

"Perhaps," Councilwoman Adrian Hite asked in a sarcastic voice from her seated position, "Chief Sager would now be willing to offer some explanation as to why his officers apparently butchered four young men in our city streets last Thursday night? Four, young, unarmed men, I might add." Hite looked up at the slowly boiling chief through the red-framed glasses that matched her carefully dyed hair, and smiled in anticipation. Sheffield noticed that copies of the front pages of several local papers were spread out in front of her on the table.

Chief Sager glared at the incessantly mouthy female politician for a few moments without speaking. She was one of seven elected individuals who held the full authority by majority vote to hire or fire him without explanation. The look in his eyes made every unspoken word absolutely clear. When he finally spoke, his voice was calm and controlled, exactly as it had been when he confronted people like Adrian Hite on the streets as a patrolman twenty-five years ago.

"Mrs. Hite has managed to include three major errors in her brief speech," he said in a graveled voice to the entire group, his eyes remaining fixed upon the flickering gaze of his predictably vocal adversary. "First of all, the four suspects were shot in a gun battle. They were not executed. Secondly, at least one of the suspects was armed with an auto-loading shotgun which we are having examined by an outside agency to confirm that it was used in the shooting. Finally, Mrs. Hite has apparently forgotten that one of our city employees, Officer Jacob Farber, was killed in this shooting and his partner, Daniel Branchowski, is now in intensive care with severe chest and head wounds."

Having finished his reply, the chief conveyed a weathered and patient expression to each of the other politicians and administrators at the table. Sager, for all of his rough-and-tumble jargon at council meetings, was a seasoned veteran of the political side of law enforcement. As such, he was perfectly comfortable with the verbal sparring and word games that were constant elements of city politics. He rarely was in as vulnerable a position as he found himself this morning.

"I'm sure that we are all very distressed by the death of Officer Farber." The dark red lips spoke in a voice more sarcastic than sympathetic. "And Officer . . . uh . . ."

"Branchowski," Sager's voice rumbled briefly through tightly clenched jaws. From his rearward position, Sheffield was able to observe the remarkably similar facial reactions of Chief Sager and Andersen as both men fought to control their tempers. Hernandez had simply turned a darker shade of red around the back of his neck.

"Yes, of course. However," Hite continued forcefully, "I am equally distressed by the apparent disregard for human life that your officers displayed in responding to what I am told was a simple case of three intoxicated boys, none of whom had ever owned or handled a firearm." She spoke with emphasis which implied that a considerable amount of background investigating had been done by one of her associates or informers. "They just happened to get involved in some minor vandalism. Following which, I am told, your SWAT officers"—she spoke these words with a distinctive venom—"kicked in the door of another young man who may or may not have been involved in the incident. Unfortunately, we may never know because your officers immediately killed him, and then later claimed that he had a weapon of some sort taped to both of his hands. I believe that is correct, is it not?'' Hite looked up from her notes, adjusted her glasses and stared, unintimidated, back at the chief.

Andersen spoke up. ''Ms. Hite,'' he said, exerting a considerable amount of internal control to maintain the tone of his voice at a calm matter-of-fact level, ''I'm Sergeant Walter Andersen. As the field supervisor of the investigating team on this case, I believe that until Chief Sager has been fully briefed on all of the information gathered so far, I might be in a better position to answer your questions.'' Andersen looked over at Sager and received a go-ahead nod.

''That would be fine, Sergeant.'' The richly coated lips thinned momentarily in frustration and then opened up in amused anticipation. Hite was hungry for some hard-hitting publicity to lead off her campaign for the county supervisor's office, and she had prepped herself carefully for this rare opportunity to get under Sager's skin. She was not at all pleased by the young sergeant's sudden decision to defend his chief.

''I'm sure that you are well prepared to enlighten all of us in this matter,'' she continued after completing her brief visual evaluation of her new adversary. ''Please do so now.''

''To begin with,'' Andersen said, ''we are not at all certain that the three young men our officers initially tried to contact were unarmed at the time of the shooting. The evidence we have found so far suggests that at least one other weapon was involved in addition to the shotgun in the possession of the fourth suspect.''

''You say your evidence indicates that these boys might have been armed. Can you explain why you apparently failed to find these . . . uh . . . presumed weapons? And furthermore, why none of their friends or relatives ever saw any of them handle any type of firearm before?'' The predatory smile was firmly in place.

''At the moment, we cannot explain why we were unable to find any other weapons,'' Andersen admitted candidly. ''Unfortunately, we have received very little cooperation from the friends and relatives you mentioned. We would, of course, appreciate the opportunity to add their statements to our case file. However, I might add that we are in the process of conducting a separate scientific examination to determine which of the individuals involved in this case did, in fact, discharge a firearm.''

"Oh, really?" The predatory eyes and ears waited alertly.

"As a matter of fact, Chief Sager requested that I have the supervisor of our crime laboratory, Brian Sheffield"—Andersen motioned for Sheffield to join him at the end of the table—"attend this meeting to explain the scientific details of our evidence in this case."

"We appreciate your willingness to help us here," the mayor broke in, directing his words to Sheffield. He was uncomfortably aware that his rival Hite had effectively managed to dominate the meeting so far. The mayor had a few unannounced plans of his own for the county supervisor's office. "Perhaps you could give us a brief description of what you have done to determine who was actually involved in the shooting?"

"Yes, Mr. Sheffield," Hite added, "I'm sure that we would all benefit from some unbiased forensic testimony at this point." The patient expression on her face could only be described as smug.

"I'm not here to testify, Mrs. Hite," Sheffield said quietly, mentally shrugging at the unintentioned lie as he settled himself into his calm, professional, expert-witness demeanor. "But I'll try to be as helpful as I can."

Sheffield carefully described, in nonscientific terms whenever possible, the technique involved in collecting evidence for gunshot residue testing. After politely requesting permission, as he would have done in a courtroom, he moved over to a wall-mounted chalkboard and used a small piece of white chalk to make a series of neat sketches, visually explaining the process by which a discharged handgun or shotgun could leave gunshot residues on a suspect's or victim's hands.

"Once we collected the swabs at the autopsies, we turned them over to the Orange County Crime Lab for analysis," he continued, replacing the chalk on the narrow rail and walking back to stand next to Andersen's chair. Andersen was sitting down, relaxed and amused by the fact that Sheffield had the entire group—even Sager—listening intently.

"When can we expect the results of these tests?" the mayor asked, and Sheffield winced visibly.

"I received a verbal report by phone just before I arrived

here,'' Sheffield answered, feeling a knot of tension begin to grow deep in his stomach. He had tried to imply that the results wouldn't be ready for another two or three days without actually saying so. "I haven't had time to discuss the results with Sergeant Andersen and my staff. I'd prefer to wait until I have a written report before I say anything about the test results."

Hite had seemed ready to nod agreeably, but then she suddenly changed her mind, as if she sensed that she had been lulled into complacency by the personable scientist. "I'd like to hear what you have right now, if you don't mind. I'm sure that we are all here to be informed."

Sheffield looked at Andersen for support, and then to the chief, but both men seemed to be oblivious of Sheffield's sudden discomfort.

"Is there something the matter, Mr. Sheffield?" Hite asked.

"No, ma'am. It's just that some of the results were unexpected and I haven't had a chance—''

"What do you mean, unexpected?" Hite was now sitting forward in her chair, ears tuned and mind working furiously as she cursed herself for allowing the young scientist's delivery to abate her inherent suspicions regarding anyone who was the least bit involved in law enforcement.

Sheffield took a deep breath, aware that Andersen and Sager were now alert and wondering what the hell was going on.

"According to the verbal report that I received a few moments ago over the phone, all but one of the swab sets came back negative."

Outside of Andersen, Sager, and Hernandez, who now sat upright in their chairs, wide-eyed and stunned, no one in the room seemed to grasp the significance of Sheffield's statement. They were all settled comfortably around the table, waiting expectantly for Sheffield to finish his report. All except Hite, whose mind was frantically trying to fit all of the pieces together, vaguely aware that somewhere in her subconscious the pieces had meshed with a solid clunk and an alarm had gone off.

"I'm afraid that I don't understand," Hite said carefully. "All but one?"

"All but one of the swabs were negative for gunshot

residues,'' Sheffield explained reluctantly, knowing that there was nothing that he could do now except lay it all out. "Of the six individuals swabbed for gunshot residues, the tests indicate that Officer Branchowski was the only one who discharged a firearm that evening.''

Hite sat momentarily stunned, unable to believe that her entire campaign had been handed to her on a forensic platter. She recovered rapidly.

"Are you telling us you have confirmed that none of the three boys found near the liquor store fired a weapon at our police officers?"

"It appears that way, unless the residues were washed off by the rain that evening.''

Hite brushed off the qualification in her single-minded determination to solidify her information. "And the young man in the room, the one that you claim had a shotgun taped in his hands?''

"According to the verbal report from the county lab, he did not fire the shotgun,'' Sheffield finished, his stomach feeling as sick as the expressions on the stunned faces of Sager, Andersen, and Hernandez.

Alone on the winding dirt road, Johnny Baumgaertel sucked cool morning air deep into his lungs and continued to run up the hill, driving his tightening legs through another punishing 10,000-meter practice run. He concentrated on his pace, referring frequently to the stopwatch bouncing against his sweat-slickened chest, as he passed one familiar road marker after another. He was working on his best event, but the dream was still there, beckoning. The image of the torch flickered in his mind . . . rising high, touching the edge of the polished metal bowl . . . the stadium cheering . . .

The young athlete shook his head and forced his mind back on the road. The 9,000-meter mark swung by, and he picked up his pace, forcing his legs to demand more oxygen from his straining lungs. Johnny Baumgaertel was determined. The most important moment in his life was approaching. He had seven more days to prepare. He was going to be ready.

BALEFIRE

Minus 7 Days

Saturday Afternoon

1550 hours

"What exactly are the chances of those test results being wrong?"

"Almost none, Chief," Sheffield answered. He sat across from Sager in an uncomfortable folding chair, his cold hands thrust deep into his jacket pockets. Andersen and Hernandez, sitting on either side of the downcast criminalist, appeared to be equally uncomfortable for reasons that had little to do with the unpredictable weather or the furniture. "The guy at the county lab who ran the swabs knows what he's doing. Besides, he's already run the second swab on Williker—the kid with the shotgun. Same results exactly. Trace amounts of gunshot residue on the right palm, which would be consistent with Williker holding a shotgun that had already been fired. Nothing at all on the back of the hand and fingers, which would be impossible if he had fired that auto-loader. We test-fired it three times. Unburned gunpowder all over our hands every time the ejector kicked out a spent casing."

"Somebody fired that fucking gun at Branch," Hernandez interjected. "If Williker didn't, who the hell else did?"

"That's the problem," Sheffield said. "We can't even prove that those deer slugs or the buckshot in Farber came out of that shotgun. We've got two expended deer slug casings on the floor of the apartment that we matched to the shotgun by breech and extractor marks, but there's no way to say when they were fired. Someone could have fired them through that shotgun the day before, and then dumped them on the floor to confuse us. Circumstantial evidence at best."

"Hell of a coincidence that we've got two deer slugs in the street, and two expended deer slug casings that match a shotgun in a room with an open window overlooking the scene of a shooting," Sager commented gruffly.

"We'd never get past the prelim," Andersen said, still mad at himself for ignoring Sheffield's warning, causing the anguished scientist to catch the full brunt of Hite's subsequent burst of outrage before she abruptly stomped out of the conference room, her soon-to-be campaign manager close behind. "The way it stands right now, Branchowski shot three unarmed kids in the middle of Main Street."

"After someone else shot Farber in the face with a shotgun," Hernandez added.

"What about that shotgun, Brian?" Sager looked up from his rapidly cooling coffee.

"Which one?"

"The one that was used to shoot Jake." Sager's voice betrayed a sense of personal loss and anger. Sager spent almost all of his free time on his twenty-foot sailboat, and Farber had crewed with him on several weekend races to Catalina. As a consequence, their relationship had been considerably closer than what might have been expected between a police chief and a patrolman.

"For all we know right now"—Sheffield raised his opened hands in frustration—"it could have been his own shotgun. The distance is too far for Williker to have done it from the window, even if we had found residues on his hands. It's possible that whoever did the shooting could have run upstairs and taped the auto-loader to Williker's hands."

"While Branch is busy blowing away three kids in the street?" Andersen wasn't being sarcastic. He was simply expressing the overpowering frustration that all three investigators felt. They had already gone over the same line of reasoning several times. And they continued to run full force into the same dead end.

"Plus we still have a missing shotgun casing," Sheffield added.

Sager looked over at Sheffield. He hadn't been aware of any missing evidence.

"A buckshot round," Sheffield explained. "We can account for the two shotgun rounds that Branchowski fired. At

least we're reasonably sure from distances and patterns that
he fired both of the rounds at the kid in the middle of the
street. The location of the two casings are consistent with the
Remington's ejection pattern. If we assume that the two deer
slug casings in the hotel room caused Branchowski's wounds,
then we're still missing the buckshot casing that killed Farber."

"So the easy answer is that we've got a cop killer still
running around loose," Sager said.

"That would explain a lot," Andersen agreed. "But it
doesn't help Branchowski, or any of the rest of us for that
matter. That Hite bitch is probably sitting in some editor's
office right now."

"No, she uses Hammon to do her dirty work." Sager
shook his head. "I got a call from Jim Woolsey before I
left." Woolsey was the managing editor of the local newspaper.
Andersen knew that he was usually sympathetic to law
enforcement, but he wasn't the type who would bury a good
story. "He's giving us an hour, then he's going to go with
the leak from Hammon's office. I wonder if that son of a
bitch Hammon ever heard of conflict of interest."

"So, what do we do now?" Andersen asked.

"Right now, you get your asses back on the street and
keep doing your job," Sager growled. "If you come across
something new in the next thirty-five minutes, let me know."

The three investigators nodded silently and got up from the
table, walking outside to their patrol car. Sager remained
sitting in his chair, staring through the rising steam of his
freshly refilled cup.

The calls began coming in at 1643 hours, Saturday afternoon,
slightly less than fifteen minutes after the first copies of the
late-afternoon edition began to land on doorsteps.

There were two primary telephone numbers listed for the
Huntington Beach Police Department. The first was a public
information and business number answered by the officer
assigned to the front desk. Within ten minutes of the first
indignant phone call, all six extension lines that rotated off of
the main number were blinking brightly, indicating calls on
hold. A Records clerk and two cadets were put on the front
desk to screen the calls for the officer, but they were subse-

quently replaced by a lieutenant and two sergeants when the less inhibited protesters began showing up in person to register their displeasure. Outside the entrance to the station, crude picket signs blossomed among the growing, angry crowd of Huntington Beach residents. Among the more original sentiments displayed on the crudely scrawled signs were such declarations as "Cops Kill," "Don't Shoot, I Live Here," and "Huntington Beach Is Not Vietnam."

Unfortunately, there was no practical way to trace the incoming calls or determine the places of residence of the rapidly gathering protesters. Had such information been available, Andersen would have been very interested to learn that almost half of the calls in the first fifteen minutes originated from six separate telephone booths near Dana Point. In addition, many of the more vocal demonstrators had been recruited from a group of university students at nearby Irvine who were always receptive to hard cash in exchange for a little political activism.

The police emergency number represented a much more serious problem. When outraged citizens were unable to get through on the business line, they began dialing the emergency number that was prominently displayed on their telephones.

The emergency lines fed directly into the Control Center where the three dispatchers in the secure basement communications room suddenly found their switchboard jammed with routine calls.

Those callers who refused to be shunted off to one of the few administrative officers still on duty were switched over to the Watch Commander, who punched one glowing button after another on his desk phone with growing irritation, clarifying the situation with phrases that were anything but polite. As he dealt with a seemingly unending succession of callers, he suddenly realized that the number of available units had been reduced from eight patrol cars to one while he had been on the phone. Cutting off a complaining housewife with a curt apology, he slammed down the phone and reached for the roster of home numbers for his off-duty officers. Within fifteen minutes, he managed to reach enough officers to fill out six additional two-man units, but it would be at least another half hour before they all would manage to grab their gear and report in.

While the Watch Commander was busy dialing numbers, a man dressed in expensive rubber-soled loafers, dark slacks, and a dark windbreaker stepped out of his small sports car, a low-slung black Porsche.

In all outward respects, the man appeared to be a well-to-do businessman who had decided to return to his office and take care of some last-minute paperwork. Because all of the small businesses and stores in the darkened and isolated neighborhood shopping center closed at six-thirty sharp, it was not at all unusual that the man was alone as he walked with no particular urgency along the deserted sidewalks. The only unusual thing a security guard might have noticed about the man, had the association of store owners been willing to part with the money necessary to hire a security guard, was that he parked in the alley behind the stores instead of the empty parking lot, and he didn't lock his car door.

Thanatos walked slowly, appearing to take a casual interest in the illuminated store windows and their assorted displays. Then, when he reached the end of the walkway, he turned and noted with approval that his position was effectively hidden by the L-shaped design of the shopping center and a large bank building located in the center of the parking lot. Satisfied, he removed a small, ball peen hammer from the inside pocket of his jacket and quickly began to retrace his steps.

The senior dispatcher had just alerted the Watch Commander to the fact that the patrol units were reporting an unusually high number of calls where they were unable to locate either the suspect or the reporting party. Suddenly, the first of what immediately proved to be a string of nine silent alarm lights lit up the grid board which monitored almost eight hundred silent and audible alarm systems in homes and businesses in Huntington Beach. The dispatcher jabbed at a button on her console, killing the alert buzzer, and immediately checked her coding book against the numbers below each of the orange flashing lights. Then she depressed the foot pedal of her headset microphone.

"Seven Charles and any unit to follow. Audible alarms in the Arendale Shopping Center. Start rolling now. TP to follow."

"Seven Charles, copy. I'm ten-eight from Egret and Marsh, ETA about four."

"Eleven Charles, Warner and Sage. I'm clear to back."

"Eleven Charles, Seven Charles, ten-four." The dispatcher's fingers flew across the keyboard on her console, transferring the call information to the unit teleprinters. The duplicate teleprinter in the dispatch room began whirring.

"Seven Charles, be advised that the teleprinter in my unit is out of order. What do you have?"

"Seven Charles, confirm you have out of order printer. Hold one." The dispatcher looked quickly over at the alarm grid for a final confirmation on the reset status. "Seven Charles, be advised we have nine audibles, no reset, at the following locations: Jason Brothers Cleaners, Maxwell Pets . . ." She read off the list of nine business establishments; all were located along one wing of the shopping center, according to the video-screen map that she keyed up on the large overhead projector.

"Seven Charles, copy. All of those alarms should be tied to one main circuit. Probably a short. I'll check it out."

The dispatcher checked her stand-by screen and noted that there were five calls backed up, waiting for a unit. At least one of the calls was potentially serious enough to justify a code response. She made a quick decision.

"Seven Charles, confirm you are en route to Arendale Shopping Center, code two. Be advised that I am cancelling your backup for a priority-one call now holding."

"Seven Charles. No problem. I'll call in if I need someone to hold my hand."

The senior dispatcher grinned, then she reassigned Eleven Charles to respond immediately to the residence of an elderly sounding man who reported two young men breaking into a garage across the street from his house. Typically, the man had mumbled his address and then hung up before the dispatcher could get his name and phone number.

Under normal circumstances, the dispatcher would have quickly run an index check to get the phone number at that address, and then called the informant back to confirm his report before dispatching a unit. This evening, however, the switchboard was going berserk, and she had a third of her available units pulled in for station security and crowd control. Having made the decision to reroute Eleven Charles without the confirmation call, she punched one of the blinking extension buttons on her phone. As she took another emergency line call, she visualized the face of Seven Charles, otherwise known as Larry Guyerly, an aggressively confident young officer who periodically shared the rewards of her kitchen and bedroom—and she grinned again.

By the time that the single black-and-white rolled cautiously into the empty Arendale Center parking lot with all lights shut off, Thanatos had removed his dark jacket, exposing a clean white shirt, an expensive tie, and casually rolled sleeves. Waiting until the darkened patrol unit had cruised past the bank and into the isolated parking area, he stepped out of the shadows and began running toward the slowly moving vehicle, waving his arms to attract the officer's attention.

In virtually every contact made by a law enforcement officer with members of the public, the initial observation and evaluation that the officer makes in the first few moments will determine his subsequent actions, and occasionally, his likelihood of survival.

Larry Guyerly responded exactly as he had been trained, and exactly as Thanatos had expected. Had someone leaped out of the shadows wearing jeans and a T-shirt or an old jacket, Guyerly would have been on the radio immediately, and then would have left his unit to confront the individual with either a baton or a revolver in his hand. Instead, the man that Guyerly observed running toward his unit appeared to be anything but the burglar or vandal who was the cause of the nine alarms ringing noisily in the background. Criminals who wandered around in the evening did not wear highly visible white shirts and constricting ties, and they did not run toward a police car with open and waving hands. Accordingly, Guyerly brought the unit to a gentle stop and waited for the man to reach his open side window.

"Officer!" Thanatos gasped excitedly, apparently out of breath as a result of his frantic dash across the parking lot. "We've got him over there, behind the pet store!"

"Take it easy," Guyerly smiled, shutting off his engine. "Who did you get?"

"I'm sorry," Thanatos rasped, breathing heavily. "I guess that I'm getting too old for this sort of thing." He held up a palm to excuse himself and then took several deep breaths before continuing. "My sons and I had stopped by my office to pick up some papers, and we saw two young boys smashing windows in the shopping center. We chased them and caught one of them. My older boy's sitting on him right now. I was running over here to call the police"—he motioned toward the public telephone booth next to the bank building— "when I saw you drive up."

"And you are . . . ?" Guyerly asked, reaching for the dash-mounted mike.

"Oh, yes, of course. I'm Dr. Wheeler. James Wheeler. I'm setting up a family practice here in this shopping center."

"All right, Doctor, hold on just a minute." Guyerly brought the palm-sized mike up to his mustached upper lip and pressed the key button. "Seven Charles. It's code four at the shopping center. Contacted an informant. Apparently two young kids breaking windows. Possibly one in custody. You might have the alarm company respond to shut everything off."

"Seven Charles, code four at Arendale. Will advise alarm company."

"Okay, Dr. Wheeler, let's go take a look at what you've got here." Guyerly stepped out of the unit, picked up his flashlight, and followed the excited doctor across the parking lot. As they walked past the sidewalk on their way to the rear of the complex, Guyerly could see the shattered row of storefront windows.

"Goddamned kids," Guyerly muttered darkly as the two men stopped for a moment to observe the damage. "No wonder insurance is so high."

"I'm afraid that I don't even have that consolation, officer," Thanatos said ruefully, shaking his head. "I bought a two-hundred-dollar-deductible policy to save a little money on the premiums."

"And you'll probably have a hundred-and-ninety-dollar broken window." Guyerly nodded sympathetically, as they continued around the side of the building.

"I suppose I should be grateful we didn't get here earlier,"

Thanatos said, as they walked past the black Porsche. "They probably would have smashed the windows on my car, too."

"Your car?" Guyerly asked, stopping to take a quick look at the type of automobile that most cops dreamed about. Guyerly had turned slightly away from the doctor to get a good look at the Porsche's interior, when it suddenly occurred to him that he should have heard the sounds of excited young voices by now.

"Where did you say—" Guyerly started to ask, and then screamed as the hard edge of a shoe was driven sharply into the side of his left knee, tearing ligaments and tendons loose. There was the sickening sound of bone grating against cartilage. Guyerly grabbed at his horribly torn knee with both hands before his survival instincts brought his right hand back up toward his holstered revolver. He neither heard nor felt the baton being slipped out of his belt ring. He was still fumbling for the strap that secured his holstered handgun when the heavy blunt end of the unbreakable, plastic baton was driven straight into the vulnerable area just below the intersection of his lower ribs and breastbone. He folded, then vomited helplessly with spasmodic convulsions as he dropped to the asphalt.

An older, more experienced officer might have remained down, mercifully slipping into a state of pain-induced unconsciousness, or faking that response in order to gain some time. Guyerly was young, bull-chested, and totally incapable of accepting defeat. He tried to come back up, eyes bulging, lips pulled savagely back against bared teeth, clawed hand reaching blindly for the man that he was going to kill bare-handed. The deadly blunt end of the baton struck again, crushing in the thin wall of bone that comprised the temporal region of Guyerly's skull just below the protective helmet. The young officer was dead before his suddenly loosened body dropped to the asphalt, face down and irrevocably stilled.

Working with calm but hurried efficiency, Thanatos checked for the carotid pulse. Finding none, he savagely smashed the baton into the legs, arm, shoulders, and neck of the limp figure. Then he carefully replaced the baton into the empty chrome belt ring, looked around to confirm there were no witnesses to the brief, fatal assault, and then walked over to pick up the ball peen hammer. He drove the side of the hammer sharply into Guyerly's rib cage four times before flinging the tool up onto the rooftop of the damaged building. Then he put his jacket back on and quickly walked over to the waiting Porsche.

By the time that the senior dispatcher began calling for units in the area to make a safety check on Seven Charles, the black Porsche had been abandoned in a rented garage in the neighboring town of Fountain Valley. The expensive clothes had been placed in a large, brown paper shopping bag that had earlier contained a completely contrasting set of clothes. Five blocks away from the expended garage space, the paper bag had been dropped into a handy garbage dumpster.

The small tan Volkswagen was slowly turning into the driveway of the Huntington Harbour home by the time that the backup units pulled up next to Guyerly's black-and-white. Thanatos was reaching for a chilled can of beer in the refrigerator when the first officer shone his flashlight beam on the broken body of Officer Larry Guyerly and started cursing. The terrorist was tilting his head back to enjoy the first chilling swallow of the thirst-quenching beer at the same moment that the officer keyed his pack-set radio, broadcasting a helplessly enraged message that set into motion a tangled series of emotionally generated events.

Four teenaged youths who had been stopped in an old grey Plymouth for suspicion of drunken driving were sullenly arguing with the officers about the number of times their tires had crossed back and forth over the yellow lines when all heard the broadcast over the senior officer's belt radio. One of the more intoxicated teenagers made a slurred comment about making pigs into bacon, and subsequently found himself bleeding seriously from the mouth and both nostrils and missing four of his front teeth before the senior officer managed to get his partner under control.

It took the combined strength of the Watch Commander and both dispatchers to hold the hysterical senior dispatcher immobile on the floor of the communications room until her screaming and convulsive thrashing was finally reduced to shaking sobs. The two pale, shaken dispatchers immediately returned to the communication terminals that were noisily demanding attention. The Watch Commander remained kneeling by the stricken girl until the jail duty nurse managed to call in a confirmation to the nearby hospital medical staff. She then administered a fast-acting sedative while the dispatcher was being strapped securely onto a transportation litter.

A phone call was made to the home of newscaster Jack Paradee. He answered grumpily, and then listened silently for a few moments. Three minutes later, he was pulling on a heavy overcoat and running out to fumble hurriedly with the rusty lock on his garage door.

Andersen, Hernandez, O'Rorke, Sheffield, Malinger, and Dorsey each received phone calls within sixty seconds of each other. Sheffield was the last one to be located because he and Meiko had returned to the lab after eating a quick dinner to keep working on the pile of over two hundred photographed, labeled, and packaged items of evidence that had been collected so far on the Farber and Branchowski shootings. When Malinger came bursting into the laboratory less than fifteen minutes later, the lab van was packed and ready to roll.

Meiko, having already disobeyed her doctor's orders to remain at home for at least one more day, tried to convince Sheffield that she was perfectly all right and capable of working a scene. Sheffield-the-boyfriend would have lost the argument hands down. Sheffield-the-lab-supervisor told her to get her undamaged behind back into her chair and get to work because they would have a lot more evidence to put on that table within the next few hours.

In the basement of the Dana Point home, a small group of men gathered around an expensive piece of electronic equipment that was little more than a highly sensitive police-band receiver. While the members of the Committee listened to the emotional transmissions, a small teleprinter virtually identical to the smaller models mounted in the Huntington Beach black-and-whites continued to whirr as it spewed out a long strip of printed paper. The men listened, occasionally making animated sounds and gestures of approval as Huntington Beach officers vented their frustrated anger against citizens, dispatchers, and each other.

The members of the Committee became quiet and thoughtful as the Watch Commander took over a dispatch terminal personally, and rapidly brought order and coordination to the confused situation. They listened carefully, and then checked radio call numbers against their copy of the police personnel roster, as first Andersen, then Hernandez and Sheffield reported in with calm, determined voices to advise that they had arrived at the scene. As they continued to listen, one of the technicians responsible for monitoring the tapped telephones in the police building walked quietly over to the group of men and handed Kaem a hurriedly printed report. The technician quickly returned to his station while the rest of the Committee gathered around Kaem.

The news was significant. One of the members of the opposition had made a move that could be manipulated to the advantage of Balefire. The timing was unfortunate because the opening ceremonies for the Olympic Games were still seven days away, but the opportunity was too favorable to waste. Sequences would have to be altered, but that was why the Committee had located themselves adjacent to the target area—to observe, to evaluate, and to make decisions. After a hurried consultation, Kaem walked upstairs to make his second phone call of the evening.

BALEFIRE

Minus 7 Days

Saturday Evening

2015 hours

Jack Paradee was a very poor, very fast, and very careless driver. He was, however, a very lucky driver, because in the fifteen minutes that it took him to brake, swerve, and accelerate the rusted station wagon to the designated meeting point, he did not once cross the essentially random pathway of a patrolling HBPD black-and-white.

From the vantage point of hindsight, it might have been argued that Paradee's success in avoiding a police unit that evening was one of the most unfortunate events in his long and varied life. Certainly Paradee himself would later have ample reason to question the fates that had allowed him to reach his intended destination.

He had parked at the end of a long, winding, gravel and asphalt road that accessed a small maintenance shed, concealed by numerous trees and bushes in the middle of the city's Central Park. Now he waited in darkness that was unusually quiet for a densely populated suburban city like Huntington Beach, contemplating the urgency of the information that had prompted the panicky phone call and the unscheduled meeting.

At night in an isolated setting where the normal background sounds of a city are absent, a sudden noise is often magnified as much by a startled imagination as by the still air. To Paradee, the crunch of a heavy shoe against roughly shifting gravel sounded like the footstep of a man twice the size that he was expecting.

"Jack?" The whispered voice was deeply nasal, questioning,

and—as evidenced by Paradee's quietly released breath—
reassuringly familiar.

Paradee stepped out of his car and walked over to the
almost invisible park bench where the dark shadowy figure
was barely visible in moonlight that was obscured by slowly
shifting cloud masses.

"Yeah, it's me." Paradee sat down on the cold wooden
bench next to the hunched figure of Sergeant Patrick Lagucii,
whose readily identifiable white hair was concealed beneath a
woolen ski cap. "What have you got?"

"Some hot information and some problems," Lagucii
muttered, his normally enthusiastic voice noticeably subdued.
"For one thing, the shit really hit the fan in Sager's meeting
with Hite and the mayor." Lagucii recited the details he had
managed to obtain from the secretary who transcribed
Andersen's dictated report of the meeting and his summary of
Homicide's intended actions.

Paradee listened impatiently. He wasn't about to inform
Lagucii that he had already received a full report of the
meeting from a much more dependable source. That would
only suggest to the officer that his role in Paradee's future
plans was something less than Lagucii envisioned; something
that Paradee did not want to happen at all.

Lagucii was, Paradee had to admit, a rare find. It wasn't
often that one ran across a man whose occupation, political
ambitions, and unbounded self-esteem, plus a mediocre level
of intelligence and common sense, made for an ideally placed
and easily manipulated informant.

The manipulation was almost childishly simple. Lagucii's
carrot was media coverage—something prohibitively expensive for an unsponsored hopeful aiming for political status,
but freely available from a source like Paradee. The fact that
Lagucii could get to information that would be totally inacces-
sible to a man of Paradee's reputation easily justified some
prime time coverage for the seemingly newsworthy officer.

No, Paradee did not want to disillusion an irreplaceable
source of information within the police department. However,
the meeting between Sager and Hite was not the mind-boggling
bit of whispered intelligence that had caused Paradee to leave
a warm fireplace and a generous glass of expensive Scotch

and sit on a park bench that was cold all the way through his woolen pants.

"What about the officer?" he asked when he judged that Lagucii had reached the end of his material on the meeting and was starting to rephrase the same information.

"Yeah, that's something else." Lagucii paused for a few moments, unconsciously adding to the subtle chill of the darkness as he pondered the wisdom of his next statements. "His name is Larry Guyerly, twenty-four years old, three years in the department. Good kid. Usually pretty careful about following standard procedures; not the type to let himself get into trouble like that. Of course, neither were Farber and Branchowski."

"What the hell happened to him?" Paradee demanded, becoming increasingly impatient with Lagucii's sudden desire to ramble and reminisce.

"He responded to an alarm call. Bunch of broken windows in a shopping center." A growing vein of insecurity was now readily apparent in Lagucii's voice. "He called in a code four, and that was the last we heard from him. Nothing to indicate he was in any kind of trouble." Lagucii paused again, taking in and then quickly releasing a deep nervous breath. He was relating information still being withheld from the public under Sager's direct order. "Backup officers found him beaten to death behind one of the stores. Coroner's investigator thinks there might be several people involved due to the extent of the injuries. Might be related to all of the public flack we received over the Farber and Branchowski shootings."

"Christ Almighty," Paradee whispered.

"In the entire history of the department," Lagucii added, "we've only had one officer killed on duty, and that was by a goddamned drunk in a traffic accident. Now we've had two fatals and one critical in a week, not to mention those shootings . . ." Lagucii's voice trailed off, then suddenly bounded back with the old Lagucii self-confidence.

"It's the people, Jack. They're not going to take this sort of thing from their police department. I mean, look at the mob outside the station earlier this evening. It was like one of the Fourth of July riots on the pier. One misstatement or a single bad judgment at the front desk, and we could have had someone hurt like Guyerly. There's a real bad undercurrent of unrest out there, Jack. Real dissatisfaction with the way that the department's been handling the whole situation with those kids in the Main Street shooting. That's why I thought this would be an opportune time for us to start our project—''

"What the fuck are you talking about?" Paradee was trying to absorb the implications and story-angles of another dead Huntington Beach officer. He had barely been listening to Lagucii after hearing about Guyerly's death, and was startled by the white-haired sergeant's sudden shift into politics. "Are you saying that Guyerly was beaten to death by a mob of Huntington Beach citizens?" Paradee's eyes glowed at the nationwide possibilities of such a story.

"Well, no, not exactly. I mean, we really don't know yet. It just seems like a logical possibility, considering everything that's been happening. That's why I thought—''

"Forget the project." Paradee spoke in a firm, no-nonsense voice. "I want to know more about these cops getting killed, especially if it looks like local citizens may be involved. And I need to see a copy of the crime report. How soon can you get it?"

"That's another thing I wanted to talk to you about," Lagucii said, unable to keep the bitter disappointment out of his voice. He had been thinking expansively about his future all evening, already envisioning himself wearing the gold-braided hat and the four gold stars on his uniform collar. "I think that Andersen and a couple of the other guys may be starting to build a jacket on me. I've been pretty careful so far, so anything they've got has to be circumstantial. But I don't think that this is a good time—''

"Lagucii," Paradee said with emphasis that left no room for misinterpretation, "it doesn't matter what you think. I don't care if Andersen and his friends are tying bells on your shoelaces. I need that crime report, and you're the one who has to get it. Do you understand what I'm saying?"

Lagucii understood perfectly. As much as he feared the idea of being exposed as a news media informant, the idea of giving up the press coverage and the dream of being voted in as the new police chief by a Paradee-manipulated city council was much more unthinkable. Lagucii muttered his assent, stood up, and stomped off into the darkness.

Paradee closed his eyes and rubbed his forehead, trying to block out the distracting irritations that were often an aftereffect of dealing with Lagucii. He was only vaguely aware of the diminishing sounds of Lagucii's feet stomping through the underbrush; he did not hear at all the barely perceptible noise of gravel being disturbed near his station wagon. He was trying to think.

One thing that twenty-five years of news reporting had taught Paradee was that coincidence was more often than not the by-product of some level of coordinated activity. Seemingly isolated events that had a similar theme were frequently tied together by a common thread of intent that might be so obscure that even the individuals involved weren't aware of the connection. The trick was to sort out that thread from all of the crossover patterns that were simply the result of random human behavior in an enclosed environment.

The violent deaths of HBPD officers Jacob Farber and Larry Guyerly were two highly unusual events separated by a very small amount of time and distance in a peaceful bedroom city where such things simply did not occur. In downtown LA, yes, but not Huntington Beach. Even the most remedial application of deductive logic suggested—in fact, almost demanded—that there was a tiny connecting thread somewhere in the wealth of information that typically was being withheld from the public.

Perplexed and not a little frustrated, Paradee rose from the chilling bench that had been slowly absorbing his body heat, walked back through the shifting gravel toward his car, and then came to a sudden heart-surging stop when he realized that a dark figure was standing next to the driver-side door, staring at him from less than ten feet away.

"Paradee."

It was not a question.

An uncontrollable sound escaped from Paradee's throat, a bodily response to mind shock. Lagucii had walked away in the opposite direction; therefore, there should not have been anyone standing in the darkness next to the station wagon. The physiological reactions were instinctive, rather than practiced. Paradee was not a physical coward, and his mind recovered rapidly.

"Who are you? What do you want?" he demanded.

"I thought that newsmen tried to avoid trite phrases," the voice responded gruffly. "I want to talk with you."

"I don't conduct business under these circumstances," Paradee growled, his voice deliberately deepened in a partially successful attempt to conceal the outward symptoms of his adrenaline-soaked nervous system.

"Oh?" The voice was now mocking, blatantly confirming Paradee's suspicion that the figure had eavesdropped on his conversation with Lagucii.

"That was a private conversation."

"So is this," the voice responded coldly.

As Paradee shifted his position slightly, the moon poked briefly through its cloud cover, with the result that the dimly diffuse moonlight revealed the identifiable shirt, creased trousers and square belt buckle partially concealed by the darkened figure's open overcoat. Paradee recognized the Huntington Beach police uniform immediately. He also noted that the badge and nameplate appeared to have been removed from the shirt. An unaccustomed sense of fear and confusion swept through Paradee's mind as he quickly digested this new information and realized that he did not like the implications at all.

"Who are you?" Paradee repeated, sounding less confident. He detected the odor of beer on the man's breath.

"Your reporting is extremely one-sided," the voice stated in the same chilled tone. "We would like you to understand our side of the situation."

Paradee tried to match the voice with one of the few Huntington Beach police officers he spoke to on occasion. Unfortunately, outside of Lagucii and Andersen, there weren't all that many officers who were willing to be seen talking to Paradee. Most were politically astute enough to realize that a seemingly minor indiscretion could have a major effect upon their already limited opportunities for promotion.

This one appeared to be relatively young, intelligent, and dangerous as hell. Paradee's evaluation was made in spite of the fact that the facial features were completely hidden by a dark-colored, full head-and-neck ski mask. The blank, sinister effect of the mask, in addition to the unnerving voice, caused Paradee's spine to tingle and his legs to feel heavy and immobile.

"I'm not really interested in your evaluation of my

reporting." Paradee forced the words past tightened vocal cords, trying to control the fear-induced demands of the body for more oxygen. He fought the impulse to turn and run.

"We would like you to listen anyway."

"You said 'we.' Who are you talking about?" A conditioned response—when under pressure, pick up on something vague and ask a question.

"We believe there is an active conspiracy working to disrupt and embarrass the department." The figure spoke in the unvarying vocal tones, ignoring the question. "We also believe that you are a part of this group, either active or supporting."

"What?" Paradee said, shocked into a nervous burst of laughter. "What the hell are you talking about?"

The figure stood silently in the darkness, and Paradee made a sudden decision to try to bluff his way out.

"Listen, if you want to talk with me about all this, you can make an appointment." Paradee stepped forward and reached for the door handle of the station wagon.

Four stiffened, leather-gloved fingers slashed deep into Paradee's solar plexus. The swift and unexpected nature of the punishing body blow immediately produced the anticipated effects, most of which centered around Paradee's subsequent inability to breathe. Emitting a high-pitched scream that ended abruptly when his lungs ran out of air, Paradee dropped to the ground like a sack of fertilizer.

The dark figure remained standing, seemingly detached from the convulsive activity at his feet. Paradee twisted about, clutching at his stomach with open-mouthed agony as he tried to force his lungs to function. Thanatos waited until Paradee's legs stopped thrashing, a reasonable indication that his diaphragm had resumed its now painful, not quite rhythmic function. Then he reached down, grabbed the dazed newsman by the collar and belt, lifted him easily, and threw Paradee across the hood of the station wagon.

Paradee was sufficiently alert to realize that he had made a serious mistake in choosing not to turn and run when he first observed the masked figure. Sprawled face down on the cold metal hood, Paradee also recognized the logic involved in feigning unconsciousness. Unfortunately, like Guyerly, he chose not to do so, telegraphing his decision by bracing his palms against the side of the car, throwing himself backwards and twisting around painfully to swing at his assailant.

Thanatos made three quick, successive moves. He slammed the heel of an opened right hand across Paradee's lower face, splitting both lips and snapping the nose cartilage. Then he drove a clenched left fist into the vulnerable stomach of the upraised and staggered newsman, causing Paradee's head to swing down in a swift arc. Timing his third move perfectly, the terrorist brought his right knee up sharply at the last second to connect with Paradee's face, breaking the rest of the nose cartilage and several capped front teeth. Paradee was unconscious before his head struck the graveled road for the second time that evening.

"Hold it right there."

Thanatos froze in mid-stride, allowing only his head to turn slowly until the carefully moving figure of Sergeant Patrick Lagucii was in full view. The sergeant had both of his arms out and fully extended, holding the absurdly small .25 Beretta automatic pistol in a tight, two-handed grip. In spite of the tiny size of Lagucii's off-duty weapon, Thanatos was perfectly aware of the damage the quarter-inch diameter, jacketed bullets could inflict upon a human body. He remained absolutely still, his arms extended slightly. Only his eyes followed the slowly moving Lagucii.

"Turn around and face the car."

Thanatos did so, moving his feet carefully to avoid tripping over the unconscious Paradee.

"Move forward . . . slowly."

In spite of his demonstrated incompetence as a supervisor, Lagucii had no difficulty at all functioning as a street cop. He knew all of the procedures that had been developed through trial and error by generations of sturdy policemen who walked a beat. And unlike many seasoned officers, Lagucii rarely deviated from these standardized procedures in the field, preferring to take as much time as was necessary to do things right. There was nothing inconsistent about Lagucii's self-serving character and his proficiency as a street cop. Police work on the street was often a matter of survival, and every neuron and muscle fiber in Lagucii's body had been programmed long ago to look out for Number One.

"Stop," the sergeant commanded, as he moved cautiously

along the gravel path, keeping a safe distance between himself and the ski-masked figure. "Now, lean forward and place the palms of your hands against the roof of the car."

As so often happens, a quirk of fate had caused Lagucii to reconsider his situation and turn back to argue again with his intended political benefactor. The direction of the offshore winds had carried the sounds of the two voices back to Lagucii before his noisy footsteps had been detectable. So Lagucii had moved in quietly, more out of curiosity than any sense of impending danger, coming around the maintenance shed just in time to see the easily identifiable silhouette of Paradee being flung backwards off the impact point of another man's knee.

Like almost every other officer on the department, Lagucii carried a small caliber off-duty weapon as a matter of habit. He did not, however, carry a pair of handcuffs or any of the other hardware extremely useful when attempting to arrest an individual in a dark park in the middle of the night. His sole weapon contained one underpowered round in the chamber and five in the clip, and it was inaccurate as hell beyond fifteen yards. It was not the type of weapon an officer would select before going into a fight. But then, an off-duty weapon was usually selected on the basis of comfort and weight rather than caliber.

"You okay, Jack?" Lagucii's eyes flicked down to the still form, and then quickly back to the masked figure who had compliantly assumed the standard off-balance search position. There was no audible response from Paradee. Lagucii prodded his fallen associate with the front of one shoe, and was awarded by some semiconscious stirring and moaning.

Ignoring Paradee's condition for the moment, Lagucii stepped forward and braced his free hand against the lower back of the figure who had so far maintained a calm silence.

"If you even think about moving . . ." Lagucii spoke softly, deliberately leaving the remainder of the warning unspoken. Realizing the man showed every intention of being cooperative, Lagucii placed his far leg between the suspect's legs and commenced to search for weapons with one hand, keeping the little automatic braced tightly against his hip, out of the suspect's reach. Lagucii's hand brushed across and almost went past the familiar object nestled in the upper leg side pocket.

"What the hell?" Lagucii's hand tightened around the immediately recognized standard-issue police blackjack. Then his hand quickly went under the coat, touched the equally familiar uniform cloth, and went instinctively up to the leather shoulder holster. Uncomprehending, Lagucii grabbed the masked figure by the shoulder and spun him around, his eyes immediately taking in the uniform shirt, the pants, the missing nameplate and badge.

"Jesus Christ! What—" Lagucii reflexively shifted his right hand to point the loaded and cocked automatic away from his fellow officer, reaching up with his free hand to rip away the mask.

Lagucii's hand had closed on the lower edge of the mask and had started to lift upwards when the terrorist's hands suddenly blurred into motion. One stiffened forearm moved laterally to knock Lagucii's gun hand aside. The other hand moved swiftly down to the side of his leg as his right knee came up and connected solidly, crushing the sergeant's genitals against an unyielding pubic bone mass. Lagucii was in the middle of a shocked scream when the blackjack came up, then smashed down on the fragile wrist bones of his blocked-out hand. The automatic discharged harmlessly into the ground as it spun out of the numbed fingers of the shattered hand, disappearing into the surrounding darkness.

Lagucii dropped to his knees, head down, his undamaged hand grasping the broken wrist, and at the same time pressing against the agonizing and suddenly nauseating pain in his groin. As Lagucii began to vomit uncontrollably, Thanatos hesitated with the blackjack poised, his eyes searching for the source of the all too familiar sounds that had unexpectedly emerged from the soothing random mixture of night noises.

Helicopter.

The sweeping eyes coordinated with data generated by differential vibration pressures on his eardrums, and he immediately located the blinking white taillight of the chopper in a sky filled with clouds, stars, and higher flying aircraft. His mind quickly judged position, direction, and approximate vector distance of the running lights. He hesitated an additional three seconds to estimate speed and flight path.

The Committee had provided Thanatos with a briefing paper dealing with the routing of air traffic over the city. In addition to the small private aircraft flying out of Meadowlark Airport, two oil companies and the Marine Corps base at El Toro routinely flew helicopters over the city. However, according to the briefing materials, the military pilots stayed well above and out of the way of the flight paths used by the private pilots at Meadowlark. The only rotorcraft that routinely flew at a low altitude over Huntington Beach at night was Ten Henry, the radio code designation for the HBPD helicopter.

Lagucii tried to come up just as the blackjack swept down in a fast and slightly angled arc, glancing off of the sergeant's cheek before thudding into his collarbone with a crunching sound of breaking bone. The waves of pain created by the sharp edges of the shattered bone grating against nerve tissue would have been horribly agonizing had Lagucii been in any condition to experience the additional pain stimulus. Mercifully, the glancing blow against his cheek had been sufficient to send the white-haired officer into blissful unconsciousness before the leather-wrapped lead completed its destructive swing.

Thanatos was absolutely certain that the sound of the gunshot from Lagucii's automatic could not have been heard by the crew of the police helicopter. He knew from experience that inside the plastic bubble the altitude and the penetrating noise of the rotor blades would completely mask all but the most explosive ground noises. It was difficult enough to hear radio transmissions through the earphones in the incessantly vibrating machines. It was very possible, however, that the pilot or the observer had been looking in the right direction when the muzzle blast of the Beretta had flashed across the darkened background of the park.

The whump-whump sound of the rotor blades shifted in pitch as the helicopter banked and then headed directly for the park, confirming the terrorist's suspicions. Kneeling, he quickly wrapped one of Paradee's limp hands around the handle of the blackjack, stood up, kicked Paradee sharply in the head, and then dove to the ground, rolling beneath Paradee's station wagon just before the observer switched on the chopper's high-powered searchlight, bathing the entire area in glaring white light.

The observer manipulated the searchlight's joystick, sweeping the adjustable cone of light through the barely visible parking lot area adjacent to the large city park, searching for the source of the yellow streak of light that had flashed across the pilot's field of vision moments earlier.

"See anything?" The pilot used his foot pedal to activate the internal communication system which linked the helmet-mounted headsets of the pilot and the observer. Both men had a similar set of pedals under their feet. One pedal controlled the ship-to-station communication, and one enabled them to talk with each other. Because of the tightly fitting military crash helmets and the steady rumbling of the engine and rotor blades, it would have been impossible to communicate in any other manner.

"Over there at four o'clock," the observer said, shifting the searchlight so that the blinding white disc surrounded the station wagon. As the pilot banked the aircraft around, two still figures on the ground came into view.

"Oh, shit," the observer mumbled into his microphone, forgetting to depress the mike pedal as he shifted the searchlight stick instinctively to compensate for the sudden violent movements of the helicopter, keeping the two horizontal figures and the vehicle in the spotlight as the pilot fought for altitude.

The immediate, instinctive reactions of the pilot were based upon an intimate knowledge of his aircraft and its vulnerability to a single bullet from the ground. Unlike its military cousins, the HBPD helicopter was not designed to absorb projectile damage and still stay up in the air.

As the helicopter churned to a higher and safer altitude, the observer struggled to keep the spotlight on the two figures. The pilot keyed his mike.

"Ten Henry requesting units to respond to Central Park. Two men down in the southeast corner at the base of the maintenance road. Possible shots fired."

"Ten Henry, do you have a suspect in sight?"

"That's a negative. We're conducting a sweep search now. Be advised that there is a light-colored station wagon." The pilot looked over at his observer who had his face pressed against the eyepiece of the gyro-controlled binoculars mounted through the floor of the helicopter.

"Five-five . . . eight . . . Sam-Echo-Sam." The observer spoke into his mike, coordinating the binoculars and the searchlight controls with both hands as he continued to make a search of the area around the station wagon while the pilot completed his evasive maneuvering, ending up in a tight turning pattern over the park at a reasonably safe altitude. "California," the observer added, as his field of vision swept across the front license plate of the immobile vehicle.

"A light-colored station wagon next to the two nine-two-sevens," the pilot continued. "California license five-five-eight-Sam-Echo-Sam. No apparent movement in or around the vehicle."

Thanatos waited patiently beneath the confining frame of the station wagon, his arms, legs, and torso positioned like a lizard. He was waiting for the roving cone of light to shift away from his position for a few moments, knowing full well that a patrol unit could arrive at the scene at any moment.

The heavy weight of the Browning automatic provided a calming sense of security as he gripped the oiled, precision weapon in his right hand. The hammer was pulled back into the full-cock position, and his thumb rested comfortably against the safety release.

Thanatos forced himself to keep the weapon on safety. If at all possible, he wanted to avoid using the familiar and dependable pistol. He had not bothered to bring along one of his disposable weapons, and it was much too early in the mission to resort to the use of a weapon which he had no intention of discarding. He was confident in his ability to put at least half of the Browning's fifteen rounds into the bubble or fuel tanks of the hovering helicopter, but he also realized that any advantage to the mission gained by the meeting of Lagucii and Paradee would most certainly be lost by such action. In addition, the discovery of 9mm copper-jacketed slugs in the helicopter wreckage would almost completely negate Lagucii and Paradee's belief that their assailant was a Huntington Beach police officer. Calmed by the knowledge that he had a great deal to gain by avoiding combat, the terrorist continued to wait in the darkness with predatorlike patience.

The area adjacent to the right side of the station wagon suddenly shifted into relative blackness as the helicopter banked around to make a wider search of the area. Thanatos made his move immediately, his efforts hampered by the narrowness of the available crawl space beneath the vehicle. Using his elbows like ski poles, he swiftly propelled himself halfway out from under the low-slung vehicle, and then froze as a new source of light swept across the rear of the station wagon. He made a quick evaluation of his position, estimating the amount of open space between the station wagon and the nearest clump of bushes which might offer reasonable concealment, and then quickly crabbed his way back under the automobile as the patrol unit came roaring down the gravel road and slid to a rock-grinding stop.

He heard a muffled voice, then the sound of two doors being opened and shut. There was a sharp metallic clack-clack. A round was being pumped into the chamber of a shotgun, Thanatos realized, tensing his body up against the still warm oil pan. He forced himself to remain absolutely motionless, breathing slowly with an opened mouth as he listened to two sets of footsteps, one set much heavier than the other, move slowly along the gravel pathway.

Barry Barlowe and John Parham moved in toward the station wagon cautiously, covering each other as they approached the two motionless figures lying on the ground. Parham, the officer with the shotgun, remained standing, sweeping the barrel of his lethal weapon across the area being illuminated by the helicopter searchlight as his partner quickly moved forward and knelt down beside the nearest still form. Barlowe, the older and senior officer of the pair, gripped his revolver tightly in his gloved right hand as he used his teeth to remove the black leather glove from his left hand.

Under reasonably normal conditions, the two officers might have approached the vehicle and bodies with less caution, reassured by the presence of the helicopter and the continued aerial surveillance reports coming in on their belt radios. The fact that neither officer relaxed his vigilance for a moment was directly attributable to the lessons provided by the recent deaths of Farber and Guyerly. Barlowe kept his eyes on the surrounding area as he felt for and found a carotid pulse. Only then did he shift his eyes downward as he reached for his flashlight, shining the light across the face of the victim.

"For Christ's sake, it's Lagucii!"

"What?"

Parham ran forward and crouched down next to his partner, staring unbelievingly at the battered face of the frequently ridiculed field supervisor. Both flashlights were quickly directed to the face of the other crumpled figure.

"Well, I'll be goddamned."

"What's the matter?" Parham hadn't recognized the second face. His flashlight beam had shifted over to the fallen man's hand.

"That there is Mr. Jack Asshole Paradee," Barlowe drawled with some apparent amusement and satisfaction. "Six-O'Clock News. Far as he's concerned, every man wearing a badge is a fascist, a crook, or a hustler."

"Sounds about right."

The younger officer grinned, but his eyes remained serious and alert as he continued to search the areas being illuminated by the observer in Ten Henry, watching intently for any sign of movement near the shifting border between darkness and light.

"Is he alive?" Parham asked as he maintained his vigilance, acutely aware that he was responsible for his partner's safety as well as his own.

"Yeah. Good steady pulse, but his breathing's kinda ragged." Barlowe reached for his radio.

"You see the gonzales?" Parham asked.

"No, where?"

Flicking his eyes away from the path of the helicopter searchlight for a moment, Parham directed his flashlight beam at the blackjack lying beneath Paradee's limp hand.

Barlowe shook his head in bewilderment, then keyed his radio. First Guyerly and now this, he thought. What a fucking night!

"Eight Adam, Ten Henry. Be advised we have two male adults. Both unconscious. One of them is Sergeant Lagucii." Barlowe decided it would be unwise to broadcast Paradee's name on the publicly monitored airwaves.

"Eight Adam," the dispatcher broke in, "confirming that Sergeant Lagucii is down at the scene."

"Eight Adam, that is affirmative. Both subjects are down with unknown injuries. No apparent gunshot wounds. Uh . . . possible mutual combat situation."

"Eight Adam, ten-twenty-three." The dispatcher didn't

believe what she had heard over her earphones, and asked for a repeat.

"Eight Adam. It is possible this is a mutual combat situation," Barlowe repeated carefully. "Requesting paramedics and a supervisor."

"Eight Adam, ten-four. Can you advise the name or description of the second subject?"

"Eight Adam, hold on." Barlowe looked up at his partner. "Is Lagucii supposed to be on duty tonight?"

"He went off two hours ago." Parham shook his head. "You think he's on a special assignment with Paradee?"

"Hell, I don't know." Barlowe stared down at the unconscious newsman, shining his flashlight across the bloody nose and lips. "Lagucii would kiss a dog's ass to get on tv, but I never saw him pack a gonzales." He motioned over to Lagucii's still form. "Check him out and see if he's carrying. Should be a twenty-five caliber Beretta in a hip holster."

Thanatos focused his attention on the reflective black shoes and the lower legs of the two officers as they made a quick pat-down search of the unconscious men. He tried to separate real movement from shifting shadows as the helicopter continued to circle, its high-amp searchlight blazing down into the darkness. For the moment, the observer's attention had apparently shifted from the surrounding area to the two still figures lying much too close to the station wagon. It was only a matter of time before one of the officers on the ground accidentally or deliberately directed his flashlight beneath the automobile. When that happened, Thanatos would have less than a second to take advantage of his position and the element of surprise.

It would be easy now to simply shift his arm and fire. He could put three rounds into the chest of the nearest officer, the older one, and at least four into his partner before the younger officer could get his hand on the trigger grip of his shotgun. The first officer would die quickly under the impact of the 9mm parabellum rounds. Like many of the old-timers on the force, the senior member of this patrol team clearly preferred to sacrifice safety for comfort. He was not wearing a vest. The younger officer had apparently gone to the trouble and expense of having his bullet-resistant vest tailored to his relatively thin frame. The telltale outline of the thick woven

pads were barely visible under the starched and ironed uniform shirt. It was likely that the edges of the pads overlapped,
eliminating the effectiveness of a side shot into the rib cage.
It would have to be a head shot; tricky in the darkness,
especially if the younger, and presumably more agile, officer
was warned in time by his partner's death.

Thanatos listened as their conversation turned to the death
of one of their comrades. Officer Guyerly, he noted, recognizing that the tone of their voices reflected a high degree of
anger and nervous tension. Both officers were alert and on
edge, and therefore very dangerous.

Time was still the prevailing factor. In a few minutes, the
area would be filled with the vehicles and personnel of the
Huntington Beach police and fire departments. Any effective
action had to be initiated in the next one or two minutes to
allow enough time for an escape.

The necessary emphasis of the initial stages of Balefire was
on escape rather than violent and deadly confrontation; this
immediately negated the option of killing the two officers
from the concealment of the station wagon. Thanatos knew
that even if he managed to drop both officers before they had
a chance to use their radios or weapons—a likely possibility,
considering his proficiency with the familiar Browning and
the added advantage of surprise—the muzzle flash of the
heavy automatic pistol would almost certainly be observed by
the helicopter crew. The end result, assuming that the air
crew was experienced and careful—a fact already demonstrated by their observation of the previous muzzle flash and
their reaction to the two bodies that had suddenly appeared in
their searchlight beam—would be a manhunt where the enemy had the continuous advantage of air surveillance.

Thanatos had spent too many stomach-wrenching days and
nights as the focal object of inhumanly persistent Israeli
retaliation squads to relish another run for his life in a situation where the enemy had all of the advantages. The Huntington Beach police officers were no match at all for the
vengeance-driven Israeli commandos who would crawl in
their own blood for one last chance to kill a terrorist. But the
police officers here had the advantage of mobility, communications, familiarity with the area, and most important, a

continuous source of directional guidance from the damnable helicopter.

The maddening reality was that the helicopter was perfectly capable of neutralizing any escape plan by simply climbing to a safe altitude and maintaining a watch for any movement within the widened circle of light generated by its powerful searchlight. Once the aircraft was in position and had him spotted, Thanatos knew that capture or death was an almost inevitable conclusion. If he ran into a house to escape the probing beam of light, the helicopter would simply climb higher until the illuminating cone covered all four sides of the house. Using his radio, the pilot would then direct units into the area and coordinate the isolation of almost any escape hole.

The terrorist listened as the officers determined that Lagucii's hip holster was empty, and reported that fact to the dispatcher. Then he tensed as the helicopter began to widen its search pattern, causing the infernal light to angle deeper underneath the station wagon. He held his breath as the shifting light brushed across his unmoving knee. There was a possibility that one of the officers might happen to be looking in the direction of the station wagon at precisely the wrong moment. However, it was much more likely that one of the alert officers would hear the sound of shifting gravel if he tried to move to a less visible position beneath the vehicle.

"Eight Adam, do you have an ID on the second subject?" the dispatcher asked again.

"Uh . . . negative at this time," Barlowe responded after an additional moment's hesitation. Parham looked over at his partner and nodded in understanding and agreement.

"Eight Adam, ten-four. Be advised that Sergeant Torres is en route to your ten-twenty. ETA on the paramedics about five."

"Eight Adam, copy."

Thanatos began the slow cautious movements necessary to remove the ski mask as the dispatcher started her message. The temporary helplessness was the most disconcerting factor as the knitted wool slid across his eyes, blocking out his already limited vision. The movements involved in removing the mask were dangerous, in spite of the covering noises of the helicopter engine and rotors, but they were absolutely

essential. One minute—count on two to be safe—were barely
enough time to carry out a quickly devised plan that offered
a short-range chance for a non-violent escape and some
difficult long-range problems that would have to be resolved
at the first opportunity. There were no other obvious choices.

Distraction was critical. Thanatos waited with growing
impatience for the officers to transmit or receive on their
pack-sets or for the helicopter crew to bring their noisy
machinery into closer range.

Finally, after the helicopter had completed two complete
sweeps around the perimeter of the small section of park
land, the en route sergeant provided an opening, requesting an
exact ten-twenty from Eight Adam.

Making the logical assumption that the drumming beat of
the helicopter blades and ever-present radio transmission static
would mask the unavoidable gravel noises, Thanatos carefully placed the cocked Browning down on the coarse rock
next to the outside edge of the station wagon's wide, right
front tire. Then he pushed himself up onto his toes and
fingertips, and quickly slid out from under the vehicle just
as the helicopter swung around to the aerial quadrant containing the opposite side of Paradee's vehicle and the two
officers.

Coming up rapidly into a crouched stance next to the front
passenger door of the station wagon, he grabbed the automatic pistol, slid it with practiced efficiency into the worn
and sweat-stained leather shoulder holster and then stood
straight up, all in one quick and smooth movement.

Both officers were facing in the opposite direction. Neither
of them picked up the sudden vertical movement with their
peripheral vision. Thanatos began to walk backwards away
from the station wagon, taking slow careful steps, keeping his
eyes locked on the two reflective helmets.

The uniform! Thanatos froze in mid-step, realizing that he
had forgotten about the partial police uniform that he wore
underneath his unbuttoned jacket. One good look at the uniform shirt, pants and shoes by either one of the officers who
were now watching the path of the helicopter searchlight
beam that was rapidly circling back in his direction, and his
escape plan would fail instantly. His hands moved hurriedly

to remove and discard the thin black gloves that police officers preferentially wore to ensure a tight and sensitive grip on a gun butt or a baton.

He had taken seven slow, cautious steps backward, his fingers working furiously to button up the knee-length overcoat as he forced himself to remain casually erect, when his rear shoe crunched down on a patch of loose gravel. The nearest officer, Parham, whipped around, spotted a dark upright figure outlined against a slightly less dark background, and leveled the shotgun.

The nonchalant "Good evening, officers, what's—?" and the harsh command "Freeze!" echoed across the brush-covered park at virtually the same instant. Thanatos willed himself to ignore the survival instincts that screamed for him to either lock his hands behind the back of his head or dive behind the protective bulk of the station wagon. Instead, he stood in what he hoped would appear to be shocked and confused immobility, one upraised hand frozen in a wave of greeting.

"I'm sorry," he said quickly, raising his voice in pitch. "I saw your lights. I was out looking for my dogs. Kids left the gate open." He moved his head and raised hand slightly in the direction of the nearby housing tract across from the park, a good two hundred yards away. "I thought that I'd come down and say hello," he stammered when neither of the cautiously approaching officers responded. "I didn't mean . . ."

"What's your name," Barlowe asked in a steady, cold, businesslike tone, the beam of his flashlight immediately directed at the man's open hands and then his face.

"Bob. Bob Saladin. I . . . uh . . . live in the Tammarack tract up—Oh, my God!" Thanatos tried not to overdo his reaction to the two sprawled bodies barely visible behind the two officers. "Are they dead?"

"What's your address, Mr. Saladin?"

"I . . . they're . . ." He shook his head. "I'm sorry. I live on Nightingale, twenty-five-thirty-three Nightingale," he said, repeating from memory the address he had selected for this evening's work. The names and addresses on his list consisted of individuals who had recently moved into the city. The assumption was that neither of these officers would have come in contact with a new resident named Bob Saladin during the last four weeks.

"Could I see some ID, Mr. Saladin?"

Parham had shifted the Remington so that the cavernlike barrel wasn't quite pointing in the man's direction. However, his carefully selected position provided a clear field of fire, completely excluding his partner, and it would only require a quick movement of two steady wrists and one tensed finger to sweep the shotgun through a 12-degree arc and pull the trigger. Thanatos did not find it difficult at all to act appropriately nervous. The expression on Parham's face provided all of the necessary motivation.

"Yes, certainly . . . oh, no." The terrorist's hand came to a sudden halt in the middle of a deliberately open and slow grab for his right rear pant pocket. "I . . . uh . . . I'm afraid that I left my wallet back at the house," he said sheepishly, nervously shifting his eyes down to the two unmoving figures on the ground and then back up at the standing pair of officers.

"I was in a hurry," he started to explain, shrugging his shoulders. "I . . . we . . . can go right over to my house," he continued in an attempt to be helpful. "It's just up the hill a little ways . . . if it's really important," he added hesitantly, looking at each of the officers for confirmation.

Uncertain. Nervous. Anxious to please. And more than a little curious in spite of the obvious fear that he had been mistaken for someone else. The typical profile of a middle-class homeowner who happens to come across a pair of police officers working a scene at night.

Parham looked over at his partner, who nodded in agreement. The shotgun was shifted to a less threatening position, and Parham bent down to check on Paradee and Lagucii.

Thanatos had no illusions about the casualness of the act. The officer had not switched the safety on. At most he had added a half-second delay before the shotgun could be brought to a point-shoulder position and fired.

Barlowe appraised the apparent Bob Saladin for a few moments, and then continued with his questioning, exchanging his now holstered sidearm for a notebook and pen.

"Did you happen to hear or see anything unusual this evening, Mr. Saladin?"

"You mean, regarding these two . . . uh . . . men?"

"That's right."

"No, I'm sorry. I didn't. Like I said, I was going out to chase after my dogs. A pair of dachshunds. Kids let them out all the time, and then they get lost in the park. The only thing I saw was your lights, and since I was coming this way anyway . . ." Thanatos grinned self-consciously—a wasted acting effort in the shadowy darkness, but it helped him to maintain the character.

"And you're sure you didn't hear anything unusual?"

"No, not really. Well, I did hear a loud noise a few minutes before I left the house, but I really didn't pay too much attention to it. I was too busy yelling at the kids."

"Could it have been a gunshot?"

"I guess it could have been. But I couldn't say for sure. I'm not all that familiar with guns—" The terrorist's explanation was interrupted by Barlowe's radio.

"Eight-Twelve Sam, Eight Adam."

"Excuse me a moment, Mr. Saladin." Barlowe reached for the radio and brought it up to his mouth, depressing the microphone key with his thumb.

"Eight Adam."

"Eight-Twelve Sam, Eight Adam. Give me a repeat on your ten-twenty. I can't find you."

Barlowe glanced up at the slowly revolving red and blue lights on the top of his unit, lights that had to be clearly visible for miles, and shook his head. Just my goddamned luck, he thought. Have the department turd and a guy like Paradee as suspects in a mutual combat situation, and then draw a responding supervisor who can't find his way around the city. Barlowe repeated his location obediently, listening as the frantic wailing sounds of the paramedics became audible in the distance. What a goddamned crazy night, he thought to himself, remembering the squad briefing on Guyerly and the unnecessary warning to be alert.

"Can I do anything to help, officer?"

"Huh? No, I don't think so, Mr. Saladin. Hold on just a

second." Barlowe keyed his radio again and contacted the helicopter that continued to circle above the park.

"Eight Adam, Ten Henry. I've got a male adult down here. Dark coat, dark hair. You see where he came from?"

"Ten Henry, Eight Adam. That's a negative. First time we saw him, he was walking in your direction."

"Ten-four." Barlowe turned back to the man. "All right, Mr. Saladin, you can go now. I'd appreciate it if you'd stay out of the area for a little while until we get things straightened out."

"Certainly, officer." Thanatos smiled weakly. "I'll just let those mutts run loose tonight. Serve them right if they get picked up by the dog catcher. Oh, by the way, are you going to need some sort of signed statement?"

"No, not right now. I'll put your name and address in our report. A detective may come by to see you later on."

"That will be fine. Any time at all. In fact, you're both welcome for coffee later on this evening, if you have the time."

"Thanks, maybe a rain check." Barlowe smiled for the first time, enjoying the satisfaction of seeing a sudden confrontation with a citizen turn into a friendly contact—something that had been occurring with less and less frequency lately. Ever since Farber and Branchowski shot those three kids less than forty-eight hours ago, he realized, thinking about the dead officer and the newspaper stories anticipating the coroner's inquest that was scheduled soon. Sighing to himself as he waited for the arrival of the wandering sergeant, Barlowe didn't notice that the departing Mr. Saladin took a careful look at their badge numbers and the license plate on their unit.

It took Thanatos almost ten minutes to walk out of the park and into the middle of the nearby housing tract in which he had claimed to reside. He forced himself to walk slowly, and he even stopped a couple of times to turn and look back at the two officers.

As he approached the new neo-Spanish style home where the real Robert Saladin was presumably watching tv, sleeping, or indulging in some other activity appropriate for eleven o'clock on a Saturday evening, the terrorist appeared outwardly to be calm, composed, and unhurried.

The fact of the matter was that Thanatos was in very much of a hurry. It was only the realization that his departure was very likely being watched by at least one of the officers on the ground, in addition to the almost certain scrutiny of the helicopter crew, which prevented him from breaking out into a laughing sprint to his waiting vehicle.

It had been close, much too close. He had barely crossed the street when the second black-and-white roared out of the darkness, coming around a corner, accelerating and then braking impatiently as it passed the mailbox where he stood. The unit had turned sharply, throwing dirt and gravel, as it followed the road down into the park where the two officers waited.

Had he been anywhere near the two officers when the sergeant arrived, Thanatos knew he would almost certainly have been required to remain and repeat his story. The field supervisor would have undoubtedly been more strict about requiring proper identification, possibly even insisting on a cursory pat-down search. And the additional delay would have simply increased the already much too high numbers—the number of police officers who knew his face, and the increasing numerical probability that either Lagucii or Paradee would regain consciousness while he was still in the immediate area.

He was almost free, but the helicopter was still a threat. He continued to move toward the front door of 2533 Nightingale until he judged that he was completely concealed by the conveniently overgrown landscaping. Then he moved cautiously around to the side of the house and crouched down next to the wooden gate leading into the backyard of the residence.

Thanatos remained in his crouched position, listening to the low growling noises of what was hopefully a small and unexcitable dog on the other side of the gate, waiting until the helicopter reached the most distant point of its established circular pattern. Then in one quick, smooth motion, he vaulted over the gate.

Five minutes and one kick-stunned dog later, the terrorist

had hurdled three fences and was securely behind the wheel of a dark blue Pontiac Firebird. He waited patiently for a vehicle that might distract the helicopter crew to pass by, and when a late-night driver finally appeared, Thanatos reached down for the ignition key with a steady hand, his forehead glistening with sweat, and his teeth bared in a victorious grin.

BALEFIRE

Minus 7 Days

Late Saturday Evening

2345 hours

Less than five miles away from the city park where Parham and Barlowe were waiting patiently for the paramedics, Brian Sheffield, Ed Malinger, and Bob Dorsey were using wide-beam flashlights to begin a second search of the Arendale Shopping Center's rear parking lot where the body of Officer Larry Guyerly had only recently been removed. The only evidence remaining of Guyerly's presence was the crude outline of his final resting position which Sheffield had drawn on the asphalt with a piece of yellow surveyor's chalk.

Under normal circumstances, Sheffield would have requested the assistance of the patrol officers to conduct a thorough search of the scene, increasing the possibility that someone might locate some useful evidence. Counting Hernandez and Andersen, there were eleven officers in and around the rear parking area where Guyerly had been discovered by the backup units—more than enough trained and experienced manpower to search and then cross-search every square inch of the entire shopping center.

Unfortunately, nine of those available men were uniformed patrol officers whose minds were fixed upon one all-consuming goal: to hunt down, subdue, and bring back in custody—if there happened to be any witnesses present—the person or persons who had caused the death of their fellow patrol officer. The possibility that these nine officers could control their emotions in order to effectively search a crime scene for trace items of evidence was virtually nonexistent.

The whispered possibility that Guyerly's death was related

to the recent howls of outrage by Huntington Beach citizens only served to add fuel to the paranoid attitudes that were developing among the officers. More than one officer was overheard reminding his partner that it was "them" versus "us," clearly implying that "them" included anyone who was not a sworn police officer. This was an attitude that frequently surfaced during the latter stages of squad prayer meetings, when alcohol-reduced inhibitions resulted in chest-beating pronouncements of comradery, but one which—fortunately—only rarely reflected an officer's true feelings about his job and the public that he served.

Tonight, however, the feelings of vulnerability that police officers normally experienced while on night patrol had been drastically magnified by the violent and unexplainable death of Larry Guyerly.

As far as the officers surrounding Arendale Shopping Center were concerned, the cop killings were about to come to an immediate no-bullshit stop. Someone somewhere had to know what had happened to Guyerly. Before the night was over, they were going to find themselves a suspect or a witness.

"Rudy," Sheffield asked when the swarthy detective stepped away from Andersen for a moment to observe the search, "you hear anything more about Lagucii and Paradee? We gave our radio to patrol."

"Torres arrived there a few minutes ago." Hernandez shrugged, using up the bottom line on another page of his ever-present notebook. "Barlowe put it out on the air as a possible mutual combat."

"No tie-in to this?"

"Not that we know of. Why? You find something?" Hernandez looked up quickly, his eyes alert.

"No. It just seems like too much of a coincidence. First, there's the whole mess with Farber and Branchowski. Two days later, Guyerly gets beaten to death, and we haven't found a damn thing. And then Lagucii and Paradee, guys who've been buddy-buddy for years, suddenly go at each other fist-city in the middle of the night. It's crazy. It's—"

"—got to be a coincidence," Hernandez finished. "There's no pattern, no common denominator."

"What about the grand conspiracy theory?" Sheffield offered halfheartedly, not really believing it himself.

"I don't go to prayer meetings." Hernandez snorted with mild irritation. "Cops always figure someone's out to get them, but it never happens. Occupational paranoia."

"But it does happen occasionally."

"Oh, sure. Every now and then some son of a bitch'll keep a hard-on for a cop all the way through the joint. He might even go after a couple of cops if he really feels shit on. But there's always a tie-in, always something that links the victims to one guy or one case."

"Did Farber and Branchowski and Guyerly ever work anything together?"

"Not according to the all-knowing computer." Hernandez snorted again, feigning distaste for the modern piece of police equipment in spite of the fact that he had been the first to request a complete records cross-check on the three officers. "Suspects, squads, shifts, case numbers, jock size—we asked them to run everything that we could think of. No match at all."

"This kind of thing just doesn't happen in Huntington Beach, Rudy." Sheffield shook his head. "It just doesn't happen; maybe in LA, but not here."

"Come on, Doctor, you're the one who taught me probability, remember? Even a thousand pennies will all come up heads once in a while. The odds just caught up with us, that's all."

"You really believe that?" Sheffield looked at the somber detective quizzically.

"Not really." Hernandez shrugged. "But I just don't want to think about the alternative."

The telephone booth that Thanatos selected was almost completely hidden from view by the walls of the closed gas station and the row of eight-foot-tall cypress trees that separated the station from the large shopping center parking lot. Unlike the smaller Arendale Shopping Center less than three miles away, one of the small stores in this complex, a twenty-four-hour 7-Eleven, was still open. There were two cars parked in front of the store.

Thanatos waited until the owners of both vehicles had exited the store with their late-evening purchases before leaving the sanctuary of his idling vehicle and walking over to the dangerously confining phone booth.

He dialed the first number from memory, allowing the phone to ring three times before hanging up. He dialed the same number again, and it was answered immediately.

"Hello?"

"Balefire."

"I'm sorry, you have the wrong number. This is two-two-seven, three-three-seven-five."

"Are you sure it's not two-nine?"

"Yes. One moment, please."

Thanatos checked all four visual quadrants as he waited for the cutout to complete the transfer. No signs of static surveillance. None was expected because the phone booth had been selected at random at the last minute. No time for anyone to set up a camera or rig a wire. If he was being tailed, it would have to be by a car. The chopper was out because he had been monitoring the police radio frequencies and had confirmed visually that Ten Henry had resumed its routine boundary patrol of the city.

It was easy to work for the Committee, the terrorist thought, as he listened to the line click three times in succession. They were a very professional and careful group. Communication systems and access codes were simple and effective. The next time that he called in, it would be necessary to subtract the numbers, he reminded himself, as the final circuit closed with a sharp hollow-sounding click. The phone booth was now tied in to a closed-loop scrambler system that connected the Committee contact and the cutout.

"Thanatos?"

"Yes."

"Please report."

"Subject Echo-one-nine-three terminated. Echo-four-two and Bravo-five linked and down."

"Congratulations," the slightly garbled voice replied, the underlying enthusiasm readily apparent over the slight breaking effect of the scrambler. After a brief hesitation, the voice spoke again. "We have confirmed a clean line, Thanatos. You may transmit in the clear if necessary."

"Yes, thank you." The terrorist hesitated, realizing that he was too thoroughly indoctrinated in the stringent needs of total secrecy to be comfortable with these modern scrambler devices. The Committee had assured him that once a line was confirmed to be clean, the odds against an accidental match by another scrambler was in excess of ten billion to one. A big number, Thanatos nodded, but maybe the Americans now had a computer that laughed at such an easy task.

He shook his head. It was his task to create paranoia, not to fall victim to the suffocating tendrils of fear and uncertainty himself.

"I have a problem. I need a full survey on two Echoes—Barlowe and Parham." He gave the badge numbers of the officers and the license plate number of their unit. The numbers were repeated back and confirmed.

"What is the problem?"

"They obtained a full visual of my face—completely unavoidable." He explained the situation briefly.

"What about the ones in the helicopter?"

"Unlikely. Too much darkness, unless they are now equipped with advanced night-vision devices."

"Understood. What is the purpose of the survey?"

"I am requesting an immediate clearance for elimination."

There was a long pause. Thanatos expected it. Success of Balefire depended upon a carefully moderated buildup. A great deal of careful analysis and discussion had gone into the final selection, distribution, and timing of the targets. While a certain number of contingency alternatives were operable at each stage, a major change would undoubtedly require a review and decision by the entire Committee. Thanatos waited patiently, watching as a long-haired male, with both hands dug deeply into his jacket pockets, walked across the parking lot and into the 7-Eleven.

"Thanatos?"

"Yes."

"There is some uncertainty," the voice said carefully. "There will be a delay on your clearance. However, we will proceed on the assumption that it is acceptable." There was another pause. "Are you capable of initiating Stage Nine?"

"Tonight?"

"Yes, immediately."

Thanatos mentally reviewed his physical condition. Minor fatigue. Adjustable with stimulants, but not necessary. Nerves steady. Present vehicle clean. No need to make a time-consuming switch.

"I'm capable, but not fully prepared."

"What do you need?"

"A small purchase and the number."

The terrorist listened carefully as the number was repeated three times. He was about to acknowledge when a flash of color caught the corner of his eye. Blue. Red. He was barely breathing, his eyes locked on the flickering movement of the light bar, as the patrol unit that had just turned the corner was alternately hidden and then visible as it moved past the closely spaced trees. The black-and-white stopped across the street from the gas station and then moved slowly toward the shopping center with its front lights off. Turning in . . .

"Thanatos?"

. . . moving very slowly and cautiously now. Both officers visible. The shotgun was out of the rack.

"Thanatos?"

"Hold on," the terrorist breathed into the phone. Don't look around, he told himself. If there are more units, there is nothing that you can do.

He used the internal reflections of the glass in the booth as a rearview mirror. There! A second black-and-white had pulled in behind him. His mind backtracked furiously, fighting against the paralyzing numbness. Where was the mistake? He had circled the area twice to confirm that he had not been followed. It must have been the helicopter, he decided. They must have spotted him getting into the Pontiac, although he would have sworn . . .

The first unit came up even with the phone booth on the opposite side of the trees. The doors opened, two officers got out . . . and turned their backs to the phone booth as they both headed toward the 7-Eleven market!

"Thanatos, what is the matter?" The voice was insistent. The terrorist realized his hands were tingling and sweat had formed on his forehead and the back of his neck. He stood in the confining booth, mesmerized, unable to comprehend the illogical actions of the two officers.

The glass door of the booth rattled sharply under the knock

of a gloved fist. Thanatos jerked around at the sudden noise.
He had forgotten about the second unit in his confusion. He
stood there, encased in aluminum and glass, staring open-
mouthed at the police officer on the other side of the folding
glass door. The officer's other hand was gripped tightly on
the handle of his holstered revolver. For the first time in as
long as he could remember, Thanatos was frozen with
indecision. Capture and the end of Balefire, or almost certain
death if he tried to escape. The Browning was useless, buried
deep underneath his jacket. He would have to replace the
phone and go for the officer's larynx as he opened the door.

"Would you step outside, sir?" The voice was gruff and
commanding. There was no doubt at all that the question had
been delivered as an order. His partner stood back and to the
side, his hand also on a holstered weapon, but there was no
sign of animosity on either face.

"Uh, yes, just a moment." Thanatos brought the phone up
to his mouth. "I've got to go. Some police officers want to
talk to me. I'll call you back in a few minutes." He hung up
the phone and stepped out of the booth, the fingers of his
right hand tightened and flat against the side of his leg. The
timing would be critical. The other officer was too far away
to be taken without shooting.

"Is something the matter, officer?"

"We're going to have to ask you to leave the area right
away," the first officer said.

"I don't understand." The terrorist blinked, genuinely
confused.

"We have a two-eleven—"

The officer's explanation was interrupted by a shout from
one of the officers on the other side of the trees. Suddenly all
four of the uniformed men were running. One pair took
positions behind their unit and the other pair headed toward
the access at the rear of the shopping center.

Two-eleven? Thanatos remained standing, still confused.
Then he realized what was happening. The boy with the long
hair and his hands in his pockets was pulling an armed
robbery! Twenty-four 7-Eleven stores in the whole cursed
city and the stupid criminal had to pick the one next to this
phone booth! Thanatos cursed his luck as he threw himself
into the Firebird, slamming the door and throwing the car into

gear. He resisted the impulse to jam his foot down on the accelerator. There was no need to attract attention. No need to question why. Just go.

He saw the dark crouched figure break out of the front door of the market at a full run just as he began his turn into the street. He heard one of the officers shout something. There was the sound of a single gunshot. The figure halted in mid-flight, spun around, his hands pointed in the general direction of the barricaded officers. Thanatos closed his eyes for a moment, then shook his head before accelerating the Pontiac smoothly down the street in the opposite direction from the market. Behind him, the silent parking lot erupted in a sustained burst of gunfire.

The empty storage garage was the first stop, mandatory because his face was now linked to a specific vehicle. Unlike the linking problem with the two officers at the park, this problem could be solved by simply abandoning the Pontiac in its rented home.

Thanatos hated to give up the Firebird. Like the Browning automatic, the sleek powerful automobile seemed to provide a reserve of strength and security, something more and more comforting as Balefire progressed. He knew that reliance upon mechanical tools was a weakness. Like tissues, the tools purchased for Balefire were intended to be used once and then discarded, so that they could never physically link the terrorist with the deliberately separate and distinct stages of Balefire.

The separation was the important factor. It did not matter at all if the clothing, weapons, or vehicles that were involved in one particular incident were discovered by the police. A great deal of care had been taken to make certain that every tool or item of clothing was untraceable. The acts of purchasing and stockpiling the expendable equipment had been carried out by people whose sole function had been to appear, purchase, place as directed, and then disappear.

Neither the equipment nor the considerable amount of money involved was important. What was important was the absolute assurance that there would be nothing available to the police investigators that might suggest that a most terrible and inconceivable event had occurred—a terrorist, a deadly and almost invulnerable predator, had been set loose to strike again and again at the very core of America. At least, they must not be made aware too soon, Thanatos thought, smiling to himself.

The Americans were indeed fools, the terrorist concluded. They truly believed that they could sit in their warm homes and relate to the world's problems, conveniently capsulized into three-minute segments by the evening news commentator, while their own terrestrial niche remained safe and secure from the spillover of problems from the other neighborhoods of the world. By the time that these soft and complacent Americans realized that their police forces were little more than straw men in the face of a determined, professional terrorist, the predator would be searching about for even more vulnerable victims.

Thanatos laughed, as he worked quickly to switch vehicles, selecting a small golden-brown Toyota more appropriate for the neighborhood in which he soon intended to travel. Next, new clothing, lighter shades to present a less threatening image in case he was observed by a neighbor. The shoulder holster was replaced and adjusted for comfort and easy reach. Now he was ready to search out another telephone.

He chose a less visible phone booth this time to recontact the cutout and the Committee. This time, the linkup was delayed while the cutout spent an extended amount of time double-checking the access and confirmation codes.

Thanatos forced himself to control his impatience, knowing that the expendable cutout was absolutely justified in his caution.

It was the duty of the cutout to detect and fully absorb the thrust of a police probe. It was his duty not to survive if capture and interrogation were inevitable, thereby severing the single link between the Committee and the terrorist. The assumption was that if the link was severed, for whatever reason, the Committee and Thanatos would still possess the capability of reestablishing communication whenever the circumstances were such that continuation of Balefire was feasible.

It was much easier to be at the center of the action, Thanatos reminded himself. Better to act, and be prepared for reaction than to wait in a closed apartment and wonder if the next few minutes would bring an assault team tearing at the locked door. For all the cutout had known, Thanatos might well have been taken into custody during the last half hour by people who had far less compunction than the average police officer about using effective measures to obtain information. Knowing full well that every man, even Thanatos, had his breaking point, the cutout could not be faulted for his caution.

Finally satisfied, the cutout closed the communication link and hung up his phone. His duty completed for the moment, Baakar Sera-te returned to his television and his thick stack of girlie magazines, to wait for the next telephone call, which might occur at any time of the day or night.

The Committee member who had been talking to Thanatos the first time had been shaken by the turn of events. His relief at the terrorist's return call was evident, reflecting the concern of the Committee that Balefire could be derailed by a totally random and unforseen event. Not wishing to delay at the phone any longer than was absolutely necessary, Thanatos quickly explained what had happened, then severed the connection.

Secure and isolated within their double-walled townhouses, it was unlikely that more than a half dozen residents saw or heard Thanatos drive into one of the guest parking spots, exit his vehicle, and begin walking along a narrow twisting asphalt pathway that wound behind a section of the expensive and virtually identical attached homes. Of those residents who might have been looking out of their kitchen window at that late evening hour, not one would have been concerned by the sight of another adult male strolling from one house to another with a paper bag in his hand.

The one action which would have caught someone's attention took place on a section of the cement pathway concealed by trees from all but three or four rear kitchen windows. In a quick series of movements, Thanatos stepped off the path, confirmed his position by counting rear porch lights, and then vaulted silently over the five-foot board fence. Six more steps and he was crouched behind the frame of a redwood hot tub.

He didn't waste any time with the doors. The architect had specified dead-bolt locks with a two-inch throw. It would

have been necessary to rip the door off with a pry bar in order
to bypass those particular locks. Instead, the terrorist went
directly to the rear bathroom window.

In a seaside community with crisp, dependable ocean-
cooled air currents, it was a rare homeowner who failed to
keep at least one window open for natural air circulation. The
mass-produced nylon mesh screen, designed to keep out in-
truders of considerably less mass and determination, was
quickly and quietly removed with a small knife blade. Thanatos
dropped the screen cloth over a convenient bush, checked one
more time to confirm that he was not being observed, and
then pulled himself up and through the narrow window space,
taking care to step firmly onto the bathroom sink counter and
then onto the tiled floor. Then, standing silently in the dark
bathroom, Thanatos waited and listened.

The evening had already offered too many surprises, too
many opportunities for carelessness and failure. In spite of
the telephone confirmation less than fifteen minutes ago,
Thanatos could not allow himself the luxury of casual
assumption.

He stepped into the carpeted living room and paused again,
listening for any sound that might indicate he was not alone
in the two-story townhouse. There was no reason at all for
either of the residents to be home, Thanatos knew, because
he had provided more than enough work to keep both of them
busy all night. But, even though the apartment smelled and
sounded empty, he still took the time to confirm that all the
darkened rooms were uninhabited before he set to work on a
task that the Committee had decided must take place much
earlier than originally planned.

BALEFIRE

Minus 6 Days

Sunday Morning

1030 hours

Early Sunday morning, in the basement of the stark white
police building, the Watch Commander assigned to the Watch
II shift waited impatiently for ten patrol officers and two
sergeants who were taking an unusual length of time to report
in for briefing. Having just finished a long session in the
weight room and shower, the lieutenant was still blissfully
unaware of the quiet demonstrations of citizen anger and
disgust that were taking place on the mall outside the police
building.

On any particular shift, the officers of the two incoming
squads would typically arrive at the station as much as an
hour and a half before briefing. Some were simply making an
early escape from an unbearable home life. Others seemed to
be hypnotically drawn to the spirit of comradery that permeated the basement locker room at the beginning of each shift
as each officer began the ritual transition from civilian to
uniformed patrolman.

Whatever the reasons for their time schedules, the early
arriving officers for the Watch II shift quickly found themselves in an unexpectedly hostile environment.

As soon as the men climbed out of their private vehicles,
with buckled Sam Browne belts and fresh uniforms in their
hands, they were surrounded by middle-aged picketers.
However, unlike their youthful and arrogant predecessors
who had "spontaneously" gathered around the station the
previous evening, this group of approximately fifty adults,
mostly housewives, held their hand-printed signs carefully

upright and spoke with angered voices that were loud and insistent, but at the same time controlled.

From these well-disciplined protestors, many of the officers learned for the first time that Larry Guyerly was dead. They also learned that a few of the officers on Guyerly's watch had apparently rousted an entire neighborhood on the basis of an anonymous phone call in a futile attempt to apprehend the suspect. According to some of the more outspoken demonstrators, wives and husbands and even a few young children had been cursed at and shoved aside as the officers conducted a rampaging backyard-to-backyard search for the suspect.

One of the most unnerving sights in the parking lot was a seven-year-old boy. He stayed as close to his mother as possible and held her hand tightly, staring up at the officers with the one eye that was not black and swollen. The terror on his face was evident as his mother stepped forward to confront one of the bewildered younger officers who was trying to move slowly and politely through the noisy crowd.

"Young man," she said forcefully, her blue-grey eyes glaring. "One of your policemen"—she almost spat out the word—"struck my son across the face last night while he was standing in front of our house. My husband is now in jail because he defended our son and threw your officer into a trash can." She spoke with a faint smile of apparent satisfaction, but her eyes remained icy. "It took three of your people to take my husband away," she continued, "and it will take many more than that if just one of you ever steps foot inside our house again."

"I . . . I'm sorry," the stunned officer stammered, his mind still numbed by the news of Guyerly's death. He stood in the middle of the police parking lot, staring at the bruised, swollen face of the terrified boy who couldn't have been more than a few months older than his own son. "I don't understand why it happened, ma'am." He shook his head. "One of our officers was killed last night . . . but . . ." He hesitated, not knowing what to say. The crowd surrounding him was silent.

"And we didn't kill him, young man," she said angrily. "Those animals in uniform last night didn't understand that. We didn't kill him!" She threw her sign down in a final exclamation of frustrated rage, then stomped past the numbed officer, dragging her son along behind.

The crowd was muttering as the officer watched the woman slam her car door and drive away. Then he looked at each of the citizens who stood around him with signs and folded arms, absorbing the full force of the anger and contempt expressed on their faces. Finally, the shaken officer began to work his way carefully through the crowd to the back entrance of the station, trying not to ignite another incident.

Once the officers had safely isolated themselves in the locker room, the conversation exploded.

"Christ, did you see that kid's face?"

"Anyone know what happened to Guyerly?"

"I heard he got jumped by a PCP freak."

"Is he really dead?"

"Fuck, I don't know."

One of the officers began pounding his fist repeatedly into the metal door of his locker. After a few seconds, no one paid any attention.

"Desk officer says he was DOA. Somebody beat the shit out of him. Left him in the street."

"Had to be a tough mother to take out Larry." A mixture of uncertain pride and unspoken nervousness. They all paid attention to that thought. Someone who had been willing and able to kill a tough cop was still out there on the street.

"Did they find the motherfucker?"

"Hell, no. All they did was roust a whole fucking neighborhood. Did you see those people out there?"

"You see that woman? Jesus!"

"Yeah, and you think they give a shit about Guyerly? No fucking way. One of us gets nailed and they expect us to act like a bunch of candy-assed Girl Scouts. What the hell do they expect?"

"Tell ya what, people," one of the old-timers broke in, "they didn't expect us to whip ass on a seven-year-old kid."

That last comment temporarily silenced the locker room. The officers looked at each other, embarrassed by the reminder. Their job was to protect Huntington Beach citizens, not take them out like a bunch of hell-raising bikers.

The conversation started up again. Guyerly. Branchowski. Farber. The kids in front of the liquor store. The kid across the street in the hotel room with the shotgun taped to his hands. Paradee. Lagucii. The organized nature of the nighttime pickets. The kid with the black eye.

The one thing left unspoken was the underlying sense of insecurity, the fear that was eroding the self-confidence necessary for an officer to project command presence. Without that psychological advantage over the individuals they confronted every day, these officers knew they would be forced to resort to the weapons hanging ready on their belts more frequently. This in turn would only inflame the already heated emotions of the local citizens, whose anger and dwindling support were causing much of the officers' emotional disruption in the first place.

Officer Keith Baughmann, now assigned to desk duty until the departmental investigation and the district attorney's inquiry into his shooting were resolved, was not helping to control the rapidly building paranoia level at all. Frustrated and depressed by the passive role he had been forced to assume, Baughmann repeatedly offered his analysis of the situation to anyone who would listen. He was strapping the little five-shot revolver onto his belt as he explained to another half-listening officer why it was obvious that a subversive group was trying to dismantle the police department when the Watch Commander finally got tired of waiting and ordered everyone into the briefing room.

In the northwestern portion of the city, most of the Huntington Harbour families were still unaware of the events that had taken place the previous evening. They were in the process of steering boats and cars toward favorite recreation sites and harbors as several city officials walked into Jack Paradee's private room in Pacifica Hospital.

Police Chief Lars Sager and Councilwoman Adrian Hite were glaring at each other, the councilwoman still seething with white-lipped anger. They had both been present at a hastily called city council meeting earlier that morning, just after Jake Farber's funeral. Both had been completely uninhibited in expressing their widely divergent opinions as to the cause and effect of last night's killing and subsequent mini-riot. The argument had started up again on the front steps of the hospital, ending only when they entered the public reception area. As they walked down the hospital corridor in forced silence, neither of them was paying much attention to the immediate surroundings. They both tried to enter the dimly lit room at the same time, bumped shoulders, and then positioned themselves on opposite sides of the small room.

Sergeant Walter Andersen had worked through another night with only a couple of hours of rest. As a consequence, his movements were predictably slowed by fatigue, stiffness, and too many cups of black coffee. Sergeant Patrick Lagucii was able to walk only with the assistance of two hospital attendants, who helped him out of his wheelchair and made certain that he did not fall during the short walk to the bed next to the one in which Jack Paradee was resting uncomfortably.

On the basis of a quick visual examination, it was difficult to tell which of the two hospitalized men had sustained more damage. Lagucii's right hand was encased in a white plaster cast from midforearm to the end of his fingertips. His shoulder was immobilized by an inflatable plastic partial-cast, bandages, and a sling pinned at the elbow. One cheek was badly swollen; the split tissue was sewn together and protected by an adhesive patch that didn't quite cover the dark purple bruising. And judging by his slow progress to the bed, the crushed tissues in his groin were still extremely tender and not completely responding to the injections of pain-killers.

Paradee's injuries were more localized, but equally traumatic. His eyes, nose, and mouth appeared to have been used as a practice ball for a professional place-kicker. His face was almost completely covered by bruised tissue, white tape, and flecks of dried blood. Both lips were grotesquely swollen and split. Three teeth were broken, and the white area of one eye was brightly splotched with red.

Paradee made no effort to move his head, but his eyes followed all four of his visitors. He spent a great deal of time staring at the groggy Lagucii before his eyes came back to Sager.

"You're going to pay for this, Sager." Paradee's voice was raspy, slurred as much by the drugs as by his effort to keep lips and teeth apart while he talked. "You're going to pay like you won't believe."

Before Sager could respond, Hite took the opening.

"Jack, this is Adrian. Can you hear me all right?" She moved next to the bed and patted the top of Paradee's hand. There was no response from the hand or the eyes.

"Sure."

"I want you to tell us exactly what happened to you."

"Ask them." The eyes winced shut. Too much lip movement.

"I don't understand." She patted his hand again and then glared over at Sager and Andersen. "Why should I ask them?"

"Mr. Paradee apparently believes that his injuries were caused by one of our officers," Sager said, sitting back in an uncomfortable metal chair and folding his thick, hairy arms across his stomach.

"Thass right," Paradee breathed. "Thass exactly goddam right. You want to know about it? Read this." He winced again as he pointed over at a small pile of handwritten notes on the tray next to his bed.

Hite read the scribbled story first. Then she passed it over to Sager without comment. Sager read it through twice before handing the pages to Andersen, who managed to get through less than half of the pages before he exploded in anger.

"This is a bunch of horseshit, Paradee!" Andersen threw the story on the bed in disgust. He knew that he was too tired to allow himself to get mad under these circumstances. He also knew that he would probably say something that he would regret later, but he didn't really care. "No cop in the world is going to go whip on a newsman while he's in his goddamned uniform. Nobody's worth it. Not even you, pal."

"He said he was a cop, and I saw the uniform. And you motherfuckers didn't catch him, did you? And you want to know why?" Paradee tried to yell, his face infused with rage and pain. "Because it was a setup, that's why!"

"What about it, Sergeant?" Hite broke in. "Have you personally investigated the officers who took the report?"

"Mrs. Hite," Andersen replied in a barely controlled voice, "I have spent the last ten hours investigating the death of one of our officers. I have at least fifty other case files on my desk right now that I haven't had time to look at for more than a week. They include murder, kidnapping, and rape.

Every one of those cases is more important than this stupid son of a bitch getting his teeth kicked in while wandering around the park in the middle of the night!''

"Chief, I am officially requesting that you assign a competent investigator to this case immediately," Hite said, ignoring Andersen's outburst. "I assure you that I intend to personally request the district attorney to look into this matter of police intimidation and assault immediately."

Sager looked up at Hite with hooded, cold eyes.

"I think the district attorney is going to be a little too busy to worry about this," Andersen continued bitterly. "You may remember we have a couple of other things going right now. Like Jake Farber and Dan Branchowski. You remember them, don't you? They work for you. Or at least they did until they got blown away on Main Street in the middle of the night. And then there's Officer Guyerly. He worked for you, too. He was murdered last night. A lot of things seem to happen around here in the middle of the night." Andersen stopped to try to rein in his temper. Then he looked over at Paradee.

"That's right, Mr. Paradee. You didn't happen to explain what you were doing out in the park in the middle of the night with another police officer, did you?" Andersen glared over at Lagucii who remained huddled and quiet on his bed.

"What I was doing out there is none of your goddamned business, Andersen," Paradee retorted hotly, his lips starting to bleed again from the exertion. "This isn't a police state yet."

"No, it's not." Andersen nodded agreeably, trying to think as he fought to control his temper. "Look, I don't know what's happening out there in the street any more than you do. All I know is that we're getting hit by a lot of things all at once. Maybe you could get a cop mad enough to go after you. You do a good job of pissing people off. Maybe it could happen. But nobody's going to take out another cop just to get to you. You think one of us did something like that"—he pointed over at Lagucii, experiencing a twinge of self-doubt as he remembered Lagucii's well-earned reputation as a backstabber—"to one of our own guys? Just to get you?" Andersen shook his head. "No way, Paradee. I don't buy it."

"Walt," Lagucii whispered loudly.

"Yeah, what is it, Pat?" Andersen smiled ironically to

himself as he looked over at Lagucii, realizing that he had just defended Lagucii as a fellow officer from an outsider. Hell of a note to realize that when the chips were down even Lagucii was part of the team, he thought.

"The uniform," Lagucii whispered, still groggy from the medication. "I saw it, too. The guy was a cop. Had to be. I couldn't see his face, but I did see the uniform. He had to be an HB cop."

Everyone in the room was staring at Lagucii, dumbfounded by the unexpected admission. Lagucii had said nothing about a uniform after he had regained consciousness at the hospital and had been questioned by the detectives.

Then Paradee added the kicker. "Like I said, Andersen, it was a cop. And what's more, I can identify the son of a bitch, too."

Less than five miles due south of the hospital where Paradee was demanding to be shown recent photographs of all Huntington Beach police officers, Detectives Sam Kretcher and Michael O'Rorke were walking through the main corridor of the much larger Hoag Hospital in Newport Beach.

Dan Branchowski had regained consciousness sometime around four-thirty that morning, a little less than forty-eight hours after his surgery. The time was only approximate because it was difficult to tell how long the burly officer had lain quietly in bed before he began to yell Jake Farber's name and rip blindly at the wires and sensors connected to his arms, chest and forehead.

The delicate monitors responded to this sudden abuse with dramatic efficiency. In the nearby nurses station, an entire row of red lights came alive with repeating bursts of scarlet, each flashing light accompanied by its own alarm.

One of the nurses on duty—a twenty-two-year-old RN who had been assigned to the Intensive Care Unit only three weeks earlier—nearly suffered a coronary seizure of her own as the clamor began. She ran into Branchowski's room, and subsequently acquired some serious bruises in her determined efforts to restrain and protect her thrashing patient from injury until help arrived.

When Kretcher and O'Rorke entered Branchowski's cubicle,

after obtaining the reluctant permission of the resident surgeon, the girl was still on duty, standing next to Branchowski's bed, unwrapping a pressure cuff from his thick arm.

"Excuse me, hon," Kretcher said. "Would you mind leaving us alone for a few minutes while we talk with this ape?"

The girl looked up from her clipboard long enough to appraise the two unshaven and rumpled officers. In the past six hours, she had made an abrupt transition from a probationary floor nurse to a professional member of the staff.

"Yes, I would mind," she said levelly. "This patient is not to be left alone."

"Ahh . . ." Kretcher started to say, blinking from the unexpected rebuff, when Branchowski opened one swollen eyelid.

"S'at you, Kretch?" he said, opening the other eye and grinning crookedly when he recognized his two fishing and drinking buddies through the persistently hazy film that seemed to cover his eyes. "Mike?"

"Yeah, it's us," O'Rorke growled, trying to cover the emotion that threatened to break his deep gravelly voice. "How you doing?"

"Just cruisin'," Branchowski whispered hoarsely. "Hell of a time to complain, huh?" He tried to focus his eyes on the familiar faces, and failed. "Hey, don't try to run Gerri out, okay? She's good people. I already tried to throw her out this morning. Couldn't do it."

He reached across with his free hand to shakily grasp and squeeze the soft hand checking his pulse. "Gonna drag her into the sack when you guys leave." He tried to leer and wink up at the girl, with barely recognizable success. She blushed slightly, but made no effort to remove the hand.

"You try it, and see what happens to you," she replied with a grin.

Kretcher looked at O'Rorke. The senior detective shrugged his shoulders. Kretcher walked over and shut the door.

"Listen, Gerri," O'Rorke said. "We've got to talk about some things that aren't going to be very pleasant and some things that you shouldn't be listening to. Things you might be asked to testify about in court if some attorney finds out you were here."

O'Rorke eyed the girl thoughtfully. The doctor had informed the pair of detectives in detail about the early-morning free-for-all, clearly implying that he expected them to exert some control over Branchowski. From the look of the reddish-purple bruise under the girl's right eye, and the stubborn set of her jaw as she continued to hold Branchowski's wrist, O'Rorke decided that she just might be a little difficult to intimidate, even on the witness stand.

"You know," he added, "I figure if you happened to be standing over there by the door, you could keep an eye on our friend and not hear a damn thing we're saying. Be kinda hard to testify if you didn't hear anything, right?"

Thirty seconds later, the cooperative young nurse had taken up sentry duty against the closed door. Kretcher and O'Rorke were leaning forward over the backs of the thinly padded chairs on either side of Branchowski's slightly upraised bed. Kretcher had taken out a field notebook and pen.

"Feel like talking a little bit?" O'Rorke kept his voice neutral, uncertain of exactly how much Branchowski knew about what happened last Friday morning. Three days ago, he thought, shaking his head. Three days and the whole world turns to shit.

"Yeah, sure," Branchowski rasped. "How's Jake?"

"You see it happen?"

Branchowski was quiet for a few moments. Then he began to blink his eyes as the tears formed. "They killed him, didn't they?"

"The funeral was early this morning, Branch," Kretcher said softly. "Big one. Every department in the county sent people."

"Kathy?"

"She's okay," Kretcher lied, unwilling to tell Branchowski that Farber's wife had gone into shock and was still sedated and under observation.

Kathy Farber had been extremely fond of Dan Branchowski. He was invited to family dinners at least once a week. Always brought his old beat-up guitar to entertain the two kids, and insisted on helping with the dishes afterwards. Several people in the department, including O'Rorke and Kretcher, had heard Kathy claim that she wasn't the least bit concerned about Jake being out on patrol because he always had a tough old Branch to keep him out of trouble. Branch was going to blame himself anyway, Kretcher knew. No sense in making it any worse now.

"It was a head shot," Branchowski mumbled, trying to swipe at the tears. "One of the cocksuckers had a gun. Don't know why . . ."

"Did you see the gun?" O'Rorke asked quickly.

"Jake didn't see him. Jake always . . ." Branchowski continued to mumble.

"Goddamn it, Branch! Did you see the fucking gun?"

"Huh?" Branchowski jerked at the outburst from his old friend. He blinked and shook his head slowly. "No. Never saw a gun. Doesn't matter though. I got all three of the pricks. It was probably the third one—he ran down the street. I blew his ass off with the twelve-gauge."

Branchowski suddenly had a puzzled look on his face. "Hey, how'd the son of a bitch shoot me when he was dead? Had to be dead 'cause I shot him twice. Saw him fall."

"Branch," O'Rorke said softly, acutely aware of the young nurse's presence in the back of the room, "the gun's important because we didn't find any guns at the scene. Do you understand what I'm saying? The lab guys checked. None of the three kids you shot fired a gun that evening. So it's important. Did you see anyone else on the street besides those three kids?"

"No." Another hesitation. "No one else." Branchowski shook his head, unable or unwilling to comprehend what his friends were trying to tell him. "Then who . . . ?"

"Listen, buddy, the way it stands right now, you're up for charges on three counts of manslaughter or murder-two. They're delaying the coroner's inquest until you can take the stand. As far as the papers are concerned, you and Jake opened up on three unarmed kids in the middle of Main Street because you guys panicked when a kid named Toby Williker started taking pot-shots at you with a shotgun from a second-story window. Maybe he was taking pot-shots at you, but we can't prove he did any shooting either. And we're never going to be able to prove much because Baughmann and Dukata wasted him when they made a search of the hotel. So, you know where that puts you right now?"

Branchowski simply stared at O'Rorke. He tried to match

up the things that O'Rorke was telling him with the confused mixture of memories and nightmares that had been churning through his head the past few hours. There was too much that didn't make sense at all. A shotgun from the hotel across the street? Williker, that skinny, dope freak? No guns? Three dead, and no guns?

"That's right, you're up shit creek. The whole fucking city's in an uproar. And we've got about two hours before some DA investigators show up and start asking questions you can't answer. So, in the meantime, Sam and I are going to drag everything we can get out of that thick skull of yours so we can find out what the hell's going on!"

In one of the small, claustrophobic interview rooms on the second floor of the Huntington Beach police station, Detective Rudy Hernandez sipped at his cup of bitter, vending-machine coffee and reminded himself that all foul-mouthed, seventeen-year-old prostitutes started out as pretty, bright-eyed young girls in their mothers' and fathers' arms.

Hernandez—the father of three beautiful and affectionate daughters, one of whom was almost exactly the same age as the uncooperative witness who sat in smelly, nose-picking silence less than four feet away—found it difficult to believe that this girl had ever been the light of anyone's eye. The negatives were almost overwhelming: a vocabulary that would have been considered vulgar at a PD prayer meeting, an apparently total disregard for personal hygiene, clothes that had probably never seen the inside of a washing machine, tattoos that covered a considerable portion of the exposed flesh and undoubtedly much of what was mercifully covered, and a complexion that reflected a steady diet of junk food.

Hernandez was not the only one who was having difficulty stomaching Toby Williker's girlfriend. The Records clerk who had been selected to sit with Hernandez in the isolated room to protect him from being accused of verbal or sexual harassment wanted to grab the girl by her filthy hair and pound her face into the table top. Lori Sileth seemed to have an innate talent for generating violent emotions among people with whom she came into contact. Hernandez could almost believe that she had been the one who had taped the shotgun in Williker's hands.

"One more time, Lori," Hernandez said, steeling himself and remembering that the tape recorder was running. "Are you absolutely certain that you never saw a firearm of any kind in Toby's room?"

"I already told you. Toby was too loving and caring to own a gun. You fucking pigs killed him. You put the gun in his hands. He died because he was a scapegoat, and you will all burn for it," she said matter-of-factly.

"What was Toby a scapegoat for, Lori?" Speak the words at a calm, unhurried pace, Hernandez told himself. Blank out most of her answer and listen for a slip or a change in the answer. No change this time. Just a string of profanity.

"Lori, why weren't you with Toby the night he died?"

"Because if I had been, you would have killed me, too, macho man. What do you think I am, dumb?"

"No, I think that Toby was dumb."

Hernandez knew from long experience that a side thrust will work occasionally when a direct assault is hopeless. The girl was immune to any insults directed at her heritage, profession, or personal habits. Her arrest record implied that she had been interrogated often enough to know the routines by heart. She could control her emotions just fine, but the unexpected slur on her boyfriend's intelligence caused her to react.

"No, no, taco. Toby was too smart. He knew you were coming, and he sent me away while he met his karma."

Hernandez's eyes flickered at this new bit of information.

"Lori, listen to me. Toby could not have known that we were coming because we didn't know until the street shooting started. Think about it. You and Toby had been living in that room for the past four months. We've known for a long time that you were hooking and he was dealing. We could have come up to get either one of you any time we wanted. You know us pigs are lazy as hell. So why would we get out of bed in the middle of the night to arrest a small-time chippie and a two-bit pusher when we could do it just as easily after our coffee breaks?"

He saw the first sign of uncertainty in her dulled eyes.

"You're small change, hon," he went on. "Ten or twenty

at best, and I bet you don't get many repeats, right? So Toby had to be the target. There was nothing in the room. At least, nothing big. If there was, you both would have been using it. So that means Toby had something big going. He was working with someone heavy, and he didn't want you to get hurt, right?''

The girl nodded in agreement before she realized what she was doing. Flustered, she shook her head and cursed bitterly at the smiling detective. Hernandez ignored the verbal abuse. He sensed that he had hold of a thread, and he didn't want to lose it.

"That's right, hon,'' he agreed when the outraged girl finally stopped to catch her breath, "we're all a bunch of assholes. We shot your boyfriend because we thought he killed a cop and he had a shotgun in his hands. But you know what? I don't think Toby Williker hit a cop. Because you're right—he wasn't the type. You know what I think? I think Toby Williker was set up by the guy he was working with. I think Toby's connection opened up on a black-and-white, then he left Toby unconscious and chained to that chair to take the heat. What do you think about that?''

Hernandez paused for a few moments to watch the girl's expression. Her eyes were wide, her cheeks were a pale white, and her lips were curled back in a snarl. But she had stopped yelling. Maybe, just maybe.

"And you know what else I think,'' Hernandez continued hurriedly before she snapped out of the trance, "I think you were snoopy enough to have checked out who your boyfriend was working with. You could probably do a make on the guy right now, but there's no way that you're going to give it to the pigs, right? So you've just got to hope the connection doesn't figure you for a snitch and decide to see how many times you'll bounce when you go out a high window.''

The expression in the girl's eyes told Hernandez much more than he had been expecting. He started to ask another question to press his advantage, but changed his mind. Give her some time, he decided. He motioned for the Records clerk to escort Lori outside.

*   *   *

Inside the crime laboratory, Sheffield continued to stare into his microscope at the powder-smeared barrel of Toby Williker's automatic shotgun. Hearing the pounding noises on the outside door, he groaned from stiffness and fatigue and then slowly got up from the evidence table where he had been sitting for the last three and a half hours.

"Good morning, Doctor," Hernandez said as he stepped past the blurry-eyed Sheffield. "Thought I'd check to make sure you people had enough work to keep you busy. Don't want anybody getting ideas about trying to use their Olympics tickets next week."

"You come up with a nice, quiet, surveillance job with a mattress, let us know," Sheffield responded tiredly.

"No more of that easy life, Doctor." Hernandez shook his head as they both walked toward the large examination room in the rear of the laboratory. "We've got to put some people out of business muy pronto."

"Guyerly?"

"One big blank nothing."

Hernandez selected one of the large comfortable desk chairs opposite Sheffield's work area, then put his feet up on a small area of the desk top that wasn't covered with long strips of heavy brown wrapping paper and tagged items of evidence. "You pull anything out of the scene?"

"Maybe a weapon."

Hernandez's eyebrows came up. He had been forced to leave the scene of Guyerly's murder in a hurry to try to control the riot which a few patrolmen had started with some uncooperative homeowners in the area. He hadn't heard about any weapon.

"Ball peen hammer on the roof of the shoe store," Sheffield continued, rubbing his eyes sleepily. "Found it next to an air vent. Practically brand new. No rust, light film of oil on the head. A few microscopic glass fragments stuck in the oil. Couldn't have been up there very long."

"And no fingerprints, right?"

"Good guess. No blood or hair either."

"This it?" Hernandez looked over at the desk top and pointed to one of the tagged items.

Sheffield nodded.

"Okay to pick it up?"

"Sure, if you don't mind getting dirty."

Hernandez carefully lifted the small hammer, trying to avoid transferring the gritty fingerprint powder onto his clothing. Flexing his wrist slowly, he tried to estimate the potential killing force that could be generated with such a weapon. More than enough, he decided. "So what makes you think this is related?" he asked.

"Got a call from Doc Pratola this morning. He finished the autopsy on Guyerly a couple hours ago. Says he found some compression marks in the right lower ribs that could have been made by a hammer head. Dimensions fit pretty close."

"So would fifteen thousand other hammers."

"Yeah, just in this city alone," Sheffield agreed. "No way at all to make any kind of match, and it probably wouldn't matter if we could. Standard brand, available almost anywhere." He shrugged his shoulders. "You'd never be able to track it back."

"Figure this is what killed him?" Hernandez examined the hammer one more time before putting it down on the protective brown paper.

"Pratola doesn't think so. The fatal wound was to the side of the head. Pretty solid blow. Blunt instrument, but wider than the hammer marks. More like the heavy end of a cue stick."

"Or a baton?" Hernandez suggested.

Sheffield jumped out of his chair with a curse. He looked around the room quickly, searching among the several hundred tagged bags, boxes, and loose items that were scattered across every available countertop surface. Then he ran out of the room, Hernandez following at a slower pace.

"Meiko!" Sheffield yelled, opening the door to the chemistry room. "Guyerly's belt gear. Where did we put it?"

Meiko looked up from her blood typing, startled by the unexpected burst of noise. "Latent room. Lee and Bob were going to dust his gun and badge. They'll be back . . ." she started to add, but realized that Sheffield had already disappeared in the direction of the fingerprint processing room. Shaking her head with a tired sigh, she turned back to her lab table.

"They used his own baton," Sheffield said, looking up as Hernandez came into the room, his voice filled with frustra-

tion and disgust. He pointed to the end of the thick black
plastic baton sticking out of the pile of gear and weapons that
had been strapped around Guyerly's waist. Hernandez looked
closely and saw the smears of blood, barely visible against
the glossy black plastic.

"Can you do anything with it?"

"I don't know," Sheffield admitted. "I should have thought
about the goddamned baton at the scene. God knows how
many people have handled the thing."

Sheffield felt sick to his stomach. The first potentially solid
piece of evidence, and he had to screw it up because he
wasn't thinking. Goddamn it to hell, he thought, reaching
into the drawer for a dusting brush and powder.

After five minutes of cautious dipping and stroking,
Sheffield's hands and shirt were covered with the grey-white
powder. There were five partials and three good full latent
prints visible on the black plastic shaft, which he quickly
transferred onto glossy black cards with a roll of lift tape.

Sheffield spent another few minutes writing appropriate
notations on the backs of the cards before he and Hernandez
returned to the examination room. They discovered that Meiko
had finished her work in the chemistry room and was now
sitting in front of one of the compound microscopes with a
tray of slides, a notebook, and a pen beside her.

"Well, Doctor, what's the skinny?" Hernandez asked, as
they both returned to their previous sitting positions. Sheffield was busy writing up a work request directing Dorsey
and Spencer to compare the latents from the baton against any
known suspects, and then run eliminations on everyone who
was at the scene or had the opportunity to handle the baton.
That would include the paramedics and the mortuary team, he
noted.

"Tell you one thing right now. Unless we get some breaks
on some of these homicides pretty soon, you can kiss off
narcotics and drunk driving arrests. We're already starting to
get calls from the DA on stuff we haven't had time to work."

"Screw the DA. A cop killing's more important than a
couple of fucking deuce arrests."

"Agreed. But we're not getting anywhere," Sheffield
complained. "Look at this." He tossed Hernandez the two
case folders on the Farber and Guyerly killings. The first was

almost two inches thick with investigation reports, sketches, evidence lists, work requests, contact sheets, and preliminary lab reports. "And that's just the lab file. God knows what your files look like."

"Can't even see the top of Andersen's desk," Hernandez admitted.

"That's just it. All we're doing is generating paper. Christ, we've got over a hundred and seventy lift cards on Farber's case. You figure two or three latents on each card, and Lee and Bob'll be comparing prints for a year before we get through the eliminations."

"Be grateful you didn't get called out on Lagucii's free-for-all. If Paradee had his way, we'd drop the homicides and run every cop in the department on shoeprints, fingerprints, and the lie-box. And then warm up the thumbscrews."

Sheffield rolled his eyes in disgust. It was bad enough that he had been forced to send Bob Dorsey out to work the scene on that fiasco. Then he'd been asked to send Spencer out on the 7-Eleven robbery because patrol had all of their crime scene investigation units tied up. What a night, he thought, shaking his head.

"Speaking of Paradee," Meiko said, turning around in her low chair and rubbing her eyes. "I just got a call from Andersen a few minutes ago. Chief has ordered us to put a top priority on examining the evidence from Paradee's scene. That's what I'm doing right now."

"You mean we actually have something on that case?" Sheffield asked incredulously.

"Better believe it." Meiko nodded with a grimace, brushing her long hair out of her eyes. She began reciting from the sheet attached to her clipboard. "One ski mask with attached hairs, one Beretta twenty-five caliber automatic, one expended twenty-five caliber casing."

"Lagucii shot at Paradee? C'mon."

"No shit," Hernandez confirmed. "Except that he's claiming that he fired a shot accidentally when one of our officers wiped his ass across the parking lot."

"Jesus." Sheffield shook his head, trying not to laugh. He looked up at Meiko. "What do you have on the mask?"

"Report says it was found about twenty feet from Paradee's

car where the fight took place. There was also a pair of black leather gloves found in the same general area.''

"Cop gloves?" Hernandez asked.

Meiko shrugged. "I haven't looked at them yet. Still working on the ski mask. Anyway, so far I've found a few head hairs. They're human. Average about three and one half inches long. Dark and light brown, probably sun-bleached. Only thing unusual is the hairs look like they've been trimmed with real dull scissors."

Something in the back of Sheffield's fatigue-dulled brain began pounding on his skull, demanding attention. "Why do you say that?" he asked distractedly, trying to recall something which he knew was very important.

"All of the ends are kinda shredded, almost mashed," she explained. "Oh, there were a couple of short, thick, curved hairs the same color—like the ones that come out of your mustache all the time," she added with an exaggerated expression of distaste.

A cold numbness surged up through Sheffield's lower body.

The vacuum sweepings.

Sheffield sat forward in his chair and reached for the Farber and Branchowski case folder. Fighting to keep the numb feeling confined and controlled, he rapidly shuffled through the loose papers, searching for a particular set of examination notes. He missed them the first time through, but found them on the second try.

"Lab number one-seven-nine," he said aloud. "Meiko, on the Farber case, lab number one-seven-nine is the vacuum sweepings from the floor of Williker's apartment. That's right," he nodded as Meiko held up a tagged and stapled plastic bag appearing to contain filter waste from a clothes dryer. "Take a look at that under the stereo, about twenty-five power."

Hernandez stared curiously at Sheffield as Meiko carefully emptied the contents of the bag onto a folded piece of glassine paper and placed the debris under the magnifying lens of the stereo-microscope.

Hernandez was now staring at the piece of waxed paper as if it might suddenly tell him what was going on. Sheffield was watching Meiko, and he saw her stiffen as she made a careful adjustment of the magnification knob. She turned around and looked at Sheffield, an odd expression on her face.

"You're right," she said quietly, "but I don't understand."

"What are you two talking about?" Hernandez demanded, glaring at Sheffield's back as the criminalist bent over the microscope, readjusting the focus for his own eyes. Then, as Sheffield removed two hairs from the vacuumed debris and placed them under the comparison microscope next to two of the ski-cap hairs, Hernandez made the connection. "Oh, Jesus, no."

"Almost a perfect match," Sheffield said, turning to face the stunned detective. "Color, thickness, scale pattern, and length are all in the ballpark. The ends are all torn. And the goddamned mustache hairs are nearly identical."

"The same guy was at the Paradee and Williker scenes? You can testify to that?"

"Testify? Hell, no. Not enough individual detail on a hair to make a conclusive match. You know that." Sheffield's mind raced as he tried to put it all together, trying to dovetail pieces that only minutes earlier had been separate parts of two distinct puzzles.

"You couldn't ask for better circumstantial evidence," he finally said. "What are the chances of two different people with the same color and length of hair, same type of unconventional haircut, and the same type and color of mustache being present at two separate police-assault scenes less than two days apart?"

"One of us?"

Sheffield and Meiko looked at each other, startled.

"I don't think so," Sheffield said, shaking his head slowly. "I can't think of anyone who'd fit. Any of the uniformed guys?" He looked over at Meiko.

"I don't know, but we're going to find out," she said, reaching for the phone.

"What are you going to do?" Hernandez asked. Sheffield had already grabbed a pad of paper and was busily making notes.

"Head hair sample from every officer present at either one of the scenes," she answered, cupping her hand over the mouthpiece. "Mustache hairs, too, if they've got them."

"And that's the easy part," Sheffield added, looking up

from his pad. "You can bet that Dorsey pulled a whole shit-pile of latents off of Paradee's station wagon. He dusts everything that doesn't fight back."

Sheffield reached for Meiko's clipboard and quickly scanned the crime scene investigation report. "Yep, what'd I tell you? Sixteen latent cards. Okay, so we're going to compare those cards against everything from Farber and Branchowski's case. Guyerly's too. Then we're going to cross-compare every piece of evidence we've got on these cases until we find a solid connection."

"If Paradee and Lagucii are right . . ." Hernandez couldn't finish the sentence, numbed by the unthinkable possibility that someone in the department had gone rogue. He remembered Farber, face up in the street.

"You'd better get hold of Andersen," Sheffield said, just beginning to absorb the extent of the mammoth task he had committed the lab to undertake. In spite of the hours of eye-blurring effort that would be entailed, he had to acknowledge the underlying feeling of excitement. After all of the searching and marking and tagging and report writing, after all of the missed sack time, they finally had a lead.

BALEFIRE

Minus 6 Days

Sunday Morning

1110 hours

In 1978, when Dr. Jacquem Kaem made the decision to purchase the Dana Point home, the sprawling single-story ranch house with the delightful view of the Pacific Ocean had only seemed unreasonably expensive. Now, as the result of some very expensive renovating by the Committee during the past six months, the true value of the home would have stunned Kaem's well-to-do neighbors.

Under the guise of a massive landscaping project, Dr. Kaem had completely refinished the interior of the house. Some of the improvements were actually decorative. Kaem, in addition to his many other talents, had a well-developed taste for pleasing combinations of wood and brick. But most of the improvements were strictly functional, centering around a greatly expanded electrical capacity feeding off a tap of a main service line that was neither gauged, nor legal, nor traceable.

The most impressive renovation, however, was a structural change rarely contemplated by southern California homeowners. Beneath the hardwood flooring and the lush Oriental rugs was a full-sized, completely furnished, temperature-and-humidity-controlled basement. It had been patiently carved out of a solid rock foundation.

Within the luxurious confines of this subterranean habitat, five rigorously trained and fanatically dedicated technicians ate, slept, and labored over an impressive array of electronic equipment.

In the main room of the basement, twelve tape recorders

169

blinked and slowly turned at seemingly random intervals as
their distant monitors picked up significant levels of conversation. The electronic chips that surveillance specialist Hiram
Gehling had placed in twelve carefully selected telephones
within the Huntington Beach police station were much more
than simple bugging devices. The miniaturized logic chips
actually converted each of the tapped phones into a continuously open, highly sensitive receiver capable of picking up
normal conversations within a twenty-five-foot radius. As a
result, there were few significant discussions taking place
within the police station that were not being monitored by the
Committee.

Three of the Committee members, Kaem included, now
stood behind one of the technicians as he transferred incoming signals into the stereo speakers mounted on the wall
above the recorders.

"As far as I am concerned, there is no question," Kaem
said in a soft, contemplative voice as the technician made a
volume adjustment. "Their response was obviously much
faster than anticipated. Given the demands of the remaining
stages, a diversion is essential. The Opening Ceremonies are
still six days away."

"Can we be certain that the threat is valid?" Taskanian
asked. "Is it possible they have made a connection this
early?"

"Our reports indicate there is little danger at this stage,"
Kaem said. "But the timing is becoming critical. If we wait,
we could lose everything as the result of a simple car stop.
Besides," he reminded the swarthy lawyer, "we expected to
utilize some of the diversions anyway. Given the tremendous
success that we have experienced so far, I am confident that
Thanatos can make the appropriate adjustments."

Kaem's black eyes gleamed with suppressed excitement as
he considered his revised strategy once again. A grand master
in chess, Kaem utilized his skills to evaluate the terrorist's
tactical options far in advance of the current situation. Given
the emotional climate developing nicely among the local
citizens and the confusion that was beginning to cripple the
police force, Kaem could almost taste victory.

"What about his request for the sanctions?" Taskanian

asked, his lips pressed together in an expression of concern that was matched by his eyes.

"Jain, have you changed your mind regarding that matter?" Kaem asked, turning to the older man. He was referring to their previous, heated argument over the consequences of the terrorist's request.

Dr. Jain Saekia paused for a moment in contemplation. "I still believe that the sanctions are based more upon the self-interests of Thanatos than any security problem for Balefire," he finally said. "But we have agreed he is in the best position to make that judgment. I will concur with the others. Two more deaths should not make a great difference if they are handled properly."

"I would recommend the third series," Kaem said after a moment of thoughtful hesitation. "Options two, three and five." He looked at each of the men in turn, each nodding his agreement. Kaem bent over the technician's shoulder to point out the necessary signals in an opened loose-leaf notebook. Moments later, a second technician evaluated the data on his screen, made the appropriate selection, and began to type on his keyboard with calm, practiced efficiency. Several miles away, the alerted cutout sat at his own console and began to call up his programs.

Under the direction of Kaem, a third technician, whose voice was capable of rich and varied modulation, referred to his own notebook, then reached for his desk phone. The second technician, having fed the signal codes into his terminal, punched the DISPLAY button, held his index finger just above the SEND button, and waited patiently for the command.

A warm Sunday morning in Huntington Beach meant only one thing to the uniformed patrol officers on duty—traffic, and lots of it. Given the slightest incentive, the inland residents of Orange County quickly abandoned their air-conditioned homes, taking to cars, buses, and motorcycles with one common goal: the beach. This morning, Beach Boulevard, the main road feeding into the beach city, was stop-and-go, bumper-to-bumper at least five miles east of the Huntington Beach city limits.

Bobby Muscalino, the young officer who had been con-

fronted in the PD parking lot by the outraged mother earlier
that morning, guided his black-and-white in and out of the
side streets that paralleled the beach, thankful for the departmental policy that assigned motorcycle units to handle Beach
Boulevard traffic. Anything larger than a 750 Kawasaki would
immediately become immobilized among the hot and frustrated drivers, who ran stoplights and violated pedestrian
rights-of-way with abandon in order to gain a few feet.

Muscalino was thinking about the young boy with the
terrified eyes, when the voice of an excited dispatcher broke
the peaceful silence.

"All units in the area of Beach Boulevard. Unidentified
informant advises a vehicle on fire in the southbound lane.
Informant states that the vehicle is a late model four-door
sedan, and the driver is apparently unaware of the situation.
No further information at this time."

"Thirty-seven Sam. Do you have a cross street?"

"Thirty-seven Sam, that is a negative. Informant advised
that he was at a gas station, unknown location, and then hung
up."

"Sixty-three Michael. South on Beach from Talbert."

"Sixty-one Michael. I'm southbound now, Beach and
Warner. No sign of a vehicle fire."

"Sixty-three and Sixty-one Michael, ten-four."

"Thirty-seven Sam. Contact the nearest fire department
and have them stand by."

Muscalino was trying to decide on a likely intersection to
watch for the vehicle. It would probably tie up the entire
southbound traffic flow if they didn't get to it fast. He was
listening to the uninterrupted radio traffic as units called in
locations and negative sightings, when his teleprinter began
to chatter. He watched the lines of grey type, praying for a
call that would take him out of the area before his sergeant
started to organize his squad into traffic control teams.

Thirty seconds later, the teleprinter stopped printing and
Muscalino stared numbly at the stomach-wrenching message,
wishing to God that his sergeant had called first.

As he fumbled for his county map book that contained the
street maps for neighboring Fountain Valley, Muscalino tried
to call in for additional information. He tried twice, waiting
impatiently for a break in the static-ridden radio traffic. Every

time a break occurred, he barely managed to transmit his call number before another unit keyed a mike and overlapped his signal. Finally giving up, Muscalino dropped his useless mike and jabbed the ACK button on his radio console.

"Goddamned bastards," he muttered as he finally located the street intersections on the map, and snapped on his red-and-blues and siren. He could feel his heart pounding in his chest.

The trip across the city and into Fountain Valley should have taken Muscalino no more than ten minutes. It took him fifteen. He had to stop and check the map twice because he was trying to concentrate on what he was going to say to her, and he kept forgetting the unfamiliar street names.

He double-checked the address before cutting his lights and siren and turning into the driveway. He felt his limbs grow numb as he got out of the unit and walked to the door. His mouth was dry, and the palms of his hands were sweating, and he prayed she wouldn't be home. Please be shopping or at the beach or anywhere else but home, he thought, as he reached out with a shaky hand to ring the doorbell.

Then, before he could remember what he was going to say, the door opened, and she was standing there with a quizzical smile on her beautiful face.

"Yes?"

Her smile dissolved into disbelieving, open-mouthed, head-shaking shock as she took in the sight of the pale-faced young officer with the crumpled teleprinter paper in his hand, and she realized that the thing she told herself a hundred times would never happen had happened.

"Mrs. Andersen," Muscalino managed to choke out. "Your husband . . . I . . . he . . . he's been shot. I . . . I'm supposed to take you to the hospital right away. I . . ." He realized he was holding the wretched piece of paper out as though it would be easier for her to read it than for him to say it.

"My God, no." Michelle Andersen started to turn away, then started forward, and was finally aware that she had no idea where she was going. Muscalino snapped out of his own numbed shock and came forward quickly to grab her arm, vaguely realizing he was functioning on some undefinable level that was mostly reflex.

"We've got to go now," he said, pleading with his eyes for her to understand. "They said he's in critical condition."

"He's alive?" Hope flickered in her eyes, and her face became set. "You said he's alive?" she demanded, grabbing at Muscalino's shirt with strong trembling hands.

"I . . . I don't know. I guess . . . he must be," Muscalino blinked, trying to hold back his own tears. Children. He was trying to remember. Didn't Andersen have some kids? "What about your children?" he asked. "Are they home?"

"They're at the beach. Both of them." She was talking hurriedly, clutching Muscalino's arm tightly now. "I don't know where—"

"I'll find them, don't worry." He held on to her arm with both hands, and they both stumbled and ran out the door toward the black-and-white. "I'll get you to the hospital first, and then I'll go find them," he promised as he jammed the unit into reverse and then roared down the street.

He took the turns fast, trying to concentrate on his driving, ignoring the startled drivers who were forced to hit their brakes or swerve to avoid the oncoming police car. But he couldn't keep from looking over at the beautiful, golden-haired woman with her tear-stained face and shaking hands.

Michelle Andersen knew there were a lot of things that she was supposed to be thinking about, but the only thing that she could concentrate on was the possibility that Walt was still alive and that she had to be with him.

"Please hurry," she whispered softly, staring down at her clenched hands. Muscalino hit the switches with the edge of his hand and the siren came on in mid-wail, shrieking over the accelerating roar of the engine. They don't tell you about this in the academy, he thought, his face grim as he tightened both hands on the vibrating steering wheel. Then, finally starting to think ahead again, he reached down for the mike.

"Nine Charles. Brookhurst and Ellis," he yelled into the microphone, thinking about the suspect who had shot Sergeant Walt Andersen. Muscalino could visualize the sight pattern of his own revolver aiming between the suspect's two panic-stricken eyes, and he could feel the pressure on his finger as he squeezed the trigger in revenge. "Code three run to Pacifica. Clear the traffic. Now!"

The emergency room entrance of the hospital was located

next to the rear parking lot. Muscalino tapped at the brakes, barely slowing to forty to take the turn, ignoring the damage that the unit was absorbing. He gunned the engine again and then braked, coming to a tread-grinding stop in one of the slots reserved for incoming ambulances. The siren cut off with the engine, but the red and blue lights continued to revolve as Muscalino bailed out, coming around to Michelle Andersen's door. But she was already out of the unit and they both hit the double-doored entrance to the emergency room at the same time.

The sound of the incoming siren and Muscalino's heavy boots had already alerted the duty nurses, but they were still startled by the sharp thump of a solid hand slamming against the wooden door, and the sight of the muscular young officer and the panic-stricken woman as they came bursting into the treatment room.

Trained to make instantaneous decisions, both nurses moved immediately toward Michelle Andersen, recognizing the signs of shock. They didn't stop to question the officer's unnecessarily dramatic entrance. That would come later when they had everything under control.

"Where is he?" Muscalino demanded, his throat constricting as he realized that all four of the emergency examination tables were unoccupied.

Both nurses ignored Muscalino, trying to get the shaking, blond-haired woman to sit down on one of the tables. They each held on firmly to one of the unexpectedly strong arms, and they talked in soft, calm, professional voices, but the wide-eyed woman had no intention of being cooperative.

"Where is my husband?" Michelle Andersen screamed, suddenly realizing that she was being restrained instead of being guided to Walt's bed. Confused, both nurses turned and looked at Muscalino for help.

"Sergeant Walter Andersen," he said through a tightened jaw. "This is his wife."

The nurses stared at Muscalino, then at the shaking woman, and finally at each other. "You're going to have to explain—" one of the nurses started to say.

"Explain, shit!" Muscalino exploded. "Her husband is Sergeant Walter Andersen. He's been shot. I was told to bring her here immediately. Now where the hell is he?"

"Officer," the senior of the two nurses said in a calm level voice, "we don't know what you're talking about. I've been on duty since seven o'clock this morning, and I can assure you that no one has been admitted to this hospital with gunshot wounds since that time. Perhaps you have the wrong hospital," she suggested, and then quickly turned to Michelle Andersen when her practiced fingers picked up a rapidly elevating pulse rate.

Muscalino stared at the nurse in disbelief for a long, uncertain moment. His fingers reached into his shirt pocket, and he pulled out the crumpled piece of teleprinter paper. "They said Pacifica," he said. "Goddamn it, they said Pacifica!" He dove for the phone at the nurse's desk, fumbling with the receiver. He punched at the buttons, missed one of the numbers with his sweating fingers, and had to redial.

"Communications," the dispatcher answered in a calm, ready-to-be-helpful voice.

"This is Muscalino. I'm at Pacifica with Mrs. Andersen. Where is Sergeant Andersen?"

The dispatcher sat up in her console chair, alerted by the edge of panic in Muscalino's voice. She pulled Andersen's code number out of her memory and punched teletype keys.

"Sergeant Andersen is at Pacifica Hospital—" she started to say, reading from her console.

"Goddamn it, they just told me he's not here!" Muscalino yelled into the phone, startling everyone in the emergency room.

"—with the chief, interviewing Sergeant Lagucii," she finished weakly, stunned by Muscalino's burst of outrage. "They checked in less than five minutes ago," she added. There was no response. "Bobby, are you still there?"

"What about the teletype?" he asked, his voice barely a whisper. He felt like his throat was constricting around his vocal cords.

"What are you talking about?" The dispatcher signaled for her supervisor to pick up on the call.

"I got a teletype at eleven-fifteen. It said Andersen had been shot. It said he was critical, and I was supposed to take his wife to Pacifica." Muscalino realized that his hand—the one holding the smeared teletype message—was starting to shake.

The dispatcher was clear-headed and well trained. Before she said anything, she turned her chair and reached for the long continuous strip of paper that recorded every teletype message sent out. She was absolutely certain, but she checked anyway.

"Bobby," she said into the telephone as she finished scanning the record strip, "listen to me. There is no such teletype on the log. Do you understand what I'm saying. We did not send that message out to anyone. Bobby? Bobby?"

Officer Bobby Muscalino let the phone drop out of his suddenly nerveless hand. He sat, shaking his head, staring at the crumpled piece of paper, as everyone in the room slowly converged on the desk.

Sergeant Walter Andersen came into the emergency room at a run and was caught in mid-stride by his hysterical wife. He held her tightly, waiting for her uncontrolled shaking to subside. He listened as she tried to talk between sobs, and he soothed her and kissed her and helped the nurses get her settled. He waited beside the bed, holding her hand tightly, until the sedative took effect. Finally, he listened carefully as the doctor explained the recommended treatment for a nervous collapse, watching quietly as the nurses wheeled his wife out of the ER.

Then, as the double doors swung shut behind the nurses, the rigidly controlled expression on his face gave way to one of pure madness, and he whirled toward the nurse's desk.

Muscalino had listened to the hospital paging system, had watched as the nurse answered the phone and spoke quietly, and then had sat immobile as the uninjured Andersen burst into the emergency room. Muscalino was still sitting in the same spot, dazed and numb, when the clawed hand slammed into the base of his throat, closed around a handful of shirt and vest, and drove his upper body up and back into the plaster wall.

Bobby Muscalino was younger, thirty pounds heavier, and physically stronger than Andersen. But even if he had been able to dredge up the strength to fight against the steellike grip, he still would have been paralyzed by the maniacal rage in the eyes inches away from his own.

"Why?" Andersen snarled. "Just tell me why."

Muscalino tried to speak, tried to explain, but he couldn't get the words past the frightening pressure against his throat. Instead he tried to stare back into the maddened eyes, bringing up the hand still clenched around the crumbled piece of teletype paper. Realizing he had inadvertently committed the worst possible offense against a fellow officer, he tensed against the expected fist. He was relieved when the pressure against his throat suddenly released. His eyes closed, and he slumped back against the wall, as Andersen stared at the scrap of paper.

Andersen read the teletype message three times before he dropped the paper on the desk. He was almost blind with rage as he reached out for the phone. He didn't see the gnarled hand pick up the paper. All of his concentration was focused on what he was going to say to the Watch Commander. He would handle Communications in person when he got back to the station.

"Watch Commander's office. Gilcrist."

Andersen took in a preparatory breath, ready to vent his rage, when a thick hand, scarred by fishlines, clamped around his wrist. A second hand of identical character and strength removed the phone from Andersen's grasp.

"This is Sager." The voice of the man who had effortlessly stripped the phone from Andersen's clenched hand was as cold and unforgiving as the ocean.

"Yes, sir." Gilcrist flinched at the sound of Sager's voice.

"You are to relieve the entire watch immediately," Sager ordered. "Replace them with sworn officers until you can call in replacements. I want every man and woman who has stepped foot inside that communications room during the last hour in my office in exactly thirty minutes. And I mean everyone! Is that understood, Lieutenant?"

The emphasis of Sager's final words made one thing absolutely clear to Gilcrist. During the next thirty minutes, the rank and career of every officer and civilian in Command and Control stood on very uncertain ground. "Yes, sir," Gilcrist replied several times, trying to comprehend the reason for the chief's thunderous pronouncement, but the phone clicked dead in his hand.

*   *   *

While Gilcrist and the station sergeant frantically scrambled to locate replacements to man the consoles of the bewildered day watch crew, the man who was the cause of the lieutenant's distress was enjoying what he considered to be a well-deserved respite from his labors.

Thanatos had arranged his blanket on a rise of unclaimed sand immediately adjacent to a stretch of plastic windbreak staked out in angled sections along the city beach. Stretched out and relaxed, he could feel the surface warmth of the sand rise up through the thin blanket and soak into the tired muscles of his back and thighs.

Based upon his observations during the past hour and a half, Thanatos decided there was a definite territorial pecking order among the beach-goers who had taken advantage of the welcome transition into summer.

The young children and the early teenagers tended to congregate at the water's surging and retreating edge. The aggressive male teenagers and a few older men body-surfed and bobbed between surging waves in water barely over their heads. Another group of young male adults demonstrated their casual aloofness to Mother Nature by flinging Frisbees back and forth along the access road between the beach and the upper street level. Between the asphalt and the water, groups were further segregated by volleyball nets, football games, cement fire rings, and uneven rows of colorful surfboards stuck vertically into the sand.

There was one group, however, that seemed to disdain any territorial limits, walking singly, or in groups, or lying in parallel twos and threes. That group was comprised of attractive females between the ages of thirteen and nineteen just barely attired in lengths of thin cord and small colorful pieces of tightly stretched nylon.

A large percentage of the young ladies were clearly walking along the beach with the specific intent of showing off everything they had, leaving as little to the imagination as possible. One lanky, tanned blonde stood in the nearest volleyball group, wearing two strips of eye-catching black cloth over her oiled muscles. A pair of identical twins rode past on a tandem bike; they had identical bodies which had lost all

but the essential baby fat. Then there was the diminutive
dark-haired girl in the wispy one-piece length of body-clinging
nylon that looped at the neck, flowed with anatomical precision down over the full breasts and flat stomach, disappeared
between the smooth legs, and then came back up and around
to tie off at each curved lower hip.

It was obvious to Thanatos that two quick hand movements
would immediately allow the stretched cloth to flip back up in
the girl's seemingly unconcerned water-streaked face. He
watched from his horizontal position while the girl walked
with liquid-smooth strides back toward the water, and he
wondered how the young man who tagged along beside her
managed to resist the explicit temptation. Perhaps he won't,
the terrorist thought, amusing himself with the vivid fantasy
that placed him in the water with the sensuous young female,
hands sliding up the firm, tanned thighs to find and loosen the
snug bow-knots.

The appearance of three more girls in the terrorist's temporarily stabilized field of vision unaccountably caused him to
break away from his imaginative enjoyment just as the vulnerable hips disappeared under a surge of frothy white water.
Distracted and puzzled, the terrorist's eyes moved invisibly
behind the silvered lens of the sunglasses, following the
unsteady movements of the three figures in the deep loose
sand just beyond the high-tide mark.

Thanatos had survived a number of life-threatening situations by recognizing and responding to alarms generated at a
subconscious level, well before the threat became obvious
and unavoidable. He had no idea what stimulus had actually
triggered his mental alarm system. It wasn't necessarily the
girls, he knew. It could be a pattern or a significant directional movement. Alert and tense now in spite of his outwardly relaxed appearance, he began to catalog and cross-
reference facts.

Three subjects. All female. Two approximately sixteen to
eighteen. The other one younger, maybe fourteen, definitely
beyond puberty, but not yet possessing the development and
poise of the two older girls. All three dressed—if that was the
appropriate word—in the apparently fashionable one-piece
cling suits. Ignore the younger one, Thanatos decided. Concentrate on the older two.

The girls spread out their blankets approximately twenty yards away from the terrorist's position. He watched their movements, noting analytically that the older girls were healthy, well-proportioned specimens. But he had already seen a more erotic image. The physical beauty of the girls was not the factor.

Colors? Nothing significant about the bathing suits. One of the girls had long black hair, deeply tanned skin. A possibility. Mediterranean features commonly found in Spanish, Arabic and Mexican women were also shared by many of the Israelis. The girl was a beauty, regardless, he noted. The other girl was also tanned, but a more golden brown shade which matched her long, straight, blond hair. Probably the older sister to the younger one.

All three of the girls finished arranging their belongings on the blankets and then began walking in the direction of the water. Thanatos waited a few moments, casually scanning the surrounding area for the signs of surveillance. Nothing. He counted to twenty, searched again, and then got up and walked back to his vehicle, abandoning his blanket on the beach.

Thanatos spent two hours driving on freeways and side roads until he was satisfied he wasn't under surveillance. Then he returned to his Huntington Harbour home, determined to resolve the uneasy confusion generated in his mind by the faces of the three girls. Forty-five minutes later, he found the answer in a thick three-ring notebook that he had removed from a concealed floor safe, well protected by an explosive device and an inch and a half of steel plate.

The photographs of Jody and Martine Andersen were mounted on a single piece of heavy paper that also contained photos of Sergeant Walter Andersen and his wife, along with a considerable amount of information about Andersen and his family. The photographs were recent. Both of the blond-haired faces in the color photographs, taken covertly several months earlier, showed the Andersen girls in a natural pose, relaxed and smiling. Exactly as he had observed them on the beach hours earlier.

Working on a hunch, Thanatos continued to thumb through the thick reference book that contained photos of every Huntington Beach police officer and his family, searching patiently.

Five minutes later, his eyes settled on the face of a dark-eyed, dimple-cheeked girl with long dark hair, whose sensuous features stirred in the terrorist a deep sense of physical arousal. His eyes flicked down to the name typed below the photograph. He smiled maliciously as he read the name of Ramona Hernandez.

BALEFIRE

Minus 6 Days

Sunday Evening

1935 hours

The first call rang on Andersen's phone at 7:35 that Sunday evening. He had talked the doctors into letting him take his sedated wife home, assuring them that she would rest easier in a family atmosphere. He had tucked her into their king-sized bed, and was sprawled across the living room couch with an untouched bottle of beer in his hand, listening to his daughters' descriptions of their afternoon at the beach, when the phone began to ring.

It was the phone in the den. That was his phone, and when it rang, it certainly meant someone at the department had a problem. He was tempted to let it ring, because he could count on his fingers the number of hours he had been able to spend with his family during the last four days. And he wasn't even willing to admit to himself how much he had been unnerved by the expression on his wife's face at the hospital. There was nothing about his job, neither the salary nor the personal satisfaction, that would ever compensate for the shock she had suffered when Muscalino delivered the bogus teletype message.

He thought about the teletype message as he walked slowly toward the den, wondering—without any real hope—if the phone might stop ringing before he got there.

The session with the dispatchers and the other on-duty personnel who'd had the opportunity to send that message to Muscalino had solved nothing. Sager had spent less than five minutes explaining, in case anyone was still uncertain, exactly why they were in his office. He had further explained in

183

a voice totally devoid of any warmth that the individual who had transmitted that teletype had until six o'clock that evening to confess and receive an immediate three-month suspension. After six o'clock that individual, when discovered, would be summarily fired and placed under arrest.

The denials were unanimous, and the issue was further confused when Jeremy Raines, the civilian computer programmer in charge of communications, insisted that the teletype hadn't been sent from the station: There was no record of the transmission on the hard-copy log or the master disc. When questioned, Raines admitted that the recording system could be bypassed with considerable difficulty, but he didn't think that anyone in the department other than himself knew how to do that with just a keyboard. And even he would have to think about it a lot.

Sager gave Raines exactly twenty-four hours to do his thinking and come up with an answer, leaving the ''or else'' hanging, then he dismissed the meeting by walking out of his office.

In the end, the meeting had accomplished absolutely nothing except to create a lot of emotional anguish and dissension among a group of loyal, hard-working employees, Andersen thought, as he reached for the still ringing phone.

''Andersen.''

''May I speak to Jody, please?''

''Just a minute.''

Normally, Andersen would have advised the male voice to call back on the other line, the family agreement being that it was for all calls to and from boyfriends. Tonight, however, Andersen welcomed any excuse that would allow him some uninterrupted time at home. He called his daughter and handed her the phone as she came into the den, keeping his hand over the mouthpiece for a moment.

''For you, munchkin,'' he said. ''Probably wants to serenade outside your window.'' He grinned at her wrinkled nose and then picked a book up from his desk, surrendering his sanctuary to his vivacious first-born.

He was almost through the door, his mind back on the problem of the teleprinter message, when he heard his daughter call out in a strangely quiet voice.

''Dad.''

He turned and saw her standing in the middle of the den, staring down at the phone in her hand as though it had just tried to bite her. Her eyes were wide, and her normally tanned complexion had visibly paled.

He was at her side instantly, taking the phone gently out of her hand and holding it up to his ear. Nothing. Whoever it was had hung up.

"What did he say, hon?" he asked, and then immediately realized he had asked the wrong question.

"I can't say those things," she whispered, staring down at her feet. "Who was that?"

"I don't know. I thought he was one of your boyfriends. I didn't recognize the voice." Andersen felt his stomach twist and his jaw start to tighten.

Jody Andersen looked up at her father, in spite of the disgusting words and the slimy voice still echoing in her mind. "Why did he do that?" she asked in a soft voice.

"He's just one of those people that I've told you about," Andersen said, hanging up the phone and putting a protective arm around her. "They dial numbers at random"—Andersen suddenly remembered with a numbness in his chest that the voice had used his daughter's first name—"and try to get people to react." He could feel the panic start to surge in his brain, and he fought it back down. "They're sick, hon. Just weird, sick people who get their kicks trying to scare people. Nothing to worry about, okay?"

She looked uncertain for a moment, remembering the guttural voice and some of the bathroom wall words. Then she nodded, smiling weakly. "Sure, I—"

The telephone in the kitchen rang shrilly. Andersen felt his arm tighten involuntarily, and his daughter reacted by moving tight against his chest. Using willpower that he hadn't thought himself capable of, Andersen brought his vocal cords under control before he spoke.

"My turn." He smiled down at his daughter and winked.

"Be my guest," she said with forced cheerfulness, trying to match her father's nonchalance. She didn't even come close, but he pretended not to notice.

He started out toward the kitchen at a deliberately casual pace, and then hurried when he realized his younger daughter Martine was running down the hallway to get to the bedroom extension. He picked up the kitchen phone and brought it up to his ear just before he heard the extension click on the line. "I have it, Martine," he said firmly. He waited until he heard the second click, signifying that his fourteen-year-old had reluctantly obeyed. Then he waited a few more seconds. A deep, hollow silence that told him that the line was open.

"Hello." Andersen spoke the word as a neutral challenge. He waited, gripping the phone with increasing pressure, feeling the sweat beginning to form on his forehead.

"Sergeant Andersen?" The same voice. Andersen was certain of that. Not as much emphasis on the high-pitched vocal tones which had vaguely suggested a teenager before. More resonance now, deeper inflections, but the same voice. And the son of a bitch had both phone numbers, Andersen suddenly realized with a start.

Getting both of the phone numbers would be difficult. Both were unlisted. One was for Michelle and the girls to use, and the other was kept open for himself, though it was available through any of his detectives or the Watch Commander's call-out list. And the people who had access to that list included every one of the dispatchers, Andersen remembered, his mind flicking back to the teletype message. His eyes narrowed as he considered the possibilities.

"That's right."

Be calm, neutral, businesslike, Andersen reminded himself. No need to tell him that you're planning to rip out his throat. The man probably didn't have enough background or imagination to realize he was teasing someone who had already been prodded too many times. The restraining bars for a cop are only words on paper. Every good officer will honor an oath of duty to enforce and obey the law until his own family is threatened by someone who doesn't care about laws or honor. Then the rules change.

There was another period of electronic silence. Almost ten seconds. Then the voice again, taunting and cold.

"You have very pretty daughters, Sergeant. Very pretty. They both seem to take after your wife. Nice long legs. Flat stomachs." The voice broke into a quick deliberate laugh.

A rational portion of Andersen's mind wondered absently about the stress tolerance built into the handle of a telephone. Apparently it was quite high, because the brightly colored plastic didn't shatter into jagged pieces when his grip tightened. But he said nothing, professionally intent upon listening very carefully to everything that the man said, to every sound that came out of the receiver, searching for a recognizable background noise.

"Do you leave home very often, Sergeant?"

The voice was pleasant and politely inquiring. A nerve that ran under the tightened cheek muscles below Andersen's right eye twitched briefly. He continued to listen, his features impassive, as the voice launched into a lengthy, carefully descriptive narration involving Jody and Martine. Even after the voice stopped talking, and the line went dead in Andersen's hand, his eyes remained fixed. He didn't even realize that his hand had gone through the movements of hanging up the phone.

When the phone in the den rang again, less than fifteen minutes later, Andersen waited patiently for the sixth ring before he rose slowly from his chair. There was no need to hurry. The girls had been carefully instructed to watch television in their upstairs bedroom and make periodic checks on their sleeping mother. He warned them not to answer the doorbell or the telephone for the rest of the evening.

He waited for the eighth ring before lifting the receiver.

"Andersen."

"Hello, Sergeant. Remember me?"

"No." Andersen had discovered that beyond a certain mental dividing line it was almost easy to feign indifference. The voice started to say something, hesitated in what might have been confusion, and then started again.

"It occurred to me that before I came by to pick up your daughter, I should ask your permission. Just in case you're not home when I arrive."

The slight alteration in Andersen's expression could have been mistaken for a smile. Except that no one in Andersen's family, or anyone else for that matter, had ever seen him smile like that before.

"I will look forward to discussing that matter with you," Andersen answered in a voice that only suggested quiet and pleasant anticipation. Then, before the voice could respond,

Andersen's left index finger firmly depressed the disconnect
button on the receiver. He released the button, waited to
confirm that he had a clear line, and then he dialed a very
familiar number.

The phone in the kitchen rang again. He carefully placed
the receiver in his hand on the surface of the desk, then he
walked out to the kitchen without any evidence of haste. He
held the kitchen phone up to his ear and listened to the sound
of the old grandfather clock in his den tick audibly in the
background. Satisfied, he placed the receiver on the tiled
kitchen counter and returned to his den.

The heavy .45 automatic was out of its holster, cocked,
and placed next to the temporarily silenced telephone. An
unsheathed military combat knife—the blade surface deeply
blued to eliminate give-away reflection—lay next to the familiar pistol. Readjusting himself comfortably in the reclining
chair purchased by his wife and daughters for his last birthday,
Andersen picked up the knife and returned to the inwardly
satisfying and time-consuming task of stroking a thin oiled
stone along the already sharp edge.

Thanatos remained in the telephone booth after replacing
the phone, evaluating the disconcerting response of the detective sergeant.

He realized with some degree of satisfaction that his preliminary appraisals of the HBPD investigating team had proven to
be remarkably accurate. The forensic lab group had demonstrated a dogged persistence, and had been rewarded with an
unfortunate number of leads that were rapidly beginning to
cross-link. Equally unfortunate, the scientists seemed to de-
light in communicating these leads to the detectives—particularly Hernandez—who seemed to gain energy and enthusiasm
with every new bit of information. The Watch Commander,
Gilcrist—who had thus far demonstrated steady and firm
control over his field patrol units—would be a continual
problem if Balefire was to remain on schedule. But it was
Andersen, the father of the two beautiful blond girls, who
represented the most dangerous threat to himself and, therefore,
to Balefire.

Gilcrist had repeatedly slammed the phone down after

hearing the first threat toward his young soccer-playing son. Hernandez had responded with threats of dismemberment and unpleasant death. But Andersen had remained almost inhumanly calm and controlled, expressing none of the panic and helplessness that had laced the angered words of the other protective officers.

The possibility that the teletype gambit would only partially succeed, as it did, had been anticipated and accepted as a necessary risk—a horribly expensive risk, as it turned out, because they had potentially exposed one of Balefire's most useful tools much too prematurely. The gamble was made in the hope that Andersen would overreact against one of the dispatchers and get suspended. The assumption was that no one in the police department would seriously suspect that an outside transmitter had sent the havoc-causing message to Officer Muscalino.

In spite of the failure to neutralize the dangerous Andersen, the Committee was in general agreement that the secret of their duplicate teletype transmitter remained inviolate. It could be used again.

Thanatos now faced the prospect of making a direct assault against Andersen's vulnerable point with an uncharacteristic reluctance. But it was not the idea of striking at the officer's family that caused his hesitation, in spite of the concern of several members of the Committee, who felt that such an assault might trigger something in the American psyche and effectively reunite the local citizens with their police force. Thanatos was a strong believer in the theory that an enemy's weaknesses should always be exploited, regardless of their nature. Instead, his concern was directed toward the possibility that his inevitable confrontation with Andersen would occur before the final critical stage of Balefire was set into irreversible motion.

The terrorist's hesitation was not derived from a sense of self-preservation, but rather from professional pride. He knew his capabilities; he knew that his skills and expertise were essential to the successful completion of the Warning. He was being paid very handsomely to succeed. Risks, even the relatively minor risks involved in confronting Andersen, were acceptable only if they were taken in such a way as to maximize the likelihood of success.

Thanatos was ever mindful that his primary objective was to ignite Balefire. Demonstrating the vulnerability of an American city's police department to even a limited terrorist operation was of secondary importance. Therefore, it was essential that Sergeant Andersen be prevented from taking a continued, active part in the police investigation. Once Balefire was an undeniable reality in six more days, there would be opportunities for a face-to-face meeting with the tenacious sergeant, at a time when the outcome of the intriguing confrontation would only be a personal matter—of life and death.

Brian Sheffield and Meiko Harikawa allowed their stockinged feet to intertwine on the polished wood surface of their living room table next to Meiko's burlap purse. The gentle foot-touching was the extent of their sensual behavior. Neither of them had the energy or the inclination to provoke anything more demanding.

"Hungry?"

Sheffield mumbled the question through a jaw comfortably propped against his left arm. His eyes were half-shut and his body was almost totally relaxed against the firm cushions.

Meiko didn't answer. And her breathing had become suspiciously even during the last few minutes, almost in rhythm with the soft stroking movements of her feet. Sheffield gave her a couple of firm nudges with his toes and managed to get a grumbled response that he took to be affirmative. Groaning, he unfolded himself from the couch and walked stiffly toward the kitchen.

He returned a few minutes later with a perilously balanced tray containing crackers, cheese, apple slices, and two full wine glasses. Meiko had forced herself awake, and had reached down to move her purse—vaguely puzzling because she couldn't remember having left it there—to make room for the tray. Suddenly the wine glasses and food crashed to the floor as Sheffield stared in disbelief at the center of the table.

The object that held their shocked attention was unremarkable in its own right. It was a small hollow cylinder of ribbed green plastic, one end of which was capped with a supporting cup of shined brass. The other end of the plastic cylinder was flared open and covered internally with a fine greyish-black residue.

There were a number of reasons why the presence of a discharged 12-gauge magnum buckshot casing on Sheffield's living room table was disconcerting, to say the least. The most significant of those reasons was that for the last three days, a missing buckshot round from Farber's scene had been a constant source of confusion and irritation to Sheffield. A comparative examination had confirmed what had been apparent last Friday morning at the scene: all the spent buckshot casings found near Branchowski had been fired and ejected from Farber's shotgun and were also accounted for by the wounds in the dead suspect in the middle of the street.

Farber had been killed with buckshot. Which meant the shell used to kill him had almost certainly been taken from the scene. But by whom? And what about the distance factor? The shot pattern was too tight to have come from the second-story window. All the unanswered questions tumbled through Sheffield's mind as he continued to stare at an object that had no logical reason to be on his table.

"It wasn't there when we left," Meiko whispered.

"Are you sure?" Sheffield asked, realizing that the question was absurd even as he spoke. "When did you put the purse on the table?"

"I didn't . . ." Meiko hesitated, looking up to see the confusion on Sheffield's face. "At least, I don't remember putting it there." In fact, Meiko was almost certain that the last time she had seen that purse, it had been on a shelf in the hall closet. She couldn't remember for sure because she had a habit of frequently changing purses. Still . . .

Sheffield was one of those irritating and irrepressible individuals who believes there is a logical explanation for every supposedly unfathomable event. True to his nature, Sheffield seized upon the least unreasonable theory that could logically fit the facts.

"Listen, Meiko," he said, his voice low and serious. "This is important. Very important. Is there any chance at all that you picked up that casing at the scene and then forgot about it after you hit your head?"

Bewildered, Meiko started to shake her head, but Sheffield continued on before she could say anything.

"Or maybe someone found it and handed it to you?"

"No. Absolutely not. I would have remembered," she said firmly.

"What if someone put it in your purse without you knowing about it?" Sheffield persisted.

"Why would they do that? Every officer out there knows about chain-of-custody. Unless someone picked it up before we got there and then put it in my purse after I sat it on the van."

"What's the other alternative? Someone broke into our house and stuck it under your purse so that we'd find it?" Sheffield asked sarcastically.

"I don't know, but I didn't pick the damn thing up!" Meiko flared, glaring furiously at Sheffield through red-streaked eyes.

Sheffield blinked at the unexpected anger, and then they both tried to apologize at the same time.

"Look, maybe this is somebody's idea of a practical joke," Sheffield finally said. "It's probably not even the missing shell." He held his arm around her, but they both continued to stare at the unexplainable plastic and metal cylinder. "Maybe Rudy or Walt . . ." Suddenly determined and angry with himself, Sheffield got up quickly and went over to the wall phone. He tried both of Andersen's numbers twice, receiving a busy signal each time. Then he tried Hernandez's home number. The phone rang, but no one answered. He tried Andersen's numbers once again and then gave up in frustration.

"I'm going over to the lab and check this thing out," Sheffield said, wrapping the shotgun shell in a piece of tissue and placing it carefully in his pocket. "Want to come along?"

Meiko shook her head, getting up to give Sheffield an affectionate squeeze, her sudden outburst of temper forgotten. "The only thing that I want to see tonight is the bathtub and the bed. Wake me if you find out something interesting."

After Sheffield left, Meiko went upstairs to start a hot bath, and then returned downstairs to clean up the spilled food and broken glass. Halfway through cleaning up Sheffield's mess in the kitchen, she realized she had been deliberately trying to avoid looking at the familiar burlap purse still lying on the table top. For some reason she couldn't quite explain, the sight of the purse made her feel strangely uneasy.

When the kitchen was clean, Meiko shut off the lights and then walked by the table, intending to pick up the purse and return it to the closet where it had been put away—she was almost certain—for several days. But when she reached down to pick it up, she hesitated, experiencing a slight chill at a sudden irrational thought: there might be something else under it. She realized now that she would not be able to handle the sight of another unexpected object under that purse without maddeningly logical Brian being there to provide an acceptable explanation.

Feeling foolish, but at the same time oddly relieved, she decided to leave the purse where it was. Humming to herself, she turned off the lights and went up the carpeted stairs quickly, leaving the disconcerting burlap purse untouched in the now darkened downstairs living room.

Peeling off her dirty clothes and stepping into the hot soapy water helped Meiko's spirts immensely. Standing in anticipation of the pleasure to come, she observed herself in the full-length mirror, noting with approval that although it wasn't every day, her periodic exercising was still enough to maintain a tight abdomen, reasonably slender legs, and supportive chest muscles. Not the perfect figure by any means, she decided, but as long as Brian didn't complain, it was fine.

She used the large natural sponge to soap her smooth, tanned legs, arms, and upper torso. Then, unable to resist, she slid the rest of her body down into the soapy water. She had just gotten herself adjusted in a semihorizontal position where she could rest the back of her head against the rear edge of the tub, her hair strung across the narrow porcelain ledge and her firm breasts poking hill-like out of the foamy white water, when her mind recorded the fact that something about the bathroom was wrong.

She froze, her heart thumping solidly against her rib cage, while her eyes flickered around the room. When she finally recognized the source of her subconscious reaction, she almost cried with a combination of shaky relief and embarrassed laughter.

A roll of toilet paper.

The master bathroom had been one of Meiko's special home decoration projects. After consulting and clipping from several magazines and newspapers, she had decided to use carefully selected pieces of smooth, light redwood as a background for cut-glass mirrors and hanging plants, all set beneath a skylight that counterbalanced the closed-in effect of the wooden walls. The towels and racks all matched in color and texture. In that rustic setting, a roll of bright pink toilet paper was a horrible standout.

Shaking her head at Brian's total lack of color sense, Meiko slid completely down into the soothing water again and finally allowed herself to relax.

Resting his forehead against the fixed camera mount, Sheffield adjusted his sitting position in the darkened microscopy room and stared through the twin eyepieces of the comparison microscope.

In the split view, the magnified brass sides of the two expended 12-gauge shotgun shells came into partial focus.

It took Sheffield almost five minutes to position the microscopic ejector marks on the two casings. One of the casings was the one that he and Meiko had found under her purse. The other was a comparison standard which he had personally test-fired through the automatic shotgun that had been cut out of Toby Williker's hands. As Sheffield carefully adjusted the knobs on the microscope, the fine striation marks merged into almost perfect alignment. A match.

There was no doubt now. Both casings had to have been ejected, if not fired, out of the same shotgun. Toby Williker's shotgun.

The proof that the shell in question had been through that shotgun would come through a comparison of the firing pin and breech-mark impressions on the base of the shells. Sheffield considered the amount of work involved to make the additional comparisons, and he decided to wait until the next morning when his eyes would be more up to the effort. Besides, he had one more task to complete that evening.

Malinger had deposited the pile of labeled contact sheets—pages of negative-sized photos which illustrated all of the photographs taken at Farber's shooting scenes—on Sheffield's lab desk earlier that evening. Using a low-power binocular microscope, Sheffield began to examine the miniaturized photos, searching patiently for a third expended shotgun shell somewhere in the scene that wasn't recorded on anyone's investigation notes.

He had already set aside the fifth contact sheet and was determinedly reaching for the sixth, when a subconscious analytical function in his mind set off an alarm.

He blinked, trying to remember—something he saw, but really didn't see. He couldn't make the connection, so he went back to the fifth contact sheet and began to reexamine the photos, this time in reverse order.

As frame eight came into his field of view, Sheffield made a slight readjustment of focus, and this time realization struck with a tingling numbness that spread down his neck to the backs of his arms.

It was Meiko's purse. Or, to be more exact, it was not the burlap purse.

Malinger had shot frame eight with a wide-angle lens, taking in the entire rear portion of the lab van in addition to the sidewalk which had been the primary focal point of the photo. Meiko was clearly visible in the photo, standing with one foot on the rear bumper, writing something on her clipboard. She had hung her purse on the rear door handle of the van. A hand-stitched leather purse. It was not the burlap purse that had been lying on their table. Therefore, the shotgun shell casing on their coffee table—the casing that matched Toby Williker's shotgun—could not have been given to Meiko or put into her purse at the scene.

In the few seconds it took Sheffield to figure out the most logical explanation for the buckshot casing's appearance in his home, the tingling sensation moved up to his head and seemed to tighten the skin around his skull. Cursing his stupidity, he lurched up out of his chair and reached for the telephone.

The sound of the ringing phone in the otherwise silent house jarred Meiko out of a relaxed stupor. She groaned aloud at the idea of leaving the still warm water, but she managed to get out of the tub, wrap herself in a large towel and reach the nightstand next to their bed before the sixth ring. She sat down on the firm mattress and reached for the phone.

"Hummm, hello. When are you . . ." she started to say,

and then hesitated, suddenly realizing that the slow raspy breathing in the background didn't belong to Brian.

"Turn on your patio lights."

A raspy voice that matched the breathing. Not as deep as Brian's foghorn. More like a tenor, except with a sharper, more threatening pitch. She had to repeat the words to herself before she could comprehend enough to respond.

"What?"

"Turn on your patio lights," the voice repeated. No change in tone or emphasis.

"Who is this?" Meiko demanded, her lustful anticipation turning rapidly into indignant anger.

No answer.

"Why should I turn my patio lights on?" she asked in a tightly controlled voice, barely managing at the last moment not to call the man an asshole. Been hanging around cops too long, she thought.

"You be a good girl and do what I tell you, and I might bring you some more of that nice pink toilet paper."

Meiko's head snapped up, the discordant image of the bright cylindrical roll flashing across her mind. Suppressing an involuntary whimper of fear before it escaped her constricted throat, she abandoned the phone and towel on the bed and ran into the bathroom. With trembling legs, she bent down and pulled open the door to the storage cabinet under the bathroom sink. This time she couldn't control the sounds of fear that passed through her clenched teeth.

The package wrapped in clear plastic that once held four rolls of toilet paper was standing upright next to the curved drain pipe. Three of the gold-patterned rolls were still in the torn package. She remembered putting a new roll into the wooden holder. That roll of gold-patterned white paper was lying by itself on the floor of the cabinet. A bright pink roll was now in the holder.

Adrenaline shock is a survival mechanism designed to provide a last-ditch means of escape, or the push needed for a final frenzied assault, before the predator succeeds in dragging its victim down into unacceptable death. The mechanism is oriented toward muscle tissue and instinctive nerve response. Blood is pumped to legs, arms and hands. The brain is relegated to function as an off-on switch, the grey matter receiving only enough nourishment to select the direction offering the highest probability of survival and to yell "go."

In her trembling confusion, Meiko reacted blindly. She ran back to the bedroom and grabbed at the phone. She took a shuddered breath, intending to vent her contained terror and fury in a seething, passionate outburst. But the dial tone buzzed distantly in her ear.

Brian.

She fumbled with the push buttons on the receiver, dialing the lab. Busy signal.

"Goddamn it!" she screamed, throwing the phone at the bed. She suddenly, unaccountably, realized that she was naked. Panties in the top right drawer. She was putting her arms through the sleeves of her bathrobe when she remembered the door. She started for the stairs, hurrying because she couldn't remember whether Brian had locked the dead bolt. She hesitated for a moment, realizing she should have dialed the police emergency number. She started to go back, then changed her mind, because she knew if he got through the door in the next few seconds, the police wouldn't arrive in time. Only vaguely aware of her numbed body, Meiko ran down the stairs, her robe billowing open like a cape.

She had reached the bottom of the stairs and was crossing the darkened living room, not wasting time to fumble for the light switches, when she heard the footsteps on the sidewalk outside the door. She froze for a moment, moaning a barely audible no, then dove across the remaining distance and grasped at the dead-bolt latch. The tempered-steel bolt slid solidly into the reinforced door frame with a reassuring clunk.

The footsteps stopped, and Meiko backed away from the door slowly, the expression on her face shifting from fearful apprehension to a more controlled, purposeful determination. She moved backwards into the living room, bringing her breathing under control and shifting her eyes to the windows, the front door, and the sliding glass door next to the kitchen, watching for any sudden movement or shadow.

Using only her hands as a guide, Meiko felt her way back into the kitchen, keeping her eyes on the windows until she reached the sink. Then she turned and opened the top drawer beneath the drainboard, moving quickly now that her back was turned. Her hand closed around the familiar wooden handle, and the last of her fear dissolved into a feeling of calm, intense self-confidence.

The knife had been a gift from her grandfather. It was a heavy, plain, functional Japanese meat knife, forged out of thick carbon steel with a straight quarter-inch-wide top edge to provide the weight necessary to drive the razored edge through a slab of tough, sinewy meat with a single, smooth stroke. The blade was almost an inch and a half wide at the handle, ten inches long, and curved upward to a point along its sharpened edge. Unlike the ancestral pair of fighting swords mounted in peaceful retirement on her grandfather's bedroom wall, Meiko's knife was comparatively crude and ugly. But as her grandfather had explained, the temper of the steel and the sharpness of the edges were alike. If necessary, a man could be made to die before he was aware he had been cut.

She was not going to call the police and act like another one of those women at home alone who had just received a crank call, Meiko decided. There was no need to have to endure the playful harassment she would receive from the officers at the station the next morning. Brian would be home shortly, and she knew the voice on the phone could not possibly be in her house. More important, she also knew there were only so many ways of getting into the two-story townhouse. If the intruder was going to try and come in quietly to catch her by surprise, he would have to stick a very vulnerable leg or arm through one of the windows.

Gripping the knife handle tightly and smiling with unflinching anticipation at the thought, Meiko's eyes swept through the dark living room and focused on the sliding glass door leading to the patio. The curtain was drawn back, displaying the wooden patio deck and hot tub as an indistinguishable mass of darkness and shadows, barely illuminated by a distant street light. Realizing she was still nearly naked, she put down the knife long enough to secure the robe around her waist with the cloth belt.

Then, intent upon providing herself with every possible advantage, and remembering curiously the words spoken by the unemotional voice on the phone, she reached for the switch to turn on the outside lights that would illuminate the patio and hot tub.

*   *   *

Sheffield dialed his home number four times in quick succession, becoming more and more apprehensive with each repetition of the busy signal. The fifth number he dialed was the supervising officer's phone in dispatch.

"Dispatch, Sergeant Neibolt."

"Jerry, this is Brian, down in the lab."

"Hi, crime lab, what can we do for you?"

Sheffield sensed the underlying nervousness in Neibolt's voice, but he was too distracted to question the normally easy-going supervisor who frequently spent his coffee breaks down in the lab talking with Dorsey and Spencer.

"I need a unit to make a quick patrol check. Do you have somebody free in the south?" Sheffield tried to sound casual about the request, but he couldn't ignore the unquestionable fact that someone had broken into their house and left that shotgun shell.

"Bad night for that sort of thing, partner," Neibolt drawled, the tension still evident. "Calls backed up for miles. Is it important?"

"Yeah, I think so."

A short pause. "Tell you what, I've got an Adam unit clearing from the harbor in about two. Where do you want them?"

Sheffield did some quick mental calculations. A fifteen-minute ETA at best, and they'd have to blow several lights to make that.

"Okay, fine," he said quickly. "My place. One-two-seven-three-five Sand Dollar. We had a break-in today that may tie in to Farber's case. The guy may still be hanging around. Meiko's there, so have them step on it, okay?"

"On their way, partner."

Sheffield tried his home number one more time. The insistent busy signal provided the final impetus. He ran out into the reception area of the lab and fumbled for his keys. The door to the Identification Office was always locked, but Dorsey never bothered to lock his desk. Sheffield pulled open the large lower drawer and found what he was after.

Bob Dorsey hadn't worn a uniform in over six years, but he still kept his Sam Browne gear polished and ready in his

desk. The six-inch Smith & Wesson revolver was predictably
clean, lightly oiled, and strapped securely into its clamshell
holster. Sheffield drew the long-barreled weapon, checked to
make certain it was loaded, snapped the cylinder shut, and
ran for the exit.

The diffuse light from the two green-tinted bulbs concealed
in the open-beamed lathing which surrounded the hot tub,
was more than sufficient to illuminate clearly the two small
objects sitting upright on the tub's wooden cover. In spite of
the fact that the objects were only about three inches tall and
almost fifteen feet away from the sliding glass door, Meiko
had no difficulty at all making an immediate identification.

Meiko stared at the green and brass cylinders with exactly
the same expression of horror she would have exhibited if she
had been faced with a pair of poisonous snakes. Two live
12-gauge shotgun shells. In her mind, she reexperienced the
vision of the expended casing under the burlap purse, and the
pair of expended buckshot rounds lying in the gutter next to
Farber's shattered, bleeding face.

The realization that the voice, the pink toilet paper, the
burlap purse, the shotgun shell on the coffee table, and the
two 12-gauge shotgun shells on the hot tub were all related to
the violent death of Jacob Farber was enough to disintegrate
every fiber of determination and self-confidence in her body.
The realization that she was a very vulnerable target against a
man in the dark with a shotgun, a man vicious enough to play
sick, terrifying games, drove her to run stumbling across
the dark living room to the phone, unaware that her grandfather's knife had dropped out of her nerveless hands onto
the floor.

The small self-adhesive tag on the wall phone listed the
police emergency number in large black numbers against an
iridescent yellow background. She punched every one of the
numbers before she realized with a chest-constricting numbness that the phone was buzzing, an unresponsive piece of
plastic in her hand. The phone upstairs. Off the hook. Lying
on the bed where she had thrown it.

Wavering on the edge of total panic, Meiko heard the key

slide noisily into the lock mechanism behind her. Unable to contain a deep emotional whimper of relief, she turned and ran toward the door.

Pinko Rutsche carefully closed the wooden entry gate and walked along the sidewalk into the small courtyard between the garage and the narrow two-story townhouse. As he walked past the garage window, he noted with satisfaction that the information he had been given over the phone appeared to be righteous. The garage was empty. That meant the dude would be gone for at least another hour and the girl would be there all alone with the dope. She was supposed to be a real honey. Pinko smiled, rubbing himself in anticipation.

Pinko Rutsche had lived the vast majority of his thirty-four years with the conviction that somebody, somewhere, owed him a big one. He wasn't exactly sure who that somebody was or what he was owed, but Pinko was absolutely certain that there was someone out there anxious to do him a big favor.

The phone call had taken thirty-four years to come, but Pinko accepted the delay the way he always accepted things. Even so, he had been forced to admit to his disbelieving companions that the offer of a lot of money to do a simple job did seem a little too good to be true. He had been cautious enough to take his single-barreled sawed-off when he went to see if the promised "good-faith" money had been delivered.

He had turned over the trash can in the alley behind the Main Street Bakery, and sure enough, the roll of twenties— all ten of them—had been there, just as the voice had promised. He had been tempted to take the cash, buy some real fine powder, and forget about the rest of the deal. But the promise of an additional five grand and a share of all of the coke in the house was too big a draw. He couldn't resist the offer, and he wasn't about to let any of his friends in on his "big one."

Pinko had developed a sufficient amount of self-serving paranoia during his thirty-four years to realize that something this big had to have a bad catch somewhere. A guy didn't deal in pounds of cocaine, make a score, and then leave the entire stash in a broad's townhouse without putting on a little protection. She probably had a gun, he reasoned. Didn't matter. All he had to do, according to the second phone call, was to pick up the key at another drop, and then wait at a designated phone booth for a third call. Once he got the go-ahead, he would walk in, catch her by surprise, and use the available time to locate thirty-two one-ounce plastic bags of white lumpy powder and a carved wooden figure of an Oriental fisherman that was an essential part of the deal. The girl, and whatever time remained of his safety limit, was a bonus for efficiency.

As he approached the door, it occurred to Pinko to wonder how his contact had managed to get the key, and why he was willing to trust Pinko to turn over the dope. He shrugged, deciding that it wasn't his problem. Holding the sawed-off 20-gauge shotgun in his puffy left hand, Pinko eased the key into the dead-bolt lock, turned the key until he heard the click, and then pushed the door inward with a quick thrust of his palm.

He caught the girl in mid-stride reaching to open the door. The joyful welcome on her face instantly melted into an open-mouthed, wide-eyed look of horror. He got his right arm around her just as she started to turn away, slamming the door shut with the back of his boot.

Jesus God, she's a beauty, he thought as he used his ample torso to jam her struggling body against a wall, his right hand coming up to clamp over her mouth. He could feel her squirming against his stomach, and he turned her so that she faced him. He started to breathe faster when he realized that her robe had pulled open, and he was badly tempted to take his bonus first. If it was anything else but powder . . . He slid the barrel of the shotgun up against the girl's neck, brushing aside the long black hair.

"Listen to me good, honey," he said in a rough whisper. "I'm not going to hurt you any, okay? You tell me where he keeps the stash, and I'll be gone. You understand?" Adjusting himself carefully to prevent the girl from bringing up a knee, Pinko leaned his weight against the trembling, deliciously firm body, and slowly removed his hand from her mouth.

Meiko tried to twist loose, to escape from the obscenely fat, sweaty stomach, but the weight was too much, and the rough, burred end of the shotgun barrel dug menacingly into her throat.

"Don't know . . . what you mean . . . no stash here," she gasped between deep shuddering breaths, her eyes staring upward, wide open with fear.

Pinko smiled crookedly and slid his right hand down across the exposed warm breast, laughing softly as she cringed and tried to turn away.

"No way, baby," he whispered. "That's not going to do it." He rubbed the palm of his hand against the hardening nipple, ignorantly mistaking a bodily response to fear for one of sexual attraction. Distracted by anticipation, he failed to hear a car come to a fast bouncing stop in the driveway on the other side of the courtyard.

"Your dude doesn't come here just to dip his wick, does he?" Pinko continued, grinding himself slowly against the girl. "Nah, of course not. You see, I know you've got a couple of pounds of good rock coke in this place. And you're going to give it all to me," he added with a knowing smirk. "You can tell me where it is now . . . or later."

"You're crazy," Meiko wheezed, trying to breathe against the unyielding weight pressing insistently against her chest and diaphragm. "We don't even use grass." She tried to take a few more shallow breaths.

"Okay, baby," Pink smiled, running his tongue across his rough uneven teeth, "if that's the way you want it. We'll just talk about it again . . . afterwards." He pressed the shotgun barrel tight under her jaw and moved his hand downward from her breast, feeling himself respond to her groaned protest.

Sheffield came out of the unit with the awkwardly heavy Smith & Wesson in his hand, uncertain and a little self-conscious when he realized that the entire block appeared to be typically quiet and peaceful.

Neighbors'll think I'm insane if they see me, he thought, as he went through the gate and headed for the front door. He was halfway across the open courtyard when he realized the rear patio lights were on. Less anxious now that he was home, his immediate reaction was to assume that Meiko had turned on the heat pump and was waiting for him in the hot

tub with a chilled glass of wine. He looked down at the
weapon in his hand and shook his head, beginning to feel
foolish in spite of the fact that the break-in and the threatening presence of the shotgun casing was still on his mind.

He walked around the side of the house quickly, intending
to ditch the revolver in one of the wooden planters before he
surprised Meiko. He had changed his grip on the pistol,
holding it with one hand around the frame and cylinder. He
turned the corner, walked a few steps and stopped abruptly
when his eyes focused on the cover of the hot tub.

"What?" he said aloud, incredulous. He moved forward,
stepping up onto the redwood deck to get a closer look.

"No, don't," Meiko moaned, shaking her head, straining
ineffectively against the rough, insistent fingers that were
pulling at the waistband of her tight panties. Pinko laughed
hoarsely between quick excited breaths. He started to move
back a little to give himself some leverage, when a sound and
movement in the corner of his eye caught his attention. He
jerked his head around, and both he and Meiko saw Sheffield
through the sliding glass door at the same instant.

Meiko saw Brian reach out to pick up the pair of shotgun
shells on the tub, oblivious to the struggle going on in the
darkened house. Then she saw Pinko's fat hand extend the
sawed-off shotgun, and this time the adrenaline-shock-frenzy
had something solid to fight against.

"Brian!" she screamed. Her suddenly freed hand lunged at
the cocked weapon, and at the same time she sunk her teeth
savagely into the flabby skin of Pinko's chest. His bellowed
scream of pain was drowned out by the explosive roar of the
sawed-off shotgun and the high-pitched crackle of shattering
safety glass.

Trying to keep his eyes on the spot behind the wooden tub
where the unsuspecting target had disappeared, arms and legs
flailing in an obscuring spray of reflective glass fragments,
Pinko fought to pry Meiko's jaws loose from his painfully
lacerated chest. Struggling, but unable to force his fingers
between her tightly clenched teeth, he slammed the barrel of
the shotgun against the side of her head in desperation. He

screamed again in agony as her teeth tore loose from his chest with a final ripping of fatty tissue.

"Bitch!" He flung her sprawling into the shadowy darkness, hearing her crash into a table and lamp. There were more sounds of pain and breaking glass as he fumbled to pull one of the extra shotgun rounds out of the tight front pocket of his jeans. Wincing, Pinko managed to work one of the shells loose. Using both shaking hands to break open the short weapon, he snorted with angered amusement as he heard the girl move around on the floor with soft whimpered moans.

"Just wait." He chuckled loudly, watching the shadowy area around the wooden tub with intense interest. "You don't know what pain is yet." He hurried to pull the discharged round out of the smoking chamber, acutely aware that the amount of light over the patio had been considerably reduced by the destructive effect of the wide shot pattern. Better go out and finish the guy off first, he decided, reloading and cocking the shotgun with two sharp clicks.

Pinko stepped confidently toward the shattered glass door, shoving against the dark kneeling form of the girl with his leg. Then he shrieked from sudden, excruciating belly pain as the heavy, cold blade sliced cleanly through layers of denim, stretched skin, fat, and abdominal muscles. Mouth opened wide, eyes bulging in horrified disbelief, Pinko dropped the shotgun and clutched protectively—much too late—at his critically torn groin and stomach.

Meiko released her grip on the knife and scrambled backward out of reach, as Pinko's hands closed around the protruding wooden handle. He appeared ready to pull out the knife and slash at her, but the sound of crashing glass turned Pinko's anguished eyes up to the patio door as a man staggered sideways through the remaining glass in the sliding door, an arm upraised to protect his face. Then Sheffield turned, and Pinko saw the long-barreled revolver come up in two clenched hands, heard the snarl in the darkness.

Pinko tried to turn away, and he felt the edge of the knife cut deeper. Warm, thick liquid began to flow faster through his pressing fingers.

As the intruder screamed again, Sheffield's battered mind recorded the sight of Meiko sprawled against the wall, her robe torn open, and the sawed-off shotgun less than three

feet away from the bent form of the man who had shot him.
Dorsey's revolver roared and recoiled against Sheffield's hands.

The muzzle flash of the revolver seemed to reach out for
Pinko's face as the first streaking, twisting bullet cut a ragged
groove across the side of his bulging neck with a burst of
sprayed blood. Pinko gurgled another scream as he was flung
back into the bathroom door. He managed to claw and twist
and slide into the relative sanctuary of the bathroom, functioning only on survival instincts.

The image of Meiko's bared breasts and torn panties flashed
across Sheffield's eyes. He deliberately and coldly pulled the
trigger five more times, aiming down into the partially closed
door, wincing at the blasts as the wooden door splintered
from the bullet impacts, offering no protection at all for the
soft target inside that screamed and screamed and finally
stopped.

Sheffield's mind was fixed on the carnage only dimly
visible from where he stood. He was still standing there, his
weight balanced on one leg against the wall, his arms loose at
his sides, when Meiko hit the light switch.

Turning on the lights made everything—the reflections
from the shattered glass, the glistening pools of bright red
blood—seem worse. Sheffield was too stunned, too shocked
to comprehend fully what had happened.

Sheffield's ears were ringing madly. He couldn't understand what it was that Meiko was trying to tell him, why she
was being so insistent. But his eyes followed her wildly
gesturing hands, and he looked down and saw the small torn
holes in his right pants leg, the dark blood-matted areas that
ran from his hip to below his knee.

He then relived the sudden unexpected shock and pain—
the total incomprehension when he heard Meiko scream, his
surprise when the sliding glass door exploded outward, the
moment when something irresistible grabbed him by the leg
and yanked him across the top of the wooden tub in a shower
of flying glass. He remembered fumbling for the gun, remembered that his leg hurt terribly. But the pain hadn't mattered
at the time because he had expected to be shot again when he
went in through the broken glass door.

Funny, he thought, as he dropped the revolver onto the

floor and allowed Meiko to help him lay down on the couch, I can't remember . . .

He was still trying to understand what and why, vaguely aware through the foggy haze that Meiko was cutting away the leg of his pants with a large bloody knife. Then the fog thickened, and the first of many Huntington Beach police officers came in through the front door.

BALEFIRE

Minus 6 Days

Sunday Evening

2133 hours

Sergeant Jerry Neibolt sat at his control desk, his face infused with anxiety, and looked out at the backs of the four female dispatchers who were working intently to bounce units back and forth from one high-priority call to another, and the one young female cadet monitoring the station security screens.

Neibolt, a family man with five young children and an understandable interest in his career, had every reason to be anxious. He had relieved a communications watch supervisor who was now facing the very real possibility of suspension over a teleprinter message that the supervisor didn't know a damn thing about. Neibolt knew several of the dispatchers occasionally sent out coded see-you-tonight-at-ten-my-place type messages. But, Christ, never anything like the teletype sent to Muscalino. Neibolt shook his head, fully aware and for the first time concerned that any one of the four individuals sitting in front of the dispatch keyboards could type out another practical joke that could end his law enforcement career.

Neibolt almost missed the frantic signal from the dispatcher monitoring the police emergency line. She gestured at her earphones, and Neibolt quickly patched himself into the incoming call.

Neibolt recognized Meiko's voice immediately, in spite of the fact that she was hysterical. He listened to the ragged flow of information which the dispatcher was quickly typing onto her console screen. Then he used his desk-mounted microphone to order his one free unit out of the north on a

code run to back up Four Adam, who had already acknowledged the code order issued by the alert secondary dispatch
team, filling the airwaves with the piercing sound of his
activated siren before he released the key button on his mike.

An indignant housewife in the harbor area had delayed the
unit asked to respond to Sheffield's requested patrol check,
refusing to accept the officers' insistence that they could not
do anything about the obnoxious and persistent encyclopedia
salesman who had been calling every ten minutes for the past
hour. By the time the exasperated officers received the clearance to roll the lights and siren on Sheffield's call, the best
estimated time of arrival that they could give was at least
another five minutes.

Neibolt quickly guessed distances on the wall-sized map of
Huntington Beach mounted over the dispatch consoles, and
estimated the Adam and backup units would hit the security
gate entrance to the townhouse complex within thirty seconds
of each other.

Neibolt tried to mentally block out the panicked sound of
Meiko's voice, reaching for his desk phone and the roster of
off-duty phone numbers. He noticed his hand starting to
shake as he searched for Andersen, Walter.

Officer John Parham reached down to adjust the volume on
Eight Adam's radio, listening with wistful interest as Four
Adam and Nine-Thirteen Charles took the hot call.

"Always in the south," Parham muttered, adjusting the
dial so that he and his partner could hear the broadcasts
clearly over the night traffic noise coming through their opened
side windows.

"Bitch and moan." Barry Barlowe shook his head, continuing to maneuver the black-and-white with casual indifference
toward the location given on their assigned call. They were to
check out suspicious circumstances, a man observed wandering in an industrial construction project. "Hell, after that call
last night with Paradee and Lagucii, you ought to be grateful
for a little peace and quiet. Besides, we gotta rest up. Olympics detail starts next weekend."

"Yeah, assuming they still let us go after all the shit that's
been going down around here," Parham nodded moodily.

"Which reminds me, I still want to check out that Saladin guy."

"What for? Paradee claims one of us did him in, remember?"

"Yeah, I know, but it was a hell of a coincidence for that guy to pop out of nowhere like that."

"Especially right around the area where the lab guys found those gloves and the mask," Barlowe nodded thoughtfully. "You put him in the report?"

"Just name and address. Contacted at the scene and released."

"Yeah," Barlowe nodded, "I think I'll ask Sarge to kick us loose after dinner. Go down to Nightingale and get a good ID, and maybe take a look at Saladin's shoes while we're at it. In the meantime, here we are." Barlowe motioned with his head at the entrance of the partially completed industrial complex.

"Okay, boss man," Parham said. He reached down for the mike. "Eight Adam. We're ten-ninety-seven in the area." Parham paused as Barlowe shut the lights and turned sharply into the complex. They drove slowly in the darkness along the dirt and crushed rock road, each officer searching his side for any sign of movement.

"Eight Adam," the radio blared, and Parham reached down quickly to lower the volume. "Ten-ninety-seven. Ten-four."

"Eight Adam." Parham spoke softly into the mike. "Be advised subject appears to be GOA. We'll be getting out and looking around for a few."

The dispatcher acknowledged, and Barlowe parked the unit next to one of the portable outhouses. Both officers got out of the unit, snapping on helmets, sliding batons into belt rings, and taking out long four-cell flashlights. Without speaking, they split up, each taking one side of a row of framed buildings that were in the process of being wired.

Aside from the occasional chirping of a few crickets and the sound made by Parham's boots as he walked carefully through the construction refuse flicking the beam of the flashlight back and forth, there were no other noises in the area. Probably a guy picking up some building materials for his den, Parham thought, breaking off his search pattern frequently to illuminate the ground in front of his feet, trying to avoid stepping on the nails that were sticking out of some of the discarded boards. He was looking down at a particularly threatening piece of lumber when he suddenly realized that there was a small bright scarlet spot flickering on his chest just under the badge.

"What the—" Parham started to say, raising his head, when his ears heard a soft thwap, followed by a rushing whirr, and then a loud thunk as he received a powerful blow to the chest. Parham staggered backwards and then stared down, horrified, at the thick metal shaft that had replaced the scarlet spot and was protruding out of his uniform shirt. He died before his body fell backwards and struck the ground.

"John?"

Barlowe had heard the sound of Parham's flashlight striking against a chunk of concrete. He came around the side of the building with his revolver in his hand and his own flashlight held out away from his body. Distracted by the angled beam of Parham's flashlight, Barlowe never saw the pencil-thin dot of red light come up and center on the side of his helmet. He saw the limp form of his partner on the ground and instinctively swung his light across the disorderly stacks of lumber, searching for the expected moving form. He never heard the soft thwap, whirr, and thunk that caused him to twist suddenly and then fall lifeless onto the ground.

Thanatos worked fast. He had listened to the radio calls on his car scanner, confirming as best he could without a portable teleprinter that all the other patrol cars in the immediate vicinity had been drawn out of their assigned areas by service calls. Most of which, he knew, had been called in by the Committee. He expected to have plenty of uninterrupted time, but the terrorist still hurried from reflex and the knowledge that he had another, more pleasurable task ahead.

The pressure of time was always the difficult part, Thanatos reminded himself, as he worked to jam one of the limp, uniformed bodies into the opened trunk of the black-and-white, and the other into the floor space in front of the rear seat. Then, using one of the heavy flashlights, he backtracked, working with a small piece of jagged plywood to obscure footprints and the surprisingly few spots of blood in the rough sandy dirt. He shoved three pieces of two-by-fours bearing telltale reddish stains deep into a pile of wood scrap. Finally satisfied, he returned to the police vehicle, putting on the undamaged helmet—a close but comfortable fit—and Barlowe's black nylon jacket which he had set aside before loading the bodies.

The short drive in the black-and-white to the waiting empty storage garage was the chanciest aspect of the entire operation. Thanatos knew that unless they were otherwise occupied, patrolling police officers were compulsively curious about the radio calls, food habits and love lives of their fellow patrol officers. If two patrol units happened to cross paths anywhere within the city, they would invariably signal each other with spot lights, wave, meet in a nearby parking lot to chat briefly or arrange to stop for coffee. Aside from a casual wave, any one of those other activities would have caused the terrorist a great deal of difficulty. To his relief, he managed to drive the black-and-white up to the door of the storage garage, thumb the automatic door opener in his shirt pocket, drive the unit in and shut the heavy door without seeing any other patrol units.

Once inside the garage, Thanatos again worked quickly. This time the work was unnecessary, but he looked upon his efforts as time well spent. The bodies of the two officers were heavy, but he managed to get both of them strapped into the front seat of the black-and-white without too much difficulty. Then, moving with a casual haste that spoke of repetition and confidence, he changed clothes, tossing the used garments into the back seat of the unit. Next, he quickly distributed the six metal one-gallon cans of gasoline in a random pattern across the open floor space of the garage. Finally, he removed the laser sight from the stock of the crossbow and then placed the deadly modernized version of the ancient battle weapon in Parham's lap, noting with satisfaction that the solid sharpened pencillike metal bolt had penetrated further through Parham's nylon-layered vest than had the bolts he had tested against a similar vest in his basement.

After mounting the explosive device in the middle of the cement floor under the vehicle, Thanatos set the activating mechanism, shut off the lights and stepped outside, carefully shutting the small back door. When the door clicked shut, the explosive device was armed. At that point, any attempt to force either the large main door or the small rear door would result in an instantaneous primary explosion and a secondary fireball created by the ignition of six gallons of gasoline, added to whatever happened to be in the patrol unit's gas tank. The fire would incinerate any useful trace evidence, leaving only the gruesome sight of two burned bodies sitting in whatever remained of the police car.

Satisfied that he was not under observation, Thanatos returned on foot to the parking lot of the industrial complex and buried the cylindrical laser-beam generator under a bag of trash in one of the large metal dumpsters. Making one final check, he then walked over and stepped into his waiting automobile.

Sergeant Jerry Neibolt's hands were still shaking when he gave up trying to get through to Walt Andersen on either of his listed phone numbers. Neibolt thought for a moment about sending a black-and-white out to Andersen's house. But then he took another look across his desk at the miniaturized dispatch console screen and shook his head. The vertical slice of screen space which listed units available for a call was blank. Every one of the unit call numbers was listed in bright green numbers in either the EN ROUTE or the SCENE columns. There was no one available to send.

Feeling his chest tighten with anxiety, Neibolt tried to block out the memory of the irate and threatening calls he had been receiving from Huntington Beach citizens all evening. Every one of the callers had voiced his distaste, anger, and contempt at the manner in which police officers were responding to service calls, traffic stops, and other routine, normally low-keyed situations.

He tried to explain to every caller that the recent surge of violence against the police force, and especially the deaths of two officers during the past week, had put everyone in the station on edge. But he knew, even as he spoke, that the excuses sounded lame and inadequate. As a patrol supervisor, he didn't have to be told that police officers were hired, trained, and paid to handle difficult, even hazardous situations. That was why police officers were given expensive insurance benefits and an early retirement system, the callers reminded him, almost unanimously adding the pointed suggestion that officers who were incapable of distinguishing between law-abiding citizens and criminals should immediately resign or be fired.

All the phones in the dispatch room were monitored by tape; every action he took this evening would almost certainly be scrutinized by the Watch Commander and the division captains. With a sinking feeling, Neibolt moved his finger down the call-out list and reached for his phone again.

As conditioned as Neibolt had become to verbal abuse over the phone, he was totally unprepared for the blast of profanity that he received when Detective Rudy Hernandez answered his home phone.

"For Christ's sake, Rudy!" Neibolt blurted out when Hernandez finally paused for breath. "What the hell's the matter with you? This is Jerry Neibolt at the station."

Neibolt listened, shaking his head as an apologetic Hernandez calmed down and explained about the phone calls he had been receiving all evening. Then, as Hernandez listened in shocked silence, Neibolt relayed the information he had so far on Meiko's call.

"Holy Jesus, are they okay?" Hernandez whispered when Neibolt finished.

"I don't know. Just a second, I think Mary's getting a report now from one of the units at the scene."

Neibolt keyed his console for the running log on the case and quickly scanned the lines of information fed into the system by the dispatcher. Four Adam and Nine-Thirteen Charles had arrived less than two minutes earlier, so the information was understandably brief.

"Sounds like Meiko's all right," Neibolt said, "but she's got a fairly severe head wound. Sheffield took a shotgun round in the upper leg from the son of a bitch, but he's alive. They've got the paramedics rolling now."

"Who was it?" Hernandez growled, caught in a turmoil of emotions. He knew why Neibolt was calling.

"A downtown puke named Pinko Rutsche." Neibolt paused. "Listen, buddy, I need you down there at the scene." Neibolt waited for a response. Nothing.

"Rudy . . ." he started again.

"Get Andersen."

"I can't, man. I've been trying his place for the last ten minutes. We've got to get a detective out there."

"I can't leave," Hernandez said softly, anguished by the conflicting need to protect his family from the voice on the phone and the knowledge that somebody in the department needed his help.

"Jesus, Rudy. I've got to get somebody out there before the Watch Commander fucks things up royally!" Neibolt sucked in his breath and closed his eyes as he realized what he had said into the tape-recorded phone. Too late now, he thought to himself, shaking his head sadly.

"Look, tell me what you've got, and I'll try to run it from my house until you get hold of Andersen, or until I can get one of my brothers to come over and stay with the family."

"Okay," Neibolt agreed. "As far as we can tell, this guy Rutsche made some threatening phone calls to Meiko—"

"What?!"

Neibolt suddenly made the connection. Goddamn it! he thought, I must be getting senile. Can't even put one and one together when it's kicking me in the face. "Yeah, that's right. Jesus, Rudy, I didn't even think—"

"And you're sure they got him?"

"Hell, yes. Meiko cut the bastard's guts out with a Japanese butcher knife and Brian nailed him with a three-five-seven. They wasted him good."

"All right!" Hernandez laughed enthusiastically, feeling an immense pressure lift away. "Listen, buddy, do me a favor. Call the guys at the scene and find out if Meiko knows for sure if it was the same guy that made the phone calls, okay?"

Neibolt agreed and keyed his desk mike. Two minutes later, he was back with Rudy.

"He sounds good for it," Neibolt said. "She's pretty confused and shook up, but she's pretty sure it's the same guy. Something about some shotgun shells and Jake Farber's shooting. She wants to talk with you and Andersen real bad," Neibolt added, not understanding but assuming that the information was important.

"You tell her I'll be at their place in twenty minutes," Hernandez said. "And in the meantime, keep trying to get hold of that goldbricking Andersen."

*   *   *

Thanatos sat in his car, almost totally hidden by the darkness and the other cars parked along the street, and watched carefully through the night-vision scope as Hernandez stepped out of his house, waved at someone inside, and then ran out to his car. The terrorist slid down in his seat as Hernandez drove past, and then waited another five minutes before he sat up and reached for the ignition key. It took him another few minutes to get to a certain telephone booth at a closed gas station. Checking his watch again, he dropped coins into the telephone and dialed a number.

"Mrs. Hernandez?"

"Yes?" The voice was hesitant.

"Mrs. Hernandez, this is Officer Prichard from the police department. I'm relaying a message from Detective Hernandez."

Juanita Hernandez smiled at the sound of the polite officer's voice, and at the respect she could hear when he mentioned her husband's name. It made her feel warm and proud, causing her to forget about the horrible phone calls that had driven her husband into fits of helpless rage.

"Yes, go ahead, officer," she said kindly.

"Ah, yes, ma'am. Apparently one of the girls in our crime lab, Meiko Harikawa, was involved in a shooting incident. I guess she's still pretty upset, because Detective Hernandez said for me to call you and ask you to come out and stay with her for a couple of hours . . . and to bring the younger girls?" The voice added the last phrase hesitantly, as if not sure of the message.

"Of course, you tell Detective Hernandez"—she smiled to herself—"that I will come right away. Do you have the address?" She listened, writing quickly on a scratch pad near the phone. "We're on our way right now," she said, and hung up the phone.

Thanatos had been back in his previous surveillance position for less than two minutes before he saw Mrs. Hernandez and two young girls walk out of the front door, clad in light coats. He moved the visible field of the scope from face to face as they opened up the garage door.

Wonderful. He smiled to himself with malicious satisfaction.

He had not wanted to risk arousing the woman's suspicions by providing a reason why the older girl should remain at home. If the older girl was still in the house, his plan for the distraction of Detective Rudolfo Hernandez was certain to be highly effective and satisfying. If she was not there, then the house should be empty and there were other alternatives.

He left his car and moved rapidly toward the side of the house as soon as the old four-door station wagon with Mrs. Hernandez and her two daughters turned the corner. The time factor on this one was going to be extremely tight. He figured on twenty-five minutes at the outside. Anything longer and the risk became unacceptable.

As Thanatos entered the side gate quietly, watching for any sign of a curious neighbor, he thought about the two officers who were no longer in a position to make a positive identification of the fake Bob Saladin. The only uncertainty remaining now was the newsman, Paradee. In spite of the urgent warning by the Committee, Thanatos was almost certain that neither Paradee nor the white-haired Sergeant Lagucii had seen enough of his face beneath the ski mask to make an identification. Still, there was a chance . . .

He was uncomfortably aware of a conflict. There was the concern of the Committee that he not be identified and apprehended until Balefire had been successfully set into motion, versus his own personal concern that he not be identified at all. If he could be identified, he knew he would have to sacrifice his plan to retire on the California coastline. But only if it was absolutely necessary, he reminded himself, as he tried the knob to the side door of the garage with his gloved hand. There were other alternatives that the Committee would not have to know about. The time was almost at hand. Too close to fail now.

The knob turned and the door swung open on hinges that squeaked slightly. Thanatos made a last adjustment of his ski mask and then moved purposefully through the darkened garage toward the entrance to the house. He stopped at the door, put his hand on the knob, and listened carefully. No sounds of movement. No lights coming through the crack in the door jamb.

He pulled the door open and stepped noiselessly onto the linoleum floor, hearing as he did so the unmistakable sounds of a television set in one of the back bedrooms. American children are so very predictable, he thought, as he continued to move silently through the meticulously neat rooms. The Browning was out of the holster now, insurance against the possibility that Hernandez had requested one of his male friends or relatives to watch the house while he was gone.

When Thanatos finally reached the doorway to the far back bedroom, he took one quick look around the corner of the door jamb and then quietly slid the heavy automatic pistol back into its holster. A weapon would not be necessary.

One pair of bare legs, clearly female, were lying on top of the bed, which faced toward the far end of the room where a small color television was blaring.

Ramona Hernandez was lying comfortably on her bed, wearing her favorite hip-length silky nightgown that had been a secret gift from her boyfriend, sipping from a cold can of diet soda, and totally absorbed in the antics of a pair of comedians while she absentmindedly brushed her long, shiny hair. She didn't hear the soft footsteps. She became aware of the terrorist's presence only when a strong gloved hand clamped hard over her mouth. Her eyes bulged as she saw the masked face.

She tried to scream, couldn't, and then tried to twist away from the other hand that circled under her waist. She was thrashing wildly with her arms and legs, her back to the black-clad intruder, feeling helplessly exposed with her night-gown bunched up around her rib cage, when the hand clamped over her mouth suddenly released. She took a deep breath to scream, and then gasped as the inner elbow of the solid arm pulled tightly into her throat beneath her chin. She felt the arm grasp at something behind her head, then the other arm came around behind her neck, and the room disappeared in a sudden constricting, suffocating blackness.

Thanatos released the carotid choke hold immediately, allowing the girl to fall limply back onto the bed. He adjusted her so that she was lying flat on her back, arms at her side, and then checked her pulse. Steady. Good.

Leaving her on the bed for a moment, the terrorist rummaged through the girl's dresser drawers, coming up with a handful of nylon pantyhose and a single white cotton sock. He used the nylons to tie the girl's feet to each of the short bed posts at the foot of the bed. Two more nylons were used to tie the girl's hands together and secure them to the headboard. He placed the sock carefully in the girl's slack mouth, making certain the air passageway was not accidentally blocked. Another nylon stocking was tied around her mouth to keep the sock in place. The girl would be able to breathe through her mouth, but any attempts to scream would be considerably muted.

Thanatos double-checked his knots to make certain he hadn't interrupted any blood circulation. Then he pulled a folding knife out of his pocket and opened one of the stone-sharpened blades.

The blade cut through the thin fabric of the nightgown cleanly, exposing skin between the girl's breasts and all the way down to her lower abdomen. Two more cuts at the shoulders and the terrorist was able to pull the garment out from underneath the girl. The knife blade slid carefully under narrow strips of nylon at each hip, and the panties joined the remains of the nightgown on the floor.

Thanatos allowed himself a few moments to enjoy the fullness of the girl's firm body, remembering how she had looked in her bathing suit the day before. Then he got up from the bed and began to search through the numerous bottles and jars on her dresser. Finding what he was after, he returned to the bed and reached over to switch off the bedroom light.

Illuminated now only by the flickering patterns of colored light from the television set, the softly breathing, selectively tanned body of the girl took on a crude, erotic appearance. Thanatos removed the cap from the bottle and poured the oily contents over the firm curves and fleshy valleys. He placed the empty bottle of perfumed oil on the floor. Only then did he remove the glove from his right hand.

Ramona Hernandez regained consciousness slowly, unable to realize immediately where she was or what was happening. She realized it was almost totally dark, and she couldn't seem to breathe very easily. She tried to move and realized that her hands were secured and so were her legs. Her heart was pounding, and she was breathing heavily. Then she became aware of the hand sliding smoothly across her stomach, coming around the outer curve of her left breast, and moving firmly against the sensitive nipple.

She jerked convulsively, trying to twist herself away from the terrifyingly frictionless hand now moving across the liquid surface of her trembling, heaving chest to caress and squeeze the other hardening nipple. She couldn't comprehend her emotions—the terror and spine-tingling fear mixed uncontrollably with the growing sensations of excitement and arousal. She could feel her breasts swelling tightly against the slipperiness of the slow, patient, circular movements of the hand, and she fought unsuccessfully to blank out the instinctive, involuntary reactions, vaguely aware that she was moaning sporadically.

She tried to stare into the flickering colored darkness to see a face, but all she could see was a large shadowy form that suddenly shifted heavily on the mattress. Then she tensed, gasping and whimpering helplessly, as she realized that the hand was moving downward.

Thanatos allowed his hand to slide to a slow halt along the trembling surface of the oily, firmly muscled thigh. He brought his left hand up to the eye slits in his mask and checked the time. Then, increasing the pressure of his right hand against the throbbing silky flesh, he began to reach for his belt buckle with his other hand, only partially aware of the subtle change in the sounds coming from the gagged mouth as he listened with equal intensity to the sounds of the street outside.

The large muscular male was lean, sunburned and stringy-haired from years of exposure to the sun and the saltwater that propelled his short Fiberglas surfboard. He entered Sergeant Walter Andersen's house by prying a partially opened kitchen window, and he survived the entry only because in the darkness he faintly resembled one of the Andersen girls' less intelligent boyfriends. He came through the window with the heavy metal pry bar still held tightly in his hand. Thus, it was the intruder's last-minute decision to wear the Halloween eye-mask that saved his life.

The overaged surf bum entered the window confidently. The voice on the phone had carefully assured him that he would find a collection of gold coins and a small, faggy resident who wouldn't put up much of a fight at all.

Instead of the promised easy victim, the intruder found himself staring into the unbelievably huge barrel of a .45 caliber automatic held in the steady, extended hand of a man who looked exactly like a towering, infuriated, protective, streetwise cop who was savagely intent upon hurting people who threatened his daughter on the phone and then came in through his kitchen window with a potentially lethal weapon.

Stunned and frozen into total immobility, the would-be burglar dropped the pry bar and made no effort to avoid the hand with the combat knife that reached to cut the black mask away from his face. He stared hopelessly at the smoldering eyes and saw a flicker of something that he misinterpreted as being sympathy. In reality, Andersen's eyes simply registered the fact that he had never seen this particular individual in the company of either one of his daughters.

The unmasked, smiling face tried desperately and unsuccessfully to avoid the slashing frame of the automatic. The rectangular chunk of milled steel caught the young man solidly just below the left eye, crushing cheek bone, jaw bone, and back teeth. He dropped at Andersen's feet, mercifully unconscious and unaware of the damage to his once-handsome face.

Jody and Martine Andersen came downstairs long enough to confirm their father's assumption that the unconscious and bleeding man was a total stranger. Martine was young enough to be intrigued by the fact that a blond-haired surfer had made an obscene phone call to her sister and had then tried to break into their house. She was ordered back upstairs. Jody, on the other hand, still had the memory of the obscene voice fresh in her mind. She took one look at the mangled face that was bleeding steadily from the mouth and nose onto the kitchen floor and required no further urging to return to her room to keep a close eye on her sister and sedated mother.

Andersen waited until both of his daughters were upstairs. Then he handcuffed the limp hands of the sprawled man behind his back, closing the steel ratchet cuffs tightly around each wrist, and went out to the garage to open the rear door of his unmarked detective unit.

Considering the disabling extent of the injuries Andersen

had inflicted, the handcuffs were redundant and unnecessary. It was highly unlikely that the intruder would regain consciousness soon or be in any condition to escape. Andersen would not have bothered to use the cuffs, in spite of the departmental regulations mandating their use in every felony arrest, except for the fact that they also provided a useful handhold.

Returning to the kitchen, Andersen reached down and grasped the handcuff chain in one hand and the intruder's wide leather belt in the other. Lifting the hundred and sixty pounds of limp flesh, he walked back to the garage and heaved the flaccid body head first into the back seat of the unit, calmly indifferent to the solid thump made by the head as it struck the far door.

Andersen was in the process of filling out the short booking form, having advised the supervising detention officer that the still unconscious suspect in the holding cell would require medical attention, when he overheard two patrol officers talking about the shooting at Sheffield's house. Five minutes later, having interrogated both officers and then bursting in on a relieved Neibolt in the Watch Commander's office, Andersen was back in his unit and racing madly toward the townhouse complex.

Hernandez was standing inside the doorway of Sheffield's home, humming cheerfully to himself. He periodically glanced down at the blood-smeared body of Pinko Rutsch while continuing to write in his field notebook. He nodded and grinned at the sight of his winded supervisor as Andersen brushed past the officer guarding the front gate and walked quickly to the door.

"Glad to see you could make it, Walt," Hernandez said, waving the glaring sergeant into the hallway. "You're just in time to witness the grand finale of Pinko's criminal career." He gestured down at the grotesquely deflated body with the hands still clutched under the torn draining belly. The toothy smile on Hernandez's tanned face was oddly inconsistent with the icy gleam in his eyes.

Andersen took in the thick pools of blood on the carpet and the ragged bullet holes in the bathroom door. Then he looked across the room at the shattered sliding glass door next to the couch where Meiko was seated, still wrapped in her bathrobe, talking to a uniformed officer who was writing furiously in his leather-bound notebook.

"How's Sheffield doing?" Andersen asked, ignoring for the moment his detective's inconsonant attitude of amusement. It was readily apparent that Hernandez, as expected, had the scene well under control.

"He should be all right," Hernandez said, suddenly turning serious. "Paramedics got the bleeding stopped and ran him down to Pacifica a few minutes ago. They said he's got about fifteen holes in his right leg and hip, but they're pretty sure there wasn't any major nerve damage. Meiko got a tourniquet on him before he lost too much blood."

"She okay?" Andersen gestured with his head toward Meiko, who was holding a bloody towel against the side of her head as she talked.

"Yeah, she's one tough little broad," Hernandez said, grinning again. "Paramedics checked her over. We're going to get her over to the hospital in a few minutes."

"So what happened?" Andersen demanded.

"This asshole," Hernandez said, pointing down at Pinko, "apparently broke into their place yesterday evening while they were out on Guyerly's shooting. Meiko thinks he must have pulled one of their spare house keys out of their dresser drawer. He used a key to get in this time. Anyway, he apparently made some sort of threatening call to her this evening while Brian was at the lab. Spooked her with some shit about pink toilet paper and some shotgun shells."

Andersen's eyebrows came up as he stared at Hernandez with a perplexed expression. Hernandez shrugged.

"Got me," he said, shaking his head. "All I know is that she and Brian seem to think he's got something to do with Branch and Farber. Anyway, she tried to make a call to the lab, couldn't get through, and then this asshole comes in through the front door claiming she's hiding a dope stash and tries to rape her."

Andersen felt the back of his neck start to tingle. He started to say something, but Hernandez continued talking enthusiastically.

"When old numb-nuts here saw Brian come around the

back door, he capped off a round at him, but Meiko says she
hit the shotgun before it went off. Probably saved Brian's
life. Pinko knocked her down and was reloading when she
tried to deball him with that goddamned meat knife of hers.
Damn near did it, too. Then ol' Sheffield comes busting in
through the glass like the fuckin' cavalry and empties a Smith
into him at point-blank range. Even our mad scientist couldn't
miss a target like that. That'll teach this asshole to go around
making obscene phone calls to cop families.'' Hernandez
smiled approvingly.

"What are you talking about?" Andersen demanded, the
expression on his face shifting from perplexity to a sudden
anxious concern. He could feel the cold tingling feeling
spreading down his spine. "I thought you said he made a
threatening call to Meiko?"

"Yeah, I did," Hernandez admitted, looking slightly
sheepish. "But I got a couple of calls earlier this evening.
Same type of thing, except he wanted to know when I'd be
gone so he could come after Juanita and the kids." Hernandez's
voice drifted as he realized that Andersen's face had gone
deathly pale. "What's the matter?" he asked, his chest starting to tighten, uncertainty replacing his feeling of satisfied
revenge.

"Shit, I just laid out a guy in my house not more than
twenty minutes ago," Andersen whispered, furiously trying
to think, to put everything in some sort of logical sequence.
"He tried to come in through the kitchen window. We got the
same kind of calls earlier this evening. Wanting to know
when I was leaving, talking about Jody."

"Hi, Walt. Is it all right if I come in?" a shy voice asked.

Both Andersen and Hernandez turned sharply and stared.
Juanita Hernandez was standing hesitantly outside the front
door, her two younger daughters craning their heads around
her blocking arm, trying to see inside the house.

"What are you doing here?" Hernandez yelled, running up
to the doorway and staring at his startled wife. She stepped
back instinctively, the confusion evident on her warm, trusting face.

"You . . . you asked us to come here," she finally managed to say, unable to understand what she had done to anger
her husband.

"What?!"

"The officer . . . ah . . . Prichard," she finally remembered, her voice shaking. "He said you wanted us to come here and help look after one of the crime lab girls. Meiko."

"We don't have an officer named Prichard!" Hernandez looked wildly around and saw his two younger daughters cowering back against the wall of the house. "Where's Ramona?" he demanded.

"She's back at the house. She didn't want to come." Juanita Hernandez started to explain, and then she remembered the phone calls. "Oh, no," she whispered, suddenly understanding. She started to say something else, but her husband had already rushed past her, running for the gate.

"Rudy!" Andersen yelled, and then gave up as first Hernandez and then his wife disappeared through the gate. He started after them, then stopped. "Mackerson, get out here!" he yelled back toward the house. The patrolman who had been interviewing Meiko stuck his head through the doorway.

"You watch these two girls," Andersen yelled, pointing at the two younger girls who were clumped together in an uncertain huddle next to a tree. "Keep them out of that house." He hesitated. "No, take them to my place. You stay with them every second until I get back. And you"—he pointed at the rookie officer who was supposed to be guarding the gate, but was now staring confusedly at Hernandez and his wife as they fumbled frantically with the locked doors of their black Mustang—"you get on the horn and get more officers out here. Get someone to take Meiko to the hospital. Then call in O'Rorke and tell him to get the county teams rolling. Understand?"

"Yes, sir!" the young officer said, and nodded quickly.

"Good. Now get your ass in gear!" Andersen yelled, as he ran out through the gate, almost knocking over the Watch Commander and the area patrol sergeant who had wandered over from their cars where they had been drinking cups of coffee, curious as to the reason for all of the commotion. They turned and watched in confusion as Andersen jumped into the closest black-and-white and roared off after the tire-screeching Mustang.

Andersen waited until he had the Mustang in sight before

he took a hand off the wheel and grabbed for the microphone. "Oh-Five Delta to any unit in the vicinity of eighty-five-forty-four Raintree."

The radio crackled and a voice quickly came on the air.

"Eight-Twelve Sam, Oh-Five Delta. I'm in the area. What have you got, Walt?"

"Eight-Twelve Sam, respond to the location immediately. Suspect possibly attempting two-seventeen on One-Three Delta's daughter. Be advised Rudy's en route in a black Mustang, no radio. I'm about one behind him, Golden West and Ellis."

"Eight-Twelve Sam. Springdale and Bolsa," the patrol sergeant replied. "I'm rolling now."

Andersen tossed the mike aside and concentrated on his driving, trying to catch up with the taillights of the Mustang. In spite of a sixty-second lead and his skill as a driver, Hernandez was still delayed by the necessity of having to brake and look at each red intersection light, whereas Andersen had a flashing light bar on the overhead rack to announce his oncoming presence and intentions. By the time that Hernandez turned onto his street, Andersen was no more than ten seconds behind.

Andersen turned the corner in time to see Hernandez take his own front door off its hinges with his shoulder, the momentum of his enraged charge splintering the thin wood of the door frame and sending the gun-wielding detective crashing into his living room. Andersen accelerated up onto Hernandez's lawn, braked and bailed out of the unit in time to catch Juanita Hernandez coming around the Mustang. He held her back long enough to go in through the door ahead of her, thumbing the safety off his .45 as he stumbled over broken pieces of wood.

"Rudy! Where are you?" Andersen yelled, searching in the darkness for movement. He heard a choked sob in one of the back bedrooms and moved quickly down the hallway, Juanita Hernandez close behind. He came to the bedroom and saw Hernandez tugging frantically at the bonds that held the nude, still girl to the bed.

Andersen heard Juanita scream behind him, but all of his attention was focused on the girl and the tears flowing down Rudy Hernandez's face. Was she dead? He couldn't tell at first, then he saw the girl's legs start to tremble and he realized she was in shock. He managed to pull the frenzied detective aside long enough to use his pocket knife to cut through the stretched nylon stockings, freeing the girl to be taken into her father's arms and held tightly until Juanita was able to wrap her shaking and whimpering daughter in a blanket.

Andersen had to shake Hernandez several times before he was able to get him to release his daughter and let her lie back down on the bed, where she continued to cry softly, her eyes tightly shut and her legs and arms trembling.

"She's okay, Rudy," Andersen whispered, pulling the detective away from the bed so that Juanita could provide some soothing comfort. Hernandez was in no condition to soothe anyone. The veins on his neck and forehead were bulging with rage.

"I'm going to kill him," Hernandez rasped softly so that only Andersen could hear. "When I get my hands on the—"

The sound of two rapid gunshots out in the street galvanized the two officers into a frenzy of action, each grabbing frantically for his weapon and slamming against one another as they ran for the doorway. Hernandez was first through the front door, Andersen right behind him. They both heard the car engine turn on, and each saw the small dark Porsche screech away from the curb, making a sharp U-turn around the black-and-white stopped in the middle of the street with its windshield shattered.

Andersen ran for the unit in the street, immediately deciding not to shoot at the small, rapidly moving target in the darkness, unaware that Hernandez was sprinting toward the Mustang. By the time that he reached the black-and-white, Sergeant Michael Christopher had pulled himself out of the unit and was slumped against the open door, blood streaming from his shattered right forearm as he tried to pull at his holstered revolver with his left hand. He gave up and was trying to grab at the dangling mike when Andersen reached the car door.

Andersen took one look at the glassy-eyed field supervisor, then reached across the seat for the microphone just as Hernandez smoked the rear tires of the Mustang and accelerated down the street in pursuit of the Porsche.

"Oh-Five Delta. All units in the north. Two-seventeen, two-sixty-one suspect in a dark-colored Porsche, late model, proceeding southbound on Algonquin from Raintree. Be advised that One-Three Delta is in pursuit in a black Mustang. Eight-Twelve Sam is down at Raintree. Roll paramedics!"

In virtually every police agency in the United States, a mandatory operational procedure exists that is rarely understood by the public. When an officer is down, seriously wounded, and the suspect is seen fleeing, the injured officer's partner is obligated to abandon his comrade and pursue the suspect. The official justification is that the officers are duty-bound to risk their own lives in order to protect the public from the danger of a fleeing felon who will be seeking shelter. The unofficial justification is based upon the unwritten assertion that no one will shoot at a police officer and escape without being hunted down and brought to justice, wherever and however that may occur.

Andersen hesitated long enough to tell Christopher he would call in the location for the paramedics when there was a break in the radio traffic. Then he sprinted for the black-and-white he had left parked on Hernandez's front lawn. By the time he managed to get rolling southbound on Algonquin, the Mustang and the Porsche had disappeared.

"Oh-Five Delta," Andersen yelled into the mike as he continued south. "Eight-Twelve Sam is down in front of eighty-five-forty-four Raintree. Bullet wound in the right arm. I've lost the pursuit on Algonquin. Can you get Ten Henry over the area?"

"Oh-Five Delta. Be advised paramedics en route. Ten Henry is up and approaching from the south. Any units in the area, advise if you spot the pursuit."

Thanatos power-shifted the Porsche into two sharp turns, cursing himself for becoming distracted with the girl and allowing the time to run too close to the limit. He had barely gone out the back door when he heard the squealing tires and had been forced to hide in some nearby bushes until the occupants of the two vehicles—one of whom was the persistent Sergeant Andersen, Thanatos had noted thoughtfully—had run into the house. Then the terrorist had dashed across the street, only to be nearly run over by the police car turning the corner without using its siren or any light. He had been forced to shoot at the officer in order to escape.

And now I've got one of them behind me, he thought, reaching down to adjust the volume on the police radio. It was probably the father, Hernandez, in the black Mustang which he hadn't been able to shake so far. That was unfortunate because the father was undoubtedly irrational by now, and therefore exceedingly dangerous.

I should have executed both of them when they ran for the house, Thanatos decided, as he shifted again and jammed the accelerator of the small powerful racing car to the floor, grinning at the surge of horsepower. He knew his situation was precarious, invigoratingly so, but it was by no means critical. The Porsche could outrun anything the police department had to offer, especially on turns. Even the heavy-engined Mustang would have to brake and downshift to avoid spinning out. All he had to do was to lose them for thirty seconds, and he would be home free.

Earlier, in his reconnaissance of the target area, Thanatos had taken the trouble to preselect evasive-action routes on the Huntington Beach map in anticipation of exactly this type of situation. In doing so, he had looked for routes which offered a maximum number of sharp turns, alleys, and exit points. He had also looked for sites with tree coverage. The last was especially critical in the event he was spotted by the helicopter. He had heard Andersen's request for Ten Henry, and he was keeping a periodic check for the running lights of the helicopter as he wound the engine of the Porsche to the RPM red line.

Thanatos took a quick look in the rearview mirror. The lights of the Mustang were still there, almost a hundred yards back. Less than thirty seconds, he estimated, and he would be in the playground.

The excited voice burst out over the airwaves, jarring at the terrorist's ears.

"Seven Charles! Dark Porsche eastbound on Jannasee! High rate of speed!"

Thanatos spotted the black-and-white at the corner as he barreled through the intersection, ignoring the four-way stop signs. He took the next corner at full acceleration, feeling all

four tires tear at the pavement for traction as the Porsche's
extremely low center of gravity kept it from flipping over. He
didn't have to look back to know the black-and-white was in
pursuit. He could hear the screaming whine of the siren and
could see the reflections of the flashing red and blue lights in
his windshield.

Thanatos took his hand off the gearshift knob long enough
to tighten his safety belt around his waist. He was approaching the first cutoff. All he had to do was to put a little
distance between himself and the black-and-white, and he
would be free. He bared his teeth in an anticipatory smile and
tightened his grip on the shift knob.

"Oh-Five Delta, Seven Charles. Report your cross street!"
Andersen yelled into his radio mike as he accelerated the
black-and-white down Algonquin. Jannasee intersected Algonquin five blocks south of his location. Once he had the cross
street of the last sighting, he might be able to intercept the
Porsche.

"Seven Charles!" The officer in pursuit was young, excited,
and breathing fast. It was his first pursuit in a one-man unit
and he had the luck to draw a rape and attempted murder
against a police officer. Hot damn! he thought, I gotta get this
guy! "Suspect vehicle is turning south on Bayleaf from
Jannasee," he yelled into his mike.

Andersen could barely hear the voice over the siren in the
background, but the alert dispatcher with better reception
equipment helped out.

"All units involved in the pursuit, be advised the vehicle is
now southbound on Bayleaf from Jannasee. Any units in the
area, move in to intercept. Eight Adam, if you copy, be
advised the suspect vehicle is heading toward your last reported ten-twenty. Join in pursuit and intercept."

The dispatcher released the foot pedal on her microphone
and listened hopefully. No response. She had been trying to
contact Eight Adam, Barlowe and Parham, for the past fifteen
minutes, not realizing in the confusion of the evening that the
two officers hadn't reported in for over an hour. She would
have been more concerned except the unit they were driving
had a history of radio transmission problems, and neither of

the officers had checked out a pack-set. More than likely, they were in hot pursuit and were simply unable to report their position. She crossed her fingers hopefully and continued to monitor her screen.

Within five minutes of the dispatcher's transmission, four black-and-whites were on interception courses with the anticipated direction of the pursuit and suspect vehicles, Andersen's black-and-white included. The airwaves were being jammed with unit responses. Ten Henry was now over the area, directing the responding units on the basis of Seven Charles's flashing lights.

Hernandez was less than twenty yards behind Seven Charles and gaining rapidly on the less experienced officer, blindly intent upon taking the lead in the pursuit. He could see the taillights of the Porsche in the distance, and he prayed he would have at least one clear shot before the other units closed in on the bastard.

Thanatos entered his playground—an area within which he had memorized every street name, intersection, dead end and turnout. He felt his confidence surge, in spite of the fact that the radio traffic indicated there were now six black-and-whites in addition to the relentless Mustang and the police helicopter working to intercept and box him off. He had been only counting on darkness to provide him with the opportunity to disappear and go to ground. The raindrops beginning to bead up on his windshield were an added blessing, providing him with all of the advantage he needed. He turned on the windshield wipers and laughed out loud, enjoying the adrenaline thrill of a chase that he knew he would win.

Of all of the units involved in the pursuit, the helicopter represented the greatest source of concern for the terrorist, especially on the straight, open, and right-angled suburban streets that covered most of the coastline city. In this particular section of Huntington Beach, however, the roads were old, curved, and poorly maintained. In addition, the old-fashioned street lights were far apart, and in many cases were almost covered by a massive overgrowth of twenty- and thirty-year-old trees. And, just as important, all of the utility wires in this area were still above ground, looped across high poles that would prevent the helicopter pilot from coming down too low.

It was going to be a matter of exact timing, the terrorist knew, watching the road intently, both hands gripping the steering wheel as the rain began to fall faster. Ready now, he reached down and pulled the concealed microphone out of the glove compartment. He was rapidly approaching the split—a high hump in the road that suddenly branched off in three different directions as it dropped down on the other side. He checked his rearview mirror one last time, estimating that he had plenty of distance. Then he red-lined the tachometer as he accelerated up over the hump, continued to accelerate as he came down the back side, and then killed his lights after taking one last quick look at the road in front of him.

In the sudden and almost total darkness, the road disappeared into a swirl of black and grey shadows. Thanatos counted off the seconds, dropping the mike in his lap and reaching for the gear shift. At the count of four, he downshifted, braked, and then accelerated into a hairpin turn to the left, westbound. The tires started to slide, and he poured on the gas, playing the fishtailing with the steering wheel until the tires regained traction. He kept his foot on the gas pedal and the front tires centered over the white line—the only part of the road that he could see—and keyed his mike.

"Suspect vehicle eastbound at intersection off of Bayleaf!" he yelled into the microphone.

Seven Charles came over the hump fast, looked, and saw darkness instead of the expected taillights he had been following for the past five minutes. His eyes caught a shadowy movement going left, out of range of his headlights. Then he heard the radio broadcast and froze in indecision.

Still accelerating, the wide-eyed young officer started to turn left, changed his mind, tried to go right, and then lost it.

The slippery asphalt, the wide tires, and the high center of gravity built into the police unit, combined with the young officer's lack of experience in pursuit driving, sent the heavy back end of the patrol unit sliding. A back wheel caught the edge of a run-off ditch, dropped, and the unit flipped over instantly, rolling once, twice, and finally coming to rest upside down in a swirling cloud of plowed dirt.

Swinging head down in his shoulder harness, Seven Charles

heard someone yell out his call numbers. He tried to reach his mike, but couldn't find it, and then his spasmodically jerking hand found the ignition switch before he blacked out. By some miracle, the crumpled vehicle didn't explode.

Hernandez heard the screeching of tires and as he came over the hump, and then saw the tumbling black-and-white, its headlight beams swinging wildly in the darkness, as he came down into the split. In the split second he had to decide upon evasive action, he realized the Porsche's lights had disappeared. Having nothing to base a decision on, he arbitrarily spun the wheel of the Mustang to the left. He hit the accelerator just in time to miss the still sliding rear fender of the crippled black-and-white by less than three feet as he took the westbound branch of the road.

In the confusion that followed the spinout of Seven Charles, two of the intercepting black-and-whites barely avoided a high-speed broadside—which would have almost certainly killed all three of the officers involved—when the officers tried to respond to the conflicting suspect-last-seen directives coming out over the air. Each driver saw the other enter the blind intersection in time to swerve out of the broadside, but neither could avoid the other altogether. The units collided side-to-side in a resounding clamor of squealing tires, screeching sheet metal, and breaking glass. The total damage was two broken noses, several cracked and loosened teeth, one broken arm, two concussions, innumerable bruises, and two more demolished police units.

Up in the helicopter, the observer was screaming into his helmet microphone, trying to direct the remaining units back to the area where he had last observed the Porsche before it had disappeared into the trees. But every time he tried to transmit, other units on the ground covered with their own ten-twenties and last-seens.

"It's a fucking Chinese fire drill down there," he complained to the pilot, giving up his attempt to communicate with an exasperated slam of his palm against the Plexiglas bubble.

"Looks like we're the only ones left, partner," the pilot sighed, exaggerating his Texas drawl over the ship's intercom. "Hold on to your ass."

He kicked the rudder pedals and maneuvered the joystick to send the two-man Bell swooping toward the ground, oblivious of the observer's prayerfully muttered, "Oh, shit."

Thanatos checked his rearview mirror three times before he was convinced he had lost his pursuers, in spite of the helicopter observer's determined efforts to organize the now random crisscrossing search by the remaining black-and-whites. He parked the Porsche under a stand of trees in the entrance to a long gravel driveway and waited. He heard the helicopter roar overhead barely above tree level, and he saw the searchlight stab back and forth into a group of trees about two hundred yards away.

He continued to wait, impatient because sanctuary was only a thirty-second run, but cautious because during fifteen of those seconds, he would be out in the open and vulnerable. He watched the searchlight beam swing around to the west, waited a few more seconds to confirm the direction of flight, and then jammed the Porsche into gear.

He made the run with all lights on, and at the legal speed limit, hoping to blend in with whatever nighttime traffic happened to be on the street, just in case the helicopter turned around. He checked that there were no on-coming headlights in either direction, and confirmed that the helicopter had maintained a westerly search pattern. Then he made the last turn at normal speed, thumbed the small plastic transmitter, and drove the Porsche underneath the opening garage door.

He thumbed the transmitter immediately, and as the door shut, he settled down into the low seat with a relaxed sigh, confident that he had managed to conceal the Porsche without being detected. Now all he had to do was set the booby-trap devices and then work his way back to the south end of the city on foot—a time-consuming task in view of the need to avoid patrol checks—and retrieve his trustworthy Volkswagen. Child's play in comparison to the events of the last half hour.

Intent upon assuring himself every possible advantage, the terrorist took the time necessary to change his clothing. It was always possible that the Hernandez girl would be able to provide a description of the dark sweater and pants, and there was also the likelihood of evidence to consider. There was no need to take any hasty risks now. He left the gas cans stacked next to the rear door, taking a few extra moments to double-check the activating switches for the explosive devices before he turned the doorknob and pulled the small rear door open.

He stepped through the doorway and closed the door gently. As the activating switches clicked shut, he turned, and froze. An empty black Mustang was parked twenty feet away.

Being careful to keep his hands down and away from his sides, Thanatos turned his head slowly and saw the heavy-set figure of Rudy Hernandez step away from the corner of the building, the long-barreled revolver held out at mid-chest level in both hands. Thanatos remained motionless, watching the slow menacing approach of the detective, noting that the aim point of the revolver never shifted.

Hernandez came within twenty feet of the dark, unmoving figure and then stopped. Thanatos could see Hernandez's face clearly now. There was nothing in his expression except coldly focused, malevolent anger. There was no question at all as to the intent of the officer.

"Before you do that," Thanatos said evenly, forcing himself to remain absolutely still, "there's something you should know."

"Say it," Hernandez rasped, his lips pulled back in a snarl, anticipating the moment when he would squeeze the trigger for the first time. He had the impact points all picked out.

"Your daughter was a great piece of ass."

Something inside the detective's head snapped. His eyes widened with a savage uncontrollable hatred, and he lurched forward to drive the frame of the heavy Smith & Wesson through the man's face.

At the instant that the barrel of the revolver shifted away from the center of his chest, Thanatos twisted down and away. He rolled desperately sideways, as he jammed his hand underneath his jacket, trying to pull the Browning free of the leather holster in time.

Hernandez's first shot tore a chunk of asphalt out of the road less than an inch from the terrorist's left ear. The second slug would have ripped through his sternum and torn away a section of the aorta had he not suddenly twisted back the other way, firing the Browning automatic beneath his armpit

through his jacket three times in quick succession as the
intended death bullet from Hernandez cut a shallow furrow
across the terrorist's lower chest before ricochetting into the
darkness.

The three jacketed 9mm bullets caught Hernandez in the
stomach, right lung, and right collarbone, spinning him backwards and sideways onto the sloping wet hood of the Mustang.
He felt the cold painted metal against his teeth and tried to
push himself off, his mind still focused on vengeance. His
left hand—the only one that would respond—slipped on the
rain-slickened surface, and he rolled sideways, landing face
down and still on the wet asphalt.

Thanatos pulled himself to his feet, shaken but still alert,
and immediately bent over from the pain that was radiating
across his protesting chest muscles. He blinked his eyes and
shook his head repeatedly, trying to hold back the physiological effects of the shock which was beginning to weaken his
stomach and legs. Not now! Plenty of time to get sick and let
your legs tremble when you get to the safe house, he told
himself, shaken by the nearness of certain death, unable to
understand why a grazing wound hurt so badly and why the
rain had started to make whomping sounds around his ears.

Rotor blades.

The suggestion was made by deep-seated, survival-oriented
neurons in his brain. Look up, damn it!

He looked and saw the helicopter. The pilot had flared the
blades, causing the airship to rear back and hover about fifty
feet above the storage garage. The blades were sweeping
rhythmically and noisily through the water-laden air currents,
working to maintain position.

Thanatos started to raise the Browning, ignoring his torn
and protesting chest muscles. Then, before he could bring the
sights of the Browning to bear on the Plexiglas bubble, the
unbelievably bright searchlight beam leaped from the belly of
the ship to his face, driving the super-concentrated light into
his retinas.

The terrorist staggered backwards, blinded, unable to judge
angle or direction to fire at the damnable machine. He crouched
down, trying to shield his eyes, ignoring the loudspeaker
voice from above demanding that he drop the gun. Squinting
his eyes beneath one arm, he tried to get his bearings, but he

was only able to make out the small rear door of one of the rented garage spaces. An escape opportunity—a very dangerous one—formed in his mind. The distance factor was bad, but capture or surrender was unthinkable. Better death at his own hand.

Still crouched down, Thanatos steadied the butt of the automatic pistol against his leg and began squeezing the trigger, trying to aim for the upper edge of the door frame, barely able to see the rapidly appearing bullet holes climb the door in the horrible glare of the searchlight.

The explosion flung the terrorist backwards off his feet, tumbling, then sprawling loosely across the rough asphalt.

Thanatos survived the detonation only because the shape of the charges and the cement floor of the building vectored most of the blast force upwards, blowing shreds of roofing material, wallboard, car parts, and concussion waves up at the helicopter. The airship was tossing around like a toy, causing the observer to forget all about the searchlight stick as the pilot fought the controls.

Deafened, groggy, and still partially blinded, Thanatos neither heard nor saw the police helicopter tumble in the air and then churn noisily as the pilot used every ounce of skill and luck he possessed to keep the damaged aircraft from tearing itself apart while he searched desperately for a landing spot.

Dimly aware that he had survived and that time was still a critical factor, Thanatos scrambled on the ground until he found the Browning that had been wrenched from his grasp. Then, and only then, did he rise up on his shaky legs and begin to run.

By the time the helicopter pilot managed to put his severely mangled aircraft down in a barely controlled crash landing—the observer screaming "May day!" and radioing their position into his helmet mike all the way down—the terrorist had disappeared into the darkness, gaining at least a ten-minute head start before the black-and-white with Andersen at the wheel came screaming and flashing to a stop next to the Mustang and the burning remains of the building.

BALEFIRE

Minus 6 Days

Late Sunday Evening

2354 hours

It took the exhausted, blood-soaked and partially deafened terrorist almost three minutes to convince a fearfully stubborn Baakar Sera-te that it was an emergency. And that he needed competent medical attention right away.

The cutout had been very adamant at first, nervously responding in accordance to his specific and detailed instructions and also to a forboding sense of imminent and personal disaster. Thanatos was calling from his home. That was expressly forbidden. Sending a doctor to the house to treat minor wounds was out of the question. The contingency plans specified that all noncritical medical treatment would take place outside the city limits at preselected locations. Thanatos would have to travel to a designated meeting point. It would take time to make the arrangements. Didn't he realize he was endangering Balefire? Didn't he realize he was also needlessly endangering the function and the life of the cutout?

Thanatos ignored the cutout. In fact, he was barely able to hear the cutout's blasphemous words over the severe buzzing in his ears. He brought his fiery temper under tight control, and repeated his message.

The situation was an emergency. The bullet wound was superficial, but the explosion had caused severe dizziness and nausea in addition to the impaired hearing and numerous bruises and lacerations. He needed professional medical attention immediately. At the house. He was still bleeding and could not dress all of his own wounds. There was no question of walking or driving anywhere.

The terrorist then added the promise that a certain individual, who was worth less than a warm dog turd, would have his belly slashed open and his entrails yanked out by the handful if he didn't get the message through to the Committee right now! Did that individual understand? Good!

Thanatos slammed the phone down and collapsed back on the reddened bedspread. For the hundredth time, he cursed his decision to intensify the recommended diversion of the Hernandez family and to handle the assault himself rather than depend upon another unwitting surrogate. It had been a foolish and unnecessary decision that ultimately threatened a mission far more important than a thousand beautiful, young, dark-eyed women. The risk had been all the more foolish because the Hernandez girl, the terrorist readily admitted to himself, had been the decisive factor in his selecting and carrying out the Committee's cautiously authorized option.

The unacceptable possibility that he might not be capable of carrying out the final, most important task—igniting Balefire— tore at Thanatos far more than his numerous wounds and his dizzy, aching head. Less than six days remained. Too much was at stake, and too much had already been accomplished to fail now.

The concept of the Balefire Warning had originated among small groups of respected men who sat close together around hidden campfires and cursed the all-powerful nation that sent hundreds of warplanes and thousands of other modern weapons to their hated enemy with impunity, while at the same time loudly proclaiming a doctrine of peace to which all other nations should adhere. Gestation of the Warning had been far more difficult. The needs of secrecy, planning, materials, leadership, and money—especially money—had severely strained the resources and temperaments of men who were not accustomed to following through on their heatedly spoken words of the night.

In point of fact, the birth of the Warning would simply have not occurred—dying instead from the insidious diseases of disorganization, inertia, and tribal rivalry—had it not been for the announcement that the same high-minded nation would host the 1984 Olympic Games in Los Angeles, a city readily identified with the Zionist cause. At once, the burning resolve was reignited. A group of men with political connections came together in a secret place. Money was pledged. A second group of professional men with sympathetic ideals and convenient places of residence were selected to comprise the Committee. The rough outlines of the Warning were formed.

A full year was allocated to set the stage. During that time, more meetings were held. Trade-offs between effectiveness and vulnerability were evaluated. A target was selected. The Committee members were extensively briefed and set into place, and the meetings began again. This time, however, the discussions centered around the minutiae of operational plans and the availability of desired resources with the understanding that money would no longer be a limiting factor.

Finally, it had come time for the most critical decision— the selection of a single man capable of fulfilling the goals and the objectives of the Warning. A man professionally competent above all others and psychologically driven to succeed against seemingly overwhelming odds. A man who would go forth as a single warrior, facing a modern police department of over two hundred police officers, well trained, well armed, and dedicated. A man who would expose their vulnerability and ignite Balefire.

The Committee had chosen well.

The man they ultimately selected to carry out their psychological assault upon a nation had already accomplished the first objectives of the Warning. The highly professional police officers, who were sworn to protect the target city, had been shaken and demoralized as the result of the unexpected attacks by a man who rose up out of the night, struck, and then faded back into the darkness. Hampered by regulations and the inherent limitations of their training, the officers tried to strike back, but succeeded only in outraging the very people they were sworn to protect—the uncomprehending citizens of Huntington Beach.

As the Committee had planned, one man had accomplished all of this and would accomplish much more, but not for the reasons the Committee would have liked to believe.

Like most other professional terrorists, Thanatos was very much aware that it was not the money but the act itself—the theatrics, the publicity—that drove him to risk his life against tremendous odds in order to attain a moment of pure, unparalleled accomplishment. The Balefire Warning was to be his moment, his time to step out on the stage and alter the flow of all that had gone on before. If the act were successful—as it must be!—there would be few in the world audience who would know who he was or even exactly what he had done.

But a few would know. A few men much like himself who would pass on the story to generations of those select few who would be given the opportunity to alter history itself! They would talk about him in small gatherings around concealed campfires in the cold desert, around wooden tables piled with saucers and drained cups. They would talk with wonder and pride about the man who had proven that the sprawling, rich, modern cities of the United States of America were helpless against a single man, a professional terrorist.

It was the secret itself, the secret supposedly known to only a few like himself, that made Thanatos laugh in spite of his pain. The ill-kept secret was that he, like the others, cared little or nothing for causes. No sense of nationalism or religious fever could drive a man like Thanatos. It was the act itself that offered the terrorist his sense of fullness and accomplishment. The cause, any cause, was simply a vehicle.

Thanatos smiled at his knowledge, and then closed his eyes against the pain as he poured the remaining portion of the iodine solution across the bleeding gouge in his chest. The gods are ironic, he decided, allowing a single girl with a warm beautiful body like so many others to be the cause of such problems. Accepting his agony as payment for his foolish error, Thanatos pressed the blood-soaked bandage tight against his chest, reviewing the details of the final objectives of Balefire in his mind as he waited.

The police response to the assault on Ramona Hernandez, the shootings of Patrol Sergeant Christopher and Detective Hernandez, and the downing of Ten Henry, was almost as violent and uncontrolled as the explosion which had initiated the terrorist's escape, far exceeding the Committee's most optimistic expectations.

Secure and comfortable in the Dana Point command center, the members of the Committee sat together and listened as their scanners and phone taps relayed the frenzied sense of confusion and the mindless anger of the police officers.

The Committee members had been listening with a sense of nervous anticipation from the moment that one of the technicians picked up Sergeant Andersen's pursuit of his vengeance-maddened detective on the patrol frequency. Alerted to the possibility that their reluctance to approve the terrorist's requested diversion might have been prophetic, the men hurriedly assembled to monitor the consequences of their decision. From the soft chairs surrounding the bank of communications equipment, the Committee had been able to listen to and visualize the sequence of chaotic events Thanatos had set into motion.

They listened with a sense of detachment when Andersen screamed for paramedics on his car radio, more intent upon listening for the announcement that their terrorist had been located or captured or killed. Once they were reasonably assured that Thanatos had escaped the massed pursuit, they listened with a more personal sense of accomplishment as more and more off-duty officers took to the streets in search of a suspect—and revenge.

The search for the terrorist increased in intensity as additional information from the scene started coming in over the radio. The dazed and badly shaken helicopter observer reported that the suspect, an adult male, had been armed with a pistol, make and model unknown. Spent casings found near Hernandez's Mustang were determined to be 9mm parabellum. Within a half hour of the broadcast, virtually every adult male on the streets, whether in or out of a vehicle, within a mile radius of the still smoldering storage garage had been stopped and thoroughly searched at gunpoint for a 9mm pistol.

Several of the searches were conducted by officers whose only means of identification was a loud, demanding voice, a badge hastily pinned to a shirt or jacket, and a loaded weapon extended out in both hands. This only served to further aggravate and terrify those citizens who were already convinced that Huntington Beach was taking on all of the unpleasant aspects of a police state. Many of those who were stopped tried to stand on their rights and refused to be searched. Immediately they found themselves being flung to the ground, their arms handcuffed behind their backs, and placed under arrest for interfering with the duties of a police officer.

Detective Rudy Hernandez had been worked on at the

scene by a team of furiously determined paramedics, prior to being rapidly transported to Pacifica Hospital where an emergency surgery team had already been alerted and was waiting. Almost exactly half an hour after the police vehicles, paramedic wagons, and fire trucks had converged on the burning storage garage, a suspect-last-seen broadcast came over the unit teleprinters. A witness had phoned in a report that an unidentified male, armed with an automatic pistol, had run down the sidewalk and entered a house on Claymore Street less than half a mile away from the scene of the burning building.

In a sincere attempt to be helpful, the dispatcher had broadcast the message to all of the police units in the field in addition to the SWAT team that was standing by for just such a situation. By the time the armed and eager SWAT officers arrived at the location on Claymore, fifteen patrol officers had already surrounded the house. They attracted the attention of the occupant with a bullhorn, and entered the house in a simultaneous crash of splintered wood and broken window glass. Suddenly, a second occupant, who fortunately was unarmed as well as unclothed, tried a frantic escape through the back door.

The SWAT team leader stomped into the house through the loosely swinging front door, ready to unleash his pent-up fury on the impatient officers, just in time to learn that the unsuccessful escapee from what was obviously a homosexual liaison was the oldest son of Councilwoman Adrian Hite.

The enormity of the compounded error was clearly evident in the voice of the officer who was trying to report to Dispatch without really saying anything over the public-monitored airwaves. The officer hesitated several times before he finally advised the dispatcher he would report in by phone, but the message came across perfectly clear to the members of the Committee, and they immediately broke into a relieved, loud, and sustained clamor of laughing, back-pounding congratulations.

Of the fifty-odd people working in the Huntington Beach police station when the distraught officer finally reported from a nearby phone booth, only one individual was totally oblivious to the turmoil taking place in the field. That one individual was sitting moodily in the locked basement computer room, surrounded by stacks of opened operation manuals, electrical circuit maps, and at least two hundred yards of rolled, crumpled, and torn computer pages covering virtually every square foot of available floor space.

Jeremy Raines, the civilian computer programmer who was responsible for the operation of the department's Command and Control System, sat before the jumble on his desk and glared red-eyed at the display screen of the unresponsive computer. Four partially drained cups of cold coffee and an ashtray filled with cigarette butts gave mute testimony to the number of solitary hours Raines had already spent in the secured room.

In spite of the frustrated look on Jeremy Raines's face, the young programmer had discovered several things. First, he had run an exhaustive test series on the link circuits for every terminal console in the Command and Control Room to determine if one of his dispatchers could have possibly bypassed the recording system. Conclusion number one: short of introducing a modified program into the mainframe to avoid the protection loops, a bypass was impossible. There was no indication at all that the protected computer had accepted any new programming data during the past one hundred hours of operation. Therefore, conclusion number two: there was no way the teleprinter message could have been sent through the HBPD dispatch system unless Jeremy Raines had done it himself. Which he hadn't. This logically led to conclusion number three: someone out there had a transmitter tuned to the restricted HBPD frequencies and keyed to their scrambler code.

The questions were who and how and why.

Why was not Jeremy Raines's problem, at least not at the moment, so he immediately narrowed his areas of interest. How wasn't likely to be all that difficult. There were only so many ways of tampering with a system designed by game-playing experts to defeat game-players. The who was going to be difficult.

Raines had already concluded that the computer was not going to be of any further help until he got his hands on a little more data. The thing to do was to start at the source. Releasing the last puff of smoke from another cigarette with a sound of renewed determination, he flipped through his rotary card file in search of a number, and then reached for his phone.

BALEFIRE

Minus 5 Days

Monday Morning

0935 hours

The first meeting that Sergeant Walter Andersen attended Monday morning was a command performance. He had been ordered to attend by the captain of the Investigation Division, who in turn had received his orders from apoplectic Chief Sager.

The meeting was held in the largest conference room that was available in the new Civic Center Building. Large as it was, the room barely held all of the attendees—the police chief, his three division captains, Andersen, the city administrator, the city personnel officer, the city public relations officer, the fire chief, eight administrative staff members, the entire city council, the mayor, and four delighted members of the local press.

With the notable exception of Andersen, every person in the room was either glaring at someone else or was waiting with barely repressed enthusiasm for the blood-letting to begin. Andersen simply stared at the opposite wall, the thoughts that were running nonstop through his mind having little, if anything, to do with the undercurrent of excitement and antagonism that permeated the room.

Sager started things off by standing up and pointing a thick, battle-scarred finger at the four reporters who had grouped together at the back of the room. "Who the hell invited them?" he demanded from the room at large, but he stared directly at the mayor and Councilwoman Hite.

"I did," Hite said, her eyes glistening with defiance.

"Get them out of here." The graveled voice spoke exactly the way that Sager would have spoken to a rookie officer.

"This is a public meeting. They have a right to be here," Hite retorted, her facial expression reflecting a mixture of confidence and blatant hatred.

Adrian Hite was still trying to recover emotionally from the recent shock of learning that her oldest son was gay, and that his previously well-kept secret had been exposed by last night's police raid which Hite was certain had been planned well in advance.

The 2:30 A.M. call from Sager had, without a doubt, been one of the most nauseating and disorientating moments of her life—and certainly the worst moment of her political life. In spite of Sager's insistence that her son's exposure had been the unintentional result of a citizen calling in an incorrect spotting of a suspect—Sager had offered and subsequently provided her with a tape recording of the call—and his personal assurance that the information regarding her son would not be released to the press, Hite was convinced that the raid on the house had been nothing more than an elaborately planned political maneuver.

From Hite's point of view, the damage was done whether Sager released the information or not. The reality of the situation was that the politically astute police chief now had a twist that could be used to destroy her political ambitions, if it was handled properly. And the trouble was, she knew exactly how she would handle that type of information if she were in Sager's position.

Adrian Hite was no stranger to political blackmail. She had been a willing and eager participant in the destruction of more than one opponent's political career. Thus, she assumed that Sager would not hesitate to use her son's unfortunate sexual preferences as a weapon if the right opportunity were presented.

The councilwoman's first impulse was to expose the incident herself, angling for a sympathy vote by portraying her son as a confused and helpless victim of police harassment. But that tactic, tempting as it was, could easily backfire. She knew that her liberal attitudes, political and otherwise, did not quite mesh with the prevailing views of the voters in her district on this particular issue. The safer approach would be to assess the damage carefully, remain alert for Sager's move, watch patiently for an opening, and make her own attack from a different direction.

"I have no intention whatsoever of discussing ongoing homicide investigations in the presence of members of the press," Sager said.

Before Hite could erupt into a tirade, the mayor quickly stood up. "I believe that we have already reached an understanding on this matter with the gentlemen—and lady," he added quickly with a brief smile, "in the back of the room. Everything discussed within this room will remain strictly off the record until such time as an item is specifically released in writing by the city administrator's office. I trust that is satisfactory with everyone present?" The mayor looked around, finally receiving a grudging nod of agreement from Sager and an even less enthusiastic nod from Hite, and then sat back down.

"Mrs. Hite," the mayor finished from his chair, "I believe you have something to say?" The sarcasm in his voice was readily apparent to everyone in the room.

"Yes, I certainly do," Hite smiled coldly, standing up and looking around the room. "I would like to start out by stating categorically that the recent actions by members of the Huntington Beach Police Department are a disgrace to our city as well as to our nation. In the period of one week," she continued determinedly before Sager could interrupt, "the police have succeeded in completely terrorizing every law-abiding private citizen in Huntington Beach. They have violated civil rights, state laws, the city charter, and common decency. And they have murdered—yes, that's right, murdered— four innocent young men in the middle of Main Street."

Hite paused to take a deep breath, daring anyone, especially Sager, to disagree with her. Sager simply sat in his chair with his arms folded, favoring the councilwoman with an expression he usually reserved for child molesters.

"We have had innocent and helpless women and children beaten," she continued. "Families dragged out of their cars at gunpoint. Doors of private homes broken in. All of these things supposedly justified by what our policemen call 'hot pursuit,' or 'suspicious circumstances,' or 'probable cause,' or even 'active investigation of a homicide,' " she added with a particularly venomous emphasis in her voice.

"In case all of this is news to any of the ladies and gentlemen in this room, may I suggest you read the headlines and articles that have been appearing in the newspapers during the past week or listen to some of the television commentaries. You might pay particular attention to the article which will appear in this afternoon's edition of the *Coast Telegram*. I'm speaking of an article written by Jack Paradee. He wrote it, I might add, instead of delivering it on his news show, because at the moment he is incapable of speaking. And the reason he cannot speak is because he was savagely beaten by a member of our fine police department who doesn't happen to believe in the Bill of Rights!" She emphasized these last words by slamming her fist on the table.

The room was totally silent.

"Oh yes," she started again, this time in a much softer voice, almost a whisper. "I almost forgot. I understand the civilian members of our illustrious police department are not above taking part in a little mayhem and murder either. It seems that two members of our crime laboratory staff"—she started to say that they happened to be living together without benefit of marriage, but changed her mind, realizing the sexual reference offered Sager a much too tempting opportunity—"decided to execute a confused young man who had the serious misfortune to knock on their door and ask for some money to feed himself. Obviously a heinous crime deserving of instant justice."

Andersen finally seemed to shake himself out of his lethargic stupor. He looked up at Hite as though he were only suddenly aware of her presence.

"Councilwoman," he said calmly, "it may interest you to know that these police officers you are describing have been subjected, and are still being subjected, to deliberate, premeditated acts of terrorism. That's right. Terrorism. To put it more plainly, an individual or a group of individuals is making a very determined and successful attempt to confuse us, frighten us, and kill us."

A clamor broke out in the back of the room, joined by most of the other attendees until Sager stood up and yelled, "Shut up and listen, goddamn it!" The clamor died down immediately, and Andersen continued.

"If you will carefully examine the dates and times involved, you will find we have had two officers killed and eleven officers seriously injured during the past week. Right now my senior detective is lying in an intensive care ward, losing blood as fast as he is taking it in. Last night he tried to apprehend one of those individuals I have described to you, after that individual assaulted his daughter in her own bedroom. What I am trying to tell you, Mrs. Hite, is that in every one of those cases you described, the actions of our officers, regrettable as they may be, have represented only a reaction to an assault upon themselves, their families, or their fellow officers. I am not saying their actions are excusable, but they are understandable."

"Sergeant, the only word that I can use to describe what you just said is paranoia." Hite spoke softly, staring at Andersen and shaking her head, her mind sharply alert now, waiting.

"No, Mrs. Hite," Andersen said, shaking his own head sadly, "not paranoia. What I have described to you has absolutely nothing to do with my imagination. We have collected a large amount of very real physical evidence in these cases. In fact, the 'homicidal' pair of criminalists you just described were in the process of cross-comparing this evidence when that 'confused young man' you described entered their home with a key to their door and a sawed-off shotgun. Fortunately, they survived and he did not. And I say fortunate in more than the personal sense. You see, with their assistance and that of the other members of the lab plus what remains of my detective squad, we are going to find the sons of bitches who are doing all of this, and we are going to put a stop to it."

"And just how do you plan on doing that, Sergeant?"

"I beg your pardon?" Andersen looked up at Hite quizzically.

"First of all, it is my understanding that your own rules mandate that any member of the department who is involved in the death of another individual is to be suspended from duty until the matter is fully resolved. I believe that the matter involving Mr. Sheffield and Ms. Harikawa is still under investigation. Is that not correct, Sergeant?"

Andersen turned his head and stared at Sager. The grizzled

chief stared back at Andersen, his jaws clenched, and nodded his head slightly.

"Oh, and we mustn't forget the question of your own duty status, Sergeant. I am also led to believe there is a man being incarcerated in the county medical center who received a broken jaw and a serious concussion as a result of being pistol-whipped by you only last night. I can't imagine that you would seriously think you would be allowed to return to duty until that matter is thoroughly investigated.

"And as for your investigation into the terrorism focused on our officers: I think that we have gone far past the point where we can expect an unbiased investigation into the circumstances of these cases by our own officers. I am, therefore, recommending that the city council immediately request that a panel of state or county law enforcement officials take over the entire investigation into these matters. And furthermore—"

Hite stopped in mid-sentence, staring with sudden apprehension and disbelief at the sight of Andersen, who had stood up and removed a small revolver from his belt. As she watched in frozen silence, Andersen broke open the weapon, emptied the rounds out of the cylinder, and then let the weapon fall out of his hand to join the clattering bullets on the table with a loud clank. A pair of handcuffs followed. He tossed his badge on the table in front of Hite, the leather case falling open and exposing the shiny gold shield with the three blue enameled chevrons.

"May I suggest that you try wearing that badge around the city at night, Councilwoman," Andersen said drily. "You may find it to be a very eye-opening experience." Then he turned and walked out of the room.

At a little after eleven o'clock that Monday morning, Andersen walked down to the end of the Huntington Beach pier and walked through the wide weather-beaten screen door of the Bait and Tackle Cafe. He nodded to the owner and then took a chair at the far corner table. Sager was already there, sipping reflectively at his coffee as he carved paper-thin slices from a small chunk of hardwood, using the heavy folding knife with the brass and wood handle his wife had given him for Christmas the year before her death.

The two law enforcement officers sat at the stained oak table for almost two hours, talking and sipping at their refills with an outward casualness that gave no indication of the seriousness of their discussion. Finally, Andersen stood up, shook Sager's hand firmly, picked up the familiar leather badge case from the table, and then walked back out the screen door.

It took Jeremy Raines seven phone calls before he was able to find a sales manager who had access to the data the communications chief was after and also had the necessary authority to discuss such matters.

Yes, the sales manager confirmed, there were a large number of law enforcement agencies throughout the United States who had purchased communications equipment that could use the specific high-band frequency utilized by the Huntington Beach Police Department for their teleprinter operation. That particular frequency was very popular, in spite of its rather limited range, due to its isolated position on the waveband. Very little interference from commercial or private broadcasting. Yes, most agencies had also ordered the scrambler option. The number? Seventy-five or so. Maybe a hundred. No, the scrambler code listing was not available. Security reasons; surely he could understand.

Jeremy Raines stubbed out his cigarette and closed his eyes in momentary frustration. Resigning himself to putting in the extra hours rather than trying to push the issue, he asked another question.

The complete list of agencies who had purchased communications equipment from the company? Certainly, no problem there. In fact, if a phone patch could be arranged, the entire list could be remote printed on the department's AJ-73 system. No, no problem at all. Glad to be of service.

Raines waited for the dot-matrix printer to stop churning out paper before he tried to read the last number. Four hundred and seventy-two. He decided to try to narrow the odds a little first, before he started on the telephone. He turned to his desk console and began composing a standard message, classified urgent, requesting information on any communications equipment of the following makes and models, containing any of the following crystal frequencies, and including any one of the following scrambler capabilities, lost or stolen during the past twelve months. Then Raines started to feed in the agency code numbers that were included on the salesman's list.

Almost two hours later, Jeremy Raines sat back, lit another cigarette with a sweaty hand, double-checked the screen message, and then hit the SEND key. Instantaneously, four hundred and seventy-two law enforcement teletype systems throughout the nation began to type out the HBPD request on rolls of teletype paper.

Three hours and forty-five minutes later, Jeremy Raines had some numbers he could deal with. Sixty-seven agencies had failed to respond to his teletype request, and therefore still remained on his list of possibles. He thought momentarily about the telephone bill the department was going to receive, shrugged, and then reached for his phone to begin calling long-distance numbers.

At five-thirty that Monday afternoon, Jeremy Raines struck pay dirt in a manner that was totally unexpected. Thinking at first that he had dialed a wrong area code, he tried again and got the same message from a now slightly irritated receptionist. Still uncertain of exactly what he had, Raines went back and cross-referenced the address against his own copy of the Agency Code Book and made a very interesting discovery.

Once again, Raines called the communications equipment company.

"Mr. Manfelt," Raines said pleasantly when the sales manager finally came on the line, "I thought you might be interested to learn that your company sold a couple hundred thousand dollars worth of restricted police communications equipment to a town in New Mexico with a population of twenty-seven that has never had a police department and has never heard of your company."

Late Wednesday afternoon, three days after the surge of violence at the burned-out storage garage, a private meeting was held in the living room of Brian Sheffield's and Meiko Harikawa's townhouse.

The setting for the meeting was not likely to appeal to most meeting goers. Less than seventy-two hours earlier, the living room had been the site of an attempted rape, an attempted murder, a shooting, a stabbing in self-defense, and a thorough crime scene investigation conducted by Lee Spencer, Bob Dorsey, and a team from the sheriff's department. The end result was a room that met, or possibly exceeded, the most rigorous definition of the word 'carnage.'

In spite of Meiko's efforts, the living room still bore the unmistakable look of a battle scene. The broken sliding glass door had been temporarily boarded over with a four-by-eight piece of plywood. Most of the dried blood had been cleaned up from the floor and walls of the downstairs bathroom, but the thick, light brown, living room carpet still had ominously dark stains in several areas. The five splintered, clustered bullet holes in the lower portion of the downstairs bathroom door had been temporarily ignored. All in all, the living room was not the most pleasant environment within which to hold a meeting; however, it suited this particular group just fine.

Sheffield was sitting on one of the couches, his heavily bandaged leg resting on a pillow-covered foot stool, per the doctor's explicit orders. Dan Branchowski sat groggily in his wheel chair next to Sheffield, his head shaved and bandaged.

Keith Baughmann, Michael O'Rorke, Ed Malinger, Bob Dorsey, and Sam Kretcher sat on a mixed collection of chairs and cushions. Meiko, Michelle Andersen, and Juanita Hernandez worked quickly in the small kitchen to fix drinks for everyone before they joined the group, taking the remaining couch.

The Andersen and Hernandez girls were upstairs in the master bedroom, making a halfhearted attempt to get interested in the night's tv offerings. The girls had been deliberately and emphatically excluded from taking part in the meeting, but they had been given no choice in the matter of being present with their parents that evening. Until the nightmare was over, Juanita Hernandez and her daughters would stay with the Andersens. None of the girls would be left alone or allowed to go anywhere without an armed escort. Understandably, in view of their recent experiences, not one of the girls complained. They simply arranged themselves on the large bed and floor, turned the tv down, and tried to listen in on as much of the downstairs conversation as possible.

Ramona Hernandez had been sent upstairs with the other girls in spite of her argument that she had a right to take part in the meeting. The young girl had demonstrated a remarkable degree of inner strength and maturity, character traits that everyone agreed she had inherited from her father.

Andersen stood next to the blackboard he had borrowed from a cooperative high school coach, waiting until everyone had a drink and chair.

"Before we start," he said. "We just received word from the hospital a few minutes ago that Rudy's condition has stabilized. They managed to get the internal bleeding stopped, and his pressure's been steady for almost twelve hours."

Andersen smiled at the subdued cheering and words of encouragement offered to Juanita Hernandez. Everyone in the room knew Rudy was still in critical condition, but they all tried to put on an optimistic front in spite of their generally somber and worried feelings.

"What about Barlowe and Parham, Walt?" Baughmann asked. "Any more word on them?"

"No." Andersen shook his head. "Patrol's been working an expanded street-by-street search from their last known location. Nothing so far."

The fact that the two patrol officers were still missing with their unit was almost as damaging to the morale of the group as it was to the squads of patrol officers out on the street, searching for their comrades. It was as though the darkness had swallowed the pair. Andersen sensed the deteriorating mood of the group and hurried on.

"All right. Let's get started. First off, are we missing anyone who should be here?" He looked around at the quiet group, waiting for suggestions.

"What about Lee?" Bob Dorsey asked, curious about the obvious absence of his dependable ID Unit partner.

"And Herb Gilcrist. He's got a definite interest in this," Sheffield offered, referring to the calls that the lieutenant, like the others, had received.

Andersen nodded. "Lee and Herb have already been contacted. They've agreed to play this thing straight. That'll give us two dependable sources of current information from the station—administration and the lab."

The group nodded at each other approvingly. In spite of their generalized state of frustrated depression, they all seemed to realize that Andersen's determination and organization might give them a chance. That was all they wanted.

"Anyone else?"

"What about Lagucii?" Malinger suggested, not bothering to conceal the distasteful look on his face.

"Fuck Lagucii!" Branchowski's rough voice burst out weakly. Then he looked around sheepishly and apologized to the three women in the group.

"I agree completely," Meiko said, and even Juanita joined in on the brief laughter.

"All right," Andersen smiled. "Any more . . . ah . . . suggestions?"

"Be nice to have some support from the chief on this," Baughmann said, the bitterness evident in his voice. There was a general murmur of agreement throughout the group. Only Andersen and O'Rorke remained silent.

"Don't count Sager out on this," Andersen suggested quietly. He started to say something else, and then changed his mind. His face turned serious.

"Before we go any further," he began, "I want to be certain everyone here understands one thing: what we are intending to do is absolutely, unquestionably illegal. In reality, it is nothing more than a vigilante action, regardless of our own justifications and motives. If it blows up on us—and it could, make no mistake about that—we are totally on our own. We will receive no support whatsoever from the department. Is that clearly understood by everyone?"

Andersen looked from face to face, making a point of including his wife. The vocal confirmations were unanimous.

"At the risk of insulting someone, I want to emphasize this is an especially important consideration to four of us," he continued. He glanced again at each of four unresponsive faces. "None of these four have been personally involved in any of this yet."

"Yet?" Sam Kretcher asked patiently. "You saying we lack motivation, Walt?" he inquired, his eyebrows rising toward his balding forehead, his arms folded over the back of the kitchen chair.

"No, just giving you a last dignified chance to hang on to your careers, such as they are," Andersen replied, trying to suppress a grin.

Kretcher smiled, apparently satisfied. "In," he said.

"Ed?" Andersen looked over at the lanky photographer who sat sprawled across a large beanbag chair.

"I was looking for a job when I came here," Malinger shrugged. "Besides, I wouldn't miss the party for anything. Bound to get a Pulitzer for the photos."

"Bob?"

"My wife got an interesting call last night. She said the guy was pretty good at heavy breathing, but not very imaginative," Dorsey explained, ignoring Andersen's surprised look. "Besides, I've got to do something with all of my vacation time."

"You want her to move in here?" Andersen asked, looking concerned, but Dorsey held up a declining hand.

"I already suggested it. Even tried to make her take a trip back East to visit her mother. She told me to stuff it somewhere in the vicinity of my wallet pocket. That's what I get for marrying a girl out of the hills, I guess," Dorsey went on. "Say's she can out-shoot half the guys in the department, and she can't wait for the son of a bitch to show."

"Your decision," Andersen said, still looking a little worried. "Mike?"

O'Rorke favored Andersen with an indignant glare. "Let's get this turkey shoot on the road," he growled.

"Okay," Andersen nodded, relieved that part was over with. "We'll start with Brian. He'll give us a rundown on what we've got so far in the way of physical evidence."

"To begin with," Sheffield said, shifting painfully on the couch to hand a staple-sealed plastic bag to Branchowski, "we can rule out Toby Williker as being directly involved in Jake's and Dan's shootings. I called one of the guys at the coroner's tox-lab. He said they pulled enough morphine out of Williker's urine to dose half a dozen hypes."

"Heroin OD?" Kretcher asked, puzzled.

"No. Doc Pratola confirmed he was still alive when he got hit." Everyone looked over at Baughmann, who shrugged self-consciously.

"People at the lab figure it was a maintenance dosage—a series of injections to keep him unconscious, but not kill him," Sheffield explained when he realized everyone looked confused. "At that dosage level, he had to be comatose for several hours. No way for him to have done the shooting."

"So where the hell—" Branchowski started, still staring at the contents of the plastic bag.

"All three shots came from Williker's apartment window," Sheffield said. "I'm almost certain of that. Someone was cooperative enough to deliver the evidence." He pointed to the disassembled shotgun shell in Branchowski's hand. "It's a specialized hand-loaded buckshot round. Whoever put it together used a heavy cylinder of plastic to keep the shot clumped for a few extra yards before spreading out into a pattern. We don't have enough to test accurately, but Bob test-fired one of the two we found on our hot tub. The pattern narrowed down by almost fifty percent, which would fit with the distance and pattern at Jake's scene."

Sheffield hesitated, uncomfortable about discussing the mechanism of Jake Farber's death while his injured partner sat nearby. But Dan Branchowski didn't seem to be affected. He sat quietly, his face composed as he listened intently.

"I don't understand," Michelle Andersen broke in. "Why

would this Pinko Rutsche put those shotgun shells out on your patio if he already left one under Meiko's purse?''

"I don't think he had anything to do with those shells," Sheffield said. "Or the phone calls either, for that matter. It doesn't make sense. Why would he break into the house ~~once~~, ~~leave~~ a shotgun shell fired through Toby Williker's shotgun on the table under Meiko's purse, take an extra key out of our dresser upstairs, leave two shotgun shells out on the hot tub, and then come back later, bust in, and start yelling about a dope stash? If he thought we had cocaine in the house, he would have torn the place apart the first time.''

"Also, I'm pretty sure that his voice was different from the one on the phone," Meiko added.

"It has to be scare tactics," Andersen said. "Whoever pulled that deal off on you two was trying to scare you away from something. And I'm not talking about Pinko Rutsche either. It took someone with brains and imagination to pull that toilet paper trick. I'd say the guy who made the calls was the one who convinced Pinko there was dope in your house.''

"And paid him two hundred dollars for something," O'Rorke added. "I've busted that asshole more times than I can count, and he never had more than a couple of dollars on him. Ever.''

"The call we received wasn't from Rutsche," Andersen added. "Whoever it was, he was very calm, like he knew exactly what he was doing.''

"Same with mine," Meiko said, shivering slightly as she remembered the cold, distant voice.

"Ours too," Juanita Hernandez added quietly. "I answered the first call. Now that I think back on it, it was almost like he wasn't really interested, or really didn't care . . .'' She stopped, unable to continue with the part that involved her eldest daughter.

"And then what happened?" Andersen went on. "Somebody sends in a couple of throwaways to take Brian, Meiko, and me out of the picture. Or help us take ourselves out," he added ruefully.

"Except the guy who set up Ramona and then shot Rudy wasn't a dummy like the other two," Kretcher commented. "A guy who can lose six units and the chopper in a pursuit, get the jump on Rudy, take at least one round, blow up a building underneath the chopper, and then get away, is a couple of light years out of Pinko's and Toby's league.''

"That's right," Andersen nodded. "That's why I'm suggesting the guy who got to Rudy is the one we're after. One man."

"A terrorist," Baughmann nodded, relieved that someone else was finally willing to go along with his reasoning.

"One man taking on the whole police department? That's crazy!" Michelle Andersen blurted out, unable to restrain herself.

"Is it?" Andersen asked. "What kind of people are we trained to deal with? Drunks, dopers, petty thieves. People who flip out because they can't handle their lives any more. Wife beaters, child molesters, freaks, kids—how many times do we come across a professional? Even our homicides are almost always husband and wife, boyfriend and girlfriend, or dope burns. They blow up in an emotional flash, and then they run scared until we manage to pick up enough of the pieces to track them down. But this guy doesn't even come close to fitting that pattern.''

"Maybe that's what he's trying to make us think, though," Meiko offered. "Maybe he wants us to think that he's just a freak who's lucky enough to stay ahead of us so he can play with us instead of the FBI.''

"Either that, or he's just trying to spook us, put us into a holding pattern, while he sets something else up," Baughmann said.

"One thing for sure, the guy's a hell of a shot," O'Rorke commented. "Thirty to forty yards with a smooth bore at night with both guys moving . . .''

"I think he had help on that one, though," Sheffield said. "Like either a Starlight or a laser scope. More likely the laser.''

"You sure about that?" Kretcher asked. "Those things aren't all that easy to get hold of.''

"I'd bet on it," Sheffield nodded. "I couldn't figure out why there were fresh scratch marks on the barrel end of Williker's shotgun. Then I remembered a company in Fountain Valley that mounts laser aiming devices on shotguns for police departments. I called them up for the dimensions on the screw mounts, and then had Lee measure the shotgun.

The distance between the scratch marks matches exactly with the mounting points."

"You sure he used one of those things on us?" Branchowski asked, his voice sounding fatigued. "I don't remember seeing any red light beam."

"You wouldn't necessarily see the light," Sheffield said. "Usually only the dot, and you'd probably miss that unless you were looking for it. Oh, yeah, and one more thing," Sheffield added. "Don't just think shotguns. These scopes can be mounted on rifles, pistols, even a hunting bow. Same principle."

"Shit," O'Rorke commented.

"What about the rest of the stuff, Brian?" Andersen asked, no happier than anyone else in the room about the idea of being hunted by a moving red dot.

"Still working on it as best we can," Sheffield added ruefully. The idea of being suspended and locked out of his laboratory still hadn't settled well. "Ed's been shooting film all afternoon."

"I've got all of the latent cards on Farber, Guyerly, and Williker's scenes on negatives," Malinger said. "Lee's going to shoot the stuff he collected from this house and Ramona's bedroom. It'll take another six or seven hours to get everything blown up into prints. We'll do eight-by-tens so Bob won't strain his eyes, and it'll make it easier for the girls, since they're going to do some of the comparison work. I've still got the latents from Paradee's car and all of the victim and officer elimination prints to shoot. Then we'll get started on the shoe prints."

"Okay, fine," Andersen nodded approvingly. "Just so everyone understands what's going on. If the theory holds that one guy is doing all of this, then there has to be something that will link all of the incidents together. We're going to cross-check every violent incident during the past week that involved a member of the department, from the standpoint of both physical evidence and the crime reports. We'll cross-reference the officer's past assignments, suspect history, and anything else we can think of to find that link."

"We'll work out of my house," Andersen went on when everyone nodded their heads in understanding. "The kids are going to help Bob with the latent comparisons. That'll keep

them busy and at home where we can keep an eye on them.
Michelle and Juanita are going to work with Brian and Meiko
on the crime reports and follow-ups. We've got a stack of
copies almost eighteen inches thick. Brian's worked out a
computer program with Jeremy Raines so that we can record
data on computer cards and run them through the city's
computer.''

"How are we going to get to the city computer? Break
in?'' Baughmann asked, looking as though the idea appealed
to him.

"That's been taken care of,'' Andersen replied. ''One of
those situations where the fewer people who know, the better
off we all are.''

"Gotcha,'' Baughmann nodded, satisfied.

"One more thing,'' Andersen said. ''We're going on the
assumption that these attacks were carried out for a specific
reason. Too many people from the investigation team have
been involved for this to be just a series of random attacks on
the police department. The logical assumption is that we were
getting in the way of something, or we were about to discover
something during our investigations. Which means whoever
is pulling all of this shit hasn't finished whatever it is he
intends to do.''

"Assuming that he's still alive,'' Dorsey added. ''There
was a hell of a lot of blood out there that didn't come from
Rudy. And nothing's happened since Sunday.''

"We can hope,'' Andersen nodded, ''but we can't make
any assumptions. He may just be holing up somewhere. Until
we know for sure, we have to assume he's still active.''

"Maybe he just wants to disrupt the city?'' Baughmann
suggested. ''Maybe play off the Olympic Games? It's a
standard terrorist technique. Hit and run. Turn the cops and
the citizens against each other. And he's sure as hell managed
to accomplish that!''

"That would fit,'' Andersen agreed, nodding his head.
"Everything except the publicity. That's what bothers me. If
all the guy wanted to do was to terrorize a town, he'd have
been playing it up to the press by now, taking credit for
everything. That's why I think whoever's doing this is holding off for something else. Probably something bigger.''

Baughmann nodded his head in agreement. He had to

admit it sounded logical, though he hated to think what that bigger 'something else' might be.

"Okay," Andersen continued. "We could probably assume that whoever's doing all of this figures we're out of the picture and not worth bothering with any more, but we can't take that chance. From now on, everyone in this room, and that includes the women," he added pointedly, "will be armed or escorted twenty-four hours a day. Brian and Meiko will double on guard duty to give Bob a hand with security. Dan can help out after the doctors clear him to start moving around. Ed'll be going back and forth to the lab and maintaining liaison with Lee and Herb. And that means you watch your ass when you travel," Andersen added, warning the photographer. "Mike, Sam, Keith, and I are going to go out and start talking with people. Teams of two. We'll check in every three hours and update you on everything we find. Any questions?"

There were none.

"Okay, go home, clean out your refrigerators, pick up sleeping bags, personal gear and any extra canned goods you've got lying around. We'll meet back at my place at ten o'clock this evening. And remember one thing. This son of a bitch is good, but we're going to stop him."

Jeremy Raines had come to the conclusion that whoever had manipulated the purchase of the restricted police communications equipment was a cut or two above the normal criminal mentality.

Four hours ago, he had received a final list from a nervous sales manager. The list of equipment delivered to the nonexistent police department was impressive: two complete computer-operated transmitters, each equipped with eight restricted police frequencies in addition to the separate, scrambled teleprinter frequency; twenty push-button police unit radios; four pack-set radios with a wide selection of short-range frequencies; twelve highly sensitive tape recorders designed specifically for wire-tapping and surveillance monitoring; six dispatch consoles.

Raines shook his head as he went through the complete list from memory. There was nothing to indicate that any of this equipment had gotten anywhere near Huntington Beach. But then, no one at the communications firm had any idea where the hell the truckload of electronic gadgetry had been delivered. It had been paid for in advance and unaccountably picked up at the warehouse by the presumed buyer.

As far as Jeremy Raines was concerned, he had found out how. He couldn't prove it yet, but he was absolutely certain in his own mind that the diverted scrambler equipment had been used to transmit Muscalino's bogus teletype message. Now, the problem was to find out where.

It was not going to be all that difficult, Raines thought to himself, as he tightened another locknut on the mount of the directional antenna, enjoying the coolness of the night breeze. He had the nine frequencies. Two of the crystal-controlled frequencies were used by Huntington Beach PD as the station-to-unit and unit-to-unit channels. One was the scrambled teletype channel. None of the remaining six frequencies was used by any law enforcement agency within a hundred-mile radius of the city. It was not going to be all that difficult.

During the past four hours, Jeremy Raines had been extremely busy. He had already jury-rigged and mounted two directional antenna monitoring systems at the two inland boundary corners of the city. He was in the process of mounting the third antenna system on the roof of the Civic Center Building.

The monitors were crude, but they would work well enough for what Raines had in mind. Every time a transmission went out on one of the nine target frequencies—within range of at least one of the antenna receivers—the entire signal would be tape-recorded and its relative direction of origin recorded. All teletype transmissions and direction-of-origin data would be dumped into the memory of the police computer. The computer was programmed to delete any signals originating from the station transmitter, which would cut out a lot of the unwanted data, but would not eliminate the accumulation of unit-to-unit and unit-to-station transmissions. These would have to be evaluated and deleted manually.

Once he finished setting up the third antenna, Jeremy Raines knew it was just a matter of time and patience. With any luck, whoever was playing games with the HBPD communications system would transmit again on one of the nine monitored frequencies. With a little more luck, at least two of the antennas would pick up and evaluate the signal. Then Jeremy Raines would draw straight lines on the appropriate compass headings going away from each antenna in the direction of the signal. According to the laws of triangulation, the lines should intersect at the exact spot where the illegal transmitting antenna was located.

At that point, Jeremy Raines would have done his job. It would be up to the blood-maddened investigators to find out who and why.

Within the concealing walls of the Huntington Harbour home, the wounded terrorist slept fitfully, tormented by pain and the ever-present dream. This night, however, the form that rose up out of the darkness had a number burned into its flesh. Three. Three more days. In his nightmare, the terrorist dreamed that a mysterious form was getting closer, that he would not be ready, and that the Olympic flame would not be ignited.

Minus 2 Days

Early Thursday Evening

1835 hours

The heavy-set, white-haired detective displayed his badge to the bored duty-nurse at the County Medical Center and mentioned a name. She checked her list and then took the large brass master key out of her desk drawer, motioning for the two officers to follow. They walked down the empty, silent corridor, stopping outside a heavy metal door with a small barred window mounted at eye level. The nurse unlocked the door, followed the officers inside, checked her patient quickly, and then shut and locked the security door behind her before returning to the magazine on her desk.

George Pouling's eyes followed the movements of the two blurred figures with a lazy, drugged indifference. He had talked with at least fifteen investigators, reporters, doctors, and parole officers during the last three days. Over that time, he had realized that while he was definitely in trouble and facing the possibility his parole would be revoked, the cop who had busted in the side of his face was almost certainly going to get into a lot more trouble. If talking with two more people was going to help that process along, then so be it. Pouling would be more than happy to cooperate. All he wanted to do was to get back on his surfboard and forget about the whole bungled scene.

He watched with curiosity as one of the figures did something to the door. It sounded like he was taping something over the window. Probably another vision test, he decided, feeling a certain sense of disappointment that these men were probably doctors. Hope they can do something about my eyes, he thought. Can't seem to focus on anything. He adjusted himself on the bed, trying to get more comfortable in spite of the pair of handcuffs chaining him securely to the bed frame.

He smiled complacently around the wires and straps holding his broken jaw together, watching as the blurred figures approached his bed. He shut one eye, clearing his vision considerably. Then both eyes widened with shocked terror as he recognized one of the faces.

"You can't—" he started to slur, his mouth painfully restrained by the tight wires. Then he stopped and sucked in a gurgling breath as the heavy barrel of a .45 automatic scraped slowly down his forehead and came to rest at the bridge of his nose, exactly between his eyes.

"Yes, we can," Andersen said. "And we can do it without anyone knowing what happened." He paused to let O'Rorke finish unwrapping the small package on the food-tray table next to the bed. There was a disposable plastic syringe with a plastic-capped needle and a small brown ampul of serum which sparkled in the shaded light of the isolation room.

Andersen allowed the sun-wrinkled beach bum to stare at the threatening items for a few moments, and then handed him a field notebook and a pen.

"I want you to write in that book—who, what, when, where and why," he said menacingly. "You've got fifteen minutes."

Pouling stared one-eyed at the face of each man, searching for some sign that this was all a joke or a bluff they wouldn't dare carry out. He saw nothing in either face that offered any reassurance at all. Having long ago outlived his youthful notions about life and fair play, he began to write furiously about the phone calls, the money, the gold coin collection, and everything else he could possibly remember.

That same Thursday evening, Lori Sileth was busy earning twenty-five dollars from a middle-aged air-conditioning salesman when the pounding on her warped apartment door interrupted her rhythm.

"You expecting somebody?" the fleshy salesman asked, his puffy cheeks reddened from exertion, his eyes wary.

"Nah, don't worry about it," Lori shook her head, angered by the interruption that would necessarily drag the whole scene out longer. "Door's locked. He'll go away after a while." She had begun to reapply her efforts when the door burst inward and crashed against the wall.

"That's all right. Don't get up, Lori." Sam Kretcher smiled, replacing the snub-nosed revolver in his hip holster, as Keith Baughmann closed the door.

"You stay put, too, sport," Kretcher added, waving his opened badge case at the stunned and now thoroughly deflated client.

"You bastards!" Lori screamed, starting into an abusive tirade as she launched herself at the amused detective, fingers outstretched and teeth bared. Kretcher tossed his badge case to Baughmann, stepped aside, caught one of Lori's extended wrists, twisted and folded it behind her back, and then threw her sprawling and still screaming back into the salesman's already abused lap.

She started to disengage herself from the salesman's thin, flailing legs, but then she looked up, saw the calm, bemused expression on Kretcher's face, and decided to stay put. She crouched back into the corner of the sagging bed, trying to cover herself as she glared first at Kretcher, and then at Baughmann who had begun to rummage casually through her dresser, dropping some ragged items of clothing on the floor.

Kretcher reached down, picked up a likely combination of clothing and tossed it to the girl. "Here, put some clothes on, for Christ's sake," he said. "You too, buddy." He nodded to the salesman, who began to comply with feverish haste.

"You bastards can't do this without a warrant," Lori snarled, as she quickly pulled on the pair of faded jeans and the T-shirt that Kretcher had thrown to her.

"Of course we can, honey," Kretcher said reassuringly, sitting down and leaning across the back of an unsteady kitchen chair. He took the wallet that Baughmann removed from the pair of pants lying across the dresser, and began to look through the contents.

"Mr. . . . ah . . . Talsbert, here, Walter J., of ninety-two-seventy-five Bannister Street, Redwood City, California, happens to be working as an undercover operator for us this week. Isn't that right, Mr. Talsbert?'' Kretcher inquired, looking over at the salesman.

Talsbert was trying to locate his underpants within the unsavory-looking sheets. "Huh?" he said, looking up from his quest. "Oh, sure, that's right," he finally said with a sudden enthusiasm that sounded more confused than sincere. He found his pants, and fumbled around in an effort to maintain some degree of dignity while carefully avoiding the girl's sullen glare.

"Which, of course, gives us sufficient cause to believe that you're not a very nice girl," Kretcher continued, smiling cheerfully as Baughmann tossed a vial that contained a small amount of a white crystallike powder, a sandwich bag about half full of some moldy vegetable material, two American Express cards, and three Visa cards down onto a dirty rug between the bed and Kretcher's chair. The salesman's eyes flickered down to the cards on the floor and then back up at the MasterCharge card that Kretcher waved in his fingers, smiling as he did so, before replacing the card and tossing the wallet back to Baughmann. The salesman's eyes followed the path of the wallet, and he sagged visibly as the billfold joined the growing pile of evidence on the floor.

Lori Sileth stared despondently at the felony charges rapidly accumulating on the filthy rug, looked up, and realized that Kretcher was watching her, a patient smile on his face.

"This is some sort of twist, isn't it?"

"Sure is, hon."

"What happens if I talk to you?" she asked cautiously, the inbred con within her approaching the bait with a mixture of hope and distrust.

"Then we dispose of this unsanitary rug for you, Mr. Talsbert goes home to Redwood City, and we go on about our business," Kretcher explained calmly.

"I only know a couple of heavy dealers," she began.

"Lori," Kretcher said softly as Baughmann motioned the salesman outside, "I am not the least bit interested in dope or your connections, unless they happen to involve the asshole that Toby Williker met with just before he died. You know who I'm talking about, don't you?"

She nodded her head, still looking down at the rug, her throat constricting as she thought about what she didn't want to say. She should have bugged out and started up someplace else, she thought. Now it was too late.

"You followed them, didn't you?" Kretcher asked the question gently, sympathetically. He could have just as easily, without any greater display of emotion, twisted her arm back behind her head until the shoulder snapped, and then asked the question. This way there was less fuss and no mess to clean up.

She nodded again, and looked up at the detective.

"He was the one who killed those cops, wasn't he?" she asked. "Not Toby? Just like that Chicano cop said?"

Her eyes stared at Kretcher, pleading. Kretcher didn't say anything, but his patient expression answered her question.

"Then if he finds out . . ." she started to say, looking as though she was going to start to cry or throw up.

"Lori," Kretcher said, maintaining the gentle, paternal voice, "this man has already killed two police officers. If he decides to go after you, you're not going to be able to stay away from him, no matter what you do."

"If I show you where he went after he left Toby?"

"Then we're going to take him out, and you won't have to worry about him any more," Kretcher said matter-of-factly, watching the girl carefully, waiting patiently for her to make her decision.

Late that Thursday evening Dr. Jacquem Kaem drove the expensive Buick with the tinted windows into the underground garage of the Huntington Harbour home, now furious with himself over his decision to handle the medical check on the terrorist himself.

Kaem had argued to accept the personal risk, reminding the Committee that they could not afford to involve any more people in Balefire at this late stage. They had already used their only available medical doctor, and had dispatched him immediately out of the country. There was no one else capable of making an accurate evaluation of the terrorist's ability to carry out the final stage of the Warning. The Committee had finally agreed, but only after expressing their concern and advising extreme caution.

The danger, of course, was the possibility that Thanatos

was already under surveillance and that Kaem would be spotted and identified. It would not be difficult for the police officers to trace Kaem back to his Dana Point home, thereby exposing the Committee and destroying Balefire in the last few hours before the Warning became a reality. Certainly, Kaem could not risk a return to his home. Like the terrorist, the individual members of the Committee were expendable. The Committee as a whole was not.

Kaem, of course, would have to abandon his role as an active member of the Committee. As soon as he completed his voluntary task, he would meet the pickup who would deliver him to the ship waiting offshore in international waters. There he would continue to monitor Balefire, waiting for Thanatos to complete his mission and join the ship, whereupon they would both savor the victorious journey home.

Two more days, he repeatedly told himself. Only two more days.

Kaem had expected to make the trip to the terrorist's home full of pride, sensing for the first time the addictive excitement of exposing one's self to physical danger. He had looked forward to treating the wounds of Thanatos with the exuberant knowledge that he was contributing more than his share toward the success of Balefire. But now, having had time to consider fully the consequences of being linked to the terrorist, he was far less enthusiastic about his new role.

Kaem walked up the stairs from the garage, used the special key to unlock the door and bypass the security systems, and walked hurriedly upstairs to the bedroom. Much more realistic and thoughtful now, Kaem wanted only to complete his task and get on board the waiting ship as soon as possible.

As expected, Thanatos awaited Kaem's arrival with the Browning automatic lying next to his hand on the bed.

"You look well," Kaem said as he removed the bandages from the terrorist's chest. There is no lie to my words, Kaem thought. The man appears to be remarkably recovered, based upon the descriptions of the wounds provided by the first doctor. The major wound was thankfully shallow and had crusted nicely. There were no visible signs of infection and very little apparent tenderness.

"I am fine," Thanatos spoke gruffly, wincing as Kaem

applied fresh dressings and bandages. "What is the decision of the Committee?"

Kaem continued to wrap the bandages, remaining mute for almost a minute. Let him worry a little, he decided. He deserves to wonder, to experience fear and uncertainty like the rest of us.

"We are in agreement," Kaem finally said. "The Warning is well along, and does not seem to have been damaged by your activities. There is still plenty of time, almost two full days, before the Opening Ceremonies begin. The missing officers have caused great consternation within the police department, possibly greater than that which resulted from the first deaths. Your request proved to be doubly effective." Kaem paused. "There are, however, two problems."

"Yes?" The eyes of Thanatos bored into Kaem, searching for and demanding information.

"First of all, it seems you have not deterred the Sergeant Andersen. He continues to actively investigate the deaths of his comrades in spite of his official suspension."

"He is the major threat," Thanatos agreed, smiling slightly to himself. "As we suspected in the beginning. Nothing is changed. He does not represent an insurmountable problem. He can be eliminated at any time."

"We agree, but we do not wish to cause any more obvious deaths at this time. The Councilwoman Hite is pushing for an independent investigation. If we are not careful, we will most certainly attract the attention of the federal agencies. The Los Angeles Police Department has taken an interest in our activities. Also, we do not wish a direct confrontation with Andersen. He is fully alerted to the possibility of danger now, and you are"—Kaem hesitated again, choosing his words carefully—"possibly at a slight disadvantage with your wounds. While we do not doubt the outcome, we feel even the slightest risk is too much to accept at this point."

"The time, then?"

"It has not changed." Kaem nodded. "It must be Saturday night. Two nights from now. Can you be ready?"

"Without question," Thanatos said, relaxed and smiling now that he was certain he would have his turn on the stage.

"Excellent!" Kaem could feel some of his recent excitement return. Balefire was so close now! "Also, as you requested," he continued, "the Committee has made a complete evaluation of the targets. The successful ignition of either target will satisfy the requirements of Balefire."

"Then it will be accomplished easily," Thanatos said quietly. "You need not be concerned at all."

"Good. Then there is one final thing. We will arrange for a small boat to be offshore Saturday evening. The recognition signal will be a pair of yellow lights mounted vertically, one over the other. Your signal will be two flashlight blinks, repeated once. In the event it is necessary or desirable, the boat can take you out to international waters. I will be waiting for you on the tanker until two a.m. Sunday morning—at which time we will depart for home."

"I am looking forward to that moment," Thanatos said, reaching across and shaking hands firmly with Kaem.

Thanatos waited until Kaem had departed. Then he began to disassemble the trusted Browning, wincing openly now at the pain he had been unwilling to display before the Committee member. Balefire was his now. There would be no further questions of failure.

Andersen and O'Rorke drove to the arranged late-night meeting place with Kretcher and Baughmann, frustrated and depressed by their failure to extract any useful information from Pouling. Fortunately, Kretcher's message, relayed through Meiko at the house, seemed to offer some promise of another lead. It had better, Andersen thought, as O'Rorke drove through the rain-dampened streets. There weren't all that many unexplored leads left, and there was a limit as to how long they could operate outside the law before their activities were brought to a halt.

When they drove up next to Kretcher and Baughmann's car, the two officers were talking with a small, frail-looking girl.

"You got something?" Andersen asked as he and O'Rorke walked up to the three people standing in front of a storage garage.

Kretcher nodded to Andersen and O'Rorke and then glanced down at the girl who seemed to be trying to hide within the faded, green fatigue jacket, outwardly shivering in spite of the relative warmth of the night air. "You tell him, hon," Kretcher said to the girl.

"This was the place," Lori Sileth said, barely able to keep her teeth from chattering. "This was where the guy went after he finished talking with Toby. He walked up to about where we're standing right now and did something with a package he had in his hand. Then one of the middle doors opened. I don't remember which side, but I think it was this way," she said, pointing with a trembling finger at the southern row of storage spaces. "He went inside, and then a few minutes later, he drove out in a car—a Firebird, I think. That's the last time I ever saw him."

Andersen looked across the row of rental garage spaces, remembering the location of Rudy's ambush and the helicopter explosion scene still being investigated by federal agents, and suddenly a lot of pieces began to fall into place.

BALEFIRE

Minus 1 Day

Friday Morning

0930 hours

At nine-thirty Friday morning, Kretcher and Baughmann escorted Lori Sileth into an office that appeared to serve both as a psychiatrist's examination room and an artist's workshop. Feeling safe and secure in the presence of police officers for the first time in her life, Lori adjusted herself comfortably in the raised couch and allowed herself to be put into a deep hypnotic trance.

As the hypnotist worked to bring the girl's hazy memory of the man and the garage incident to the surface of her conscious mind where it could be focused and examined in minute detail, the hypnotist's assistant worked at a sketch pad. Occasionally, the artist would feed a question to Lori via the hypnotist and then quickly apply eraser and pencil to make a slight alteration to the outline of the face that was slowly coming to life.

At the end of three hours, both Lori and the hypnotist were satisfied with the finished sketch. The only failure, as far as the two officers were concerned, was the fact that no matter how hard she tried, Lori had been unable to zoom in on the mental image of the Firebird and read the number of the license plate.

By eleven-thirty that morning, Andersen and O'Rorke finally managed to get their hands on the list of people renting the thirty private garage spaces in the Madderdale Park complex. It had not been easy.

They had no trouble at all in determining who owned the two buildings. The owner's name and telephone number was prominently displayed on the side of each building, advising the reader to inquire immediately to get on the list for the next available space.

Andersen inquired and discovered that the owner had departed for a two-month vacation in Europe. No, the answering service said, as far as they knew, there was no one available to take a new listing. And no, they could not give out the owner's mailing address over the phone without permission. No, the fact that the police want it makes no difference at all. Sorry. Click.

A quick check of the telephone book had confirmed Andersen's suspicions. The owner did not list his home address or phone number in either the white or the yellow pages.

Frustrated and impatient, Andersen called Lee Spencer at the lab and asked him to contact Lieutenant Gilcrist and have him call a certain number from a phone that wasn't hooked up to the department taping system.

Forty-five minutes later, Gilcrist called back with the address. The building owner listed his home address on his business license. 4219 Elm. Also, the owner had a silent alarm tied into the PD alarm board. Unfortunately, due to a sudden malfunction, that particular alarm would be disconnected for the next two hours.

When Andersen and O'Rorke arrived at the back gate of 4219 Elm, they discovered broken glass fragments glued to the top of the high wooden fence, and a sign that warned, "WATCH DOG! DO NOT ENTER!" They whistled softly and rattled the gate. No response. Then they observed that the water dish was dry and there were no piles of dog shit anywhere on the weed-filled lawn. They went through the gate.

"I'm surprised the paranoid bastard didn't put in a moat and drawbridge," O'Rorke commented sarcastically, using a medium-sized plumber's wrench to twist the doorknob on the back door, while Andersen kept an eye out for curious neighbors and roaming patrol units. Five seconds later, both officers entered the home.

They worked quickly, searching the residence with methodical determination, finally locating the list in a bound ledger underneath a dusty telephone. Then they spent an additional fifteen minutes copying names and numbers into their ever-present notebooks. Finally, they replaced the ledger carefully back in its original location, placed two $20 bills on the kitchen table to pay for the damaged lock, unplugged the alarm system to cover the PD's failure to respond to the break-in, and then made a hasty, unobserved exit into the back alley where their unit was waiting.

Locating the individuals who had rented the storage spaces proved to be almost as difficult as obtaining the list. By late afternoon, the two investigators had received permission to inspect all but four of the storage spaces. After the first renter slammed the phone down in O'Rorke's ear, they gave up identifying themselves as police officers, and started using the title of city fire inspector. After being assured cooperation, the officers advised each renter that he or she would be contacted for the date and time of the inspection.

According to phone company records that Gilcrist obtained, the number provided by one renter, who held a six-month lease on the four spaces still outstanding on their list, was no longer in service. There was no new number. Also, there were no other city, county or state records filed under that name and address. As expected, the listed address proved to be a phony.

Gilcrist's discovery that the renter of the four garage spaces was conveniently nonexistent was almost superfluous information. Andersen and O'Rorke had already determined that the storage spaces in question were located in the center of the garage building—exactly the area where Lori Sileth watched the man disappear. A closer examination revealed that unlike every other storage space in the complex, these four were equipped with automatic door openers rather than padlocks. A phone call eventually confirmed that the garage space involved in the explosion last Sunday evening had also been equipped with an automatic door opener.

At six-thirty in the evening, Andersen, O'Rorke, Kretcher, and Baughmann sat down in Andersen's living room and conferred with the remainder of their group. After considerable discussion, they came to a general agreement that the four doors were probably booby-trapped, assuming there was actually something being stored in the garage spaces.

The only real disagreement was over the method of entry.
It came down to two choices. Either get permission from one
of the renters on either side of the four attached spaces, or use
a pair of bolt cutters on one of the two padlocks and everybody cross their fingers.

By quarter of eight that Friday evening, Kretcher and
O'Rorke had stationed themselves at either end of the driveway leading to the storage buildings, each armed with a
flashlight, a copy of the sketch produced with the help of Lori
Sileth, and a loaded 12-gauge shotgun. Nighttime visitors
who bore no resemblance to the sketch whatsoever would be
shown a nice shiny badge, advised that a narcotics surveillance operation was in progress, and asked to leave the area
immediately. A visitor displaying more than a passing resemblance to the sketch would be shown the business end of a
Remington 12-gauge shotgun and asked to step out of his car
very slowly and carefully.

As soon as Kretcher and O'Rorke were in position, Andersen,
Baughmann, and Dorsey walked quickly to the garage door to
the immediate right of the four target spaces. After making a
superficial check for any obvious burglar alarms, Baughmann
took out a pair of heavy-duty bolt cutters and snapped the
Yale lock. Looking around one last time, all three men—clad
almost identically in jeans, work shirts, tennis shoes, gloves,
and hip-holstered pistols—picked up their boxes of tools and
other miscellaneous items, went under the opened tension-
spring doors, and then closed the door behind them quickly.

Dorsey started to move forward and immediately stumbled
into a pile of boxes whose location he had forgotten to note
when the door had been open. Picking himself up, thoroughly
embarrassed, he prudently waited until Andersen snapped on
his flashlight.

"Nothing we can do about light showing through the doors,"
Andersen said as they began to clear an area away from the
wall adjoining the first of the four storage spaces. "Just try to
keep it hidden as much as possible."

The walls of the storage spaces were comprised of two-by-
four studs with plasterboard nailed crudely on each side. The
joints between the pieces of plasterboard had been taped and
covered with a thin white layer of plaster. No attempt had
been made to paint the wallboard, which would make it easy

to conceal their cuts later if they decided that such action was necessary.

Dorsey made the first cut at about neck height, just above a horizontal two-by-four fire block nailed between two of the studs. Dorsey estimated the position of the studs and the fire block from the position of the visible nail heads, and then used a plasterboard cutter with a sharp disposable blade to cut out a rectangle of plaster approximately fifteen inches wide and thirty inches high. They had decided to make the cuts high on the hopeful assumption that the repair would be less noticeable than if it was at the floor level and to play it safe just in case someone had decided to wire the garages at the lower, more logical, break-in points.

"You know," Dorsey said, as he changed blades on the cutter, preparing to cut into the piece of wallboard on the other side of the studs, "if they've hooked up sonic or vibration alarms in these things, we're screwed."

"Too much chance of somebody accidentally setting the thing off by backing into a door," Andersen said, hoping he was right. "If they're wired, they've got to be mechanical systems." Dorsey shrugged in hopeful agreement and went back to work on the wall.

Dorsey cut the hole through into the first garage space approximately four inches square. Then he used a flashlight to try to see as much of the interior as possible. The first thing he picked out was a flat rectangular object in the center of the concrete floor with some sort of cable running in a straight line toward the back wall.

"It's there," he said softly. "Just like the one the son of a bitch blew up under Ten Henry. Device mounted on the floor. Wires probably run back to a trip device over the rear door. Nothing else that I can see. Ready?"

"Go to it," Andersen said tensely, as Dorsey made long cuts with the sharp blade. No wire.

They used two stepladders to climb up and through the hole, first passing the tools to Dorsey, and then climbing through themselves. They used their flashlights to look around carefully before moving very far from their entry position, noting with shaking heads and long soft whistles the trigger devices set at both doors and wired to the explosive charge set in the middle of the floor. They found a clean, unused set

of clothing in a paper shopping bag while Dorsey was getting
the camera and strobe ready, and then stood back while the
ID technician recorded the interior, paying particular attention
to the components of the booby trap.

Andersen cut the second pair of holes, and was only slightly
surprised to see the smoothly curved body of a new Datsun
280-ZX. This time, they were more careful with their entry,
avoiding any contact with the automobile until they had a
chance to look it over carefully.

Baughmann made the first important discovery when he
carefully opened up the glove compartment and found the
concealed police radio. "No wonder the bastard outran those
black-and-whites," he muttered, moving back so that Dorsey
could take a picture. "I'll bet when the feds get finished
sifting through the debris from that explosion, they'll find
pieces of one of our radios in whatever's left of the Porsche."

"No bet," Andersen said. "Shut the door, wipe off your
prints, and let's get going. We've got two more to do."

Baughmann cut the third hole. Working faster now that
they were reasonably certain only the doors were wired,
Baughmann cut the second piece of plasterboard quickly,
punched it out, wrinkled his nose at the sudden horribly
familiar odor, took one look inside the third storage space
with his flashlight, and almost threw up.

"Jesus," he whispered, frozen on the ladder as he stared
down through the rectangular hole.

Andersen finally pulled the younger officer down off the
ladder and took his place, shining the flashlight into the
garage area for almost a minute before he stepped down.

"Barlowe and Parham," he said, his face set in a cold,
distant expression as he made room for Dorsey. The case-
hardened ID technician was back down the ladder in less than
ten seconds.

"What do we do now?" Dorsey asked, looking shaken in
the dim artificial light, but nowhere near as bad as the
nauseated Baughmann.

"We go in, search, photograph, and then cut through to
number four," Andersen replied. "Then we'll sit down and
talk about it."

It took the team of officers—Baughmann included, in spite
of his inability to look directly into the front seat of the

black-and-white—almost a half hour to search the third storage space, noting and photographing the crossbow, the nature
of the projectiles which had caused the deaths of the two
missing officers, and the presence of the discarded clothing in
the back seat of the unit. They rapidly confirmed that the
fourth space contained another new and apparently unused
high-performance automobile. Then they began to work
backwards, cleaning up the plaster dust and replacing the
cutout pieces of plasterboard back in the original positions as
best they could. Their original plan to retape and plaster over
the cuts was forgotten in their mutual, unspoken desire to get
out of the storage spaces and back to Andersen's house as
soon as possible.

As they retreated, Andersen made two minor alterations to
the scenes, alterations he hoped would not be detected. He
removed his radio identification key from his key ring and
placed it into a concealed key slot in the police radio console
mounted under the dash of the car sitting in the fourth space.
Then, as they continued to work backwards, trying to conceal
their entry into the storage spaces, Andersen took Baughmann's
key and slid it into the PD radio mounted in the Datsun's
glove compartment.

Finally reaching the garage space they had used as their
initial entry, the three officers opened up the large spring-
controlled door and hurriedly placed the ladders, boxes of
tools and equipment into the back of O'Rorke's pickup truck.
They signaled Kretcher and O'Rorke, had a quick conference,
placed a new Yale lock on the violated garage door, divided
themselves into the detective unit and the truck, and then
sped off into the night.

In the basement of his Huntington Harbour home, Thanatos
unlocked a large plywood storage locker and began removing
the devices, one at a time, from their protective wooden
boxes and Styrofoam packing. There were sixteen devices in
all. He laid them out in a long row, opening the dark-green,
waterproof, plastic lid of each magnet-backed box to expose
the digital timing mechanisms, the brightly colored wires,
and a portion of the soft, claylike substance which was a
tremendously efficient explosive.

With the lids of the boxes opened, the two digital display strips in each of the devices were also visible. The upper display was a twenty-four-hour clock. Brilliant red numerals began to display the time in hours, minutes, and seconds as soon as the terrorist snapped a battery into each of the sixteen devices. The red numerals flashed wildly, each displaying a different time.

Smiling at the electronic disorder, Thanatos took a large black box out of the locker and patiently hooked the sixteen dangling lead wires into the plug receptacle. After consulting his digital wristwatch, he adjusted a row of dials on the main box and pushed a small green button. Instantly, all sixteen timing clocks flickered and then began to pulse identical hour-minute-second readings which changed in synchronized rhythm at exactly one-second intervals.

The arming sequence required much more time—and caution. Thanatos used a small metric allen wrench to set identical ignition times on each of the lower display strips, double-checking to make certain each of the nonpulsing numerals was identical, accurate, and unchanging. In doing so, he carefully avoided the large red arming button on each device. Finally, he took the arming wire from the first bomb, plugged it into the black box and double-checked to be absolutely certain there was no current flowing through the wire. Only then did he carefully attach the small detonator to the end of the wire, and then bury the entire length of the detonator into the exposed portion of the soft, pliable explosive. He repeated the sequence fifteen more times and then stepped back to examine his work.

The means of igniting the Balefire Warning was ready. All that was required now was for the red arming button to be depressed, the lid snapped and locked shut, and the device slapped against a metal target. Once the button mechanically closed the arming circuit, the secondary timing strip would be activated. At the precise second when the upper and lower display strips showed exactly the same time, a primary and backup circuit would close, current would flow into the detonator, and the meticulously produced device would disintegrate in a powerful explosion.

There were two further electronic refinements which would

ensure that the devices would not be disarmed or removed from their intended explosion point.

The first modification consisted of an additional circuit, activated when the arming button was depressed. The circuit was tied into the detonator, and would close instantly if an attempt was made to tamper with the timing mechanism.

The second modification was a simple protruding spring-activated rod at the back of each box that automatically recessed when the device was placed against a solid metal surface and armed another circuit. Any attempt to remove the device after the arming button was pushed would result in the metal rod sliding out to its original position and igniting the detonator. In effect, once the bomb was set and the arming button punched, there was no obvious way to remove the device or to prevent it from detonating at the set time.

Satisfied with the mechanisms, Thanatos carefully shut the protective lids and then placed the bombs into sixteen slots cut into the foam liner of a large metal camera case. He snapped the lid of the case shut and then carried it upstairs to wait for the signal to begin the final stage of Balefire.

At exactly 11:43 that Friday evening, Baakar Sera-te received the message from the Committee to alert the small pickup boat waiting patiently off Catalina Island as to the confirmed date, time, and recognition signal. Less than twenty-four more hours, he thought with a mixture of eager anticipation and relief as he typed the message onto his console screen. Twenty-four hours and Balefire would be a reality. And he, Baakar Sera-te, would have accomplished his critical task and survived.

Humming to himself, the youth selected and keyed in the correct transmission frequency, double-checked the accuracy of the message against the unscrambled words on the second video-screen, and then punched the SEND button with a firm downward movement of his index finger.

On the roof of the fourteen-story Santa Ana building, a transmission antenna spit out a brief signal. Ninety miles away and almost sixty miles offshore, the antenna on the waiting pickup boat received the signal and fed it down to the alert radio operator. The operator quickly translated the sim-

ple Morse code and reported the message to the boat's captain
who smiled, shrugged his shoulders indifferently, and then
rechecked the tension on his trolling line as he took another
swig from his steaming coffee mug.

Fifteen, twenty, and twenty-two miles away from the penthouse location of Baakar Sera-te, three directional antennae
homed in on the brief signal. Each of the three antennae
efficiently determined the relative compass heading of the
signal and instantly transmitted the electronic dots and dashes
to Raines's patiently waiting computer.

Not having been programmed to translate Morse code, the
computer confirmed that the signal had not been transmitted
from the station, and then printed out the message on a
teleprinter as a series of ones, zeros, and spaces. Then,
having performed exactly as programmed, the computer ceased
printing, waiting for the next transmission from the monitoring antennae. Unlike Jeremy Raines, who would not return to
the basement communications room until 0800 hours the
following morning, the computer was not capable of realizing
that the message was significant.

BALEFIRE

T Minus 14 hours

Saturday Morning

0800 hours

Saturday morning, the day that the Olympic Games began in Los Angeles, Jeremy Raines turned his waxed and polished Volkswagen Rabbit into the police parking lot just as the carillon in the high school tower across the street tolled eight o'clock. Tired and frustrated, the computer programmer parked and walked toward the police building, wondering morosely how much of his weekend he would end up devoting to his search for the elusive transmitter. He had long since given up on the idea of attending the Opening Ceremonies scheduled for ten o'clock this evening at the new Olympic Stadium. Now he could only hope he would be home in time to watch the ceremonies on television.

Raines walked past the tightened station security and rode the elevator to the basement, took stock of his options for the day, and shook his head in disgust. If he found something on his isolated teleprinter that didn't correspond to a PD broadcast, he would end up spending most of the morning tracking down the signal source with a bunch of clue-hungry detectives and probably end up with a ham operator. If he didn't find anything, then either he could sit around and stare at the computer or he could go home and wonder how long he was going to have a job. Either way, he wasn't going to be much company for a deliciously friendly young woman who had already let it be known that she was understanding but not exactly thrilled about being stood up three nights in a row.

Tired and despondent, Raines unlocked the door to the computer room, turned on the lights, walked over to the

teleprinter, and instantly forgot all about the physical and
emotional attributes of his female friend.

"I'll be a son of a bitch," he whispered to himself as he
stared at the block of single-spaced ones and zeros that stood
out on the long strip of ACKNOWLEDGE and UNIT STA-
TUS code calls like a parking ticket on his windshield. He
read the first line. Three-one-zero. That was the relative
compass heading. One-zero-zero-zero; zero-zero-one-zero; one-
zero-zero-one-zero . . .

Jeremy Raines had not played with a Morse code key for
over seventeen years—ever since he had abandoned his home-
made crystal set for a prurient interest in a young, inquisitive
neighborhood girl. The code was still etched in his cerebrum,
however, somewhere. It just took some time.

One-zero-zero-zero.

Dash-dot-dot-dot.

B!

In his haste to find a pencil and paper, Raines almost
knocked a cup of day-old coffee onto a two-thousand-dollar
computer console. He found a pencil, gave up on the pad of
paper and quickly grabbed several feet of teletype paper. Two
minutes later, he had decoded the message.

                310:BF/LIFEGUARD
                    DATE/CONFIRM/SATURDAY
                    IDENT/SIG/CHANGE
                    TWO/YELLOW/VERTICAL/BOW
                    CONFIRM/TWO/X/TWO
                    END/ACK/BF

"BF? Lifeguard?" Raines muttered to himself, feeling
both elated and confused as he checked and confirmed that
the same message had been picked up by the other two
antennae . . . at compass headings of 295 and 321. The only
thing he could figure was that the Huntington Beach life-
guards must have bought a police frequency transmitter. He
didn't realize for a few moments that there was an additional,
much shorter coded message. Then he spotted the second
group of numbers, and decoded the signal in his head before
he put it down on paper beneath the first message.

101:LIFEGUARD/BF/ACK/

Curiously, there was only one compass heading for the second message. Apparently, the brief signal had only been picked up by the antenna on the Civic Center. The heading of 101 degrees was almost due west. Coming from the ocean?

It was immediately obvious to Jeremy Raines that the second message was some sort of acknowledge signal. But that was the only thing obvious about the messages. Shaking his head, Raines tore the paper off the teleprinter and headed back to his desk and the telephone. He didn't have the slightest idea what the intercepted message was saying, but he had three compass readings that would intersect some-where in the vicinity of Santa Ana. He figured that would be enough to interest Sager.

By nine o'clock Saturday morning, the living room in Andersen's house had taken on the appearance of a poorly organized disaster. The once clean chalkboard was filled with blocks of small printing, as were five large pieces of white butcher paper tacked onto the nearby wall. There were hand-fuls of crime reports and photo contact sheets separated into neat and not-so-neat piles across most of the floor space. Empty glasses and dirty plates were left stacked and forgotten on the brick hearth of the fireplace.

Dorsey and the five younger girls had taken over the kitchen table. The two younger Hernandez girls were marking squares on hand-drawn charts with small x's. Dorsey, Ra-mona Hernandez and Jody and Martine Andersen continued to make comparison after eye-blurring comparison between the blowups of the latent fingerprint lift cards and the copies of the elimination prints of every officer, victim, and suspect known to have been at the scenes in question.

In one very small stack at one isolated end of the table, the few lift cards containing usable fingerprints that could not be matched with anyone on their list were marked with large red question marks. Dorsey had already confirmed that a print on one of the cards—the one Sheffield had lifted off Guyerly's baton—matched a clear bloody fingerprint found on an empty 9mm Browning automatic clip located about thirty yards

away from the scene of Rudy Hernandez's shooting. It was
one of the very few useful bits of information they had
managed to isolate after almost forty hours of exhaustive
work.

In one corner of the living room, Meiko, Sheffield and a
slowly recovering Dan Branchowski continued to underline
segments of information from crime reports, witnesses'
statements, telephone records, evidence lists and investigative
summaries. They handed the marked pages to Juanita Hernandez
and Michelle Andersen, who in turn consulted their master
sheets and continued to mark the slowly dwindling stack of
computer data cards.

In the meantime, Andersen, Baughmann, Kretcher, and
O'Rorke had divided up the city by marking area maps with a
wide felt pen. They were making a determined effort to locate
and examine the doors of every rental storage garage space in
Huntington Beach and the neighboring cities of Fountain
Valley and Westminister. They had left Malinger staked out
on the roof of a small machine shop across the street and
catercorner to the Madderdale Park storage spaces. He was
armed with his camera—now equipped with an auto-winder
and a zoom telephoto lens—a radio, a loaded .38 Chief's
Special, and a copy of Lori Sileth's sketch.

O'Rorke and Kretcher had just finished checking off another area on their map and were en route in their unmarked
detective unit to check in with the Fountain Valley Watch
Commander when they received a message on their teleprinter:

ELEVEN DELTA AND SEVENTEEN DELTA:
TEN-TWENTY-THREE THE W/C'S OFFICE IMMEDIATELY.

O'Rorke and Kretcher looked at each other.
"You know what that's about?" O'Rorke asked, gesturing
down at the now silent teleprinter.
Kretcher shook his head and rolled his eyes as he reached
for the radio to notify Andersen and Baughmann of their new
en route status, while O'Rorke turned the unit around in the
direction of the HBPD station.

*   *   *

Zakar Taskanian stood by himself at the living room window of the Dana Point house, staring out at the curved infinity of the greyish-blue expanse of water below. He was contemplating the nature of his new responsibilities and the need to make a decision.

The prospect of assuming leadership of the Committee had not concerned Taskanian two days ago when Kaem carried out his decision to evaluate personally the condition of their terrorist. At that time, Balefire had seemed all but inevitable. The stage was set. The plans were drawn. The options were identified. And the equipment was in position. All that remained was the need to confirm that Thanatos was physically capable of igniting Balefire. In the sweet anticipation of imminent success, the loss of Kaem's sharp tactical mind during these last hours had not seemed too high a price to pay for a final confirmation. But now . . .

Zakar Taskanian had never in his life been a timid man. He had never shied away from the soul-wrenching demands of leadership. He accepted the knowledge that a wrong decision could mean the loss of so much life. And it was not the fear of death for himself or for any of the others that caused him to hesitate now. Rather, it was the realization that an error in judgment could destroy something that meant so much more than life to so many of his people. There was also the realization that something unexpected was taking place at the police station. Something he was certain forebode danger to their man and, therefore, Balefire.

By monitoring conversations over the tapped telephones scattered throughout the police station, the Committee had already learned that the persistent Sergeant Andersen had been secretly returned to duty by the chief of police. That was not a problem by itself; a few carefully placed phone calls could expose the sergeant's activities to the right people, if they were able to find out what he was doing. But that was precisely the problem. During the past five days, the dangerous sergeant had not returned once to the monitored police station nor had he broadcast any type of message over the police radio. He had simply disappeared at a time when the

Committee could not afford to have a significant threat to Thanatos running loose.

And now one of the technicians had reported another unusual situation. The police chief, Sager, had returned to the station on a Saturday, which was an unprecedented deviation from his normal weekend sailing. The technicians determined that the chief had gone down to the Command and Control Center, the area which housed the dispatch equipment and the computer, and unfortunately, one of the critical areas where Gehling had been unable to install one of the small monitoring chips. Then, minutes later, the technicians reported that two of Andersen's trusted detectives, O'Rorke and Kretcher, had been called in from the field.

Taskanian had been waiting now for almost an hour, hoping to learn the cause of the unusual activity that was very likely directed at Thanatos. But so far, nothing. It was exactly this kind of situation in which Kaem's chess-sharpened intellect was so useful.

Taskanian knew he himself was a man of action and direct assault rather than a tactician. His instincts told him to release Thanatos to complete his mission. Yet, he was deeply afraid his instincts were wrong.

He turned one more time to the technician who waited respectfully at the top of the stairs.

"Is there anything more?" he asked.

The technician shook his head, waiting quietly to be told what to do.

"We can wait no longer," Taskanian nodded, accepting the burden. "Advise him now. The primary target. He is to ignite Balefire tonight as planned."

Michael O'Rorke rolled down the window of the worn detective unit, cursing the heat and the broken air conditioner, as Sam Kretcher continued to drive in the direction of Santa Ana, heading toward the location on the map where three straight lines converged and crisscrossed.

They had already contacted the Santa Ana PD by pay phone and obtained the most probable location—an exclusive fourteen-story apartment complex. Santa Ana had run a quick patrol check and had confirmed the presence of a large an-

tenna on the roof. They now had a SWAT team and uniformed support standing by, waiting eagerly for the arrival of
the two Huntington Beach detectives.

That was one of the more satisfying aspects about being a
police officer, Kretcher thought to himself, humming in quiet
contemplation. It didn't really matter what city or county or
state you worked for. If some stupid bastard started taking
potshots at a cop, he would rapidly discover how small the
world really was when you had a hundred thousand vindictive
badges after your ass.

"So, what do you think?" he asked O'Rorke, who was in
the process of dumping extra buckshot rounds from the box in
the glove compartment into the pockets of his thin black
nylon windbreaker.

"About what?"

"Andersen."

"He's okay," O'Rorke said with a shrug. "Having Rudy
taken out like that, and then finding Barlowe and Parham just
hit him hard. He's the man in charge of finding this asshole.
You gotta expect him to take it personal. He'll handle it
okay, though. Walt's not going to flip out on us."

"I don't know," Kretcher shook his head. "That twist on
Michelle really set him off. Bobby said Walt damn near took
his head off before he saw the TP message. Besides, when's
the last time he let you work a door," Kretcher added,
referring to the illegal entry committed by O'Rorke and Andersen to obtain the records on the storage spaces.

"He wants that son of a bitch real bad." O'Rorke nodded,
adjusting his folding-stock shotgun to a more comfortable
position between his legs.

"That's what I'm worried about. Walt's already pushing
the line with the city council, especially with Hite. Way he's
acting now, he'd waste the guy in a courtroom surrendering
to a judge."

"No problem. We just gotta make sure we find the scum-
bag first—in less public circumstances."

"Tell you what, if this location's good, we're going to
have to climb over forty Santa Ana cops to get a shot in."

O'Rorke laughed. "Didn't I tell you? My old buddy
Brubaker's in charge of the Santa Ana team. He and I had a

little private discussion. Far as he's concerned, a white flag won't mean shit.''

"So what do you think? About the location, I mean.''

"Makes sense. At least the part about the guy using the radio to screw us around. Thing is, though, I gotta agree with Raines. This triangulation bit bothers me, too. I can't figure out why the guy would want to nail himself down on top of a building when he could have used a mobile system instead. Transmit once and then move the whole rig to a different city. We'd never spot him.''

"Maybe that's the idea,'' Kretcher suggested thoughtfully. "Maybe he figures he can take a few more of us with him if he draws us all into one location.''

"Could be,'' O'Rorke nodded, looking over at Kretcher and matching his cold, anticipatory smile.

In the fourteenth-story penthouse that was the focal point for the converging law enforcement teams, Baakar Sera-te was blissfully unaware of his impending fate. He glanced up from the *Playboy* magazine he was rereading, and saw the signal from the Committee appear and unscramble into green letters and numbers on his console screen.

As he fed the required program disc into the drive slot, preparing to transmit what he fervently hoped would be his next-to-the-last message, the cutout reviewed his escape plan one more time. He would remain locked in the apartment until he received the terrorist's signal confirming that Balefire had been ignited. He would then transmit the message to the Committee, set the timing devices in the apartment for one hundred and fifty minutes, pick up his passport and his meager belongings which were already packed in a small briefcase, get into his car, and drive south for San Diego. If all went as planned, he would be sitting in the airport terminal, waiting to get on the first available plane, when the simultaneous explosions would obliterate all evidence of his association with the terrorist and the Committee.

Waiting now for the computer to accept the program and to confirm an untapped communications linkup with the terrorist, Baakar dropped his well-worn magazine on the floor, stood up, and walked over to his panoramic window view of north-

west Santa Ana. He allowed his eyes to sweep across the
smog-tinged horizon and then drift back down to his favorite
view: the miniaturized expanse of houses, streets, and
automobiles.

Baakar Sera-te froze as he saw the police units. He counted
six, seven, eight. With a growing numbness, he watched the
cars pull into gas stations, parking lots, and side streets,
disgorging in all directions small figures armed with rifles
and shotguns.

Shaking his head in disbelief, Baakar stared at the terrifying scene for a few more seconds. Then he ran back to the
communications terminal, feeling his heart beating wildly as
he cleared the program from the computer and began to
punch keys at a furious pace.

      POLICE SURROUNDING MY LOCATION NOW.
      AT LEAST EIGHT VEHICLES. PLEASE ADVISE.

There was a fifty-second pause. The cutout stared dry-
mouthed at the blank screen, unable to look out the window.
Then a reply flashed on the console.

  ARE THEY AFTER YOU?
  I DON'T KNOW. THEY HAVE SURROUNDED THE BUILDING.
    WHAT SHOULD I DO?
  HAVE YOU SENT GO SIGNAL TO BALEFIRE?
  NEGATIVE. MUST I DESTRUCT?

Another pause, this one almost twice as long. The confusion was a direct result of the Committee's loss of their
tactician. Kaem would not have hesitated to sacrifice the
young cutout, supremely confident that Balefire would be
carried out now of its own momentum. Taskanian, however,
was far less confident that Thanatos had a clear path. He
wanted to monitor the final stage of the project, and provide
communications support if necessary. To do so safely, he
would need the cutout.

  NEGATIVE! YOU ARE STILL NEEDED. SEND SIGNAL
  TO BALEFIRE AT ONCE! WAIT TO BE SURE IT IS YOU

THEY ARE AFTER. THEN ERASE ALL MEMORIES AS A
PRECAUTION.

It took the security guard at the apartment building—
a retired Santa Ana police officer—less than sixty seconds
to absorb the information provided by Sergeant Brubaker
and come up with the probable location of the suspect's
residence. By locking himself in his apartment and canceling
his mail delivery, Baakar Sera-te accomplished something
that he had tried very hard to avoid. He had attracted the
curious attention of a retired street cop who had grown
accustomed to dealing with friendly, outgoing tenants, and
who had very little else to occupy his suspicious and skeptical
mind.

Three minutes later, Brubaker, O'Rorke, Kretcher, and
the security guard had worked out a plan of attack. With
the exception of the suspect in 14D, and an elderly lady
in 13A, the top two floors of the building, to the best
of the guard's knowledge, were empty of residents and
guests. There would be no need to evacuate the other
floors.

Two minutes from now, at exactly 2:45:00, O'Rorke,
Kretcher, and four uniforms with shotguns would use the
guard's elevator key to go directly up to the thirteenth floor in
elevator number one, and then split off to take the two
stairwells.

At 2:48:00, Brubaker, his SWAT team, and the suddenly
rejuvenated security guard who had abandoned his little five-
shot revolver in favor of a scarred and familiar .357 Magnum
from his lower desk drawer, would ride elevator number two
all the way up. The remainder of the uniformed officers
would take up stations within the first floor and surrounding
the outside of the building.

At 2:48:45, O'Rorke and Kretcher would open the stairwell
doors on the fourteenth floor to cover the hallways and the
elevators.

At 2:49:00, elevator number two would open on the fourteenth floor, and the assault team would take their positions
around the single entrance to 14D.

At 2:50:00, they would take the door.

*   *   *

Baakar Sera-te worked frantically with trembling fingers to comply with the Committee's orders, rekeying the transmit program and bringing the prearranged go signal up on his screen, knowing with a hollow certainty he was near death.

He knew that the policemen were coming for him. His one slim chance to live rested on his ability to get the message off to the terrorist quickly, and then erase from the memory banks of his computer any reference to the man or to the Committee before the officers kicked down his door. Properly erased, the equipment could be explained away as the source of income of a self-employed computer programmer. If the officers let him come to the door instead of kicking it down. If they didn't know precisely what they were looking for. If they didn't question the significance of the red and yellow buttons and the detonator wires. If he got the message off in time.

He looked up at the digital clock above the console.

2:48:47.

The terrorist would be at home, waiting.

He checked the message one last time, swiftly double-checked the frequency with a sweep of his sweat-blurred eyes, and then he jabbed at the SEND button, realizing only as his trembling index finger hit the square plastic button that he had forgotten to key in the scrambler. Stunned and whimpering, he realized he had transmitted the go signal to the terrorist in the clear!

Horrified by the enormity of his error, Baakar Sera-te was sitting in his chair, his shaking hands moving back and forth over the keyboard, trying to figure out how he could do the impossible—call the message back—when he heard the elevator open in the hallway outside his door.

The memory banks!

He had forgotten that he had to erase the disc memories before he answered the door. Leaping up out of his chair, Baakar Sera-te lunged across his console, palm outstretched to slam against the glowing yellow button. He felt his foot slip on something—the *Playboy* magazine he had been reading. Thereafter, he had only milliseconds to realize that his hand had struck the scarlet button instead of the yellow one before the massive explosion sent him into oblivion.

BALEFIRE

T Minus 6.5 hours

Saturday Afternoon

1530 hours

By the time Andersen and Baughmann received the notification, drove a fast twenty-one miles, and then managed to work their detective unit in close to the devastated Santa Ana apartment building, the city fire department had the secondary fires under control. The two Huntington Beach officers ran, shoved, and pulled their way through the mass of curious onlookers, and were finally able to badge their way through the ring of Santa Ana crowd-control uniforms just as the rescue team brought down the first body.

As Andersen and Baughmann watched, seven sheet-covered stretchers were carefully lifted over and around the scattered chunks of building rubble in the street, and then set down in a neat row next to a pair of unneeded ambulances. The sheets were blood-soaked. Andersen could see bloodied shreds of body armor and uniform cloth hanging from the sides of the stretchers.

"Sergeant Andersen?"

Andersen turned around slowly to stare at the incongruously neat and pressed uniform of the huge Santa Ana lieutenant. However, the murderous look in the black eyes and the chilled voice did not correspond with the outward image of a desk-bound administrative officer.

"Yeah."

"Lieutenant Ramirez, Sergeant. I have a message from your chief. He said to tell you to report to him immediately, but not at the station. He said you'd know where to go." Ramirez delivered the message perfunctorily. It was clear the lieutenant had other things on his mind, like taking apart with his bare hands the people who had booby-trapped his officers.

"My men . . ." Andersen spoke softly, unable to take his eyes off of the row of sheet-covered figures. He had just noticed that one of the bodies had been wearing a black nylon windbreaker.

Ramirez's face softened slightly. "They transported one of your detectives"—Ramirez glanced at his field notebook—"Sam Kretcher, about ten minutes ago. They dug him out of the stairwell. He was conscious. Lot of cuts and bruises. No apparent internal injuries. Paramedics had him transported to be checked out anyway."

"What about O'Rorke?" Andersen asked, still staring at the torn sleeve of the familiar looking windbreaker that had slid out from underneath the darkly stained sheet.

"He didn't make it," Ramirez said quietly. "Brubaker sent him up the other stairwell with two of our uniforms. They said O'Rorke made them stay back while he checked out the hallway, just before the place went up."

"Sounds about right," Andersen nodded, his voice dulled. "What about the asshole they went after?"

"If these people work at it real hard, they might scrape up enough to put in a coffee cup. I don't think anybody's gonna bother."

Andersen stared at the sheet-covered body of Detective Michael O'Rorke for a few more seconds, and then shook his head slowly.

"It wasn't worth it," he whispered, more to himself than anyone else. Then he turned around and walked back toward his unit, Baughmann following along silently.

"Yeah, tell me about it," Ramirez muttered, as he stared down at the covered bodies of Sergeant Brubaker, a sixty-three-year-old security guard, and four of his uniformed SWAT officers.

The radio-alarm clock woke Thanatos out of an uneasy nap at two minutes after four o'clock. Remaining face down on the top of the bed, the terrorist realized he had been dreaming again, the same persistently haunting nightmare. But this time there had been something new added. An explosion? He tried, but he couldn't reconstruct the pieces of this new variation of his dream.

Frustrated, he tried to focus his attention on something else, a news report on the radio. Something about the Santa Ana fire department and a damage estimate for a building. Shaking his head, Thanatos gave up the effort and shut off the radio. He had many important things to do today, assuming there would be a final confirmation from the Committee.

Stretching and feeling the still painful tightness across his chest, Thanatos rose from the bed and walked into the den adjoining his bedroom. There, on the polished top of a heavy oak desk, a typewriter-sized computer console waited with electronic patience. Outwardly identical to the terminals used by the Committee and their cutout, this particular console had been carefully programmed to function as a receiver only, eliminating the possibility of an accidental signal being triangulated to the Huntington Harbour home.

Thanatos smiled widely as he observed the flashing letters on the screen:

MESSAGE WAITING

Humming to himself, he leaned on the desk top with one hand, using the other to call up the message held in the memory banks. His fingers automatically shifted over to hit the decode key that would direct the computer to unscramble the anticipated matrix of meaningless letters and numbers. But his hand froze above the key when his eyes focused on the screen.

BALEFIRE: IGNITE THE WARNING. PRIMARY TARGET.
BALEFIRE!

Thanatos could not believe his eyes. After all the careful preparations, all the orchestrated efforts to build upon the fear of an unseen predator, the wretched dog of a cutout had transmitted the go message unscrambled! The terrorist's fist slammed into the keyboard, blanking the screen out in a sudden swirl of flickering light-points.

He debated taking the time to travel to a telephone booth, and then impatiently rejected the idea as he ran back into the bedroom and reached for the telephone on the nightstand. Even if the cutout's lines were tapped, Thanatos would not be on the phone long enough to be traced. Just long enough to vent his rage at the incompetent and worthless fool.

He dialed his primary contact number, and then listened in sudden alarm and confusion as a tape-recorded voice advised him that the number he had dialed was temporarily out of service. He quickly dialed the other three emergency numbers, and received the same message each time. There was definitely something wrong. At least one of the numbers should have connected, even if the cutout wasn't available, unless . . .

The radio news bulletin. A building in Santa Ana destroyed. The dreamed explosion.

Thanatos quickly reached to turn the radio back on, but the news report had given way to a commercial. He dialed across the entire AM band, and then switched over to FM. Nothing but music, commercials, and long-winded disc jockeys. Cursing, he ran downstairs and turned on the television set. Less than ten minutes later, his impatient dial-turning was rewarded.

As Thanatos watched with a growing sense of imminent danger, an announcer came on the air to describe the violent and tragic result of the Santa Ana police department's attempt to raid the apartment of a bombing suspect. Then the station provided confirmation by panning their camera across the jagged top of the fourteenth floor of the apartment building that little more than an hour ago had housed the terrorist's only link to the Committee.

Baughmann drove the detective unit back into Huntington Beach and down to the end of the pier in silence. He parked the unit in front of the Bait and Tackle Cafe. Then he and a somber Andersen walked in through the door, ignoring the fishermen leaning against the pier railings outside. They found Sager, Gilcrist, and Raines waiting for them. Aside from those three, the cafe was empty.

"You hear about O'Rorke?" Andersen asked as he dropped down heavily in one of the empty chairs, gesturing for Baughmann to join him.

Sager nodded, not saying anything.

"Sam Kretcher's at the U.C.I. Medical Center," Andersen continued solemnly, picking up an empty coffee cup and clenching it in his thick, veined hands. "A unit went out to pick him up." He hesitated for a moment, staring down into the cup. "We paid a hell of a price to get that bastard."

"You didn't get him," Sager stated flatly from across the table.

"What?" Andersen's head snapped up and his eyes locked on Sager's. "What the hell do you mean we didn't get him?" he demanded. "That son of a bitch shredded himself over a couple square blocks. They found—"

"Read this," Sager ordered, ignoring the outburst as he tossed a piece of teletype paper on the table in front of Andersen. "The guy in the apartment transmitted that before he blew himself up," Sager continued, as Andersen grabbed at the torn piece of paper and stared at the typed words. "Jeremy picked it up on his monitors. Different frequency from the one sent out last night, but it was from the same location." Raines handed Andersen the second teletype message.

It took Andersen a few moments.

"A command center. Or a fucking cutout," he finally whispered as the enormity of the two teletyped messages struck home. "Then he's still out there." Andersen started to come up out of his chair, a savage look of hatred on his face.

"Sit down!" Sager ordered gruffly.

For a moment, it appeared as though Andersen was completely out of control. Then the feral look cleared from his eyes, and he sat back down, blinking and taking slow deep breaths of calming air.

"He's already tried to break you, Sergeant," Sager said in a deliberately authoritative voice. "Are you going to hand it to him on a platter this time?"

Andersen sighed deeply, shook his head and brought his eyes up to Sager's again.

"No."

"All right, Walt, that's better." Sager nodded. "Now tell me what you think."

"If there's someone else out there backing this guy, then he's got to be after something big. Especially if that someone was on the other side of a cutout," Andersen said, the pieces starting to fit together. "The Olympics."

"Seems like a logical conclusion," Sager nodded, allowing Andersen to catch up at his own pace.

Andersen was thinking furiously now, staring down at the two pieces of paper in his hand. "Balefire?" he mumbled out loud. "What the hell's a balefire?"

"It's a funeral pyre or it's a signal fire," Jeremy Raines offered when no one else at the table spoke up. "They used to light them on the cliffs along the coast, to warn off ships during storms."

Andersen's head came up slowly as he stared at the young programmer. "A fire? Some son of a bitch is going to ignite a warning fire? Against the Olympics? What the—" Realization was visible in Andersen's eyes. "My God, the oil wells."

Sager nodded. "We think so."

"Why?" Andersen asked the question rhetorically. It didn't matter why. The only thing that really mattered was when and where and how they were going to stop him.

Sager shrugged his shoulders. "Keith's theory about a terrorist may not be all that far off," he said, nodding over at Baughmann. "No other reason I can think of why Huntington Beach would be singled out as a target. Aside from the oil wells, the power plant, and the pier, we're pretty much like any other coastal city."

"Jesus," Andersen said, "if he sets off a well—"

"—we're going to have one hell of a fire," Sager finished, nodding his head. "I talked with the fire chief a few minutes ago. He said a lot of the wells are close enough to each other to go off in a chain reaction. Probably just what this bastard has in mind with his 'Balefire Warning.' "

"The other message says something about the date being Saturday," Baughmann added. "If that means today, we don't have a hell of a lot of time to set anything up. The Opening Ceremonies are this evening."

"He's done everything else at night," Andersen nodded. "That gives us at least a couple more hours. What about some help from Mutual Aid?"

"Already in the works," Sager said. "Everybody's short-handed now because of the Olympic security details, so it's going to take some time."

Andersen's eyes widened. The Olympics. A direct tie-in between a terrorist in Huntington Beach and the Olympic Games in Los Angeles was something that he had never considered seriously until now.

"Jesus," he whispered, "you really think this thing's related?"

"It's a possibility," Sager shrugged. "LA's been notified of the situation. They want us to keep them advised, but there's another problem we've got to deal with first." He reached down beside his chair and brought up a disconnected telephone that was partially disassembled.

"Our in-house electronics expert here," Sager said, nodding over at Jeremy, "started thinking we've been behind the eight ball a little too often on all this. He ran an electronic sweep of the station, looking for wiretaps and bugs, and made an interesting discovery. It seems we now have twelve telephones in the station acting like very efficient transmitters. One of those phones was in my office."

Andersen shook his head in silent amazement. He was finally beginning to comprehend the magnitude of the operation they were up against.

"Then we have to assume whoever's behind all of this knows we're getting close," Andersen said, gesturing with his hand at the telephone.

"Not necessarily." Sager shook his head. "We had an accident with this phone in the Records Bureau. A clerk was coached to use some appropriate language when she knocked the phone on the floor and then 'discovered' it wouldn't work. According to Jeremy, the transmitter chip was probably working fine up to the point when we had the phone company come in to switch phones. If they were listening, they got an earful from a pissed-off repairman who had to get up in the middle of the night. They might have bought it."

"But, regardless, if you're going to leave the other taps open, we're going to have to be careful about what's said around the station." Andersen sighed, beginning to understand the complexity of organizing a Mutual Aid response under that type of internal handicap.

"Exactly. And don't forget about the radios," Sager added. "We've got to assume they can monitor and transmit on any of our standard frequencies. But we're going to have people on top of those oil wells with radios they shouldn't be able to monitor.''

"New crystals?'' Andersen asked, interested in anything that might give him a better shot at the bastard.

"On the pack-sets,'' Sager nodded. "Jeremy's working out the details now. Trouble is, we've got a lot of wells in this city. Two or three hundred at least. Unless we get help, we're going to have to spread people and radios pretty thin.''

"I think we'd be better off with fewer people anyway,'' Andersen suggested.

"Why's that?''

"If this son of a bitch spots a surveillance, he's going to jack-rabbit on us, and we'll never find him. Unless he decides to hit us again, which could be any day he chooses from now on. Right now, there's a good chance he's set for today. Let's back off a little, give him a chance to show, and then box him in.''

Sager nodded his head, smiling to himself. He had learned long ago that the key to effective leadership was to encourage good people to come up with your plan on their own. "Fine,'' he agreed. "I'll get you enough people to sit on the wells and the power plant. But you and Keith aren't going to be part of the surveillance.''

"Hite can go—'' Andersen started to say, but Sager cut him off.

"I don't give a shit about Councilwoman Hite's opinions,'' Sager growled, "but she can hurt us if one of her fucking sources spots either of you out there. Besides, you're going to be too busy to be sitting around on your ass.''

Sager paused for a moment, shifting his gaze from Andersen to Baughmann, then back to Andersen.

"As soon as it gets dark,'' Sager went on, "you two are going to set up in a roving fire-team unit. Take Kretcher with you if he's okay. Use one of the rented cars from Vice. Herb'll help you get whatever you need or want out of the armory.'' He gestured with his head over at Gilcrist, who nodded agreeably.

"There's a Lieutenant Ramirez at Santa Ana,'' Andersen said absentmindedly, remembering the row of covered stretchers. "He lost a bunch of people this afternoon. Any objection to inviting him in on this?"

"Up to you," Sager shrugged. "But when surveillance spots this bastard, I want you on him. No game rules. No warnings. No 'come out with your hands up.' " Sager paused. "You spot him, you take him out. For legal purposes, that is a direct order. Understood?"

Both Andersen and Baughmann nodded silently. Neither of them smiled.

"Then get your asses out of here," Sager growled softly. "And take this mangy excuse for a lieutenant with you. You've got less than two hours to be ready." He motioned for Raines to remain seated as Andersen, Baughmann, and Gilcrist stood up.

Sager waited until the three officers disappeared through the wooden door before turning to the visibly concerned programmer.

"Don't worry about it, son," Sager said. "Anybody asks you any questions, you just go ahead and tell them what you heard. It won't make any difference."

"It's not that, Chief," Raines said, shaking his head. "I must have been up getting coffee while you guys were talking. I didn't hear a thing. I was just wondering why you wanted me to stick around. I've got to pick up those crystals and get them switched."

"One more job, son," Sager said, having to work at keeping the appreciative warmth out of his voice. The young civilian had earned the right to be treated like the others. He picked up one of the pieces of teletype paper on the table and scratched on it with his pen. Then he handed it to Raines. "Can you transmit this for me on the same frequency, only this time directionally?"

Jeremy Raines read the altered teletype message. "You want it sent exactly like this? Three blue?"

"That's right."

"What main heading?"

"One-one-zero, no more than plus or minus thirty."

"Sure, no problem. But the only place this'll hit is Catalina."

"Do it," Sager nodded, satisfied, "and then get your ass to work on those radios."

*   *   *

In the living room of Kaem's Dana Point home, the remaining members of the Committee sat quietly as the TV newscaster finished his updated story on the police raid and explosion in Santa Ana. The Committee had learned nothing new from the story, except that their suspicions regarding the knowledge and intentions of the police were reaffirmed. Taskanian got up to turn the tv off and returned to his chair. The three men sat in silence for a few moments, each lost in his own thoughts.

Finally, Dr. Jain Saekia spoke. "It is confirmed then? Baakar sent the go signal to Thanatos before he died?"

"The signal was sent," Taskanian nodded. "We have confirmed the transmission from the tapes. Unfortunately, we also confirmed that he failed to use the scrambling device. We have no way to know if the signal was intercepted."

"I am not certain this is a critical matter," Saekia said after a few moments. "We have not determined as yet whether the police traced one of Baakar's earlier transmissions or whether the raid was based on other information. In any event, it is highly unlikely they have been monitoring all possible frequencies. And even if they were, what would that message tell them? That somewhere at some time a person is going to ignite a fire? I think we are being overly cautious."

The youngest Committee member, whose face bore the scars of previous encounters with policemen, raised his hand to speak.

"I must agree with Dr. Saekia," he said. "There is no doubt the police are beginning to converge on our man. But they still have far to go, and they are out of time. Also, they have lost the majority of their investigating team, and surely much of their previous self-confidence."

He looked around at his attentive audience and continued. "Thanatos has been given the signal. He has his target. Kaem had already confirmed Thanatos is capable and ready. I believe there is little the police can do to find him and stop him now. Therefore, I suggest our task should be the most difficult one of all. We must sit and wait for news of victory.''

They all turned to Taskanian, who remained sitting quietly in his chair. Finally he looked around at the others and nodded his head in worried agreement.

BALEFIRE

T Minus 4 hours

Early Saturday Evening

1730 hours

At five-thirty Saturday afternoon, almost exactly two and a half hours after Baakar Sera-te unintentionally and permanently severed the communication link with the Committee, Thanatos made his decision.

In point of fact, he had already decided to carry out the final phase of Balefire, in spite of the new uncertainties, an hour and a half earlier. He had spent the last sixty minutes listening intently to the police scanner in his den, trying to glean some last-minute intelligence on the activities of the patrol units near the target area. Also, more importantly, he was trying to locate Sergeant Walter Andersen.

The latest news broadcast reported one Huntington Beach police detective killed in the Santa Ana apartment explosion and another injured. No names had been released, pending notification of the families. It was logical to assume that Andersen would have been involved in the raid on the apartment; therefore, it was possible that Andersen was already eliminated. But that was an assumption the professional terrorist was not prepared to make.

The psychological profile on Andersen emphasized the sergeant's strong sense of personal involvement with his family and the men under his command. The harassment directed at Andersen's wife and at the families of his investigators had served to confirm this evaluation. Unfortunately, it had also demonstrated the sergeant's capacity for self-control under pressure.

The unexpected confrontation with Detective Hernandez,

in addition to the planned, deliberate assault on the crime lab scientists, had undoubtedly focused Andersen's tenacious mind on revenge. The additional loss of two more of his detectives—assuming Andersen was not one of the casualties—would only make the police sergeant more persistent and dangerous.

As the digital clock next to the scanner blinked 5:30, Thanatos shut off the scanner and stood up. He had been unable to locate Andersen, but the time spent listening to the police radio traffic had not been wasted. The patrol cars in the vicinity of the target area were making traffic stops and responding to calls in what seemed to be a normal manner and frequency. Nothing in the broadcasts suggested that the police had been alerted by the last careless transmission of the cutout. Nor was there any reason they should have been, even if they had somehow managed to intercept the vague message sent on a frequency unused by any other law enforcement agency in southern California.

No, Thanatos decided, as he picked up the heavy metal camera case, there was no reason at all for the police officers to be expecting anything unusual to occur in the target area tonight. By the time they did understand the significance of the Balefire message, it would be much too late.

Ed Malinger had been staked out on the flat tar-and-pebble-surfaced roof of the machine shop since nine o'clock that morning. He had taken a five-minute piss break at eleven-thirty, another at three, and had been uncomfortably aware of the pressure on his bladder for the last three-quarters of an hour. The sunburned photographer finally succumbed to the excuse that it was starting to get dark and he would soon need the night-vision scope he had left in the trunk of his car to justify a quick trip to the machine shop's small, grimy john.

He had climbed over the three-foot-high cement ledge ringing the rooftop of the building, camera slung diagonally across his chest by the wide strap, and was climbing down the steel ladder on the side of the building away from the storage spaces, when the small tan Volkswagen came down the street and turned into the alley behind the storage garage. Thus, the blissfully relieved photographer was first aware of the terrorist's presence when he glanced through the dirty front window of the machine shop on his way back to his post and saw one of the targeted garage doors start to open.

Malinger had listened to Andersen's insistent warnings to be careful with an agreeable nod of understanding that had been mentally reinforced by his previous tour of duty as a combat photographer in Vietnam. Unfortunately, that previous conditioning had emphasized the value of instinctive responses in getting that one, all-encompassing photograph.

Not entirely conscious of what he was doing, Malinger dove past the startled owner of the small shop, came out of the front doorway in a crouched position, brought the viewfinder of the camera up to his eye and set the aperture with reflexive hand movements, just as the Datsun 280-ZX swung out of the driveway in the general direction of the machine shop.

The camera was loaded with high-speed film and equipped with a battery-operated motor drive. From sixty yards away, Malinger followed the approaching car with the long lens, firing two frames a second as his left hand smoothly adjusted the zoom and focus, and his right eye centered on the still concealed face of the driver. Thirty yards away, the Datsun swung right onto the cross street. A side view of a dark tanned face, framed by the open side window of the Datsun, appeared in the camera viewfinder. The next shot was a full front view as Thanatos abruptly became aware of the photographer's presence.

Malinger had spent a better part of his working hours in Vietnam photographing the facial expressions of professional killers—both American and Vietnamese. He instantly recognized the savage look in the man's widened eyes. Almost frozen by the intensity of the murderous expression filling his viewfinder, Malinger reflexively made a slight adjustment of focus, clicked off three quick frames, and then turned and ran.

Thanatos had been thinking about a piece of ground almost three miles away as he drove the low-slung sports car into the late-afternoon sunlight. The glare from the rapidly dropping sun reflected off the clean windshield, concealing the image of the crouched figure with the long-lensed camera until the moment Thanatos turned right onto the cross street. By the time he spotted Malinger in his peripheral vision, focused his eyes on the camera, and reacted, the police photographer had disappeared into the doorway of the machine shop.

In the time it took Thanatos to identify the camera and record the significance of the photographer's rapid retreat, the Datsun had traveled about ten yards down the street. He hesitated, bared his teeth into a snarl, and then jammed the wheel of the Datsun into a tire-screeching power turn.

The possibility that the photographer was part of a larger police surveillance team had been considered and immediately rejected by the terrorist in that moment of hesitation. If there were other police officers in support of the fleeing cameraman, he knew that he would have been shot at, rather than photographed. He had no illusions about Andersen or any of the other Huntington Beach officers trying to take him alive now. The fact that he had not been shot at simply confirmed his initial evaluation. The man with the camera, the man who had undoubtedly taken his picture, was alone and vulnerable.

Thanatos bailed out of the Datsun and entered the front door of the machine shop at a run, the loaded and cocked Browning in his right hand, knowing he had to obtain the film in that camera. The beefy machine shop owner, reacting to the commotion at his front door by picking up a heavy wrench and stepping around his lathe to confront the intruder, died instantly as two 9mm bullets tore through his heart. He dropped to the floor like a mechanical target. Thanatos swung around, searching for the cameraman, and immediately spotted the movement of the closing back door.

The sound of the two muffled gunshots in the shop that Malinger had burst out of only seconds earlier simply provided added incentive to the photographer's desperate, lung-wrenching sprint. Malinger hadn't thought he could run any faster, but he made the last twenty-five feet to the corner of a large metal trash dumpster in what seemed to be three long record-breaking strides.

His heart pounding in his chest, Malinger looked back around the side of the dumpster and saw the man with a gun lunge out of the back door of the machine shop. Malinger had intended to circle around the building and go back up the ladder to reach the radio pack-set he had left on the roof. He knew now he would never make it to the ladder.

Turning to run again, the frightened photographer saw the red fire alarm lever on the side of the building less than fifteen feet away. He leaped across the open ground, pulled frantically at the heavy metal handle, and then started another dash for an open doorway fifty feet away. He was only vaguely aware of the sudden ringing clamor filling the air when the bullet tore into his upper back and spun him into a wall.

Malinger had witnessed other men fall in combat and then continue fighting in spite of what appeared to be crippling wounds. He was aware that he was badly hurt, as he ricocheted off the stucco wall and fell toward the pavement. The upper right area of his back felt as though it had been ripped apart. But he knew that he had to survive. Gasping in pain as he struck the ground, the photographer fumbled frantically for the .38 Chief's Special with his left hand—his right arm refused to respond—and brought the small weapon around one-handed just as the man broke into a zigzagging run toward him from about forty yards away.

Malinger tried to aim in the general direction of the oncoming figure, who seemed surrounded by a filmy haze, and managed to squeeze off three awkward shots which he was pretty sure hit nothing. He was numbly aware that the man had twisted away at the first shot, rolling out of sight behind the far building. Determined to use the few moments he had bought with his desperate shooting, Malinger pulled himself back against the protective steel side of the trash dumpster, realizing for the first time that the asphalt all around him was covered with blood as he tried to clear his eyes and shake the buzzing sound out of his ears.

Thanatos had been moving quickly toward the dumpster, intent upon retrieving the camera and summarily executing the fallen cameraman before returning to the Datsun, when the first of the poorly aimed shots forced him to dive for cover. He came up again immediately, determined to get at the damaging piece of film, and was driven back by a fourth shot from the severely wounded Malinger.

Ultimately, it was the noise of the fire alarm that forced the decision. Given even one more minute, Thanatos would have taken the film and dispatched Malinger with ease. But he knew he didn't have the time to waste on his personal concerns.

Already, fire trucks would be en route; the nearest patrol units would not be far behind. And there was no possibility at all that he could talk his way past the body of the machinist, the wounded photographer, and the explosives in the trunk of the Datsun. Accepting the only logical course of action, Thanatos broke off his assault and ran for his car.

He was in the Datsun, and only four blocks away from the machine shop, when the first screaming and flashing fire truck roared noisily by in the opposite direction. Forcing himself to act appropriately, he pulled the Datsun over to the side of the road and turned his head to watch two more fire trucks and one black-and-white for a few moments before he took off again into the fading light.

Fifteen minutes later, Thanatos was still sitting in the driver's seat of the Datsun, now parked in the back row of the almost empty drive-in theater, listening to the police broadcasts on his radio with growing relief and satisfaction.

The responding police and fire units had located the body of the machinist almost immediately in their futile search for a fire. The reporting police officer had just gone on the air again to advise that Thirteen Ida had been found shot, alive, and unconscious.

Another one of Andersen's men, the terrorist thought, contemplating the significance of his latest brush with the elusive sergeant's dwindling team of investigators. The fact that the photographer had been staked out by himself on the building where Thanatos had previously deposited the bodies of the two officers was significant. But the important factor was the assumption the photographer was still unconscious and, therefore, unable to provide an immediate description of the Datsun or himself.

Eventually, he knew, the cursed camera would provide that information, requiring him to alter his retirement plans. But for the moment his identity was still unknown. It was highly unlikely that the film would be discovered, developed, and printed in time to be a significant threat to Balefire.

Satisfied that Balefire was still a virtual certainty, Thanatos settled himself back in the seat of the Datsun, watching the arrivals of the snuggling couples in their automobiles as they all waited with various degrees of patience for darkness.

*   *   *

In the emergency room of Pacifica Hospital, a coolly efficient ER physician and his team of nurses and internists worked quickly to stabilize the still unconscious police photographer. The doctor used pressure cuffs and packings to control the severe bleeding while his assistants cut away the blood-soaked clothing and monitored Malinger's pulse, respiration, and blood pressure. Next door, the on-call chest surgeon was studying the first set of X rays as he and the anesthesiologist hurriedly prepped for surgery.

The heavy awkward 35mm camera had been one of the first items on Malinger's limp and clammy body to fall victim to the nurse with the pair of heavy-duty bandage scissors, as the ER team worked rapidly to clear the way for the attending doctor. The camera with its severed strap had been hastily set on the floor in a nearby, out-of-the-way corner, separate from Malinger's other personal effects. Subsequently, a large plastic bag containing the bloody remains of Malinger's clothing was tossed in the same corner, concealing the camera from view, and allowing it to go unnoticed by the LPN making a list of Malinger's personal effects.

It was not until Andersen, Kretcher, Baughmann, and the Santa Ana lieutenant, Ramirez, arrived at the hospital and were finally allowed to interrogate one of the ER nurses that the camera was located. Moments later, the camera was being rushed back to the station by a small team of police officers whose determination to locate and destroy the terrorist had become an all-consuming obsession.

In the brightly illuminated operating room, the practiced fingers of a calm, aggressive surgeon worked quickly with scalpel, gauze sponges, and clamps to seal off bleeders as they traced the destructive pathway of the jacketed bullet in Ed Malinger's chest, searching for the major source of bleeding before they ran out of time. Totally absorbed in his task, the surgeon was only vaguely aware of the surrounding activity in the operating room. His eyes were fixed on the depths of the opened wound as he listened to the quiet cadence of the anesthesiologist and called for a succession of sterilized tools that were quickly slapped into his bloody, gloved hand.

*   *   *

Less than two miles away, in the moonlit darkness of a huge oil field, surrounded by rusted metal, dirt, grease, and spilled oil, another man worked with equal skill and concentration at a task designed to fulfill months of planning and preparation by dozens of dedicated and fearless men like himself. Callused hands, trained to destroy rather than to save, worked quickly to set and then mount the magnetic back of the twelfth explosive device against the painted metal surface of a massive relay pump. A barely audible click, and the device was armed.

Thanatos was reaching for the thirteenth green box, his eyes searching through the shadowy darkness for another suitable target, when the soft scuffling sound of a boot sliding across a heavy metal pipe and a muffled curse reached his ears. The terrorist's hands froze in place, his mouth opened to quiet his shallow breathing as he listened intently, searching for a moving shadow, waiting for another sound that would enable him to pinpoint the direction.

Aside from the distant sounds of the slapping ocean waves, he heard nothing.

The terrorist allowed himself a hundred-count before moving his left arm to expose his watch. The small numerals glowed 18:58:44. Two and a half hours before the timed bombs would detonate in synchronous fury. Two and a half hours before the awaited Olympic torch-lighting finale that would cap the Opening Ceremony of the 1984 Olympic Games. Probably a night watchman, but there was still plenty of time to be doubly cautious.

Fifteen minutes later, concealed in a small clump of trees and dense brush located at the edge of a high bluff overlooking the long flat expanse of oil wells, derrick frames, pipe lines and miscellaneous drilling equipment, Thanatos discovered just how far the police investigation had progressed during his six-day recovery.

From his position looking down, Thanatos could see the target area clearly with the aid of the night-vision scope. There was a tight cluster of active pumpers with their small holding tanks and pipe lines that fed into the much larger cylindrical storage tanks. Settling himself down against one of the trees, he began to scan the area surrounding the location of the twelfth explosive device.

He missed the pair of police officers on the first pass, and then picked up the arm movement of one of the small figures as he made a second sweep with the night-scope. Both of the men were well concealed within the partially disassembled frame of a drilling rig stacked alongside the narrow dirt access road. They were dressed in dark camouflage clothing and equipped with shotguns, a pack-set radio, and what appeared to be an older, military-model Starlight scope.

Ignoring a tight numbness that was beginning to spread through his prone body, Thanatos cursed silently and immediately began a grid search of the entire oil field. Using the magnification capabilities of his modern night-vision scope, and having a specific target image to search for now, he was eventually able to pinpoint fourteen additional two- and-three-man teams. Some were scattered in place throughout the huge field where they could monitor all the access roads; others were moving carefully through the dirt pathways in a methodical search pattern, shotguns held ready.

He widened his search perimeter beyond the oil field. Six fire trucks were parked along side roads surrounding the long forestlike expanse of oil derricks. With the scope at maximum magnification, he could even see the fire crews in their turn-out gear, standing by their darkened trucks and drinking from steaming paper cups.

They knew about Balefire!

Thanatos cursed madly at the memory of the bungling cutout as he reconfirmed his immediate suspicion. His target area was directly in the path of at least two of the search teams. If they found just one of the devices . . .

There was no point in trying to set the remaining explosives in another section of the oil field. In order to reenter the field, he would have to pass by at least one of the surveillance teams, carrying a heavy metal case that would slow him down and draw the attention of a half dozen police officers the first time it struck against an unseen piece of pipe. If he was spotted—a likely prospect if the search teams were similarly equipped with the night-vision scopes—he would be immediately surrounded and outnumbered in an area that offered little in the way of concealment and no dependable escape routes. In that event, he would almost certainly be killed, and all of the preliminary effort that had been devoted to Balefire would be wasted. His once-in-a-lifetime moment on the stage would be dismissed with a shrug, and even the ridicule of his peers.

Thanatos quickly reviewed his options. The explosives in the primary target area were set, but were extremely vulnerable to discovery during the remaining hundred and forty minutes. There was no way to guarantee success at the primary target, but he could increase the odds by creating a diversion. But to be certain of fulfilling his obligation to the Committee, he would have to be ready at the backup targets. Failure now was unthinkable!

To create the diversion and to reach one of the backup targets in time, he would need reliable transportation. This was a problem. If the rented storage spaces across from the machine shop had been searched, then the police had a complete description of the Datsun. If not, they soon would have when they developed the photographs taken by Andersen's cursed photographer. Thanatos didn't dare return to one of the other waiting garage spaces to exchange vehicles; he would have to assume that all of the storage buildings were now under observation. Stealing a vehicle would provide a temporary solution to his transportation needs, but it would take hours to remove the concealed police radio from the Datsun and then install it in the stolen car. He didn't have the time to spare, and he didn't want to lose his one remaining police radio just yet.

The worst disaster from the terrorist's view had been the loss of communication with the Committee. During the preliminary stages, the Committee had been a valuable source of real intelligence. If he was to succeed, it would now have to be done on the basis of his own instincts and resources.

Standing up carefully and taking one last look out over the oil field, faintly illuminated by an occasional derrick light, Thanatos shrugged his shoulders and walked back to the Datsun. He was not discouraged by any means. He had been on his own before, often with only his bare hands for weapons. He always managed to come out victorious, in spite of odds that would have disheartened a less confident and less aggressive man. He would not fail now.

During the next forty-five minutes, the terrorist worked with feverish haste. Back in his Huntington Harbour garage, he quickly masked the Datsun's windows and chrome, and then sprayed cans of black paint across the silver-grey surface. The paint was a thin, fast-drying brand intended for furniture and toys. It wouldn't last more than a couple of days on the Datsun, which was fine because Thanatos only expected to need the car for a few more hours. Next he exchanged the license plates with ready spares, and then he went into the house to complete his disguise while the paint dried.

He started with his hair first, using a packaged hair rinse to deepen the bleached effect the sun had already started. The mustache was next, disappearing under the rapid strokes of the straight-edge razor. Finally, he changed his clothes, discarding the casual shirt and slacks for jeans, boots, and a long-sleeved flannel shirt.

As he worked quickly to alter his appearance, Thanatos reviewed the tasks he would have to accomplish tonight. He had already acquired the means to approach the backup target with minimal risk of detection. The equipment was stacked and waiting in his basement. The remaining explosive devices would have to be repacked, but he had the materials for that job, too. As soon as the paint was dry in another four or five minutes, he would place himself next to the backup targets, ready to ignite Balefire if the primary explosives failed.

But first, he had one more task to carry out—a diversion that should have been accomplished long ago.

They had known from the beginning that Andersen would be one of the major sources of resistance to Balefire. Now, in the last hours before Balefire would be a reality and with almost all of his resources expended, Thanatos could not afford another setback.

Andersen was alive. Thanatos had recognized the angered voice on the radio twice while he was waiting in the drive-in theater. First, he heard Andersen confirm that he was responding to the hospital. The second time was when the detective advised that he would be off duty the rest of the evening.

Andersen was alive. And Thanatos could not afford to be surprised again by the sudden appearance of the vengeful and unswerving officer. A diversion was necessary to ensure the ignition of Balefire. The death of Sergeant Walter Andersen would serve that purpose very well.

The M-80s and cherry bombs, timed to go off over a ten-second time interval, echoed their explosions down the empty suburban street in the night, causing a few residents to turn away from their tv sets and look at each other in momentary concern. Exactly fifteen seconds later, the string of Chinese firecrackers exploded in a ragged burst of weak bangs and pops.

"Kids," the residents commented, shrugging and returning their attention to the night's television offerings. Thus, the two louder explosions following immediately thereafter were ignored by virtually all of the at-home residents of Cape Horn Drive, with one exception.

The effects produced by the detonations of the light green, stun-grenade cannisters when they crashed through the large, glass windows of Andersen's living room and kitchen were far more spectacular and devastating than the muffled explosions had suggested to the surrounding neighbors.

The blast of the first grenade staggered the occupants of the living room, all of whom immediately turned toward the sound of the breaking glass, but had no warning or reason to cover their ears. Those nearest to the cannister when it detonated—Dorsey, Sheffield, and Jody Andersen—were flung senseless to the floor. Dan Branchowski and Meiko, both still recovering from head wounds, were instantly driven unconscious by the sharp force of the contained sound waves.

The second grenade burst through the kitchen window just as the first detonated, landing at the feet of Michelle Andersen, Juanita Hernandez, and their daughters. They had been warned by the breaking glass in the living room, but had no time at all to react. The relatively small area of the kitchen confined and magnified the concussive effect of the second grenade. The five women and children were tumbled across tables and chairs and into walls, dropping to the floor amid glass fragments and strewn paper, unconscious and bleeding from ears and noses.

The secondary effects of the grenades were doubly devastating to those in the living room who remained dimly aware of their surroundings. The pieces of fibrous material that spewed out of the cannisters ignited into flarelike bursts of glaring white light, temporarily blinding anyone whose eyes were still open.

Stunned, blinded, or driven unconscious by the effects of the anti-personnel grenades, no one in either the living room or the kitchen was aware that three more grenades, resembling black rubber balls, had been thrown through the broken window pane. At least, not until the tumbling spheres began to spew out clouds of billowing white smoke into Andersen's home.

Of those few in the house who were still functionally alert, only Dorsey and Sheffield had any practical experience with the overwhelming effects of CS tear gas. Dorsey had been walking into the living room when the first stun grenade went off, and Sheffield was already drowsy and lethargic from the effects of pain-killing drugs. Thus, both men were too badly immobilized to have any chance of avoiding the incapacitating gas rapidly billowing through the entire lower floor of the house. Dazed, blinded, and trying to hold their breaths, they both scrambled for weapons, thrashing about in a mad confusion of tearing eyes and lung-wrenching smoke before they succumbed to spasmodic coughing.

Thanatos came in through the kitchen in a ready combat crouch, moving fast, the Browning automatic extended out and cocked, his face shielded by a gas mask, his eyes searching for his target. He scanned the sprawled bodies, searching for the familiar face, watching the stairs, the doorways, the closets.

"Andersen, where are you?" he bellowed. He reached down with a gloved hand and pulled Dorsey up by the hair, just as the wheezing ID technician tried to come up on his hands and knees, but then knee-dropped him into unconsciousness as Dorsey made a feeble grab for the Browning.

"Andersen!" Thanatos screamed through the muffling gas mask, infuriated by his failure to locate and execute the cursed sergeant and confused by the presence of so many people. Only Andersen's wife and two daughters should have been in the house with him. He was supposed to be off duty. He—

Thanatos spun around at the scraping sound, and saw one of the sprawled figures trying to pull himself up by the edge of the couch. One of the crime lab scientists, Sheffield. As he identified the bearded face, he lunged forward and slashed at the tottering figure with the frame of the heavy Browning. Sheffield collapsed, unconscious before he hit the floor. Enraged, the terrorist ran from room to room, then up the stairs, searching for the one man who was still a threat to Balefire.

Thanatos came back down the stairs just as one of the girls, the older one, tried to sit up, her lungs weak from coughing, blood from her nose and mouth smeared across her face. He grabbed the girl by her long, blond hair and hauled her up against a wall so that her eyes were level with his own.

"Where is your father?" he demanded, his voice sounding grotesquely inhuman behind the rubber mask.

Jody Andersen tried to draw a deep breath, to scream in terror and rage, but her lungs rebelled, and she twisted into another spasm of coughing.

"Where—" Thanatos started to scream again, determined now to find Andersen if he had to torture every man, woman and child in the house, when the hands slammed around his ankles and he was yanked away from the girl and down to the floor, the Browning knocked out of his gloved hand.

Dan Branchowski had regained consciousness to find himself in a dizzy, swirling haze of pain and confusion. His breathing was only slightly congested by the familiar swirling smoke because he was one of the few officers in the department who never seemed to be noticeably affected by CS gas. He remained face down on the floor, vaguely remembering the grenade coming in through the window, followed by the sharp, stabbing pain. He heard the boots coming down the stairs and started to move his painfully throbbing head when he heard a guttural voice and realized what was happening.

When Branchowski lunged his massive arms forward at the terrorist's legs, he had just one thought in his agonized mind—the dark figure who was threatening Walt Andersen's daughter had to be the same bastard who had killed Jake! He roared in anguish and frenzied rage as his blurred mind flashed on the face of Jake Farber. As the terrorist went down, Branchowski threw himself forward, snarling like a

wounded grizzly, onto the back of the masked figure. His
thick, uncoordinated hands reached out, clawing for the throat
and eyes.

Only the gas mask saved the terrorist's life in those first
few moments when Branchowski's weakened but still lethal
hands tore into rubber and plastic rather than human flesh.
The mask tore loose and Thanatos inhaled his first lungful of
the low-lying CS gas as he twisted and fought to escape the
crushing weight, the gouging hands, the slashing teeth of the
patrol officer. Daniel Branchowski was no longer a trained
and experienced and controlled police officer. He was now an
animal, a creature with only one intention: to kill the bastard
any way he could.

Thanatos managed to break loose, came up coughing and
teary-eyed to his feet, and was driven backward into the wall
by the bellowing bull-like charge as Branchowski kept coming after the man who had killed his partner. The terrorist
twisted away, recovered, and hammered solid punishing ka-
rate blows into Branchowski's neck and face, blows which
should have felled or killed a normal man. Then, he staggered back himself as a blindly swung fist slammed into his
wounded chest.

Thanatos circled now, crouched and coughing, trying to
keep away from the hands as he shook off the pain in his
chest. Still moving, he stared teary-eyed at the glazed eyes
and the bleeding, snarling mouth of Branchowski, unable to
comprehend the savage determination of the man with the
bandaged head who seemed immune to physical punishment,
waiting for an opening to finish him quickly. Suddenly Thanatos
caught a movement out of the corner of one blurred eye, and
snapped his head around just as the bullet streaked past the
side of his face ahead of the cannonlike explosion.

The girl! She had managed to find the Browning in the
swirling tear gas, her eyes streaming with tears from the
effort. She was across the room, less than twenty feet away,
crouched and wincing as she recovered from the ear-piercing
noise of the gunshot and jarring recoil, trying to bring the
automatic up again, two-handed.

Before Thanatos could react, he was enveloped again by
the roaring and staggering charge of Branchowski, who had
ignored the gunfire in his all-consuming resolve to kill the

terrorist with his bare hands. This time, however, Branchowski's indomitable will to destroy was not enough. His reflexes were tangled and confused by the stabbing pain in his head. His arms were too weak to do anything more than swipe heavily against the terrorist's face and chest. And in his final effort, he unknowingly shielded the terrorist from the wavering aim of the automatic in Jody Andersen's shaking hands.

Thanatos twisted his face away from the clutching hands once more, planted his feet, and heaved the relentless officer backwards into the girl with an effort that tore at the damaged muscles in his chest. Knowing he had to finish this now, he lunged forward and slammed a foot into the side of Branchowski's bandaged head just as the bearlike officer started to crawl back up again. Branchowski dropped back to the floor in a loose-limbed sprawl as the terrorist's hand closed on Jody Andersen's wrist and twisted the Browning out of her hand.

BALEFIRE

T Minus 2 hours

Saturday Evening

2000 hours

Outside the door of the police photo lab, Andersen, Baughmann, Kretcher, Ramirez, and Raines waited impatiently for the technician to finish his work. When the door finally slid open, Andersen was the first to reach for the tray of still wet black-and-white photographs.

"He's in the Datsun," Andersen confirmed in a growled voice, holding one of the dripping photos up close to check the license plate number, and then handing it to Baughmann.

"Whose key is that?" Raines asked.

"Mine. Two-two-seven," Baughmann answered, still staring at the photo of the Datsun with the shadowy figure behind the wheel.

"Gotcha," Raines nodded, marking the number down in his notebook. "Soon as he turns on that radio, we'll have him on the locator map."

"What about our radios?" Andersen asked, peeling off the photos one at a time from the wet pile. "Crystals changed?"

"Turn your frequency selector all the way to the right," Raines nodded. "Everyone staked out on the wells has a modified set. Designated channel yellow. Haven't had time to start on the patrol units yet."

"Don't worry about it," Andersen muttered, staring with intense hatred at the photograph he held in his hand. The enraged eyes of Thanatos were glaring directly into Malinger's camera.

"There he is," Andersen finally said, handing the photos

to the other three officers. "When we find him—" Andersen broke off as an out-of-breath cadet ran into the photo lab.

"Sergeant Andersen," he gasped, trying to get out his message clearly. "Right away. Your house."

Andersen spotted the swarm of neighbors standing around on his front lawn, illuminated by the soft glare of the street light, when he and Baughmann were still half a block away. He dove out of the unit with the .45 in his hand, shoving past the crowd of onlookers with a frenzy that sent a number of his neighborhood friends sprawling onto the grass. Baughmann, Kretcher, and Ramirez followed Andersen, assault weapons ready in their hands. They found almost everyone lying out on the backyard lawn, surrounded by confused neighbors and uniformed paramedics.

Andersen saw the paramedics working desperately on the still form of Branchowski, whose bandaged head was soaked through with fresh blood. He saw Dorsey and Sheffield, both sprawled face down on the grass, Meiko beside them. He saw his wife and his daughter Martine sitting upright in the middle of a group of his neighbors, both holding blood-streaked ice-packs to their faces. He started counting heads, and felt his stomach surge into a knot of violent rage and fear when he realized who was missing.

Thanatos worked with a hurried sense of determination and purpose as he struggled to transfer the second load of equipment down to the edge of the brackish water of a saltwater marsh just north of the oil fields. As the terrorist carefully placed the blackened scuba tank next to the rubberized, self-inflating Zodiac boat, he checked his watch. 20:14:22. An hour and fifteen minutes remained before the explosive devices set in the oil field would detonate. If, for any reason, the explosions failed to take place, he would have a half hour before the torch-lighting finale at the Olympic Stadium to ignite one of the backup targets. Plenty of time.

The location he had selected would suit his needs perfectly. The land was actually a tree-covered twenty-acre wildlife refuge on a peninsula that stuck out into the marsh like a large extended thumb. There was only one entrance to the refuge—a dirt road that wound its way through a long-abandoned field of rusted pipes and unproductive wells that had been capped off and temporarily forgotten.

Catching his breath and painfully stretching his chest muscles, Thanatos walked back up the hill through the trees and into the clearing in the center of the refuge where the Datsun and the girl were waiting. He had decided to twist the knife into Andersen once more before he drew the elusive sergeant to his death and the searching officers away from the Balefire target.

The girl glared at him as he walked around and opened the passenger-side door. He could see both terror and hatred in the blood-smeared face as she stopped struggling to free herself from the handcuffs that secured her hands to the steering wheel and the ropes that held her lashed to the driver's seat. She tried to scream at him through the cloth gag. He slapped her sharply into silence with the back of his hand.

"You would like another chance with the gun, wouldn't you," he laughed, and then ignored the girl as he reached for the microphone in the glove compartment and punched the ON button of the radio.

"Andersen," Thanatos spoke into the microphone. He paused, and then continued. "Andersen, listen to me. I have her." The terrorist reached across with his free hand and wrenched the gag loose from Jody Andersen's mouth.

"Dad!" she yelled and then screamed in pain as the hand slashed across her face again, while the other held the microphone open.

"Listen to me, Andersen," Thanatos continued, ignoring the girl's whimpered moans. "If you want her back, you must call off your men until we can talk. We must be alone. I will tell you where later. And one more thing, Andersen. If I see a helicopter in the sky, I will kill her." Laughing loudly, Thanatos shut off the radio, replaced the gag tightly around the girl's mouth, tossed the dead mike onto the seat, and went back to work.

*   *   *

Andersen stared at the now silent radio in his hand, and then turned the selector switch to the new yellow frequency as Baughmann continued to drive the rented vehicle silently in the darkness. Ramirez and Kretcher sat in the back seat, quietly waiting.

"Oh-Five Delta. Acknowledge. Station to unit with Oh-Five Delta." Jeremy Raines's voice came out over the air. He had taken over the dispatch console and was desperately trying to reach Andersen.

"Andersen." The response was flat, distant, and cold.

"Oh-Five Delta. Be advised, two-two-seven has just transmitted. Approximate location, north end of John Muir Lane. That's the refuge. Also be advised, Team Seven has just reported locating an explosive device attached to Ocean-William-Two-One-Nine. EOD Team responding now." Jeremy hesitated at his microphone. "Oh-Five Delta, did you copy suspect's transmission?"

"Affirmative," Andersen said, the surging anger clear in his voice. "Keep all units clear of the refuge area, and ground the choppers."

"But—"

"Ground those birds now, and keep everyone else clear!" Andersen yelled into the radio, and then tossed it aside as he reached down at his feet for the automatic rifle and the bandolier of extra magazines.

"Yes, sir!" Jeremy Raines replied needlessly, reaching for his frequency selector when he failed to receive any further response.

"Eagle One and Angel High. Emergency situation. Return to home plate and land immediately. Repeat, Eagle One and Angel High. Land immediately."

Jack Paradee and Adrian Hite were sitting in Hite's Toyota sedan, stopped at an intersection on their way to a hastily called, private political meeting, when they both saw Andersen in the front seat of an unmarked vehicle with three other men driving rapidly northbound on Pacific Coast Highway.

"Did you see what he was wearing?" Paradee mumbled, turning his head painfully to glare at the rapidly disappearing vehicle. The unexpected sight of Andersen had reignited the

rage that still smoldered in the soul of the slowly recovering
newsman.

"No," Hite shook her head. "What does it matter what
that son of a bitch is wearing?" For different reasons, Councilwoman Hite also held Andersen responsible for the sudden
downswing in her career.

"He had on some kind of military fatigues," Paradee said.
"And he was with at least two other HB cops. I thought he
wasn't supposed to be working?"

"He's not."

Adrian Hite and Jack Paradee looked at each other for a
moment, and then both broke into malicious smiles. Ignoring
the enraged honking of the car in the neighboring lane, Hite
made a quick, illegal right turn as the light turned green, and
accelerated onto Pacific Coast Highway.

As the terrorist worked intently to complete his preparations,
a blacked-out vehicle began to move slowly down the dirt
road through the abandoned oil field that led to the refuge.
The car came to a stop halfway through the field, and both
doors were opened carefully. The overhead light bulb inside
the car had already been removed, so there was no visible or
audible warning as the four armed men began to work their
way silently toward the entrance of the isolated refuge, one
taking the road and the other three disappearing into the
darkness of the trees and brush.

It had taken Thanatos more time than he had expected to
change the timing sequence on one of his four remaining
explosives. He had been forced to work carefully and slowly,
using only the dim illumination of the small flashlight attached to his thin black wet suit to complete the changeover.
He constantly checked his watch. In spite of his determination to finish Andersen, the time factor for the ignition of
Balefire was far more important. He had to be in position to
detonate the alternate targets on time, just in case . . .

The device was ready now. The upper digital display had
been changed from an accurate twenty-four-hour clock to
read a constant 00:03:00. The lower digital display read zeros
straight across. The timing principle remained the same. Once
the device was armed by depressing the red button and the

two digital displays read the same, the device would explode. The only difference was that now when the button was depressed, the top display would start counting backwards. Exactly three minutes after the device was armed, the girl— and anyone in the near vicinity, such as her father—would die.

Using the knife strapped to his lower leg, the terrorist then cut away the carpet covering the floor of the Datsun, exposing the bare metal underneath. He could have attached the device to the outside of the car instead of the interior, which he had belatedly discovered was mostly plastic and leather, but he wanted the girl and her father to know how little time they had left of their lives.

He snapped the magnetic back of the device against the metal floor and then spent thirty amusing seconds explaining to Jody Andersen how the timer worked and how the recessed plunger would prevent her father from removing the bomb from the car. Then he rolled down the passenger-side window of the Datsun, shut the door, and was about to reach through the opened window for the radio button again when his eyes caught the movement of a shadow to his left, less than a hundred yards away.

Seconds later, Thanatos had scrambled around the Datsun, into the trees, and was kneeling in the concealing brush next to his small stockpile of weapons and equipment. He slipped a pair of binocular night-vision goggles over his eyes and focused on the dark movement. He grunted in surprise as the now visible and identifiable greenish figure of Andersen moved slowly forward toward the parked Datsun in the darkness, an M-16 rifle held ready at waist level.

Somehow, Andersen had tracked the vehicle, Thanatos realized, momentarily numbed by the possibility that he was trapped. Then he shook off the feeling of uncertainty and grinned in savage amusement. The terrorist's hand reached for a rifle, identical to Andersen's except for the attached laser-sight, hesitated, and closed instead on a two-and-a-half-foot length of cylindrical green Fiberglas about two and a half inches in diameter. The U.S. Army markings identified the cylinder as an obsolete M-72 Light Anti-tank Weapon. Thanatos smiled as he quietly removed the safety pin and extended the LAW launcher to its full thirty-five-inch length, arming the

lethal weapon. Then he waited with patient anticipation as
Andersen slowly moved closer to the Datsun, his daughter,
and death.

Thanatos followed the last twenty feet of Andersen's progress with the LAW launcher on his shoulder, the weapon
aimed directly at the cautiously moving figure. As Andersen
moved up alongside the Datsun, the terrorist's hand closed
over the trigger mechanism.

The small Toyota containing Hite and Paradee roared out
of the darkness at the spot where Thanatos had first observed
Andersen, its headlights appearing in a burst of white light
that instantly filled the terrorist's light-sensitive goggles. Blinded
by the sudden explosion of green light, Thanatos tore the
goggles away from his face, shifted his aim, and sent the
armor-piercing LAW rocket streaking across the clearing to
impact at a point midway between the two headlights.

It was a matter of overkill. The LAW rocket had been
designed to stop tanks. Hite and Paradee had only an instant
to stare uncomprehendingly at the flame-trail of the oncoming
missile before the thin-skinned Toyota disintegrated in a roaring explosion of metal, bodies, and burning gasoline.

At the far end of the peninsula, hidden in the darkness,
Keith Baughmann was cautiously examining his interesting
find when the explosion behind his back sent him sprawling
into the muddy ooze. He hesitated long enough to make
quick, effective use of his sheath knife, and then began to
move quickly and cautiously toward the source of the burning
light, his finger ready on the trigger of his rifle.

Momentarily illuminated by the Toyota's headlights as he
had reached slowly for the driver-side door of the Datsun,
Andersen barely had time to recognize his daughter's bloodied,
terrified face before the LAW rocket screamed past the Datsun,
and the world behind him exploded into raw, searing flames.
Andersen stood nypnotized by the sight of the shattered,
burning auto for a moment, and then suddenly remembered
the location-source of the rocket. He dove away from the
Datsun and rolled to the ground only inches away from four
high-powered rifle bullets that whipped over his head, shattering the Datsun's front and rear windows.

Hidden in the trees, Thanatos had quickly shifted his position before firing the short burst at Andersen, who had been

briefly silhouetted by the burning Toyota. The terrorist shifted again in the darkness, eyes watching intently for movement in the area of the clearing where Andersen had disappeared. He had to kill the cursed sergeant and get away. He didn't have much time.

Time?

The terrorist's eyes flicked down at his wristwatch. 20:49:56. He could not allow himself to be tied down much longer, Thanatos realized, as his eyes quickly returned to a search of the darkened clearing. The trip across the water to the backup targets could take an hour. It was critical to the psychological impact of Balefire that the ignition take place before 10:00 P.M. An hour and ten minutes remained. He would have—

The sound of shifting twigs warned Thanatos a split second before the wooden stock of the shotgun smashed against the tree just above his ducking head. Before the terrorist could recover and bring his rifle up and around, he was enveloped and crushed to the ground by the heavy, growling, vengeance-seeking Lieutenant Jorge Ramirez.

Sam Kretcher came running across the fire-illuminated clearing and threw himself down next to Andersen, who had worked himself about twenty-five yards away from the Datsun to draw fire away from his daughter. They both could hear the grunting, cursing, thrashing and branch-snapping sounds in the blackened forest.

"You okay, Walt?" Kretcher rasped, breathing heavily after his all-out zigzag run.

"Yeah. What the hell was that all about?" Andersen whispered hoarsely, gesturing with his head back at the horribly burning auto as they both stared into the darkness, trying to pinpoint the location of the fighting.

"I think Paradee and Hite were in that car," Kretcher replied, shaking his head as he glanced back at the glowing car rubble.

Andersen grunted, keeping his eyes on the trees.

"You find Jody?"

"In the Datsun. She's alive. Tied up." Andersen blanked the image of his daughter's terrified face out of his mind. "Who's out there?"

"Gotta be Ramirez," Kretcher said, "Keith's over there." He pointed at the dimly visible figure of Baughmann who was cautiously but rapidly moving in toward the fighting noises along the far edge of the clearing about forty yards away.

"Okay," Andersen nodded, "we'll go in."

The thrashing noises in the trees suddenly ceased. For almost ninety seconds, the only sounds that could be heard in the open clearing were occasional crackles and pops as the fire died down in what remained of the Toyota. Baughmann had frozen into a crouched position next to a large tree.

"What do you think?" Kretcher finally whispered.

Andersen shook his head. He waited another fifteen seconds and then slowly came up to a semicrouched position with the assault rifle in one hand. He started toward the Datsun, his eyes on the stark, black trees. Kretcher followed closely, his shotgun out and ready.

The pair of officers had taken less than ten steps when Kretcher saw the scarlet red dot sweep across Andersen's upper left arm, and then flicker back and center around the area of his waist.

"Walt!" Kretcher screamed, throwing himself forward to knock Andersen aside and then twisting desperately away, too late, as the first of a dozen bullets ripped across the clearing. Kretcher's field jacket spewed pieces of feather down as bullets aimed at Andersen tore into the Kretcher's neck, chest and ribs, less than half of the impacting slugs being absorbed by the ceramic armored vest. Kretcher was flung backwards, dying as he fell. Andersen stumbled forward as bullets tore a bloody gouge across the back of his left arm, slammed into his thick vest just below his heart, and sliced across the upper calf muscles of his left leg. Stunned by the force of the high-velocity projectiles, Andersen was thrown sideways, losing his rifle as he rolled to the ground in pain.

Thanatos had no time to confirm the results of his directed burst of gunfire. He had stepped away from the tree, lined the laser dot on the first of the two darkened figures, triggered the automatic weapon, saw both men fall, and then scrambled back into the protective trees as Baughmann opened up with a night-rattling .30 caliber volley from his heavy assault rifle. The jacketed military bullets ripped into tree trunks, brush, earth, and the receiver of the terrorist's laser-sighted rifle as

Thanatos threw himself to the ground and rolled desperately, trying to escape the oncoming rounds.

From his position on the opposite side of the clearing, Baughmann had watched Kretcher and Andersen rise up on the other side of the Datsun, and then tumble out of sight when the muzzle flash burst out of the trees. Baughmann had fired instinctively to provide cover for his fellow officers, just as he'd done countless times in Vietnam. As is usual in night combat, he couldn't tell if his shots hit anything. He dove forward and rolled about fifteen feet, then waited, not wanting to give away his location until he had a target.

The young officer saw something move again in the clearing. Andersen. The sergeant was backlighted by the glow of the Toyota fire as he crawled toward the small black Datsun. Baughmann made his decision instantly. He sent a second covering spray of bullets into the trees at knee level, blinking to protect his night vision from the flaring bursts of fire erupting from the stabilized gun barrel. Working with reflexive movements burned into his memory during his Army tour, he released and discarded the empty magazine and fed another heavy twenty-round magazine from his belt pouch into the rifle. Then the adrenaline that had always compensated for fear coursed into his muscles, and he sprinted toward the spot where he had last seen the terrorist disappear, firing two-round bursts as he ran.

Andersen was still thirty feet away from the Datsun when Baughmann began his covering assault. He looked up from his painful, determined crawl, saw the young officer's heroic charge toward the trees, and then saw the black shadowy figure step out of the tree line at a different spot—between himself and Baughmann.

"Keith!" Andersen screamed, bringing up his right hand with the .45 to sight on the figure just as the terrorist opened fire with the Browning. Andersen saw Baughmann stagger, try to take another forward step, and then fall.

Andersen sighted at the shadow and fired, not hearing the surprised yell of pain as the dark figure was slammed against a tree by the heavy pistol bullet. Andersen continued to squeeze the trigger, his lips bared back in a snarl as the .45 sent bullet after bullet streaking into the darkness where the terrorist had fallen until the weapon recoiled empty, the slide jammed back against the empty magazine. Tossing the gun toward the Datsun, Andersen crawled shakily to his feet, drew the razor-sharpened combat knife from his belt and began to limp with grim purpose toward the brush.

He saw the reflective metal surface of the Browning first. The 9mm pistol lay on the ground twenty feet in front of the bush where Andersen could now see the dark, bloody face of the terrorist, identifiable in the glow of the smoldering car debris in spite of his now clean-shaven appearance, lying twisted on his back in the underbrush, arms twitching spasmodically.

Andersen picked up the Browning, dumped the magazine, jacked the round out of the chamber, and then threw the now useless weapon into the darkness. He started again for the sprawled body of the terrorist, knife clenched tightly in his hand. Then he heard Baughmann groan.

Andersen hesitated. He took one more look at the bloody, glassy-eyed face in the brush, resheathed the knife, and then hobbled painfully toward his fallen partner.

Andersen knelt down beside Baughmann, and was struggling to turn the semiconscious officer over, when he heard the faint sound of moving underbrush. He swung his head around and saw the black figure break into a stumbling run toward the passenger side of the Datsun.

Andersen had less than a second to decide—go for Baughmann's rifle—which might be empty, or go for the man.

The realization that the terrorist was running toward his daughter caused Andersen's mind to go cold and empty. Emitting a scream of rage, he dropped Baughmann, and lunged upward in a raging fury, oblivious to his torn, protesting leg as he ran desperately to intercept the terrorist at the car.

Thanatos managed to reach the Datsun a half-second ahead of the madly charging Andersen, the vehicle a fuzzy dark image in his dazed and throbbing head. He had just enough time to reach in through the open window and slam his hand against the red button on the explosive device before Andersen was on him, dragging him out of the window and driving a rock-hard fist into the terrorist's rib cage and then another into his face.

Had Andersen been willing to step back and take his time, he would have been able to beat the badly injured and weakened professional killer unconscious in a matter of minutes, in spite of the sharp pains that tore across his deeply bruised chest with each swing. But Andersen was no longer in control of his rational thought processes. Like Hernandez and Branchowski and Ramirez before him, Andersen wanted more than submission and victory. He wanted death by his own bare hands.

He was on top of Thanatos with his knees, sending blow after frenzied blow into the bullet-torn face and the protecting arms, when the panicked screams of his daughter reached through the blurring rage of vengeance.

Somewhere in Andersen's mind, the screaming words linked together to tell him there was a bomb, and he clawed his way to his feet and dove at the passenger door. For the first time, he saw the blinking device, and the exposed numbers.

00:01:18
00:00:00

Jody Andersen had managed to work her gag loose, and was now hoarse and almost voiceless from screaming. "It's a bomb," she choked out. "It's going to blow up in one minute. No, wait! Don't!"

Andersen had pulled open the door and had instinctively reached for the flashing device.

"You can't move it!" the girl yelled, shaking her head, panic-stricken as she saw her father's hands close around the device. "It's booby-trapped," she choked out, sobbing with momentary relief as she saw her father pull his hands quickly away from the box. "Please, Daddy, get me out of here! He said it'll go off if you move it."

Andersen heard the strangled, mocking laugh. His head snapped up, and he saw the terrorist stagger to his feet less than ten yards away.

"You lost, Andersen!" Thanatos yelled out hoarsely through his swollen and split lips, the blood from the wound across his forehead streaming down over his eyes and into his mouth. "You never had a chance!" Thanatos turned away, continuing his mocking, coughing laugh as he began to run and stumble toward the distant tree line.

Andersen's hand flew unbidden to the knife at his waist. Then he looked back down at the blinking device.

00:00:53
00:00:00

Pulling the knife clear of the sheath, Andersen limped around the Datsun and yanked open the driver-side door. He grabbed at the ropes around his daughter's waist and began sawing frantically.

00:00:44
00:00:00

The last of the ropes came away, and then Andersen saw the handcuffs. His key. He fumbled in his pockets. Where was his key ring? Panic—and then mind-numbing realization. He had left his key ring with the handcuff key back in the car so they wouldn't rattle in his pocket!

00:00:32
00:00:00

"Dad?" Jody Andersen's voice was edged with terror.
Andersen tried to pull her hands through the cuffs. Too tight. Then he wasted five seconds trying to wrench the steering wheel loose from the column.

00:00:18
00:00:00

"Dad! Please hurry!"
Andersen's mind was screaming when his hand brushed against the empty holster for the .45 and the spare magazines. His pistol!
He stumbled around the car, searching frantically for the discarded handgun in the darkness. He couldn't find it. The rifle? Kretcher's shotgun? No, too far away! The Browning? No!
Andersen had already decided to pull the device away and try to shield his daughter from the blast with his own body when his groping hands brushed across the familar cold metal frame of the .45.
Andersen threw himself over the hood of the Datsun, fed his spare magazine into the butt of the weapon, yanked back the slide, grabbed the handcuff chain tight against the steering wheel and pulled the trigger.

00:00:05
00:00:00

The steering wheel exploded into shards of plastic. Andersen grabbed at his daughter's arm, yanked her out of the Datsun, pulled her to his chest with both arms, took three stumbling strides, and then dove toward the ground. At that instant, the Datsun erupted into a thunderous, concussive roar of jagged metal, shredded plastic, and exploding gasoline.

BALEFIRE

T Minus 50 Minutes

Saturday Evening

2110 hours

The second distant explosion was too much for Lieutenant Gilcrist whose nerves were already stretched to the limit by his responsibility to direct a desperate, scrambling search for armed explosives, at night, in a huge oil field with a hundred thousand possible hiding places for objects no larger than a tennis shoe. A search for an unknown number of timed explosive devices, each one found so far reading 21:30:00 on the second strip of red numerals. A search involving every available police officer and fireman in the city, every one of whom had been advised that a cop killer had set the bombs and the apparent detonation time might not be accurate.

Explosions going off twenty minutes before the detonation time, in an area just north of the oil field where Andersen was supposed to be hunting the bastard, didn't help things one fucking bit.

"Jackson!"

The startled sergeant twisted his head around, the strain apparent on his sweat-stained face.

"Take your squad out to the refuge. Find out what's happening out there," Gilcrist ordered.

"But Andersen—" Jackson started to say.

"Now, Sergeant," Gilcrist snarled.

"Yes, sir."

Gilcrist almost smiled as Jackson tried to hide the relief on his face. Gilcrist didn't blame him one bit. There wasn't an officer out there, the firemen included, who wouldn't have preferred to face an armed killer in the dark rather than continue this search during the next fifteen minutes or so.

"Lieutenant?"

Gilcrist hurried quickly over and knelt down by two young military men, members of an Explosive Ordinance Deactivation team from the nearby El Toro marine base. Both men had been working steadily on one of the small green boxes for almost fifteen minutes, using a large flashlight and implements from a neatly organized toolbox, calmly ignoring the frantic search activities going on around them.

"You got something?" Gilcrist asked the senior noncom.

"Yes, sir." The uniformed sergeant looked up, answering in a distinctive South Carolina drawl. "We're familiar with the design. Assembly and wiring's professional. Can't cut out the timing mechanism without triggering an arming circuit. Detonator's protected too. Ninety-nine percent chance there's a release trigger on the back side."

Gilcrist closed his eyes momentarily. "Does that mean you can't move it?"

"Means we shouldn't move it," the young sergeant corrected. "But since you people haven't figured out how to move a couple hundred oil wells real fast, we thought we might try a variation of the old credit card trick." The sergeant held up a long thin strip of stiff plastic. "Y'all might want to move back a couple hundred feet."

"Hell of an idea," Gilcrist muttered as he reached down and picked up the flashlight, freeing two sets of skilled hands to work the bomb. As he reflexively steadied the light beam on the dark box, he stared down at the exposed red digital strips; the upper row flashing at one-second intervals and the lower set glowing steadily.

21:11:52
21:30:00

"By the way, Lieutenant," the sergeant asked offhandedly, as the two soldiers began to carefully work the piece of plastic between the magnetic back of the device and the pump housing, "how many of these things y'all find so far?"

"Seven," Gilcrist answered, his eyes glued to the slowly moving piece of plastic.

"Holy shit," the sergeant's assistant whispered softly.

*   *   *

Thanatos had already gone through the excruciating process of strapping the scuba tank onto his back and had attached one of the remaining explosive devices to the tank harness, before he discovered the damage to the Zodiac boat caused by Baughmann's knife. Shaking his head in a futile attempt to clear the distracting dizziness and throbbing, the terrorist quickly confirmed that both the inner and outer compartments had been slashed. He cursed. Then he checked his watch again.

21:13:22.

Shaking his head again, frustration temporarily overriding the pain, Thanatos grabbed up the military pack with the other two devices. Looking back quickly for any sign of the persistent Andersen, the terrorist started a determined, nerve-searing run through the mud, reeds, and knee-deep water of the marsh, heading toward the Pacific Coast Highway and the ocean that was less than a quarter of a mile away.

Patrol Sergeant Bobby Jackson and the three officers in his squad found Andersen and his daughter crouched over Baughmann. Andersen was cursing and cutting away at Baughmann's uniform while a shuddering, tear-streaked Jody Andersen pressed her blood-soaked sweatshirt tightly against Baughmann's neck. She had already used one of her long knee socks to tie off the wound in her father's leg.

"Bobby, you get him to Pacifica. Fast," Andersen growled, glaring up at Jackson as two of the patrol officers moved in quickly, setting aside their shotguns to take over first aid. The third officer stood alert on sentry duty. "Take Jody with you. Don't leave either one of them alone for a minute. Understand?"

"Yeah, but—" Jackson started to say, but he stopped when Andersen hobbled painfully to his feet, grabbed a flashlight and one of the discarded shotguns, and then disappeared into the darkness.

The pathway of the terrorist wasn't difficult to follow. Andersen's flashlight beam illuminated a trail of trampled reeds, churned mud, and occasional splatters, streaks, and smears of what appeared to be blood, leading straight across the marsh toward the highway. The light would almost certainly draw fire from the terrorist, if he was still armed, but Andersen left the light on, ignoring his survival training, the warning pains in his chest, and the burning sensation in his lower leg. Time was the critical factor. The son of a bitch had at least a five-minute head start. If he got to a car, he was going to be gone.

Andersen covered the last hundred yards on one hand and both knees, scrambling up the packed dirt and gravel incline to the highway, the shotgun up and ready in his free hand. He had discarded the flashlight. Plenty of light now from the highway.

At the top of the incline, out of breath and groggy, Andersen rose up quickly from a kneeling position, the shotgun level, and stared out across an empty road. Instinctively, he swiveled around, searching back along the route he had traveled. Moonlight reflected on slick mud and gently rippling water. Shadowy darkness. No movement. No terrorist.

Andersen stared back along the irregularly lit highway again, watched a car coming fast in the northbound lane, and then growled in satisfaction as the headlights reflected off shiny splatters of brown mud and bright red blood that trailed diagonally across the asphalt road.

On the other side of the highway, staring down at the base of the incline leading out across an expanse of cold, dark beach to the ocean, Andersen spotted the two boys and the single surfboard.

"A man in a black wet suit. Which way did he go?" Andersen demanded, yelling out over the increasingly loud roar of the ocean, his voice echoing a cold, self-feeding anger as he stumbled down the incline toward the youths, one of whom was on his knees next to his sprawled companion.

As he limped up next to the Fiberglas board, stuck nose first into the sand, Andersen could see the blood and vomit smeared across the lips and teeth of the small, unconscious figure. The kneeling boy was staring up at Andersen, eyes widened in horror. He had been startled by the infuriated voice bellowing out of the darkness, and was now thoroughly terrified by the sight of the muddy, blood-soaked man with a shotgun in one hand and a savage expression of pure hatred on his face. The boy sprang to his feet, looking for a way to run.

"Police officer, son, stay where you are," Andersen rasped, vaguely aware of the effect he was having on the boy, but no longer capable of any emotion other than vengeance-seeking anger. "A man in a wet suit. Where did he go?" Andersen repeated.

"Crazy man, mister." The blond-haired youth shook his head, his eyes glassy and his voice quavering. "Came out of nowhere. God, he looked awful. His face . . ." The boy's lean shoulders shook, a response to his memory of the other terrifying man. "Took Jimmy's board."

"Which way did he go?" Andersen growled, but he didn't even bother to listen to the boy's answer. He could see for himself. The heavy footprints and the drag line of the board in the sand led into the darkness toward the pounding surf.

Almost two hundred yards offshore now, surrounded and frequently swamped by the bone-chilling, surging ocean swells, Thanatos alternately stroked his fatigue-numbed arms deep into the water, and then held on desperately as each oncoming swell heaved the small surfboard backwards and sideways with cold, unmerciful, life-absorbing indifference.

Shivering uncontrollably, choking and gagging on the salt-laden water that streamed into his nose and mouth with each gasping breath, the terrorist fought with inhuman tenacity, expending his mental and physical reserves in an unrelenting effort to keep the stolen surfboard moving in the direction of the distant lights. Able to remain conscious only because of the searing agony of his wounds, the terrorist continued to stroke, continued to grab hold of the slick board edges, and then stroke again. He was blissfully unaware that another creature much like himself had begun to follow the path of the surfboard in the cold, green-black darkness.

Standing alone beside the massive oil storage tank, sweat pouring down his wind-chilled face, Lieutenant Herb Gilcrist watched as the two marines from the EOD team approached the huge curved metal surface of the tank with quick, deliberate strides. Both of the men were carrying identical green plastic boxes, strips of stiff plastic held tight against each magnetic back with steady, strong fingers. The exposed digital strips on each box glowed bright red in the semidarkness.

Gilcrist watched apprehensively as the marines gently pressed each device against the cold metal and then carefully slid the plastic strip away. Two sharp clicks echoed loudly in the cold night air as two released plungers struck the unyielding metal surface. The anticipated sounds caused Gilcrist to wince uncontrollably. His pack-set radio was already up to the side of his mouth as the two demolition experts called out.

"Ten!"

"Eleven!"

The two marines looked at Gilcrist, who was still staring at the eleven identical pairs of numbers that flashed against the towering background of the storage tank.

21:28:40
21:30:00

Eighty seconds.

Gilcrist quickly looked around the oil field once more. The search was still in progress, but every one of the search teams had worked themselves near a car with the motor running and a driver at the wheel. An odd number, he thought numbly. A fucking odd number. Had to be more. Why couldn't they have found ten, or even twelve?

"Let's get out of here!" Gilcrist yelled, waving the marines toward their waiting truck. The nerve-taut supervisor keyed his radio and repeated the command twice before jumping into the back of the EOD truck that was already moving toward the nearest exit.

The bitterly cold water, surging gently now that the dark sloping bottom sand lay deep below the surface, splashed quietly over the nose of the bobbing surfboard, pouring into the mouth, nose and eyes of the terrorist, bringing him around again, coughing and spitting weakly, as he tried to clear the burning saltwater out of his bleeding, swollen head.

He had already blanked out once. Twice? Thanatos tried to

remember as he cautiously forced his head up off the wet,
sandy, waxed surface of the rocking Fiberglas board. His
blurred eyes blinked and then focused on the lights that
blazed from the drilling platform less than a quarter of a mile
away. Remembering now, he painfully brought his left arm
around to check his watch.

21:29:50.

Ten seconds to Balefire!

The terrorist struggled painfully to bring the resisting board
around so that the nose pointed roughly toward the distant
shoreline. Feeling a sense of exuberance that overrode his
horribly depleted condition, Thanatos forced his head up
again just as two brilliant fireballs exploded in unison against
the dark sky.

As the terrorist watched, one of the explosions sent a
toylike oil derrick tumbling high into the air, spurting oil
from a severed line that ignited immediately into a smaller,
secondary flame The second explosion—the accumulated
effect of eleven blocks of high-order explosive detonating
against a large empty oil storage tank—was much larger than
the first, lighting up the sky in a thunderous burst of yellow-
white light. But instead of feeding upon thousands of barrels
of flammable oil, the seeking flames found only residues
within the ruptured, hollow metal shell and flared into extinc-
tion as the terrorist blinked in disbelief.

Two explosions? Only two? Thanatos stared out at the
shoreline, unable to comprehend why Balefire was not roaring into the sky, why Balefire was only one pitifully small
flame. As he watched, he was unaware that the fire crews
were already moving in to contain and fight the isolated
flames.

He allowed his still-bleeding forehead to drop forward onto
his numbed wrists, stunned by the magnitude of his failure.
Then he remembered why he had fought the unyielding
ocean, why he was floating on the dark, terrifying water. He
raised his head to turn and stare at the distant lights again, to
reassure himself that they had not been a hallucination, a
fevered response of his mind to unimaginable pain and fear.
The lights of the offshore drilling rigs—the backup targets—
were still there, waiting.

The terrorist's hands fumbled for the military pack strapped to the nose of the surfboard. The explosive devices were still there. Moving cautiously on the unsteady board, Thanatos armed all three bombs. They were now programed to explode at exactly ten o'clock—22:00:00 on the digital display. He blinked twice to clear his salt-reddened eyes, and then checked the timers against his watch. 21:38:08. Twenty-two minutes. Plenty of time.

Reassured, Thanatos rested his head back on the gritty waxed surface of the board, fighting the shock-induced nausea and allowing himself to rest a little longer before he began again the torturous task of paddling the surfboard toward the waiting platforms.

The realization that he had won, that he had beaten Andersen and all the others, washed over the terrorist like another surge of the cold, saltwater. He had done it! He had absorbed everything the Huntington Beach police could throw against him, and he had beaten them because he knew their weaknesses far better than they knew his.

Weakness.

The word reminded Thanatos that he was still bleeding from the agonizing head wounds. The first bullet from Andersen's gun had gouged a strip of skin away from his forehead. Another bullet had torn away most of his right ear. His mouth and nose were swollen and probably bleeding, although he couldn't tell, from the bare-knuckled fists of Andersen and the other huge police officer. And he was certain that the wound across his chest had split open again. He had barely been able to hoist the compressed air tank onto his back and snap the brass locks back on shore.

Thanatos was not greatly concerned about the loss of blood itself. It was the sudden awareness that he was leaving behind a trail of blood in the surging, dark water that inspired the terrorist to begin paddling again, ignoring his fatigued and protesting arm muscles.

He paused once more in his labors to look at his watch. 21:40:16.

In approximately twenty minutes, a young athlete would begin his run up a number of marble steps with a torch in his hand. At the top, he would turn and salute the expectant crowd below, who in turn would respond with a roar of approval. Then the young athlete would raise the torch to the lip of a massive brass bowl above his head. From that torch, a huge Olympic flame would be ignited. A flame that would be visible throughout the entire city of Los Angeles.

But before that happened, another flame would be ignited. A flame that would be visible for hundreds of miles and would burn brighter and longer than any Olympic Flame in history. A flame that would rise up to light the Los Angeles sky even as the young man raised his puny torch in salute to the stadium. A flame that would warn a nation that it could no longer inflict agony and suffering upon other nations and then run home to sanctuary. A flame to warn others that the massively powerful United States of America could not protect even one of its cities from a single man. A Balefire Warning that would be seen and understood by millions of people in scores of countries as they watched the ceremonial opening of their cherished Games.

The police could not stop him now, Thanatos realized with a bloody smile. Even if they knew his destination—they couldn't because the treacherous cutout hadn't been told—they would never be able to find him before he attached the primed explosives to the offshore drilling platforms. He was a black figure on a small, dark surfboard, wearing blackened air tanks, and riding low on a green-black sea. The moon was hidden in a cloudy sky. There were only the lights on shore and the flickering lights of the platforms to aid a fruitless search. No one would be able to find him in time. In less than twenty minutes, the three platforms would be ablaze with the glow of burning oil, and the Balefire Warning would be an irrevocable part of history.

Suddenly, the fear that plagued Thanatos in his dreams surged through his mind again, and he sensed the presence of something moving in the darkness below, searching.

No! He gripped the board tightly with both hands until he was able to force the mental images back into his subconscious. Andersen failed because he lost control, the terrorist reminded himself. There could be no failure of will now!

Determined and tightly under control again, Thanatos raised his head to check his bearings, and then froze in horror as the huge triangular shape moved to fill his vision. A whimper escaped from the terrorist's bloodied lips. "No!" he whispered, shaking his head, feeling his entire body go numb with fear. "No!"

The triangular shape whipped around in the water, and suddenly two small yellow dots of light rose up the leading edge of the triangle.

The signal!

Thanatos, the man of terror, held himself tightly to the board until the uncontrollable trembling stopped. Through his blurry, stinging eyes, the single triangular sail of the boat, no more than two hundred yards away, had first registered in his mind as a giant dorsal fin. The terrorist coughed again, and then he held tightly to the board as his body shook once more, releasing the tension that had built as though he were a tightly coiled spring.

Holding on to the board firmly now—he could not contemplate the thought of falling off the board into the water—Thanatos fumbled for his small rubber encased flashlight. He sent out the counter signal: two quick flashes of light, repeated once. He saw the boat tack about in his direction and he began to paddle again with deep, hard, painful strokes, determined now that he would complete his mission from the safety of the sailboat rather than from the dangerous low-riding surfboard. He had already defeated over two hundred police officers and a small city. He could not be stopped now!

The terrorist's eyes were locked on the sail, and he missed the flash of glistening skin the first time the small blue shark churned to the surface in search of the source of the enticing blood. Thanatos saw the small dorsal fin the second time it appeared, and he laughed at the sight of the miniaturized terror of his dreams. He was too close now to be terrified by something he could see. He stroked again, and then pulled his hands in quickly as something much larger than the small blue shark jarred heavily against the board's rear stabilizing skeg.

A part of his mind screamed that the nameless form was down there, waiting. He heard a splash of water behind him, but he refused to turn his head to see if the creature that haunted the depths of his mind had risen to the surface. The boat was close now. A few more moments and Balefire would be his! He waited tensely, hands and legs flat in the center of the board, his eyes focused on the lights of the three platforms now. His platforms. His stage.

The boat came alongside, whispering quietly through the water, and Thanatos reached up to grasp the extended forearm.

"Quickly, we must hurry," he rasped, feeling the strong salt-roughened hand tighten around his arm and pull him upwards. He reached out with his other hand to grab at the railing, and then gasped in surprised shock as he stared into the smoldering dark eyes of an ocean-hardened old man who had lost too much already and would not tolerate the loss of anything more.

Thanatos saw the blade of the folding knife flash in the hand of Police Chief Lars Sager. Reacting by instinct alone, the terrorist's free hand grabbed desperately at the thick wrist of the knife-wielding hand, and then he screamed in agonized terror as a blunt-nosed shape exploded out of the liquid darkness and slammed into his side.

Andersen used every ounce of strength that remained in his pain-racked chest and shoulder muscles to drive the nose of the borrowed surfboard into the side of the terrorist, his lungs rasping in burning agony as he lunged across the board in a savage rage, relentless in his single-minded determination to be the one who killed the predator with his bare hands. Andersen enveloped the terrorist, wrenching him out of Sager's grasp with his own clawing hands, the impact of his driving body sending himself and the terrorist tumbling off the boards into the cold, green-black water.

In the first moments of the death struggle, fought beneath the surface in icy, restricting, liquid darkness, the terror that filled the mind of Thanatos gave Andersen the advantage. It was only as the two men surfaced, gasping instinctively for air—Andersen bellowing in rage as his hands tore at the throat of the terrorist—that Thanatos saw the face of his human antagonist, and his will to fight and live returned. The two came together again, and disappeared in a flurry of churning water as they fought with hands, feet, teeth, knees. Each flailed at the other, searching for a vital spot, but each was saved again and again by the impartial ocean that slowed, diverted, and cushioned blow after deadly blow.

Thus, it was by random chance rather than any sense of purpose or fate that caused Andersen's forehead to strike the scuba tank regulator rather than the terrorist's face. The stunning impact loosened Andersen's grip on the terrorist's wrist, allowing Thanatos to grasp at the knife strapped to his leg. His hand pulled the knife free of the sheath, and he brought the knife up, ready to stab at the unyielding Andersen, when the primitive, blood-stimulated brain of the grey-white creature, watching the underwater struggle intently with cold, black eyes, reacted to the flashing metal. Thrashing its powerful vertical tail, it drove itself forward across the remaining ten feet of water.

Andersen never really saw the shark. He only saw the horrible flash of white, triangular teeth rush past his face, and then the terrorist was wrenched out of his grasp as the huge tail slammed against Andersen's chest, the sharp enameled scales on the massive body shredding away shirt cloth and skin as Andersen was spun away by the swirling water. Nor did he see the mixture of realized horror and inexplicable relief on the face of Thanatos as the dying terrorist's hands clutched spasmodically at the explosive device attached to his scuba harness, his weakening fingers searching for the wires, the escape.

The green-black water contained the explosion for a fraction of a second. Then the water rose upward, bursting to the surface less than thirty yards from the sailboat, just as Chief Lars Sager pulled the exhausted Andersen on board. As the churning water subsided, Sager reached out and cut the line holding the two yellow signal lights against his sail. He allowed the lights to blink and disappear into the depths, followed by the rope and the pack containing the remaining two explosives. Then he turned the boat about in the direction of the shore lights, leaving the ocean surface to another boat that would begin to cruise back and forth beside the offshore drilling platforms several hours later with three vertical, blue lights on its bow—as directed by Sager's revised and misleading radio transmission—searching in vain for the signal flashes in the water that would never appear.

Ten minutes later, Andersen sat in the bow of the sailboat, wrapped in blankets, trying to hold a steaming coffee cup in his trembling hands, staring out across the dark water as Sager tacked slowly back and forth, waiting for the helicopter that was responding to his radio call. Several miles offshore,

Jacquem Kaem also waited impatiently on the foredeck of the distant tanker, staring out into the darkness with a growing sense of foreboding. Thus, as the last two explosives detonated harmlessly in the ocean depths, both men were in a position to observe the warm glow that rose in the sky above the Olympic Stadium in Los Angeles when Bobby Joe Edwards turned a brass valve with his two callused hands and a proud, trembling Johnny Baumgaertel stood at the top of the high platform, reached up, and lit the Olympic Flame.

BALEFIRE

T Plus 10 hours

Sunday Morning

0800 hours

The message that each member of the Committee received at precisely eight o'clock the following Sunday morning was brief and self-explanatory:

"Do not disband. The Warning must be delivered. Remain in place until you are contacted. We will send another."

ABOUT THE AUTHOR

KENNETH GODDARD has twelve years of experience
as a forensic scientist working in police law enforcement. His experience includes three-and-one-half
years as a criminalist and criminalist/deputy sheriff
with the Riverside and San Bernardino (California)
County Sheriff's Departments. He also spent eight
years as the Chief Criminalist and supervisor of the
Huntington Beach Police Department's Scientific
Investigation Bureau.

Mr. Goddard has written and published two text
books: *Crime Scene Investigation* and *Weaponless
Control* (the latter as a co-author). Currently Mr.
Goddard is employed in Federal law enforcement.
A native Californian, he resides in Virginia with his
wife, Gena, and ten-year-old daughter, Michelle.
His second novel, *The Alchemist*, will be published
by Bantam.

A novel of terror from the bestselling author of
THE GOD PROJECT

NATHANIEL

by John Saul

Some thought him no more than legend, a folktale created by the townsfolk of Prairie Bend to frighten their children on cold winter nights. Others believed him a restless spirit, returned to avenge the past. But for eleven-year-old Michael Hall, Nathaniel is the voice that calls him across the prairie night, the voice that beckons him to follow . . . and do the unthinkable.

NATHANIEL will be available July 1, 1984, wherever Bantam Books are sold, or you may use the handy coupon below for ordering.

RELAX!

SIT DOWN

and Catch Up On Your Reading!

SPECIAL MONEY SAVING OFFER